THE PLOT TO DESTORY AMERICA

THE RED
MUTATION

BARRY LIBIN

an imprint of Sunbury Press, Inc.
Mechanicsburg, PA USA

an imprint of Sunbury Press, Inc.
Mechanicsburg, PA USA

For information about special discounts for bulk purchases, please contact Sunbury Press Orders Dept. at (855) 338-8359 or orders@sunburypress.com.

To request one of our authors for speaking engagements or book signings, please contact Sunbury Press Publicity Dept. at publicity@sunburypress.com.

FIRST AGENCY BOOKS EDITION: January 2024

Set in Adobe Garamond Pro | Interior design by Crystal Devine | Cover by Igor Andric | Edited by Lawrence Knorr.

Publisher's Cataloging-in-Publication Data
Names: Libin, Barry author.
Title: The red mutation : the plot to destroy America / Barry Libin.
Description: First trade paperback edition. | Mechanicsburg, PA : The Agency Books, 2024.
Summary: What would happen if the Chinese planned to use bioterror to achieve world domination but had yet to discover the antidote? Dr. Jeffrey Moss, of the NYPD, is assined to finding the antidote and destroying the virus before the enemy holds the world hostage by threatening a deadly epidemic.
Identifiers: ISBN : 978-1-62006-107-7 (paperback).
Subjects: FICTION / Mystery & Detective / International Crime | FICTION / Medical | FICTION / Thriller / Suspense.

Product of the United States of America
0 1 1 2 3 5 8 13 21 34 55

For the Love of Books!

To Daniel, Alexander, Sherri and Devora

ACKNOWLEDGMENTS

I would like to thank my editor, Lawrence Knorr, for the extensive work he put into managing the preparation of this manuscript, to Crystal Devine for making the manuscript into a book, and to the entire team at Sunbury Press. I also wish to thank my wife, Margery, and my entire family for reading the early drafts and giving their counsel.

AUTHOR'S NOTE

I began writing this story in July 2019. That was six months before the world had heard of COVID-19. However, it was at that time that I imagined a virus being bioengineered to be so virulent that it could destroy all earthly living matter. Aware of the laboratories that were researching the most infectious microorganisms, I believed that the most likely site for such work to be done was at the Wuhan Institute, China's most respected Biosafety Level 4 laboratory, the highest secured level of safety awarded for working with the most dangerous of pathogens.

And then January 2020 arrived and, with it, COVID-19. As a result, my fiction soon became reality. I had no choice. I stopped all work on the novel. It took two more years before my publisher called and asked about the book. In those two years, the times had changed, and the great fear of COVID-19 had dissipated.

It was then that I began rewriting The Red Mutation. My only concern: was it truth, or was it fiction?

Enjoy.

Barry Libin

THE CHARACTERS

WUHAN
Dr. Han Shi – General and Head of Wuhan Institute
Dr. Jiang Fang – Assistant to Han Shi and Chen's friend
Dr. Sang – Scientist at Wuhan Lab
Colonel Li Ming – Chief of Security at Hunan Institute
Sun Wei – Chinese undercover agent in New York

CHINA COMMUNIST PARTY (CCP)
The Chairman – Powerful head of the CCP
Yang Shu – Chairman of the NPC Standing Committee
Mr. Kim – China's former premier

NEW YORK CITY MEDICAL EXAMINER'S OFFICE
Dr. Stan Galvin – Chief
Dr. Jeffrey Moss – Assistant Medical Examiner
Dr. Sebastian Gogoli – NYC Coroner
Dr. Julio Perez – Assistant Coroner
Dr. Priya Majmadur – Chairman, Department of Epidemiology
Dr. Sarah Samuel – Epidemiology Resident
Dr. Jason Furman – Professor

NYPD
Anthony DePalma – Chief of Detectives
Joe McDougal – Detective

WALL STREET JOURNAL
Li Zhou – Reporter based in China
Nick Robinson – WSJ Managing Editor

WASHINGTON, DC

The President
Will Porter – President's Chief of Staff
Tom Crantz – Secretary of Health
James Ryan – CDC
Dr. Frederick Kosent – Director of the FDA
Peter Ward – FDA Examiner
Jerry Kagos – FDA Examiner

BROOKFIELD INSTITUTE/LEXINGTON BIO CORPORATION

Dr. Geoffrey Ballen – Director of Brookfield Institute
Dr. Chen Chu – Young Scientist at Lexington Bio
Phillip Steppler – Chairman of Lexington Bio
Tim Channing – Chen Chu's attorney
Andy Cumberland – Regulatory Adviser to Lexington Bio
Mitchell Sedgewick – Adviser to Lexington Bio
James D'Arcy – Steppler's attorney
Sam Rapolo – Investor in Lexington Bio
Vito – Rapolo's assistant
Chris – Guard at Brookfield Entrance

INTRODUCTION

July 5, 2021

At first, he appeared to be an ordinary hiker, a backpacker seeking to ascend mountain peaks or to feel the thrill of conquering hazardous terrains in the depths of night. But this was not an ordinary hiker pursuing the conquest of earth's formations. Rather, he was there to meet a more ominous challenge: to confirm that he was carrying the most powerful weapon ever created.

He was a giant of a man dressed in black and had carefully chosen his destination, the small rural village of Wulajie located outside of Kougian in the province of Jilin in China's northeast corner. The village was the only settlement along a stretch of unpaved road lying within the shadow of the Changbai Mountains, an isolated outpost of humanity that modernity had long passed, its mud-brick buildings seemingly spawned from the lifeless earth to provide shelter for the living.

As he reached the outskirts of the village, the recollection of an earlier life guided his path. It had been years since he was last there, but with clear recall, he made his way to the large well in the center square that was the sole source of village water and peered down into the endless dark tranquility of its depth. Even as a young boy, he had marveled at its construction, how, with rudimentary tools, it was possible to dig into the bedrock a dozen feet down. No one could say when it was first built, nor who the stonemason was who shaped the rocks lining the inner curvature of the shaft that prevented its collapse, nor who designed the passage to allow the large wooden bucket attached by a thick braid of hemp shredded with age to draw water. But that momentary flight to youthful memory was cast aside by the enmity he held toward the villagers who had mocked his presence. And though it had been decades that he had been gone, the resentment from what was inflicted upon him in those early years still raged. He knew there would be a time for payback, and as he gazed deep into the well, he knew that time had arrived.

"You there, what are you doing?"

The visitor turned to see a thin, frail man approaching, a lantern in his hand whose light gave definition to the colorless scene. His lined face and wrinkled skin bespoke his age, yet his voice carried the strength of endless energy. As the old man raised his lamp better to observe the visitor, a moment of recognition and then fear coursed through his being as he witnessed the deep, twisted scar that marred the visitor's appearance.

"So, it's you. You've come back."

"Ah, the herb doctor. You remember me."

"You're not one to easily forget."

"Nor you." The recollection brought the visitor's fingers down along the scarred facial wound as if tracing the course of a deep-flowing river from its origin. "You think I've forgotten what was done to me?"

"You brought it upon yourself."

"And so shall it be done to you. But that's all in the past. Now I'm here for another reason."

"What is that?"

"To honor the place of my birth as the site for my new experiment."

"I've heard about your experiments. I don't want you near our water. Get out of here before I sound the alarm."

"Of course, but it will only take a moment. No need to wake anyone. And, by the way, I have something for you."

"I don't want anything from you."

"I'm afraid it's too late. You see, what I have is something to test your herbs on to see the effect of your ancient remedies, how strong your life energy of Chi really is against death."

"What do my remedies have to do with your experiments?"

"Well, let's find out." The visitor reached into his backpack, removed a small syringe filled with a red liquid, and held it up to show the old man.

"What are you doing? You're still as crazy as you were when you lived here."

Perhaps, but enjoying it more." He stood up, towering over the old man, and in one sudden, silent motion, placed his arm around the thin neck and inserted the narrow needle through the old man's right carotid, injecting its contents. It took but a moment for the silence of death to come to its terminal state as the frail body crumbled to the earth.

"Sorry old man, guess your herbs didn't help. But think of it this way: you donated your life in the name of medical progress."

Without hesitation the visitor removed a disposable hazmat suit from his backpack and placed it on. Whatever the visitor was about to do, he would be protected from the most potent biological and chemical agents. His gloved hands took out a reinforced stainless-steel cylinder, unscrewed the cap, and removed a sealed glass vial, carefully dropping it into the dark waters below.

"Okay, Thanatos. Let's see what kind of god you are."

The visitor knew it would take until dawn for the vial's seal to resorb, letting the virus out, and several days before the results would be known, but the wait would be worth it. Making certain he was not observed, he placed the empty cylinder and his protective gear back into the knapsack, lifted the old man over his shoulder as if a sack of flour, and deposited him into the nearby woods.

* * *

As dawn broke, the villagers made an unusual discovery: the perimeter of their isolated location had been sealed by members of China's Secret Police. At the threat of death, no one was to exit or enter the village, all external communication was blocked, and no response was to be given to the cries for help that would ensue. Two weeks later, the encirclement withdrew as mysteriously as it appeared. Whatever was without had evaporated overnight; whatever was within would never return. All that remained of the village was a ghost ship, existing but void of life.

⊢{ BOOK ONE }⊣

CHAPTER ONE

Changchun City Hospital, August 16, 2021

Chen Chu's eyes fluttered and slowly opened, adjusting to the peculiarity of light. He heard a distant voice. "I think he's coming out of it."

He tried to find the source but felt restrained. "Where am I?"

There was a gentle response. "You are in the hospital in Changchun City."

"What happened?"

"You were brought here unconscious six weeks ago. It's a miracle you're alive."

"I fought them with all my might until I couldn't fight anymore."

"Whom did you fight?"

"The evil spirits."

"You must have imagined it. They brought you in convulsing with fever."

"No, it happened. It was real."

"Would you like to tell me about it?"

The young man strained to recall the memory and spoke haltingly. "I don't know, it seems so long ago."

"Take your time."

"I was awakened by an unfamiliar sound, not the rumbling of thunder but something more ominous, like an approaching army trampling the earth beneath it, an unrelenting, unceasing force. I tried to understand, but there were no senses to guide me, no smell nor taste nor feel, only a distant presence that, as it drew near, brought a rustling, as if a wind was guiding a storm through a sea of leaves. But there was no wind, and there were no trees." Chen hesitated as if trying to reconfigure what occurred next.

"Are you too tired to continue? Perhaps you would like to rest?" the voice asked.

"No, it's important that I remember. I felt like Tang, the hero in the ancient story *Journey to the West* I read as a boy. Like Tang, I was lost in a strange land, desperately wanting to get home, but I couldn't."

"Why was that?"

"Because the evil spirits wouldn't let me. They wanted to kill me, but I fought them."

"Why?"

"Because I didn't want to die." Chen paused, his face perspiring, his head moving from side to side, his breathing rapid but shallow. He felt a cool cloth gently wipe his face and heard the caring voice.

"Perhaps that's all we should speak about for now."

Chen shook his head. "No, I must tell you the rest. I tried to get away but didn't know where to go. I tried calling for my parents, but it was as if the sounds never left my mouth. I struggled, but I couldn't continue, and then . . ." Chen's eyes closed, his arms reaching out as if to block an attack.

"And then what?"

Chen's jaws tightened as he swallowed. "I realized there was no escape, that I would never see my dear mother or father again. I fought so hard . . ." He stopped speaking, and his eyes closed as he fell back into the pillow. His trembling ceased, and his breathing slowly returned to normal, as if he were finding peace in sleep.

* * *

As Chen Chu lay in his hospital bed, he fell in and out of reveries, replays of his life growing up in the rural village where his family had lived longer than anyone could remember. The villagers had farmed the land for over two thousand years, planting wheat, corn, and potatoes on small plots or raising goats or chickens to sell at the market in Kougian for their meager earnings. Although advances had come to the village, including electricity, cell phones, and television, poverty remained in spite of China's declaration to bring its poor villagers into a "new socialist countryside."

Chen's father was the village's only doctor. He practiced traditional Chinese medicine passed down from his father and his father's father before that, carrying on the ancient traditions of healing, often receiving produce in payment, and, when treatment failed, hanging the deceased's name outside for all to see, as was their way. His mother worked in the factory near the entrance to Kougian that made children's clothing, using old Sanshin sewing machines overseen by managers whose daily quotas often resulted in bleeding fingers that had to clot before the cloth oozed red. Chen's mother made eighty dollars a month, twice as much as many of the farmers in the village earned.

Chen was a quiet, frail, pale child who displayed an unusual curiosity in the activities around him. Every evening, his mother would put him to sleep by reciting ancient stories and legends that she had learned as a child. His favorite was "The Robber and the Bell," about a robber who stole a huge, beautiful bell, but when he carried it off, it began to ring. Afraid that the noise would bring attention to his stealing the bell, the robber solved the problem by tearing his shirt and plugging the pieces into his ears, thinking no one else would hear it if he couldn't. Chen was barely three when he gave a hearty laugh and told his mother that the robber was not very smart.

But Chen was smart, and at an early age, his father taught him how to read and count, add, subtract, and tell time. Soon, the boy found that he preferred browsing through his father's books inside the house rather than playing games with his cousins outside. He could read for hours, especially the Shénmó fantasy books based on the gods, immortals, and monsters of Chinese mythology. His favorite was the sixteenth-century novel *Journey to the West*, written during the Ming Dynasty and considered the greatest example of Shénmó fiction. And when Chen was not reading, he would sit in the corner in silence, observing how his father healed the local villagers of their ailments using special herbs combined into tea to restore the body's harmony between the opposing forces of yin and yang that can block Chi, the body's vital energy. His father explained that block was the cause of disease, and the herbs would remove the block and allow Chi to flow through the channels that connect to the body's organs and maintain their health. As far back as Chen could remember, he would help his father plant goji berries, ginseng, dang gui, wild yams, and lotus seeds in the small herb garden behind their house. And he remembered how, each morning, his father prepared a tea for Chen to drink.

"You are young, my son, and healthy. Your Chi is flowing freely. Now is the time to keep the energy from ever being blocked. Within this tea is the secret to a long life."

Chen recalled how, on special occasions, he would accompany his father to the market in Kougian to obtain unusual plants for a particular patient. How he loved those trips, sitting next to his father in their old faded-green Chinese Hongqi sedan with its rebuilt engine. It was at those times, driving slowly through the countryside, that his father would explain how each of the herbs had its own secret power and how the herbs, when taken in the correct proportions, could unleash the body's ability for strength and healing.

"You mean like Superman, papa?"

"Yes, my son, like Superman. And someday, you could also learn how to heal people as I did from my father and as he did from his father."

"Would it make the god Shàngdì proud of me?"

Chen's father smiled, and he placed his hand on Chen's shoulder. "Yes, my son, both Shàngdì and the ancients in Tian, heaven, would be happy to see that the traditions they taught as far back as the Shang dynasty in the eleventh and twelfth centuries were being carried on today."

Chen's face lit up. "Then I would like that."

The boy recalled everything, and when he was old enough to go to the local school in Kougian, he already knew more than the other students, almost all of whom came from peasant homes. Their parents hoped that education would make their children's lives better than theirs. In China's state-run education system, it was compulsory for students to complete at least grades one to nine. Chen's class had forty-five students learning math, history, science, and then English, which was mandatory from the sixth grade on. Chen loved to learn, especially about animals and plants, and the teacher told his parents that their son showed promise as a worthy student. Following the ninth grade, Chen was selected to attend the three-year regional high school for gifted students in the province's capital, Changchun, a large city that required a two-hour bus ride from home. Chen's parents received glowing reports from the administrator, especially about their son's ability in math and science. When Chen scored the highest of all the senior students on the Gaokao, the competitive nine-hour final exam, the administrator suggested that Chen continue his education by applying to Jiao Tong University in Shanghai, China's finest research institute known as "The MIT of the East."

"Only one other of our students was ever admitted to Jiao Tong, and he is now a doctor, a scientist, and a government leader. His name is General Han Shi, and I believe you could be as successful."

At graduation, Chen received the Qiushi Outstanding Youth Award and was admitted with a full scholarship to Jiao Tong University. Though his parents were proud of his accomplishments, they silently lamented that he would be going so far away. Modernity was outpacing tradition, and Chen's father struggled to realize that Chen would not practice the art of ancient medicine as the generations before him had. As much as the son had to deal with the challenge of a new life in a huge city, so the father had to deal with the challenge of a changing world and that his son would be part of that world. Chen knew his voyage would take him away from those traditions and in spite of his looking forward to a new future, a well of sadness from the past remained within him.

* * *

It was several hours later that Chen opened his eyes and heard quiet voices in the room. "You're still here?" he asked.

The caring voice responded, "I am."

"You think it never happened?"

"No, I believe it did."

"Then what was it?"

"It was your struggle to live. And you did, against an overwhelming and unforgiving enemy."

"What could cause such evil?"

"There was an unknown virus." The nurse perused the missing information from Chen's file. "Do you know who you are?"

The young man thought for a moment. "My name is Chen Chu. I came home to spend the summer with my parents before I begin my PhD program at university in Shanghai."

"What village are you from?"

"Wulajie."

The nurse looked at his record. "Then it was a miracle."

"What do you mean?"

"That was the epicenter."

"I see."

The nurse made a note.

"And my parents? When can I see them?"

The nurse paused before responding. "Your parents? I'm afraid they did not survive. Only you and a young girl survived. Perhaps your dream was real, for the plague swept through the village like a raging demon, killing everyone in its path. When the emergency team went in, there was no one else to save. Only the two of you were found gasping for breath. The village streets were filled with the dead. The toll was 115, and yet, oddly, no one outside of the village was infected."

Chen closed his eyes to try and stop the tears. "Will I be here much longer?"

"I don't know. We'll have the doctor look at you. He will tell you when you can leave."

* * *

By the end of the week, Chen was discharged from the hospital. The nurses had brought him new clothes, and as he thanked them, he was handed an envelope.

"This is all that we have from when they brought you to the hospital. It was in your pocket."

Chen recognized the gift that his father had given him before he left for university. He had always carried it with him, a photo of his parents and himself as a young boy planting herbs in the garden. On the back of the photo, written in his father's hand, was an old Chinese proverb: *He who sacrifices his conscience to ambition burns a picture to obtain the ashes*. He returned the photo to its envelope and carefully placed it into his pocket for safekeeping.

It was a hot and humid August when he made the final thirteen-hundred-mile journey south to the university in Shanghai to begin his new studies. There was no one to say goodbye to. Apart from the envelope, all but the memories were gone.

CHAPTER TWO

August 16, 2021

Doctor Han Shi, Chief Scientific Officer of the Hunan Institute of Virology and Major General in the Ministry of State Security's Secret Police of the People's Republic of China, sat at his desk reviewing the data. It had been more than six weeks since the experiment had been completed, and he had worked day and night at organizing the results into a well-written article for journal publication. Han titled the paper "The Wulajie Study – Thanatos 2021," and after approving the final edits, had it delivered directly to the seven most powerful men in China, the Politburo Standing Committee. It was a lifetime of work, and all he could do now was wait for a response as if he were a Ph.D. candidate awaiting the final verdict of pass or fail.

As he sat back in the comfort of his Wuhan office, he sipped a glass of Moutai and turned on the nightly news report on CCTV, China Central Television. He knew his manuscript would never be published, could never be published, nor would he receive the satisfaction of admiration from his fellow scientists around the world. There would be no CCTV report that the 117 residents of Wulajie had died, with the exception of two who remained in a coma; there would be no mention of the autopsies revealing the massive tissue destruction that had taken place, nor the biochemical assays that indicated the presence of a powerful but unknown COVID-19 viral mutation. He knew this because powerful men could control what the masses were told, and he had a benefactor who was the most powerful of those men, one who believed in the importance of the work that he was doing. That man was the Chairman of the Communist Party himself.

Even though the events in Wulajie may never be known to his peers, the thought of death to 115 villagers brought a smile to his face. And what of the two remaining comatose villagers? Surely, they would also join their neighbors in death. The fact was he had proved he could kill large numbers without a bullet. All it took was one nanoparticle. To Han, it was all so neat and clean. Of course, some would criticize the ethics of his methods, but to Han, the death of a few villagers was the cost of doing business. Everything in the name of progress.

But he knew his work remained incomplete, for though he proved the potency of his molecule in causing death, he had yet to find the antidote to sustain life. To the chairman, such control granted vast political power, but to Han, selecting who should live and who should die was personal, the ability to carry out revenge.

*　*　*

Two weeks passed before he received a response. He was to report to The Politburo Standing Committee in the Party Chamber within the Great Hall of the People of China in Beijing on Tuesday, August 30, at 4:00 P.M. The subject of his presentation would be "China's Need for a New Defense Policy in Response to a Changing World."

To Han, addressing the seven most powerful men in the People's Republic of China would be the final acknowledgment of his brilliance. And yet, deep within his psyche, there was a regret that the villagers could not see the success that met the boy they mocked.

*　*　*

Han Shi wore his newly pressed major general uniform as he approached the massive dimensions of the Great Hall at the western edge of Tiananmen Square, its huge red flags unfurling in the breeze. He walked alone through the empty corridor surrounded by twenty huge white marble pillars, the sounds of his polished black boots echoing off the stone floor. When he reached the two large steel doors that guarded the People's Chamber, he took a deep breath, appreciating the significance of the event but realizing there was no one to share it with. Perhaps there was a moment of remorse, but Han had always been a loner, never displaying an emotional attachment, never a thought of sharing his success with anyone because there never had been an anyone. There would be women, but never the consideration or ability to have a mutual relationship.

From his youth, the incident that caused his facial disfigurement led him to a life of solitary pursuits and being regarded as an object of amusement, a freak, an oddity, an outsider. Though he tried, he was not able to overcome the humiliation that caused him to harbor a life filled with hatred for those who made him an object of their contempt. And so, from an early age, he had come to realize that he alone was responsible for his achievements, and all he had to rely on was his mental brilliance and his physical strength. His would be the life of a lonely genius. To a man like Han, though he was about to receive credit for his accomplishments, such a feeling was always transitory, cut short by dissatisfaction, perpetually seeking but never achieving happiness. Yet, there was one man who believed in him, one man who encouraged him to pursue his work—the chairman himself. Han Shi returned that faith with ultimate devotion.

The two uniformed guards saluted and opened the doors. The Chamber was a large room upholstered in blue with seven chairs widely spaced in an arc, the middle chair reserved for the chairman. Han was told to take the single chair facing China's most powerful leaders. As he sat down, his eyes caught sight of the large red star at the center of the ceiling cupola, hovering as if protecting its leaders from harm. One day, he thought, he would lead these leaders.

"Thank you, General Han, for your presence." The welcome came from Yang Shu, the powerful head of the Politburo Standing Committee. "We have reviewed your defense plan, read your Wulajie study, and considered the results of your recent experiments. Is it correct to assume that, based on your conclusions, you believe your plan of a few nanoparticles will make China the leader of the world of nations without the need for our armies to build new weapons and train more troops?"

"That is correct."

"Quite an assertion, General, that the long history of the world's battles based on power can be altered as a result of your studies."

Han looked directly at Yang. "I not only believe it, I know it. Power no longer needs to be based on ever-larger missiles and more lethal nuclear explosives, nor does it need munition plants and forged steel factories." Han regarded the faces of the seated Chinese leaders. "My comrades, power is no longer macro; it is micro, and its source will be generated from the laboratories in our land, not the bullets from our guns. The unseen will be our strength, a strength for which there is no defense. China can no longer look to the past. It is time to seek the future."

"Tell me, General." It was Mr. Kim, the former premier, who retained immense influence and was a threat to the chairman's plans to stay in power. "This assumes that you not only have the mutation and the ability to release it but that you have the ability to control it. In other words, you have the antidote."

"We are working on that as we speak. That should not be a problem."

"And when will your plan be ready to activate?"

"With proper funding to bring in the top young scientists and reequip my labs, it will take four years."

Yang Shu interjected. "Another four years? One would think that should have been accomplished by now. How can you offer a defense plan when there is no defense? Did you not just tell us the unseen will be our strength, a strength for which there is no counter? It seems to me, and many others here in the room, that as of now, if you unleash your nanoparticle, we'll all die. "

Han felt the rage, the same anger he felt toward the villagers, but he clenched his fists until they were white as he contained the wrath. He looked over at the chairman, appreciating the political battle that was taking place behind the scenes for Chinese leadership, but the chairman remained staring coldly ahead.

"So tell me, Mr. Han," Kim continued, "after you have found the antidote, then you will release your mutation?"

"There will never be that need. All there will be is the threat of release. The nations of the world will fall to their knees to prevent the mass destruction of their homelands."

"But without the antidote, you will only be bluffing."

"A few small incidents, such as was demonstrated in the village of Wulajie, will be all that is necessary."

Kim turned to the chairman. "And, Mr. Chairman, you are in favor of this plan?"

Whatever undercurrent of sounds there was emanating from those in the room came to a sudden stop. The challenge had been sent. Kim gave Yang and the other leaders of the opposition a knowing glance, for he had cornered the chairman into risking his position of power behind the success of Han's new defense policy. They and others would wait their time until the next election. Five years go quickly.

"I am."

Within an hour, the Committee passed the resolution for Han's policy to lead China into the second half of the twenty-first century. Even the most critical of the members accepted Han's defense plan after the chairman put the power of his position behind it. The resolution passed, but the success or failure would be on the chairman. His enemies had what they needed.

CHAPTER THREE

May 2022

In May of 2022, Chen received his doctorate with highest honors in bioengineering, an award shared with another student, Jiang Fang. From the first day of classes, Chen and Jiang were fast friends. To an observer, the friendship of the two was not to be predicted, for their backgrounds suggested they had little in common. And yet, opposites did attract, for their yin and yang instantly balanced each other. Whereas Jiang grew up in the big city of Shanghai with its cultural advantages and modern and sophisticated way of life, Chen's background in his small rural village limited his exposure to his school, his parents, his relatives, and his books. It resulted in Chen being more guarded with others, living a more serious life, and focusing on his studies. Jiang, in contrast, was easygoing, extroverted, comfortable with others, and always had a smile on his face.

Chen appreciated Jiang's confidence and understanding of the intrigues of politics, and Jiang admired Chen's devotion to his studies, his academic brilliance, and, in some ways, his naivete. At school, they were inseparable, rooming together. Jiang even tried to introduce Chen to his female friends, but Chen appeared more interested in the chemistry of molecules than the attraction of the sexes. They spent long hours in the lab working on their studies and bouncing ideas off each other. Even their areas of research complemented each other, Jiang seeking the mechanism of viral transfer and Chen seeking to destroy the virus even before that transfer could be made. Chen's thesis on viral virulence was awarded the Chinese National Science Distinguished Award for Young Scholars, and his manuscript was accepted for publication.

It was at that time that he, Jiang, and several others of China's best and brightest were invited to the Wuhan Institute of Virology for job opportunities. On the day of their visit to Wuhan, they were approached by an official-looking giant of a man, trim with nothing but muscle, a shiny bald dome, large round eyes as black as night, wearing a suit that stretched over his sculpted body and a long disfiguring facial scar that left its memorable mark. When introduced, Chen recalled the name from his village, Han Shi. Doctor Han explained that he was looking for talented biochemical engineers to work for him in the bioengineering department of the Wuhan Institute as part of its strategy to increase its expertise in medical research. He explained that the Chinese Academy of Sciences administered the Wuhan Institute and reported to the State Council of the People's Republic of China. The young engineers would be working in China's most respected Biosafety Level 4 laboratory. Han explained with pride that the new scientists would be given the opportunity to help develop a strategy to save the world.

"My young friends, the world will soon face a turning point. In the next ten to twenty years, the entire existence of our planet will be threatened by the sins of our fathers. It's not just climate change that is delivering that threat, but also the limitation of sheer space on Earth, a competition between where this growing human population will live and where they will grow the food to feed themselves. Either we limit our population growth, or nature will do it for us. Indeed, the natural world is already carrying out the mission, but the comforts of modern living have blinded us from seeing the real causes of man's sorrow. Yet our forefathers recognized them: pestilence, sword, and famine, but the greatest loss of life is to pestilence. My friends, nature is providing man with its own means of population control: the viral pandemic. And to control such virulence is what we here at the Institute for Virology are engaged in and why we need the minds of young men and women such as yourselves to join us here in the race for survival. This past COVID-19 virus that spread throughout the world was just the beginning. We must find a way of preventing such epidemics from rising again. And, please remember, we are part of an international community; viruses have no borders. You will be associating with the finest scientific minds in the United States, Israel, and Western Europe and have the opportunity to be present at international conferences. So, with that, any questions?"

Jiang raised his hand.

"Yes, you are Jiang Fang. Is that correct?"

"Yes, sir. There were reports of a COVID-19-like virus that killed all the inhabitants of a rural village in northeast China last year. Does anyone know where it came from?"

Han looked carefully at Jiang. "No, Jiang, I'm afraid we know very little about the origins of that virus, but that is exactly what we here at the institute are trying to answer. That is why we need all of you to work with us and why there can be no greater cause for you to dedicate your lives to than preventing the eradication of mankind."

Chen was interested. The thought of preventing further pandemics from a virus that took the lives of his parents, his village, and nearly himself had haunted him since he awakened from his coma. Why was he the one who lived? Was he chosen for a reason? Was this his *mingyun*, his destiny? Did the gods choose him to find a cure to prevent such a plague from occurring again?

As the graduates toured the huge complex, Han called Chen aside. "Dr. Chu, I understand you are from the village of Wulajie. I also grew up there."

Chen recalled his high school administrator mentioning Dr. Han's name. "Yes, I was told that we went to the same high school and how successful you have become."

"That is true. And I have reports that you are also interested in bioengineering like myself. I read your article in the Journal of Virology on countering viral virulence. It certainly is a fresh approach. I thought it to be excellent work."

"Thank you. I enjoy my studies."

"That's why we need top minds like yourself to prevent the terrible tragedy that occurred to our village."

"Yes, that would be important."

"I was so sorry to hear about your parents."

"Thank you. I have not been able to find any reporting on that virus."

"I believe they are still trying to determine its cause. Once that's done, I'm certain we will get the answers we seek. I haven't been in the village since I left for university, but I remember your father."

"Yes, he had many patients in the village."

"And you survived."

"But why? That is what I have been working on."

Han thought for a moment. "I know. I also would like to know that answer, and that's why it would be an honor to have you join us at the institute."

"Thank you. I certainly will consider it."

As Han left, Jiang approached Chen. "What was that all about?"

"Not much. The general was telling me how he grew up in the same village where I grew up. He knew about my parents dying and sent his regrets and told me he wanted me to work with him. He's also interested in why I survived."

"Yeah, he wants me to work here also. I heard about this General Han: They call him Batman."

Chen was surprised. "Batman?"

"Because his expertise is in virology. I've been told that he's done more re-search on bats and their ability to harbor coronaviruses than anyone, spending time in Manhago, deep in the mountain valleys of southern China. Supposedly, he's been investigating the virus that infested the horseshoe bats living within the caves in Yunnan, part of the Enshi prefecture in Hubei Province."

Chen was intrigued. "What was he looking for?"

Jiang lowered his voice as several of the other students passed. "How long it took the bats to pass the virus they carried to other animals."

"For what purpose?"

"To time the death of the animals."

Chen's eyes widened. "Sounds dangerous, but if it can prevent the virus from killing our people, then it must be worth it."

Jiang continued in a low voice. "Except that it may not be about prevention."

"What do you mean?"

Jiang resumed. "I heard he's been experimenting on how to modify a virus, make it more powerful, more deadly."

"You mean gain-of-function research?"

"That's what I heard."

"But why?"

"They say the leaders want it for military purposes."

"Military?"

"They say Han has contacts with powerful members of the ruling party in China. He was awarded the military rank of a *shaojiang*, a major general, by the chairman himself, and he was elected president of the China Association for Science and Technology."

Chen realized that Han was to be taken most seriously. "What's he trying to accomplish?"

"The research appears to involve making bat coronaviruses more virulent, potentially having viral loads up to ten thousand times higher than normal."

"For what purpose?"

Jiang spoke quietly. "To transmit it to mice that have been 'humanized' by splicing them with human tissue. He then infects them with the altered virus. Apparently, he wants to increase transmission from one human to another, and that's why he's seeking new researchers to begin the final phase of his work."

"And what's that?"

"To time the death of the bat virus on man."

Chen was alarmed. "If that's true, then he's playing with fire. If he ever made such a potent virus transmittable to man and it got out, who could survive? We've both worked with mice; just think how many times mice have bitten technicians. That's all it would take for the virus to escape the lab. If he can really make a virus that potent, it could start a pandemic more deadly than man has ever known."

"I know. Some even call him 'The Merchant of Death,' but you can't deny it's fascinating. Can you imagine the power that China would hold if it had such a potent weapon? It could rule the world."

Chen was surprised by his friend's response. "No, Jiang, it could be its end."

Jiang answered. "Then I will learn how to control it."

* * *

As the time to decide their future employment approached, Chen realized that he and Jiang differed in their objectives. Whereas Jiang was intrigued by General Han's belief that saving the planet required destroying lives and limiting population growth, Chen had been raised with the goal of saving lives. To Chen, it appeared that Han was seeking the keys to death while he sought the keys to survival. When the final decision was made, Jiang chose to stay in China and join the institute, and Chen accepted an offer to work in a far-off location, an offer that he could not refuse. And so the two friends parted ways, promising to stay in touch, wishing each other success in their new paths. On the day of Chen's departure, Jiang drove him to the airport. They embraced each other and said their goodbyes. Each felt that a part of themselves was being lost. As Donne wrote, *no man is an island*.

* * *

July 2022

Chen's offer came from the world-famous Dr. Geoffrey Ballan, Senior Vice President of Research at the Brookfield Institute of Viral Immunology in New York and the Charles Linton Professor of Chemistry and Chemical Biology at the University Medical School. He was a tall, imposing figure with a full mane of white hair and a well-cropped beard. He was one of the giants in immunology, but as he grew frustrated with failures in present viral research, he began looking for a new approach. He searched for a scientist whose work offered original research that addressed a new hypothesis with experimental observations that would lead to new concepts and new directions. It was then that Ballan read Chen's article published in the last issue of the *Journal of Virology*, the most prestigious peer-reviewed journal in the field of viruses. Chen's article was based on his PhD thesis, whose subject he had spent a great deal of time determining. If only he could understand why he lived and the others died. What gave him the resistance to fight the virus?

It was when, by chance, he found the picture of his parents and himself as a young boy planting the herb garden that a new idea set in. He recalled his father's words: "Remember, my son, the body is capable of healing itself. Open the meridians and allow the Chi to run freely through its channels to reach all parts of the body effortlessly. Where there is freedom, there is health."

This is where Chen felt he should focus his research. He began to outline his thoughts, equating the Chi of the East with the immune system of the West. "Treat the body, not the symptom" was the wisdom his father had provided. "Give the body the opportunity to heal itself, and it will. You are young, my son, and healthy. Your Chi is flowing freely. Now is the time to keep the energy from ever being blocked. Within this tea I make for you each day is the secret to a long life." Chen smiled as he recalled how, as a young boy, he used to cry out to his father: "The tea makes me like Superman!" and his father would smile and say, "Yes, my son, to make you like Superman."

That was the beginning of his breakthrough research—refining his techniques in analyzing his father's herbs. After months of meticulous work, he discovered that the molecular structures of the herbs were derivatives of proteins found in the immune mechanism. Could this be what he was searching for? Is this why he had survived? Was it the herbs? Were his father's remedies that effective? Chen devoted himself to seeking the answer.

Ballan read Chen's article over and over, reviewing the procedures, checking the chemistry, and realizing the potential in Chen's conclusion of finding a new treatment to counter viral pathogenesis. Ballan was amazed at the simplicity of the concept, and yet it offered a totally different approach and mechanism of action than he had been aware of. He contacted Chen and learned during their virtual meetings that the young man was one of the two to survive the isolated plague that had destroyed his village. Ballan realized that Chen's research was really about Chen himself. How did he survive? Why the difference in resistance? It was then that Ballan offered Chen the opportunity: "Move to New York and continue your research at Brookfield, and if we see promise, you will have your own lab." It was an offer that could not be denied.

* * *

September 2022

The trip to America opened a whole new world for Chen. He could feel the freedom with every breath. To Chen, America was a far different culture than where he had grown up, and though he excelled in his work and appreciated the magic of New York, he missed the modesty of the life of his childhood. In response, he surrounded himself with his studies and spent long hours working alone in the laboratory. Ballan was like a father, taking the young man under his wing, spending hours with him in the laboratory, teaching him and learning from him. And Chen responded, working tirelessly with his two assistants on his father's herbs, analyzing them and learning the relationship between the chemical makeup of the herbs and the composition of the immunoglobulins that compose the body's defense system. Soon, he began to synthesize the molecules into a pharmaceutical application for injection, and when satisfied, he informed Ballan that he was ready to test his formulation on the viruses themselves.

What Chen now proposed was to go beyond what Ballan and others had contributed in activating the body's natural immunity defenses. Rather, Chen was going beyond activation, seeking amplification. In his own way, Chen was redefining gain-of-function research, but instead of making a virus more potent, he was more interested in making the body's immune system more powerful. Chen's work had taken three years before he and his staff moved into Brookfield's new Biosafety Level 4 lab.

Chen soon discovered that his newly synthesized molecule not only achieved activation but had increased the performance of all scavenger cells well beyond the control group. He had achieved amplification. Chen called it Chi Activated Immunotherapy in honor of his father, for he realized that what he had done was open the body's meridians to allow its optimum performance as his father had taught. That night, as Chen lay in bed, he sensed a profound fulfillment with the results he had achieved. He could not tell if it was a dream, but he was certain he heard his father speaking: "My dearest son, I was wrong. You have carried on the family's tradition greater than I or any of those before me could have imagined. You are bringing it to the entire world. Thank you. You have made us proud."

CHAPTER FOUR

THREE YEARS LATER

July 9, 2025, New York City
Alumni Hall, NY Medical Center

It was one fifteen in the afternoon when Dr. Jeffrey Moss, the Assistant Medical Examiner of the City of New York, entered Alumni Hall of the New York Medical Center. He was fifteen minutes late, and as he scanned the newly built acoustic-paneled auditorium with its upholstered tiered seating and latest audio and visual technology, he realized that every one of the 912 seats was filled. His seat was in the front reserved section, and Sebastian Gogoli, the Coroner of the City of New York, pointed to the saved seat next to him.

"Glad you made it. What happened?"

"Shooting on Park Avenue. Two dead."

"Motive?"

"Looks like robbery."

"Did you find the perp?"

"Not yet. It's on my list, but it's happening more every day. The city's falling apart."

"And keeping my morgue busy."

"I wish it wasn't so." Jeff scoured the room. "Big turnout. Didn't realize the place would be packed."

"They're here to hear what Priya has to say. No one wants a repeat of what we went through back in 2020."

The attendees' chatter ceased as a short, balding figure in his sixties, with a paunch as noticeable as his unmanaged bush mustache, walked to the dais.

"Welcome to this year's International Epidemiological Society Meeting, the largest gathering of epidemiologists from all over the world. Epidemiology is the basis of our public health system, helping to explain the forces that influence man's well-being, and through the use of computer-generated data, today's epidemiology can utilize this information to save lives and improve human potential. Today, we will look to the past to prepare for the future, a future that includes the unseen assassin that has affected us all so recently. Too often, we fail to respond to what is lurking below the surface, yet history has taught us that now is the time to prepare for the next assault of what has proved to be man's greatest and one of its oldest enemies—plague. To help us better understand this challenge, we are most fortunate to have as our speaker one of the world's foremost epidemiologists, Dr. Priya Majmadur. Dr. Majmadur is Professor and Chair of the Department of Epidemiology at the New York School of Medicine. Trained as a cardiovascular surgeon, she went on to receive a doctorate in molecular parasitology and virology. She has authored numerous articles, including her well-known models predicting disease outcomes of influenza. Her multidisciplinary research is recognized worldwide, especially her past work with COVID-19 infections and lung obstruction. Ladies and gentlemen, I am honored to introduce Dr. Priya Majmadur."

As applause filled the room, the speaker walked to the podium. Priya Majmadur was in her mid-thirties and petite with large black eyes and pitch-black hair set in a ponytail. She wore a white doctor's coat with her name in script printed above the left breast pocket, under which was inscribed the NY School of Medicine logo.

"Thank you, Dr. Felton, and thank you all for coming and the many more attending via video conferencing." Priya paused, looked out at the audience, her eyes momentarily recognizing Jeff, and then looked down as if collecting her thoughts.

"It has been five years since the world was held hostage by the virus that caused the 2020 COVID-19 pandemic. This world, this nation, this government, our scientists, and our healthcare providers were unprepared. As a result, over one million individuals here in the United States died, and global mortality continues to approach five hundred million with over eight million deaths. And that's with over twelve billion vaccinations being given. We must never allow that to happen again."

From her pocket, she removed a pair of designer black-rimmed glasses and placed them on as she introduced the first of a series of PowerPoint slides. She spoke in a clear, scholarly voice that reflected her command of the subject.

"Plague has long been a part of human history. As man has migrated across the globe, infectious diseases have moved with them. Today, outbreaks are so common that we have become almost immune to them, and that is both figuratively and literally. And this war between unseen microbes and man has taken a far greater toll than deaths resulting from the wars initiated by man's inhumanity to man. The first plagues, we are taught, occurred in Egypt when God warned the pharaoh to let his people go. But since then, recorded plagues have resulted in the deaths of hundreds of millions, often caused by smallpox, measles, or the Yersinia pestis bacteria spread by rats and fleas in Europe's famous Black Death of 1348, resulting in the loss of over two hundred million people. But it was only following 1492, when Europeans brought their diseases to the immunologically unprepared Americas, that the greatest mortality occurred. The rate of death was 95 percent, but the 5 percent that survived, resistant to the new variants, was enough for man to remain in existence. It was only a little over one hundred years ago, spread by the return of soldiers following the First World War, that the so-called Spanish flu, caused by the H1N1 virus spread from pigs, resulted in the deaths of up to one hundred million people. Even within our lifetimes, we were victims of the Asian flu in 1957, caused by the H2N2 virus; the 1968 Hong Kong flu, caused by the H3N2 virus; HIV beginning in 1981; the swine flu from the H1N1 virus; and the ubiquitous coronavirus causing SARS in 2002, MERS in 2015, and the COVID-19 pandemic only five years ago. Yet, despite the persistence of disease throughout history, there's one consistent trend over time—a gradual reduction in the death rate, largely a result of advances in epidemiology. Through the use of powerful tools, we have achieved improvements in healthcare and increased our understanding of the factors that cause pandemics, allowing man to mitigate their effects.

"The fact is that viruses are really quite simple; it's containing their spread that is complex. So, what did we learn from that last COVID-19 experience? It started when someone near you coughed or sneezed, followed by an invisible spray of millions of droplets of mucous or saliva that inundated the air around you and that you unsuspectingly inhaled. And in those droplets were billions of minute virus particles that were suspended in space and quickly drawn into the stream of air that is carried into your nose or mouth. They attached to a specific receptor on the surface of the cells lining the mucous membrane and were carried down the respiratory tract. But what made the proteins on the surface of the coronavirus so dangerous were the spikes that extended out like anchors and locked onto those cells, taking them hostage and installing themselves into the replicating system of the cell—producing millions more viral particles that filled the entire respiratory tract. Think of it as a vacuum cleaner hose that is full of debris. Just as the vacuum can no longer suction in dirt due to being clogged, so the pipes to the lungs are clogged, not allowing oxygen to pass into the bloodstream to nourish the cells of the body. In about five days, the patient began to feel symptoms: first, a dry cough and fever, perhaps even a sore throat, tiredness, aches, and even loss of taste and smell. In COVID-19, 80 percent of cases with symptoms were alleviated within days or weeks, but for those at risk, the aged or the medically compromised, the attack became overpowering. As it moved deeper into the lungs, perhaps two to seven days after the beginning of symptoms, viral pneumonia developed with shortness of breath until breathing was no longer possible.

On top of that, we must add the complications of the body's immune mechanism, which attempted to fight off the intruder. Molecules, called cytokines, were quickly called to the site of the infection, and with the white blood cells and inflammatory fluids that inundated the infection site in the lungs, there was further blocking of the airway until oxygen exchange became increasingly difficult. Once the lung became so damaged, the body automatically went into acute respiratory distress syndrome or ARDS. Thus far, we have no treatment for ARDS, so the patient was placed on a respirator, buying time to see if the body could heal itself. But once on a respirator, few survived.

"And finally, our country and the world have now learned that COVID-19 has become endemic and, like the flu, will require yearly vaccinations."

At this point, Priya turned off the PowerPoint, removed her glasses, and looked directly at the audience. "And that, my friends, is our challenge, to be ready for the next viral invasion. And it will most certainly occur. It behooves those of us here, scientists, health care workers, governments, and private industry, to continue to work on new vaccines, new approaches, and new therapies. For if we fail, the next mutation will be the final one for mankind."

"Tài wǎnle!" The words filled the walls of the auditorium like the echoes of a canyon. A gasp came from the attendees who understood the ominous Mandarin words. Jeff and Gogoli turned around, and Priya looked out to determine where the message came from.

"Láibují!" came a second declaration. "It's too late!"

Priya understood the shade of difference between the two Chinese phrases. The first simply said *It's too late* as if something were being worked on. The second inferred it was already too late—whatever was being worked on had been completed.

"May I ask who said that?"

"I did." From the rear of the hall, a giant of a man with a shaved head and eyes black as midnight stood. The man presented a deceptive smile. His response was in a clear, sonorous voice. "You Americans are already too late. Your government has prioritized other needs, and your private industrialists see no profit in spending their time and money on a problem that may or may not occur. As you said, Doctor, the next mutation will be the final one, but some have already prepared for that event."

"Who are you?"

The man responded to Priya with an air of superiority. "Who I am is not important, but know this: To those who have prepared will go the spoils, and you will find out very soon."

As Priya regarded the speaker, a sudden chill of fear struck her body. It wasn't the pitch-black eyes from which it emanated nor the chiseled cheekbones, but a deep, twisting, disfiguring scar carved into the left side of his face, a mutilation that provoked a singular meaning—death.

Priya's eyes followed him as he walked out of the silent hall. His warning would keep her up for many nights, but it was the sight of his face that would not be forgotten.

CHAPTER FIVE

January 2026

It was six months later when Chen received a call from an unknown cell. It was his friend Jiang at the Wuhan Institute. Jiang explained that he had to call from a secure phone due to the tight surveillance that he and the other scientists were under. He described how he had become the top assistant in the lab working with potent viruses, spending long hours under General Han's direction, responsible for supervising the work.

"And is it what you thought?" Chen asked.

"You mean in terms of gain of function? Yes, that part is true. Over the years, Han built the most potent virus against man. It's amazing; whatever animal it contacts is destroyed immediately."

Chen was impressed. "That is amazing."

"Yes, he's a genius."

"And a merchant of death?"

"Yes, I suppose that is also true."

Chen considered the response. "But his genius must be in his engineering a molecule to destroy such a potent virus."

"That remains a problem. He never did."

Chen was taken aback. "You mean he developed a killer that can't be controlled?"

Jiang answered with apparent guilt. "I'm afraid so, and in spite of all our work, we've found no answers, and the general is getting frustrated."

Chen thought for a moment. "Listen, Jiang. We've had some success here at Brookfield with some potent mutated COVID-19 viruses, though nothing like what you are speaking about. Is there any possibility that the Hunan Institute might have samples that I could test your virus on?"

Jiang immediately realized the potential Chen was describing. "If you could help on that end, it would be most important. Han is already getting criticism from the ruling committee about his not being able to control what he has made. Let me check with him, and I'll get back to you."

* * *

General Han was at his desk reviewing papers when Jiang broached the subject. "Yes, I remember Chen Chu. A very bright young man from my village. Amazingly, he survived that virus." Han paused before adding, "I have no idea how. Sorry, he didn't stay and work with us."

"He's at Brookfield now and had some success with a molecule he has synthesized against COVID-19. I thought it might be of interest to send him your virus."

That caught Han's attention. "And he's found some success with his mutations? Yes, I would be most interested in such a study. Then go ahead, let him test it against our pathogen."

Several weeks later, Chen received a package at his lab. The label read, "Containing Category A high-risk specimens, infectious substances affecting humans (UN 2814) in accordance with the US Department of Transportation's Hazardous Materials Regulations and the International Air Transport Association Dangerous Goods Regulations."

He read Jiang's instructions: *Try your molecule against this virus, but be careful. It's lethal. It's been named Thanatos. It spreads by inspiration or ingestion, including water or food. We don't have all that information yet. Perhaps isolation of the sick is the only means of controlling it. But how long can you isolate someone? See what you can do.*

CHAPTER SIX

Chen began his experiments to determine whether his molecule was effective against Jiang's virus. The early laboratory studies indicated it had great potential, seemingly destroying the virus on cellular plates. Finding the initial results of significance, Chen then went on to test the virus in a series of animal models. When injecting his new molecule into an animal, and then injecting Thanatos, the animals survived, and Thanatos was destroyed. When injecting Thanatos into an animal without Chen's molecule, it died immediately. Chen believed that he had enough evidence to plan for clinical studies, a path that could cost a hundred million dollars. That is when unseen events soon redirected the path that Chen's viral research would follow.

* * *

It was in June 2027 when it happened quite suddenly, although, in actuality, the event should have been predictable. There had not been a large-scale viral epidemic in over six years in the United States, although short-lived viral outbreaks appeared in various hot spots around the globe. Previous vaccines, therapeutic modalities, and the use of masks had sufficed to control the mutations and offered the world's population a feeling of confidence and, perhaps, invincibility. Herd immunity was working its natural defense against the viral enemy. Indeed, the warnings that Priya Majmadur had stated had come to fruition, as viral outbreaks had become so endemic that it was thought of as simply a flu. As a result, America's commercial interests and the nation's political concerns found other areas to debate and spend their dollars on. Gene therapy had become the science du jour, where a normal, functional copy of a gene was delivered into cells by a carrier to replace a mutated gene.

Chen and many other young scientists were notified that viral grant money would not be renewed. "We'll deal with it if it ever occurs again," was the political response. It was a decision that would cause untold harm, for research funding is the basis of scientific progress, the collaboration between funder and funded that spans the history of man. Inventions from the GPS to Google, from bar codes to microchips, could not have succeeded without funding the inventor. When neither government nor private investors showed further interest in viral infections, Dr. Ballan had no choice but to tell Chen that if he were not able to secure funding, he would have to give up his lab and stop further research. Chen had to inform his assistants that without a sudden inflow of funds, he would no longer be able to keep the lab open, purchase needed equipment, or continue paying their salaries. When no further funding was secured, Chen was forced to give his staff two weeks' notice. After making such great progress in destroying viruses, Chen began preparations to seal the inner door to the Biosafety Level 4 lab that contained the viruses and discontinue his research. That was when he was introduced to Phillip Steppler.

CHAPTER SEVEN

Phillip Steppler was twenty-eight years old and six feet tall with dirty blond hair, a boyish face, intense blue eyes, and an athletic build. He was the only child of Greek Orthodox parents who immigrated to the United States and settled in a working-class community in Brockton, Massachusetts, where they established a small tailor shop. The parents worked long hours and brought up their son within their traditions, attending the Annunciation Church not far from their home. But Brockton was one of the most dangerous urban areas in the state, and young Phillip had to learn how to defend himself from older students who would steal his lunch money, or he would receive a beating when he refused.

As Phillip grew, his teachers found him to be a good student. He was aware of how hard his parents worked in their small store, struggling to make a living and vowed that he would find a different life.

When Phillip was in ninth grade, his mother was diagnosed with breast cancer, and her health began to fail. Soon, her energy was depleted. She found it difficult to get out of bed, lost her appetite, and dealt with the continuous atrophy of her muscles. He was devastated and helped his mother at home instead of playing sports after school. He read to her and hopelessly watched as she slowly deteriorated in spite of medical care. During those hours of watching, he spent time on the internet seeking treatments and causes of cancer, and when she passed, he was determined to devote his life to medical research.

Nothing could fill the void of a mother, and he promised himself that he would succeed in spite of the challenges that would be set before him. His father did the best he could in raising him through high school, but he brought up his son as he was raised: never telling his son, "I love you," or "Good job," or "Nicely done." It set the tone for Phillip's seeking of approval and his fear of failure that would drive him throughout his life.

But he was bright and mature for his age and found that his schoolwork came easily. He especially had a knack for math and science. He graduated with grades that allowed him to receive a scholarship to Boston College, and armed with a degree in chemistry, he found work in a research lab. But after six months, he realized his ambition would be to own the lab rather than work for one. He dreamed big, knew what he wanted, and was admitted to Harvard Business School, followed by a job at Reston Pharmaceuticals. With his credentials in both science and business, he was quickly recognized as someone with a future and fast-tracked into the merger and acquisition department, evaluating new business opportunities for Reston to acquire. His work brought him in contact with dozens of small companies, for which he spent time analyzing business plans, reviewing balance sheets, and understanding why some succeeded and others failed.

In most cases, he believed, the reason was leadership or a lack of it. If you wanted to be successful, you needed leaders who could make the tough decisions and take the required risks. After two years at Reston, he felt ready to start on his own and began to look for the right opportunity.

* * *

July 7, 2027

It was July 7 when Ballan made the introduction, and Steppler visited the lab to discuss Chen's needs. Chen disclosed that he had received notice from the board at Brookfield that unless he were able to raise additional capital by the end of the month, he would have to give up his lab.

Steppler was surprised. "That only gives you two weeks."

Chen nodded. "I know. Dr. Ballan has been trying to help but thus far has not been successful."

"But Ballan tells me your work is promising. Tell me about it."

Chen explained how he was working on a molecule that could enhance the immune system to seek out pathogens and destroy them.

Steppler caught on immediately. "You mean a drug that clicks on a switch to make ordinary immune cells become extraordinary, like superhunters?"

Chen smiled at Steppler's new label. "Exactly, but I've gone beyond the trying stage."

"What do you mean?"

"My latest results suggest that I may have found that molecule."

"And that molecule . . ."

Chen completed the sentence. ". . . stimulates and intensifies the immune cellular response of macrophages, giant cells, anti-toxins, lymphocytes, T cells, and other factors."

Steppler continued his questioning. "And what form did you make your molecule in?"

Chen answered, "As a vaccine against viral infections."

Steppler thought for a moment. "I'm not certain that making vaccines is a profitable venture. Every time you make one vaccine, the virus mutates, and the vaccine becomes worthless."

Chen smiled. "But not this vaccine, Mr. Steppler. We tested it against the original COVID-19 virus and its mutations numerous times, and it appears to be effective regardless of the virus form. In fact, we just recently tested it against an even more powerful virus and found it to be effective."

"Really? Where would you get such a powerful virus?"

"From the Wuhan Virology Institute in China. My friend works there, and we were able to receive what he believes to be their most powerful pathogen."

"And it worked?"

"Yes, sir. It was as sensitive to the new molecule as the other viruses we tested it on, and this one exhibits much greater virulence than its COVID-19 ancestor. You place it in any animal model, and the result is almost instant death. It's more powerful than any described in the literature. It's called Thanatos."

"Thanatos?"

"A god from Greek mythology. Thanatos is the personification of death, merciless and indiscriminate, hated by all, and hateful toward everyone, mortals and gods."

Steppler recalled once reading about Thanatos in Homer's *Iliad*. "Isn't the name a little too severe? You're suggesting that the virus is impregnable. That's not what anyone wants to know here."

Chen smiled. "But Thanatos was not impregnable. You see, Thanatos had one flaw."

"And that was?"

"Thanatos could be outwitted."

"How was that?"

"By trickery. According to the myth, Thanatos was told by Zeus to chain King Sisyphus in the Underworld, as it was time for him to die. But Sisyphus tricked Thanatos by imprisoning him within his own shackles. Once Thanatos was chained, there was no more death in the world. Every mortal was protected."

"What happened?"

Chen continued. "In the end, when Ares, the Greek god of war, realized that no one died in spite of all the battles he waged, he demanded that there must be death. But as long as Thanatos was chained, there could be no death. So Ares freed Thanatos and gave King Sisyphus to him."

Steppler was fascinated. "And you think that your drug can prevent mortals from dying from viral infections?"

Chen nodded. "I believe so."

"How?"

"By chaining Thanatos."

That caught Steppler's attention. He knew that Reston and all but the largest pharmaceutical companies had long given up on producing vaccines because of the mutation problem, but this was something new. If what Chen was saying was true, it was a game changer for the entire industry. "And when you tested your molecule against this Thanatos, it was effective?"

Chen smiled as if in triumphant mode. "Mr. Steppler, it not only enhanced the immune system's ability to search out and find the mutated virus but also immediately destroyed it."

"And your one drug did this?"

"Same drug against multiple pathogens. In virology, there is a concept called gain of function when you increase the activity of a virus beyond its ordinary virulence. I've sort of changed the definition of gain of function. What our lab has attained is a gain of function of a molecule that enhances our ability to destroy the virus."

"One size fits all! The universal vaccine." Steppler's mind was racing as the potential applications ran through it. The ability of the body to eliminate such extreme diseases was unbelievable, but the idea that one drug was capable of such a result had never before been formulated. Steppler knew he had found something that could be worth a fortune.

"Have you estimated the time and cost to completion?"

Chen went to the top drawer of a cabinet and removed a file. "This is the business plan that Dr. Ballan and I put together with Tim Channing, a former graduate student of his. Tim left the bioengineering program and went to law school instead. Now, he's a big corporate attorney here in New York. If you have any legal questions, you should call him. The plan includes costs for lab equipment, additional assistants, clinical studies, a Gantt chart indicating time to marketing approval, projected sales, and the competitive environment."

Steppler perused the pages. "I see you're figuring a total cost of one hundred million dollars."

Chen nodded. "Correct, of which ten million is required within the next two weeks."

Steppler continued reading the plan, his mind working overtime. He began to pace while reading, then paused for a moment and looked back at Chen. "And you have patents?"

"No sir, never applied for them. I didn't want to file for a patent until I knew I had something that would work. And, to be honest, patents are expensive. I didn't want to spend the money."

Steppler had taken enough chemistry and biology to appreciate the significance of what Chen's research suggested, yet he remained skeptical for a very good reason. "With all these results, how is it possible that you have not been able to raise further funding? Hasn't Dr. Ballan introduced you to potential investors?"

"He has, and then I speak to them. I've even applied for other government and private grants."

"Then what's the problem?"

Chen paused before answering. "I've been turned down every time. It seems that investment dollars, especially in biotech, have largely dried up."

Steppler seemed confused. "That's true. Both life sciences equity and equity-linked deal issuance activity have been limited due to inflationary pressures and geopolitical concerns, but what you have seems extraordinary. Is there a problem in the manufacturing process?"

"Not at all. I've kept the drug synthesis secret, but there's no need for any unusual equipment to scale up manufacturing. I call the process Chi Activated Immunology."

Steppler was becoming frustrated. "Then help me out. What am I missing?"

"I think the investors don't like that the drug is based on Chinese herbal medicine."

Steppler was trying hard to find a favorable reason for becoming involved, but with this herbal medicine tag, he was beginning to realize that Chen did not know how to communicate with investors. Steppler had learned from experience that people are down on what they're not up on, and sophisticated biotech investors are not up on Chinese herbal medicine to cure the world's problems. They were into newly synthesized molecules, large new proteins, monoclonal antibodies, cancer-killing drugs, and gene therapy, not the Tao of tradition. He realized that if he were going to sell this to anyone, he would have to meet with investors by himself. Chen may be a genius in the laboratory, but he would be a disaster as a spokesperson for a new company. Steppler had to make a decision, and there was no time to wait.

"Listen, Chen, you need two weeks to raise the money. If you give me those two weeks, I will try and raise that ten million for you, and if I can, I will be responsible for raising the remainder as needed. If that is acceptable, we can enter into an agreement. How does that sound?"

Chen wasn't certain that it could be done. He had already given up and come to terms with closing his lab and ending his research. It happens often. Chen knew of many well-qualified investigators who could not continue their promising work due to a lack of funding. The reality was, if Steppler wanted to try, why not? He had nothing to lose.

"Mr. Steppler, if you can raise ten million dollars in thirteen days, then I accept your offer." Chen checked the calendar. "I have until noon of July 20 to deposit that amount into my research account."

They shook hands.

"Chen, one more thing. Perhaps it's best not to mention the words Chinese herbal medicine. I think it is more descriptive if we describe the drug as based on a new proprietary molecular formulation. How we say things makes a difference."

CHAPTER EIGHT

Steppler marked the date on the calendar. July 20, a Tuesday. He had thirteen days to pull it off. The odds were improbable, but he knew that if you want to succeed enough, you go for it.

He had two immediate problems. The first was that he was still an employee of Reston Pharmaceuticals, and his employment contract clearly stated that as long as he was employed, he was not allowed to engage in any activity that competed with his employer. There was no competition; after all, Reston was not in the virus business. But to own the new drug outright meant he would have to terminate his employment immediately, and with no income and limited funds in the bank, he would be gambling everything on the success of Chen's molecule. The second problem was easier to define: He had two weeks to raise more money than he ever dreamed of.

He went to work. By the end of the day, Steppler had sent in his resignation to Reston, thanked them for the opportunity, and had Chen sign an exclusivity agreement stating Steppler would organize a new company if he could raise the funds within the specified time. That left him with only the second problem: How to raise the money?

* * *

The way Steppler figured, there were three ways to raise funds: a bank loan, a collaboration with Big Pharma where, in exchange for sharing the profits, they would finance the studies, or hiring an investment banker to do the raising. Over the next week, Steppler arranged meetings with all three options.

His calls to the banks proved unsuccessful, as they were not willing to finance a project without sufficient collateral. The calls to his contacts at Big

Pharma were equally negative: "Call us back when you have completed human trials, and maybe at that time there would be some interest." Only his call to his old study partner at Harvard Business School, James D'Arcy, bore potential. As Steppler learned at Harvard, unless you are an Einstein, it's not what you know but who you know.

The last he heard from D'Arcy was an email two years ago announcing the New York opening of James D'Arcy and Associates, Investment Banking Group. Steppler had no idea how D'Arcy was doing, but he knew that D'Arcy's father was a successful attorney whose clients consisted of some of the wealthiest and most influential men in the country—at least Republican country. Steppler made the call.

"James, Phil Steppler. I have an opportunity that could be major, and I think you'll be interested."

By the time Steppler had finished reviewing the project and its potential, D'Arcy was interested. "How much are we talking about?"

Steppler was ready for the question. "We start with ten mil."

"That's a lot of money."

Steppler continued. "To be honest, a drug like this could require one hundred million before getting FDA approval. One other caveat. We need the money within two weeks."

D'Arcy thought he was mad. "Two weeks?"

"Yeah, ten million in two weeks, and if you can raise it, you get 8 percent. The way I figure, it's worth the risk. Once we show safety and efficacy in humans, we go public with a huge valuation. If everything goes as expected, within three years, we're talking of a company worth more than Amazon."

D'Arcy remembered Steppler as having a sharp mind but remained cautious. "Phil, 8 percent is a lot of money, and I can't promise anything with the way inflation is running these days. You have no patents, you're an early-stage company with no human data, you need a large amount of money, and you need it immediately. I'm not sure I can be of help. Even if we find someone with the funds to complete due diligence on every aspect of the research, organize a company, and interview your scientist within two weeks may not be doable, but I'll make a few phone calls."

Steppler realized the odds were poor. "Thanks, James, I appreciate it."

Though D'Arcy and Steppler were friends at school, their backgrounds could not have been more different. D'Arcy came from a prominent, wealthy family. His grandfather, Randolph D'Arcy, was a blue-blooded corporate lawyer in New York, a major contributor to the Republican Party, and the former ambassador to Belgium during the Eisenhower administration. His son, Hal D'Arcy, continued in his father's tradition—prep school at Choate, undergraduate and law school at Harvard, and senior partner at the top law firm of Hoffman, Ives, D'Arcy and Cunningham in Midtown Manhattan. James followed in the D'Arcy tradition, from prep school to Harvard to Harvard Law, which he graduated from, but barely. After working for two years at his father's law firm with wills and estates for wealthy old clients, he told his father he was leaving to get an MBA and pursue his interest in banking. He enrolled at Harvard Business School.

It wasn't only their pedigree that made the friendship unusual; it was their personalities. Whereas Steppler was a leader with a persuasive personality with huge ambitions, ideas, discipline, and the ability to take the risks needed to achieve those ambitions, D'Arcy's goals were more modest. He was already born with that silver spoon in his mouth and didn't have the go-for-broke attitude that Steppler had. Perhaps the most independent decision he ever made was to tell his father, an overpowering man, that he was leaving the family law firm. The father, to his credit, realized that his son needed to follow a different path and, after a long discussion, agreed that finance, combined with his legal background, could be a successful one.

Following his MBA, James worked for an investment banking firm and, after two years of learning the ropes, opened his own firm. With a trust fund of ten million dollars, he began his investment career. At first, he made small investments of less than one million dollars in several startups, and with sufficient success to give confidence to his investors and referrals from his father, his clients and business began to grow. But he had never done a deal for ten million dollars, and he followed the first law of investment banking: Always use someone else's money. Where was he going to find someone with that amount of capital willing to take such a risk?

CHAPTER NINE

It had been over a week since Steppler had last spoken with D'Arcy. The stress was beginning to build, but he hesitated in calling his friend, figuring if anything happened, he would hear from him. Steppler, with all of his enthusiasm, with all of his planning and determination, had run out of ideas.

But he did not run out of his drive. How does one instill that quality within oneself? Perhaps it wasn't so much the need for success as it was the need to avoid failure. Even to the last moment, Steppler stayed in the game, though the odds were becoming overwhelmingly against him.

And so it was that on July 17, with three days remaining, Steppler received a call from D'Arcy that he had found an individual who may be interested in investing. The fellow's name was Rapolo, and he was referred from his father's office. Could Steppler take a meeting this afternoon at 1:00 P.M. at D'Arcy's office in Midtown Manhattan? Steppler agreed. As the time approached, he put on his good luck business suit, polished his shoes, and carried an impressive and unused black leather briefcase with twin brass combination locks that he saved for special occasions. He was taught appearances mattered.

D'Arcy's office was on the fifteenth floor at 980 Third Avenue. He was buzzed through the large glass doors with "D'Arcy and Associates, Investment Banking" printed in neat black letters on it and greeted by a receptionist sitting behind a desk.

"Good morning, you must be Mr. Steppler. Mr. D'Arcy is expecting you."

Steppler was ushered into D'Arcy's well-appointed office with a large mahogany desk, behind which was a dark wooden bookcase neatly filled with journals, legal books, and several small glass monuments indicating deals D'Arcy participated in. Steppler sat in one of the two leather chairs facing the desk, observing the framed diplomas from law school and the MBA program as well as photos of D'Arcy with what must have been his wife and three small children.

"There you are, so good to see you." D'Arcy had red hair and a pleasant face with pink cheeks that bulged when he smiled. He was the same height as Steppler and wore a tailored, dark business suit over a body that had gained a few pounds since Steppler had last seen him. He still had a quiet way of speaking that gave the sense of a serious, thoughtful counselor. They shook hands and spent a few minutes catching up on life since school.

"Yes, married with three kids. That's why I have to work for a living. And you? Still single?"

Steppler smiled and presented his best scenario. "Keeping my options open and enjoying every minute."

D'Arcy lowered his volume. "Listen, I tried my best, but none of my clients were interested in a space about which they had little knowledge. So, the only person who is even willing to meet with you is a fellow named Sal Rapolo. I just met him for the first time, but he is a longtime client of my father, who told me that Sal may be interested in investing some extra cash if the deal is right."

D'Arcy led Steppler down the hall and into the conference room consisting of a long, modern glass table surrounded by eight large, wheeled black leather seats, with large windows overlooking Third Avenue. Two men were sitting in chairs on the windowed side of the room, and D'Arcy made the introductions.

Sal Rapolo looked like he belonged on the cover of *GQ*. Tanned to perfection, he was dressed in a fitted blue suit that seemed to pour over his well-sculpted body, a bright red tie, and a matching handkerchief neatly placed in the vest pocket. His pitch-black, greased hair was groomed as if cut within the past hour, and his manicured fingernails reflected the overhead lights. Next to him was a heavy-set man who just managed to fit into the chair. He had a leather, beaten face, a nose with a traumatic history, and a neck that disappeared somewhere between the open collar of his shirt and his faded blazer that managed to stretch over his arms but not his paunch.

D'Arcy made the introductions, and Steppler placed a copy of the business plan on the desk in front of each man, along with his new white business card: *Phillip Steppler, CEO, Lexington Bio.*

Rapolo gave an unimpressed glance at the cover page, left it on the table, and studied the card. He looked carefully at Steppler, not a facial muscle moving, and, in a quiet voice identifying his Lower East Side roots, got right to the point. Steppler realized immediately this was not someone who wasted time.

"So, Mr. Steppler, I've come to understand from James here that you need ten million dollars, and you would like it immediately. I also have come to understand from James that you may need up to a hundred million to get this drug of yours approved. Did I get that right?"

Steppler, against his better judgment, smiled. "Actually, I need eleven million upfront. James is getting 8 percent as a finder's fee."

"I see, 8 percent." He glanced at D'Arcy, who was sitting at the far end of the table. "Not bad for five minutes of work." He looked back at Steppler. "And how long is this job gonna take?"

"I estimate four years for FDA approval."

"Okay, four years. And whadda the odds this thing's gonna work?"

"I've seen the results. The drug works."

"And the feds think it's gonna work?"

Steppler now realized he had reached a fork in the road and had to decide his path. On one hand, he realized that this was the only opportunity that might allow him to be funded for the project. If that was the case, what does he tell the investors? That this is a risk that may be worth it, but maybe not? Or does he tell them that the results that have been achieved thus far would certainly get approval from the FDA? It seemed like hours to Steppler before he made his decision, a decision that, prior to that moment, would have seemed inconceivable to anyone who knew him. Certainly, it was to D'Arcy.

Steppler felt his heart pounding as he looked into the eyes of his investors. "There's no way this drug will not be approved."

"Really? No way." Rapolo looked at his associate. "See that, Vito; this guy says it's a sure thing." The big guy just kept a blank stare on Steppler.

Rapolo continued in a slow, deliberate voice. "So, how much of your company am I gonna own after I give you the ten, I mean eleven, mil?"

Steppler had to make a quick decision. He had thought about the valuation, figuring anywhere from ten percent then, as time went on, 15 percent. And now, face-to-face with the last possible investor, he responded, "For eleven million, you will own 20 percent of the company."

"And, in your estimation, how much will the company be worth?"

Steppler responded immediately. "Thirty billion dollars."

"Thirty *b*'s. In four years. That's quite a haul." Rapolo again looked at his associate. "Vito, I think we're in the wrong business. So, tell me, Mr. Steppler, I'm not that good with arithmetic. How much are you gonna give me back?"

Steppler was beginning to perspire under the interrogation. "About six billion dollars."

"Really, six billion?" Rapolo didn't know whether to take Steppler's response seriously or start laughing. He held back a smile and began to tap the edge of

Steppler's business card against the glass table, his eyes not venturing from its owner's face.

"So let me get this straight. I give you eleven mil now and another ninety million in a year or so, and you're gonna give me, on, let's say, July 20, 2031, a check for six billion dollars."

"Unless I return your money before that date. Then I would give you a four billion dollar payoff."

D'Arcy looked at Steppler as if he was nuts. Negotiating with these guys? That could kill the deal if not Steppler himself. Rapolo remained silent, scrutinizing Steppler and continuing the drumming of the card against the glass table, which reverberated through the silence of the room like the unending tick of a clock. Rapolo's gaze was continuous, keeping his focus on Steppler, his eyes never wavering from their target as if studying a slide through a microscope, seeking something untoward. It couldn't have been more than a minute, but to Steppler, who had never had someone dissect him like this, it seemed forever.

"How long before July 20?"

"Six months. February 20, 2031."

"Kid, you gotta lot of balls to keep negotiating. I like that. Sure, if you can return my profit in three and a half years, we'll settle for four *b*'s." Rapolo put his hands on the table, got up from his chair, and tapped Vito on the shoulder. "Vito, we're done here." He left the business plans on the table and, before he left the room, asked, "You hava bank, Mr. Steppler?"

"Yes, sir, First National City. All the investor information is in the business plan."

"One more thing, Mr. Steppler. I got a bad memory, always forgetting things. February 20, 2031, or July 20, 2031, either way, you wanna grab a piece a paper and just write down how many days that's gonna be before you give me my money? That would help me a great deal. Oh, and just initial it so's I can remember who gave me this."

Steppler did as he was asked and handed it to Rapolo.

Rapolo glanced at the note. "Fourteen hundred and sixty days from the day you get a check, or less three hundred and sixty-five. Sure seems like a long time. Thank you, Mr. Steppler. You'll be hearing from me. And James, say hello to your father. The man's a saint." When Rapolo left, Steppler wiped his forehead with a handkerchief and looked at D'Arcy. "What was that all about?"

D'Arcy shook his head. "I have no idea, but you were certainly clear about your drug's future. That took guts."

Steppler bit his lip. "What choice do I have? He's my only hope."

CHAPTER TEN

July 20, 2027

It was Wednesday morning, only a few hours until Chen's noon deadline, and Steppler had not heard from anyone. He was beginning to accept the fact that he had gone as far as he could. His cell rang, and when he saw it was D'Arcy, he knew it was all over.

"It's going to be a hot summer."

"What do you mean?"

"Your money's been deposited," said D'Arcy.

Steppler didn't know what to make of it. "What do you mean deposited?"

"Rapolo went for it."

"You mean he gave you a check for the whole eleven million?"

"Not to me. All I know is that we received a call from your bank this morning that the money was deposited into your new Lexington Bio business account. And, by the way, it wasn't for eleven million."

Steppler was confused. "Then how much did he give me?"

"One hundred million."

Steppler couldn't believe what he was hearing. "What?"

"You said you needed a total of one hundred million. He doesn't like to owe anybody."

"The guy must be a nut. Let me see the paperwork. Do you have his signed shareholder agreements?"

D'Arcy explained, "There is none. Apparently, he never signs anything. You wanted the money, and he gave it to you. He expects you to honor your commitment, and after meeting those guys, I suggest you do just that. Looks like you're playing with the big boys, but I gave you what you wanted. If it gets approved, you can do the papers later, not that I'm suggesting that."

Steppler was trying to appreciate what had occurred. "James, thanks. For one hundred million, you earned your 8 percent."

"Make it only for the first ten, as agreed. But you told the man you'll get an approval in four years, and I suggest you get it done. And Phil, take care of yourself. These are very different kinds of businessmen. I suspect they're in the same type of business as you are."

"What business is that?"

"Pharmaceuticals, direct to the consumer."

* * *

The moment he reached the street, he made a call. "Dr. Chu, this is Phillip Steppler. The money is in the account of our new company. I'll be right over. We have work to do, and we have four years for approval."

Chen couldn't believe what he was hearing. "You want all the studies done in four years and FDA approval? That alone takes a year these days. This is a new molecular entity. Better figure five."

Like with most entrepreneurs, reality was never an obstacle for Steppler. For the next nine months, he urged Chen and his assistants to complete the preclinical efficacy of the drug. Once the animal work was completed and, if the FDA had no objections, clinical studies on humans would begin. Only with human data would the world take notice.

Chen worked day and night in the lab, purchasing the same herbs from China that his father used, determining the proper concentrations, extracting their essential contents, testing the formulation for activity, and then processing the extracted material into an injectable dosage form. Once that was completed, he retested it to be certain that it kept the same molecular integrity and function.

When Chen had completed the formulation procedures, Steppler hired an FDA-approved drug manufacturing company to begin production of both the vial with the active ingredients and a control containing only water. This required extensive testing and recordkeeping in each step of the process to be certain that each vial of the drug made had uniformity of dose, concentration, purity, safety, stability, and sterility. The finished drug then went through final animal studies, evaluating the viral response in animals, some receiving the drug and some the vial with water. Only one person at the animal lab held the code that defined which was which. When completed, Chen and his assistant wrote up the final documentation for the FDA, including the protocol to be used for the clinical trials in humans.

The entire preclinical work took one year, and the day that the final report was electronically sent to the FDA in Rockville, Maryland, Steppler threw a party for Chen and his team. He had catered food and drinks brought in, and congratulations were given all around.

"I want to thank all of you for the amazing work that you have done, and especially to Dr. Chu for bringing the world closer to preventing the next viral outbreak. You are all to be congratulated."

Chen responded, "And I want to thank Mr. Steppler for making this possible. Also, I am pleased to announce that I have been asked to present our work at the next meeting of the International Conference on Emerging Infectious Diseases that the CDC will be hosting from May 6–9, 2028, at the Hyatt Regency Hotel in Atlanta, Georgia. It is the largest and most important scientific meeting of the year on the emergence, spread, and control of infectious diseases. It will also be the first time that our preclinical results will be made public. Scientists and clinicians from around the world will be attending, and it is an honor that we have been chosen."

Steppler was all smiles. "Well, now, that is impressive. Let's drink to that."

It was also the day that the lab had visitors. Sal Rapolo and his friend Vito stopped in.

Steppler hadn't seen or heard from Rapolo since the moment he left D'Arcy's office in July 2027.

"Mr. Rapolo, so nice to see you."

"Yeah, Vito and I were in the area, heard through the grapevine that there was a party here, and figured we should find out what was being celebrated."

"Absolutely. Can I get you something to drink?'

Rapolo put up his hands. "Thanks, but I don't drink. Not good for the ulcer. Vito, you want a ginger ale."

Vito shook his head. "No, I'm good."

Rapolo glanced around the lab. "Quite a setup you got here."

"Want a tour? Let me ask Marianne to take you around."

Marianne Franklin was a dark-haired, brown-eyed postgraduate student who had been working with Chen for the past year. She was thin with a sweet smile and spoke with a great deal of energy. She took them around the lab, giving a general explanation of what they were working on.

Vito seemed quite interested, and when they walked past a heavy metal door, he stopped. "What's in there? Looks like a bank vault with yellow poison signs all over it."

"Actually, that's the entrance to the new Biosafety Level 4 lab. It's where Dr. Chu works with the most hazardous viruses known to man. Brookfield is one of the few laboratories in the world certified to work on them."

"So you've got a dangerous job."

"I suppose. Certainly, the viruses are extremely dangerous, but that is why they are locked in a special aseptic facility. Secure precautions must be followed before anyone can enter the area. Those viruses are the deadliest mutations of the old COVID-19 virus."

"So why they here?"

"Dr. Chu wanted to test his drug against the deadliest virus that has been identified."

"Where did he get them from?"

"China. That's where a great deal of virus research is being done. Dr. Chu has a friend who works in one of the labs."

"So, how did it do?"

"Most effective. When injected into animals, they would die in minutes. When the new drug was administered, it destroyed the virus completely, and the animals lived."

"So, this drug really works."

Marianne smiled. "Oh, yes. It's very exciting. Dr. Chu just announced he has been asked to speak at an international conference on our work. That means we're getting recognition."

When they had finished the tour, they walked over to Steppler, who was speaking to Chen. "So, how was the tour?"

"Very interesting," Rapolo answered. "My friend Vito was 'specially interested. I think, Dr. Chu, that if he could start again, he would like to go into research."

Chen laughed. "We could always use a good scientist here."

Rapolo added, "And I hear you will be presenting your work at a big conference. Congratulations."

Steppler smiled. "Well, you gentlemen had perfect timing. Not only were we asked to speak, but we just sent the application to begin testing in patients to the FDA. They have thirty days to respond. If they don't, we can start dosing patients."

Rapolo looked at Vito. "Vito, Mr. Steppler says we have perfect timing." Looking back at Steppler, he continued, "And how's your timing? Are we right on schedule?"

Steppler appeared confident. "Right on schedule."

"That's wonderful, Mr. Steppler. So what's next?"

Steppler looked at Chen, who was standing nearby. "Our first test will be to assure the safety of the drug in a small group of patients, making certain there are no side effects. If none, we will begin our larger study to see if we can help them."

"And then?"

"If those results are positive, and we think they will be, we're going to bring it right to the FDA for approval six months early."

Rapolo had a big smile on his face. "See, Vito, I told you the kid was all right." He turned to Steppler. "Steppler, you're doin' good. Glad you keepin' to the schedule. Very important to keep to the schedule." He paused before continuing. "I gotta last question. Marianne tells me the drug works on even the worst virus known to man. But why would anyone need it if there's no virus? I mean, it sounds like if there's no pandemic, there's no reason to get the drug. So how would we ever get our money?"

For the moment, Steppler's smile was erased, but it was Vito who responded. He put his big hand over Steppler's shoulder. "No need to worry. After all, we saw that steel door behind which you keep those deadly viruses. I mean, the place looked like you were guarding Fort Knox. Anyway, I'm sure you could always arrange for a new pandemic to start. Ain't that right, Mr. Steppler?"

They all laughed, and then they left.

Chen seemed concerned. "Listen, Phillip, why did you tell them we're going to show the FDA data on the Phase Two study? We're going to need to follow that up with two large clinical trials. That could take another three years."

Steppler managed a smile, but it was filled with concern. "Dr. Chu, when the FDA sees the perfect results from the Phase Two study, they will have no choice but to approve it immediately."

Chen retorted. "But you know the FDA has refused almost any drug not following proper protocol."

Steppler's response was loud enough to be heard but quiet enough to suggest it was meant to be a thought. "You heard what he said. Unless there's another pandemic."

CHAPTER ELEVEN

May 6, 2028

The meeting of the International Conference on Emerging Infectious Diseases in Atlanta was a great success. Chen spoke before three thousand scientists and clinicians from around the globe, and his presentation was received with great enthusiasm, including congratulations from an old friend.

"Chen, that was quite a talk."

Chen could never forget that voice. He turned to find his old friend. "Jiang, I didn't know you would be here."

"We have a scientific delegation from the Wuhan Institute here." Jiang smiled. "It's your research that is drawing the most attention, and, to be honest, you're the main reason why we're here. General Han wanted to know how your work with Thanatos was going. I see you've made a great deal of progress."

"So far, so good," Chen responded.

Jiang then lowered his voice. "And by the way, you were right."

"About what?"

"Remember when we first toured the Wuhan Institute after graduation, and I mentioned that the work sounded exciting because if it could develop such a potent viral weapon, China could rule the world."

Chen answered. "Yes, and I answered it could destroy it, but you told me you will learn how to control it."

Jiang lowered his head and nodded slowly. "I was wrong. We can't control it, and now things are changing. The Party Chairman is getting concerned about the lack of progress, and he wants the People's Liberation Army to take over the lab."

"What about Han?"

"He's still in charge, but he believes the future lies in using viruses like Thanatos to be a bioweapon."

"Bioweapon? How can he have a weapon if he can't control it?"

"We haven't been able to do what you've done, and he's under a great deal of pressure. I swear he's a borderline psychopath, having us work day and night to find a means of control. But we've come up empty-handed. Everything we've tried has failed."

Jiang glanced around the room and, putting his arm around Chen, walked him to a quiet corner.

"Listen, Chen, there's a lot going on, but I can't be seen speaking to you about it, at least not now. Han is here with two members of his secret police. They're keeping an eye on what we say and to whom we speak. I am being watched closely. Perhaps there's a time when we can speak out of harm's way."

Chen thought for a moment. "Why don't we get together at five after today's program is over? We can meet in the bar for a drink and lose ourselves among the crowd."

"There you are, Jiang; I've been looking for you. What are you two gentlemen talking about?"

The two turned to see a tall, well-built man with jet-black hair and a revealing scar across his face. Chen recognized him from their first meeting.

Jiang seemed startled. "General Han, I was just congratulating Dr. Chu on his work."

The general looked at Chen. "Yes, well done. I understand we met years ago when we were recruiting. Too bad we lost you, but your new work is most interesting. I see you are making some headway with our virus."

"Yes, sir, I think we may soon be able to provide some answers."

"Well, then. We must talk more about it."

"That would be my pleasure."

"Wonderful. Meantime, Jiang, we are having a meeting of the delegation. Sorry to take him away, but we have work to do."

* * *

At five, Chen and Jiang met as planned. The bar was crowded with conference attendees following a long day of scientific lectures. Chen and Jiang made their way to an open table in the rear and ordered beers.

"So that's the Batman. He took you away pretty quickly," Chen said.

"He's in charge of our delegation, both in terms of the science as well as the security."

"Why is he having you watched?"

"Because he's worried that his program will not succeed, and the Central Committee is putting pressure on the chairman to get it done. That's putting pressure on the general, and that means we are bearing the brunt of it. There's been a lot of activity at the institute, and it's not just scientific, it's political. Although I'm one of the supervisors, I'm not privy to everything. But here is what I understand to be happening. There is concern regarding the chairman's leadership. He is the one who backed Han's bioterror defense policy, and now he's under the gun. In response, he's tightening his grip by purging the leadership of anyone that he feels may be a potential challenge to his power. But it's not only internal; it's also external. The chairman believes that China, along with Russia, can establish a new world order and, along with Iran and perhaps even North Korea, foster an anti-Western alliance through which Beijing can dominate the world."

"Why would they do that?"

"Because they don't believe that they can live on this planet in peace with the West, and that means the United States. Beijing believes the US belittles them in the eyes of the world by protesting China's human-rights abuses as if it was any different from the discrimination toward Blacks, Jews, and Asians in the US."

"And China believes they can establish such a new order?"

"I believe it's becoming clear that the chairman slowly but surely wants to establish an autocratic regime whose decisions are determined by one man rather than the cumbersome debates of the West's divided nations."

"How will he do that?"

"By beginning with Taiwan. The Communist Party believes that Taiwan is part of China, and they plan to bring it and the South China Sea back into China's territorial rights. I believe he will also take measures to undermine NATO and use China's economic strength to reinforce economic trade agreements and retaliate against sanctions. They see the West's attempt to contain China's economic rise as an act of aggression, and it may be time to act, for they believe that the West has never been weaker politically and ideologically. All they have to do is point to the catastrophic withdrawal of Western powers from Afghanistan to see their lack of will or the internal dissension of the radical left versus the radical right, each looking to redefine what made America great."

Chen appeared captivated by Jiang's political acumen. "So they believe that America has lost its way."

Jiang nodded. "The reports that we get certainly suggest so. The number of murders on the streets, the attempt to overthrow the government after the past elections, the prevention of democratic voting, it's as if the US Civil War accomplished nothing. And now, they want to save lives by preventing abortion but refuse to save them by stopping gun sales. The fact is, the world and certainly China realize that Washington seems increasingly incapable of governing its people. No, Han has lectured us that this is the time that the US is vulnerable."

Chen was puzzled. "But surely China saw what happened to Russia when they tried to subjugate Ukraine. The world didn't tolerate it."

Jiang smiled. "China doesn't work like Russia. You don't use a battering ram to change people's minds. They will do it differently, with greater subtlety and, shall we say, with more discretion and finesse. China was disgusted with Russia."

"And the pact between Russia and China?"

Jiang smiled. "The fact is that China and Russia have rarely been allies, and it appears that China has other plans. China never liked what Putin did in Ukraine. They know he's a thug."

"But isn't China as autocratic?"

"Yes, but they like to think they are more refined, more cultured, more respectable, if you wish than the Russian animals. Putin became a pariah. China wants to be a bully but in the politest terms."

"But China has a pact with Russia."

"For the moment. But I've seen information that China not only wishes to dominate the West but also to bring Russia into what is called a tolerable level of submission. In other words, China wants to rule the globe, and Russia is merely a pawn to be kept until no longer of value. Iran may be an even smaller pawn, but a useful one, granted its geographic position."

To Chen, this was a living chess game. "Is this possible, this new world order?"

"Oh, it's very possible; at least, the chairman believes so. His strategy is quite simple: There is no longer a need for nuclear armaments or armaments at all. He believes that there is no need to spend a huge percentage of their economic power on developing weapons of mass destruction, aircraft, missiles, navy, and other military equipment. Rather, he is developing a more, shall we say, human method to conquer the world."

"And that is?"

"Bioterror."

"As you first told me."

"Then I was merely speculating; now I know it. The fact is, Beijing can sign all the non-nuclear proliferation agreements they want, but they don't think there will be a need for it."

"And who persuaded China to go this route?"

"Han himself. And with his background in the genetic engineering of viruses, there was no one to argue with him. He's already brought in a large military medical team to Wuhan, and already Wuhan's major hospitals are being managed by the People's Liberation Army. All of a sudden, I am no longer privy to everything that is going on, but I would wager that they are developing biological weapons in Wuhan P4, a secret and ultra-secure department that even I do not have clearance for. It's a totally military operation, but I believe they are working with Thanatos, although there is a great deal of skepticism and growing opposition, especially by the heads of China's armed forces, that such a plan is workable. But the chairman has placed his bets that Han Shi and Thanatos is capable of taking over the world, and that's where you come into the picture."

"Because they think I have the antidote."

"Yes," Jiang replied. "And, I fear, General Han will do anything to get it. The chairman is the guiding force behind the policy, and thus far, he's convinced the Central Committee of the Communist Party that it can be done. There was a great deal of opposition to his use of bioterror, but enough of the top party officials gave him the go-ahead, albeit with a timeline. The United States needs to be warned. I don't know how much time is left, but I know that he has played all his political cards on this project. If his bioterror program fails, he will suffer the consequences. If it's successful, then I fear for the future."

From the corner of his eye, Jiang saw two men enter the bar, searching the crowd.

"I've got to go. Two secret police just entered. I know they're looking for me. I've got to get out of here. One day, I will find you and discuss more, but for now, remember, be careful." Jiang got to his feet and walked toward the rear entrance. The sudden movement alerted the two secret police, who quickly pushed through the crowd. Chen realized the danger that Jiang was in. As the two police rushed past Chen's table, he suddenly got out of his chair, pushing it into their path. By the time they recovered, Jiang was gone.

CHAPTER TWELVE

August 2028

The FDA had no problems with the preclinical work, and Steppler contracted with a research organization to conduct the phase one clinical study for safety on its new experimental drug LB182 with forty healthy patients to test for any side effects. There were none.

But there was a problem. The study had taken twelve months, and when Chen projected that the Phase Two study would take fourteen months, it meant a completion date at the end of 2029. That would only leave eight months to pay the investors.

"How long for the two phase three studies?" Steppler asked.

Chen took a moment to figure. "If we do them at the same time, two and a half years, minimum, and then another year for the FDA to respond, and who knows how long to have them available in pharmacies."

"But we only have one year."

Chen shook his head. "No way. You better think of something else."

"Fine. Meanwhile, let's get the Phase Two clinical done as fast as we can and get some real results. How many patients are called for?"

Chen thought for a moment. "The protocol calls for ninety patients divided into three groups, each with thirty patients. Two with different doses and one group with no drug as a control."

"What if we divided the ninety patients into two groups and forgot the controls? That would give us a more robust study."

Chen thought he didn't hear correctly. "What do you mean? You have to have controls."

Steppler was adamant. "Listen, Chen, there are no drugs that can stop this infection. I'll tell the FDA that there was no need for controls, which means we will have more patients on the experiment. Do it. Split the study into two arms, each with forty-five patients."

CHAPTER THIRTEEN

October 2029

As Chen had forecast, the Phase Two study took almost fourteen months to complete. The results showed that the lower dose was as effective as the higher dose, but not in all cases. Of the ninety patients studied, three in the low-dose and two in the high-dose group continued to carry the virus and died.

Steppler was concerned. "What happened to these five patients? Are you sure they received the drug like the others?"

Chen reviewed the study records and the patients' medical histories and found no difference in the testing protocols and nothing in the medical records to suggest anything unusual. It was only that the higher dose seemed to be slightly more effective. When Chen had completed his review, he put down the files. "I don't see any reason for these patients having a different result unless there's something wrong with the formulation or not everyone responds to the molecule. There could be a dozen reasons. What if their immune systems are different?"

Steppler reexamined everything. "Who else has seen the data?"

"No one. You're the first person I've shown it to."

Steppler was not certain if the results were sufficient for an approval. Didn't he need to have one hundred percent efficacy? "Look, Chen. We've got a problem. The investors are very concerned about getting their return on their investment."

Chen saw that Steppler was starting to perspire. "But the results are showing promise. It works, and when we do the large sample size, we should have no problem in meeting the statistical significance for approval."

Steppler nodded. "I know, but according to our investor agreement, I don't have more time."

"Then tell them we need more time. All studies take longer than assumed and always cost more."

"We have the money, but two large clinicals, four hundred patients each, two and a half more years, and then a year with the FDA? They'll never go for it." Steppler was silent for a long time. "Okay, I'll speak to them."

* * *

Friday, November 8, 2029

He called Rapolo to discuss an update, and Rapolo invited him to lunch. The meeting was held at Mario's on Arthur Avenue in the Bronx. When Steppler arrived, he found Rapolo, Vito, and a third individual.

"Mr. Steppler, thanks for coming out to meet us. You know Vito, and this is Bernard, our accountant. I asked Bernard to be here in case I couldn't add the numbers quick enough."

Steppler shook hands, sat down, and began to speak when Rapolo interrupted.

"Wait, we'll eat first, and then we can talk whatever business you want to talk about. Never talk business without a full stomach, my father used to tell me. You hungry?"

Steppler nodded, though his stomach was already upset. "I'm always ready to eat."

"Great, then we'll fill you up. You have allergies or somethin'? Lots of people are allergic to garlic or other stuff. Otherwise, if you don't mind, I'll order for you."

Steppler agreed, and Rapolo signaled for the waiter, who came directly over with the menus.

"Yes, Mr. Rapolo?"

"Yeah, thanks, Joey. We've got a guest today, so we want to show him the real Arthur Avenue. How 'bout some appetizers? That okay with everybody?" Vito nodded, and Bernard and Steppler agreed. "Great, let's have some plates of spiedini, a little calamari, and some carciofi." He looked at Steppler. "How 'bout salad? They make a great Caesar here. You want that?"

Steppler couldn't even think of food. "Maybe a little."

Rapolo looked at the waiter. "Great, bring that for the table. Anyone want soup?"

Vito shook his head. "Not today."

"Bernie, you want soup?" Bernie passed. "All right, forget it. How 'bout you, Mr. Steppler, you like pasta? This stuff is all homemade."

"Okay, Sure."

Rapolo smiled. "The pasta they make here"—he paused, kissed his fingers, and lifted them upward—"is out of this world. Joey, bring out some plates of the homemade lasagna, some of the aragosta ravioli, and a platter of the manicotti. I want our guest not to leave hungry." He turned to Steppler. "Wait till you try the manicotti; it's filled with cheese and prosciutto. Out of this world. And Joey, just biscotti and water for dessert. We have to talk business and don't want to be too full."

By the time Steppler finished lunch, he had gained five pounds and was almost too bloated to speak.

"So, Mr. Steppler, you wanted to inform us about something. Tell us what's on your mind. Everythin' going well?"

Steppler dabbed his mouth with the linen napkin and cleared his throat. "Yes, everything's going well. All the studies have excellent results."

"That's great." Rapolo looked at his accountant. "You see, Bernie, as soon as I met him, I knew he was a good investment." He looked at Steppler. "Tell Bernie how many days left in our agreement."

If Steppler wasn't sick enough from the food, he was sicker from the question. "About two years."

Rapolo smiled at Bernie. "You see, Bernie, you'll have the money in two years unless he gives it to us sooner. Ain't that right, Mr. Steppler?"

Steppler nearly choked on his words. "Well, this is what I wanted to speak to you about. There is one thing that I may have misjudged."

"And that is?"

"The amount of time needed to complete the work."

Rapolo glanced at Vito and then turned his attention to Steppler. "I don't understand, Mr. Steppler. There's still plenty of time left in our agreement."

"Well, we just finished the Phase Two study, and the results are perfect."

Rapolo pressed his lips together and nodded. "Yeah, you mentioned that, so what's the problem?"

Steppler again blotted his lips with the napkin, trying to avoid the cold, calculated intents of the others. He was certainly not going to mention the need for two more years to give them their money. "Well, actually, I didn't realize that the FDA was so busy and they will require more time to review the data for approval. So, I wanted to let you know."

Rapolo looked at his associates and took out a sheet of paper. "And, how much is more? Two years? Three?"

Steppler couldn't believe it. They were okay with up to three years. So there was a god. "Three would be perfect. That's exactly what we need."

Rapolo held his palms up and smiled. "Well, Mr. Steppler, that's very kind of you to keep us in the loop. So, let's see. According to this paper you gave me, you said I would be getting my six billion in July 2031. And now you want an extra three, is that correct?"

"Yes, three is correct."

"I don't believe that would be a problem." He looked at Vito. "What do you think, Vito? Is that doable?"

Vito looked at Steppler like he was examining a dish of questionable fish. "Sure, I say give the kid the extra time."

Rapolo looked at his accountant. "What do you think, Bernie? Do we have enough cash to cover it?"

Bernie looked very seriously at the numbers as if weighing the future of the world. "Sure, why not? It's not like he would ever screw us."

Rapolo got up. "That's for sure. Hey, Vito, has anyone ever screwed us?"

"If they have, I never saw them again." Vito gave a forced laugh. "Sort of disappeared."

"You got it, kid. Three extra months. What date is that, Bernie?"

Steppler nearly fell off his chair. Did he say months? No, he had to tell them years.

Bernie checked the calendar on his cell phone. "That makes it October 20 or so."

Rapolo smiled. "Why, that's perfect. It's my anniversary. What a perfect gift, Mr. Steppler. I can't wait to tell my Anita. Let's see, October 2031, that will be forty-two years of bliss." Rapolo erased the smile from his face. "But don't be late again. Capisce?"

There was no way Steppler could correct them. If he felt full from the meal before, now his stomach was having a serious argument with him. He tried to get the words out. "Yes, sir, I do."

"I'm sorry, I couldn't hear you. What did you say?"

Steppler almost choked, trying to speak. "Yes, sir, I do."

"That's what I thought you said. I mean, we take this very serious, don't we, Vito?"

Vito gave a stern look to Steppler. "Very serious."

Rapolo put his arm around Steppler. "Look, kid, we like you. But business is business, and we wouldn't want anything to happen to you. I mean, accidents happen all the time, ain't that right, Vito?"

Vito nodded. "Sure, kid, nothin' to worry about, but accidents happen all the time to people who don't pay on time."

Rapolo tightened his grip around Steppler's neck for a moment, then quickly released it. "October, Mr. Steppler. See you then. Six billion in four years, four billion in three."

CHAPTER FOURTEEN

Steppler struggled to walk back to his car. As he began the drive back to the lab on the West Side Highway, the experience of fear was now taking its full response. The threat had become tangible. He could not be late again. His hands were sweaty, and his shirt was already soaked through with perspiration. He still felt the lingering sensation of Rapolo's hand around his neck. Chills ran through his body, and his face was clammy to the touch. If anyone had seen him, they would have said his face was as white as a ghost. He had never felt such stress. His stomach was as tight as a knot that forced him to double over. Suddenly, he pulled over on the side of the road and opened the door just in time to leave the last bites of manicotti on the bed of grass. When he reached the lab, he went into the bathroom and washed his face. He was angry with himself for getting into this situation, forced into a box with no exit, and pounded on whatever walls were close to him.

"You okay?" Chen asked when he saw Steppler.

"Yeah, I'll be fine. Too much lunch."

"How'd the meeting go?"

"They gave us an extra three months."

Chen laughed. "For what?"

"Until approval."

Chen's laugh stopped abruptly. "Three months? That's how long it will take before we can even begin the next studies. How much do you have to give them?"

Steppler was frantically writing numbers on a sheet of paper. "Between four to six billion."

"What?"

"And if we don't, we'll be finished."

"What do you mean finished?"

"The people we're involved with are pretty tough guys. They would just as soon burn down the lab and me in it if they don't get their money."

"What are you going to do?"

"I don't know yet, but I'll figure out something."

It was a Friday afternoon, and the lab was closing up for the weekend. Chen realized he had done all he could do. "Well, we have all the data on the ninety patients on file. What do you want me to do with it? It's all written up and ready to go to the FDA. I'll send it in on Monday. Data looks mostly good, but there are some deaths that occurred, and we're not certain what the cause was."

"Could that be a problem?"

"It's possible, but you never know. Five deaths out of ninety in a pandemic that would kill everyone? That sounds good to me. Guess we'll find out soon enough."

"We can't have a possible problem. It has to be certain. We are going to need approval without the further studies. Listen, Chen, you should go home for the weekend. You've worked hard enough. I'll see you Monday morning."

CHAPTER FIFTEEN

Steppler realized he was way over his head. There was no way he could return the money on time. It was late Friday afternoon when he put a call in to James D'Arcy and told him what happened. "I don't know what to do. Maybe I should speak to your father."

D'Arcy shook his head. "My father's going to tell you that once you make a deal with those guys, either you live up to it, or you may not be living. You have to pay them."

"I know, but how? I think this guy Vito would rather arrange my accident than my paying them back. Either way, I'm up shit creek."

D'Arcy thought for a while. "Then raise the money."

"From where?"

"An IPO. If we go public and the results are as good as you say, then we go on a roadshow and start selling stock. How much is the company worth?"

Steppler guessed. "I'm not sure, but without an approval it's not worth six billion dollars."

"Then how do you get an approval without further studies?"

Steppler thought for a while. "There is a way, though it rarely happens."

D'Arcy was inquisitive. "How?"

"The FDA can authorize a drug's use in an emergency if they find the treatment to be safe and there is evidence of benefit."

"What kind of emergency?"

Steppler didn't even want to say the words. "A pandemic."

"A pandemic? But there is no pandemic." D'Arcy's voice reflected nonbelief. "I mean, we always read about outbreaks, but not a pandemic. I suppose it could be used for the outbreaks. And you said it showed benefit, didn't it?"

"Absolutely."

"And safe?"

Steppler hesitated. "Safe? Why yes, except for a few minor responses in one or two patients." Steppler failed to mention that the minor responses were deaths.

"And will you get reimbursement?"

"I would think that federal health officials would approve payment under Medicare and Medicaid."

D'Arcy tapped his pen on the desk. "Then you have no choice. Send in your results to the regulatory agencies to see if they will give you the fast approval, and I'll start to set up an IPO. With your initial results showing so much progress, we should be able to raise something. I'm just not sure how much. How much does the company have left?"

"If we don't do any more studies, about eighty million."

There was a pause on D'Arcy's end. Finally, Steppler heard the response. "Fine, come to my office first thing Monday morning, and we'll start the IPO process. Meanwhile, send in the data to the FDA ASAP. If the test results are as good as you say, and there's a fear of another pandemic, maybe they'll give you the approval."

* * *

If the test results are as good as you say, maybe they'll give you the approval. D'Arcy's words kept ringing through Steppler's ears as he lay in bed. There was no way he could sleep, even with the pills he had taken. Both his mind and his body continued to roll from one position to another as if he were on a ship in troubled waters. He looked at the clock. It was one in the morning. He got out of bed, threw on some clothes, and took a taxi to the lab. There was something on his mind. *The test results better be good. They better be really good.*

CHAPTER SIXTEEN

Except for Chris, the security guard, the place was closed for the weekend. Steppler went to the lab and sat down at his desk, trying to concentrate. Fear had taken the place of logic, blocking his ability to think. The pressure of the situation had built to a degree he had never experienced before. He was now being driven by the innate compulsion to live.

He washed his face with cold water, poured a cup of black coffee from the machine, and returned to his desk, trying to focus on the data. He needed approval, and he was convinced that approval could only be granted if the results were perfect. But what of the five patients who did not respond perfectly?

He reviewed the dose-ranging studies. In the low-dose group, three out of the forty-five patients died after taking the drug. Reviewing their medical histories, he noticed that those three had a history of a heart condition. Steppler played with the significance of that in his mind for a long time. The pathology report showed that the viral count had been reduced in all three patients, but perhaps not enough. It was marked as a one-plus, slightly more than the minimal amount of viral load remaining. If it were marked as a one, it meant the viral load was too low to detect, and that would indicate the antiviral activity worked as designed in spite of the deaths. When he reviewed the higher dose, two patients did not respond even though their viral load was also reduced.

Steppler's fear now dominated his actions. He began to cross the line that scientists must never cross. But the mind works in strange ways. He remembered a Rudyard Kipling quote his mother taught her students: "Of all the liars in the world, sometimes the worst are our own fears." And so, the well-known process of rationalization began. It started with the thought that it wasn't the virus that caused death but the history of heart failure. Once his mind believed that possibility, it was only logical that the viral count had to be reduced to a one, and therefore, to be more accurate, the viral counts needed to be marked as minimal. To Steppler, both doses worked equally as well in terms of the effect on the virus. Figuring that the lower dose is always safer for the patient, assuming the same effectiveness, Steppler believed he had to show how the lower dose was what was called for. He could not hide the deaths, but he could edit the effectiveness of the drug on the virus. What was originally written had to be edited; what was marked as a one-plus now read as a one on both patients. It certainly looked proper at one. The change was so slight, just a matter of misinterpretation, a human judgment error. To Steppler, it was a mistake of the examiners who ran the study. Fortunately, Steppler felt he was there to correct the situation. And he did. The patient histories only required a small check in the box that asked if there was any cardiac pathology prior to the study.

It was well into the early morning hours by the time he had completed his work. The study results now read, "In all instances, both higher and lower doses of the experimental drug LB182 successfully destroyed the viral count with no deleterious effects of significance. Death occurred only in patients with a history of severe heart disease. Perhaps they should have not been allowed in the study."

He turned off his computer and left a message on Chen's cell. "Thanks again. You did a great job. I took a quick look at the application. Everything looks great. Just sign off as the chief investigator, attest to the results as truthful and click send."

That was all he had to do, just a few clarifications, a few strokes on the keyboard, and it was done. He rose from his chair, locked the door to the lab, and walked into the cool silence of an early Saturday morning, believing that all was right in the greatest city in the world.

* * *

But the belief did not last. The burden of what he had done was not easily lifted. As had been said before, what seemed scenic by the moonlight soon seemed cynic by day, and the day was fraught with a knot in his stomach that would not dissipate. At night, it was worse. He tossed and turned, and when he dozed off, the dreams would haunt him awake. The tightness became tighter, the same feeling of guilt he experienced as a boy when doing something wrong. But what choice did he have? What else could he have done? He wanted to live. And, he felt, the results indicated that a lot of others could also. He was a good person.

CHAPTER SEVENTEEN

Chen reached the lab early Monday morning, excited at the progress that was made and hopeful that the study results would be sufficient for the FDA to allow continuation to the phase three studies. Finally, his dream was coming true. All those years of preparation and hours in the laboratory seeking a cure were becoming a reality. He had even brought a new pen to scribe his signature.

He took a quick look at the 220 pages of data and patient histories that had been accumulated and began to scroll down through each of the section signature pages for him to sign off as the chief investigator. Yet, something seemed improper. He reread the summary conclusion several times: "In all instances, both higher and lower doses of the experimental drug LB182 successfully destroyed the viral count with no deleterious effects of significance. Death occurred only to patients who had a history of severe heart disease. Perhaps they should have not been allowed in the study."

This was not what he had written. Chen went back to his copy of the Phase Two entry on his laptop. He couldn't believe it. Steppler had changed the results on the two reported deaths, and he expected Chen to take the responsibility of signing off on it.

* * *

"What have you done?!"

Steppler entered the lab just as Chen completed rereading the application. "What are you talking about?"

"You changed the results. You can't do that! It's dishonest!"

"I found two mistakes."

"There were no mistakes. It was all checked and rechecked. What do you think you're doing?"

"I'm doing what I have to do. I'm in charge of this company, and that's the way I'm playing it. Either these results are perfect, or both of us are in a lot of trouble."

"I won't do it."

"Listen, Chen. What are we talking about, five patients out of all of them? Obviously, it works, and, except for those five, no reports of any side effects were present. Think of all the patients who could die if the FDA doesn't approve it. That is why we have no choice. All the work that you've done, all the honor you are giving your father for your herbal remedy to save the world, would be lost. Are you going to throw it all away for a few corrections? We're the only ones who have seen the final package. The FDA will have no idea. No one is going to know."

A sudden calm overcame Chen as if his father had known long ago that this moment would occur. Did this moment occur for everyone, or was his father's proverb meant only for him? He took out the old picture, the only evidence of his childhood, and read his father's script on the back: *He who sacrifices his conscience to ambition burns a picture to obtain the ashes.* Finally, he answered in a clear, steady voice. "You are wrong. Someone will know."

Steppler's face grew concerned. "Who's that?"

"Me."

Steppler stared at Chen, not aware that his facial muscles were tightening and his teeth clenching. He walked around the lab, trying to clear his mind to appreciate the situation. Finally, with as much control as possible, he turned to Chen. "Then you will have to leave."

Chen seemed surprised. "What do you mean, leave?"

Steppler replied in a voice louder than he wanted. "If you can't deal with the reality, then I don't want you here anymore."

Chen struggled to control his anger. "You can't do this. We have a partnership. All this work is mine; all the ideas are mine. Everything is mine. We have equal say on what happens here. And now we have patents. If you do anything to ruin our work, I will have you reported."

Steppler just laughed. "You fool. Partners? Patents? You think you have a say in what goes on here?" He walked over to the cabinet, removed a file, and handed it to Chen. "Here's a copy of the corporate papers you signed. Better take a good look. You don't own shit! Even your laptop was purchased by the company. Now get out of here before I have you thrown out. This is my lab, and I don't want to see your face again."

CHAPTER EIGHTEEN

Chen read through the pages of the corporate agreement. How foolish of him to trust someone. He needed to make a phone call.

For two years, Tim Channing had been part of Dr. Ballan's bioengineering program before he realized he would prefer spending his life outside of a lab and decided to leave for law school. Utilizing his background in science, he specialized in patent law and worked in the growing field of helping pharmaceutical research companies receive patents on complicated molecular structures that only a scientist could understand. He easily made the transition to a large firm and was hired to start a patent law department.

"Tim, I have a problem, and I could use some advice."

They had met for coffee at a local Starbucks, and Chen handed him the papers. Channing went over the corporate operating agreement. "You've been raked over the coals. Your partner is not a partner. According to this, he's your boss. He owns one hundred percent of the company, all the granted patents, the lease for the lab, and if there are net profits, he will give you 15 percent. But he is able to make all decisions, make out all checks, and control the entire company. Are you aware of that?"

"To be honest, I had no idea what I was signing. It was the last hour before I had to close the lab when he informed me that he raised the money, and I had to sign the documents he gave me immediately. I was just thankful that we were able to continue. I had no idea until now that he could throw me out of the company."

Channing was surprised. "That's a drastic step. What happened?"

"He fudged some results and wanted me to send it in to the FDA."

"Wow, what a sleaze." Channing thought for a moment. "I'm not sure what you can do about ownership. It's really straightforward. You signed everything over to him. But, if you can prove what he did, that's a felony, and he would be looking at a lot of jail time."

"It's because he's doing business with the mob."

Channing put his coffee cup down, almost spilling it on the table. "What?"

"I saw them. They came into the lab when we were having a party. Steppler is afraid of them. They gave him one hundred million dollars, and he agreed to pay back six billion in four years. Well, he'll never get an approval in that time. That's why he changed the results. He needs the FDA to issue an immediate approval based on preliminary data, otherwise he will not be able to pay them what he promised."

Channing was becoming very interested. "So that's why he wants the records changed. Either get an approval now, or his life is not worth ten dollars. And I wouldn't be surprised if the hundred million is part of a laundering scheme. They must have figured what better place to legitimize a lot of cash then with very expensive pharmaceutical research."

Chen nodded his head. "So I've lost everything?"

Channing kept doodling with his pen on a napkin. "Perhaps there's something that can be done.

"What do you mean?"

"If he knows that you have evidence of the actual results and are willing to give your evidence to the authorities, then perhaps he will change his mind."

"The problem is I don't have any evidence. He has my laptop in the lab. He told me it was company property."

"And you keep no records at home?"

"Not really. Everything is on that laptop."

"And you still have the keys to the lab?"

"I do."

"And do you think he's changed the locks already?"

Chen realized what Channing was saying. "Probably not yet."

Channing spoke carefully. "Now, I'm not suggesting anything, and we're only speaking hypothetically as friends, not in any legal attorney-client relationship, but if you happened to be visiting your lab and downloaded your data, then noticed that certain proprietary information was accidentally deleted from the computer, that could be very helpful. Certainly, it would make good sense for any scientist to keep backup records at home, just in case. You see what I mean?"

"Yes, I believe so."

"And certainly, any accounts that you might have discretionary control over should be reviewed at this time. Perhaps you have a separate account for miscellaneous expenses such as lab equipment, lab assay materials, chemicals, things like that, or personal expenses that you incurred that require reimbursement."

"I understand."

"Good." Channing stood, and they shook hands. He gave a slight grin that suggested a message had been sent. "Well, I better be going. Good luck, and Chen, be careful. This fellow is desperate, and desperate people do desperate things."

CHAPTER NINETEEN

Chen waited until dark. He dressed like a ninja all in black and waited outside the entrance to the university, keeping his eye on Chris, the guard at the desk. When he saw Chris take a phone call, he entered the lobby and walked directly down the long hallway to the lab entrance, avoiding facing the security cameras.

He took out his keys and tried the outer door. The locks had not been changed. Once in, he relocked the door, turned on his flashlight, and quietly walked to the rear of the lab where his office was located. His laptop was nowhere to be found. He walked into Steppler's office and found the laptop on the desk. He turned it on, took out a USB key, began the download, and returned to his office, where he removed the research checkbook from his desk drawer. The checkbook was only used for needed lab equipment and supplies and required only his signature. There was $500,000 in the account. He had rarely used it, but this time, Chen made out a large check, leaving a balance of $5000. The download was just finishing when he heard voices outside.

"Good evening, Mr. Steppler. Working late?"

"Hi, Chris. No, just forgot something that I have to pick up."

Chen held his breath and turned off the flashlight, his mind spinning, trying to determine what to do. What was Steppler doing here at this time of night? He quickly walked back into Steppler's office. The download was still not complete.

He heard Steppler's voice. "Oh, by the way, Chris, tomorrow I would like to have the locks changed on the door. How do we do that?"

"Having a problem?"

"Well, to be honest, Dr. Chu is no longer working here, and I think it best for security."

"OK, got it. You'll have to requisition it, and we'll take care of it for you. When do you want it done?"

"Yesterday."

"In that case, you'll need to sign the requisition now if you want the work order for the morning."

Chen heard footsteps walking away. He took a deep breath and tried to think. There was only one exit, and he didn't know if he had enough time to get out without being seen. He checked the download, and it was complete. Quickly, he removed the USB key, put it into his pocket, scrolled to a particular section of his notes, and deleted the material and procedure sections. If anyone wanted to reconstitute the drug, the laptop would be of little help. Chen walked quietly to the door to make his exit. It was too late. He heard footsteps approaching and heard the key in the lock. He had to find a place to hide, and it was too late to make it to the locked viral lab. He looked around. Where? He moved quickly into his office and crouched on the floor behind his desk. As he looked out, he realized he had left his door ajar. It was too late to close it; Steppler had already entered the lab and turned on the lights.

Chen heard Steppler speaking to himself. "Now, where did I put that laptop?" He entered his office and heard Steppler's voice again. "Here it is." Moments later, he could see Steppler walking toward the outer door carrying the laptop.

Chen's legs were cramping as he crouched behind the desk. As Steppler opened the door and turned off the lights, the pain in Chen's legs forced him to stretch his legs. As he stood, he brushed against a book on his desk. It fell to the floor. Steppler stopped and switched on the light. "Somebody here? Is anyone here?"

Chen knelt behind the desk again, his legs in pain. Steppler looked around the lab but didn't see anyone. He checked his office and again saw nothing unusual. Finally, he walked into Chen's office and noticed the book on the floor. Chen felt his presence, held his breath, and tightened his grip on the flashlight. His heart was beating so loud he thought Steppler would hear it. Steppler reached down to pick up the book and placed it back on the desk.

"Everything all right in here, Mr. Steppler?"

Steppler walked out of the office to see security in the outer doorway. "Yeah, Chris, just checking." He took a quick look around and walked out the door. "Thanks, Chris, appreciate your help."

Chen waited several minutes before leaving, standing up to shake off the muscle fatigue. He heard doors opening and closing and peeked out the door. Chris was on his rounds checking the offices. He waited for Chris to take the elevator to the upper floors and quickly exited the locked building.

CHAPTER TWENTY

At nine thirty Tuesday morning, Chen walked into the Bank of First City and cashed a check for $495,000. He figured that was the minimum he was owed for services rendered. He then walked to Channing's office and, after a short wait, was shown in.

"I took a little stroll last evening. Almost got caught. I think I'm ready for a vacation."

"Any place you want to go?"

"Yes, I want to go home. It's been a long time."

"Back to China? Fine. If things start to heat up, let me know. Meanwhile, keep your eyes and ears open. An anonymous letter should be reaching your friend advising him that unless you receive what is due to you, you will be releasing the original data."

"Thank you, Tim. You have been a great help to me. I'm afraid I really messed up. How much do I owe you for all this?"

Channing smiled. "Listen, Chen, you made a mistake. But that mistake was hooking up with someone who would sell you down the river to succeed. I don't like that. And as far as the fee, it never happened, and you're not a client. I told you that. This is where my law degree can do some country justice. Enjoy your trip, and keep me up-to-date."

* * *

As Chen was boarding Delta Airlines flight 2356 to Changchun, with a stop in Pudong International Airport in Shanghai, a letter was being hand-delivered to Brookfield Institute addressed to *Lexington Bio, Phillip Steppler.*

Steppler looked at it, puzzled by the lack of a return address, and read the typed contents:

> Dear Sir,
>
> It has come to our attention that you have completed your Phase Two study with excellent results, though not perfect. It appears that five patients died, although the reason is not certain. Be aware of our continued interest in and monitoring of the future course of Lexington Bio. The truth cannot be concealed.

That was all. There was no signature or further information.

Steppler reread the letter, trying to determine who sent it. Was it Chen? He wouldn't dare. He folded the letter and placed it into his briefcase. Whoever it was had no proof. He had the computers locked away. There were no other backups. No one was allowed to leave the lab with any study information. It was all confidential.

─{ BOOK TWO }─

CHAPTER TWENTY-ONE

Chen Chu arrived in Changchun and arranged for a car rental, a midsize Toyota Corolla. It had been almost fifteen years since his high school days in the city. As he drove through, he realized that everything had changed. In his absence, Changchun had undergone overwhelming industrial and commercial growth, becoming a major Chinese manufacturing hub. As he left the outskirts of the old city, he passed the huge new Foxconn Technology plant where Apple's iPhones are assembled.

Further on, he slowed to wonder at the modern plant run by Volkswagen, followed by another space-aged factory built by Toyota. The fact was everything had been rebuilt—roads, bridges, dams, and entire new cities. Even Kougian was unrecognizable compared to what he recalled. He continued, driving along the mountainside on a well-paved four-lane highway and turned off when he saw a new large green sign with bright white letters with the name of his village, Wulajie. He soon realized it was no longer the village that he had left. What was once his home was now a planned community circled by paved solar-lit roads, a main street with small shops, food markets, a newly built school, and automobiles everywhere. In place of mud-built homes were neatly arranged single three- and four-bedroom houses made of concrete that were twice the size of the home of his youth. The small gardens and old farmhouses that had once been present were now replaced with large modern mechanized farms with scores of workers in the irrigated fields. The People's Republic of China had kept its word, investing huge sums into rebuilding its rural infrastructure. Chen drove to where he thought his home was located, but all he could find was a small office building with a sign outside: "Feng Hue, MD, Family Medicine." It was then that Chen realized that it was not just the village but also him that had changed. With cash in the bank and having experienced life in the United States, he appreciated the advantages of success.

He parked the car on a busy street and began walking past shops that previously were empty land. Visions of the past were fleeing through his mind like scenes from a film. Down the street was a dry cleaner, next to it a store selling computers, and on the corner was a new pharmacy that reminded him of the CVS around the corner from his apartment in New York. He walked in and introduced himself to the clerk behind the counter.

"Hi, my name is Chen Chu, and I used to live here before the virus hit. Would you know if there is anyone who is still here from that time?"

The woman replied that she had only moved in a few years ago when the new village was being built but directed him to the post office where the postmistress might know of someone. He followed her directions, walked into a small, neat post office, and asked the clerk.

"Wait here; there may be someone who knows about that time."

A short, heavy-set woman appeared a few minutes later. "As far as I know, there was only one person who survived that virus, and she was a young girl at the time. She also came to see what happened to the house she grew up in. That was only last month, and she left that same day."

Chen remembered the nurse had mentioned that one other child had lived. "Do you remember her name?"

The woman thought for a moment. "I believe she left a card. Let me check my desk." She soon returned. "Her name is Li Zhou. The card says she's a reporter for the *Wall Street Journal*. She asked the same questions that you did. I don't believe anyone else survived that tragedy."

Chen recalled the Zhou family that lived next door. They had a boy, Zhong, who had gone to school with him, although that was a very common name in China.

The woman looked suspiciously at Chen. "Where do you live, Mr. Chen?"

"Actually, I just arrived this morning. I've been living in the United States, so I guess I have no address at this time."

"You came for vacation?"

"For a visit. I got homesick."

"And Mr. Chen, what do you do?"

"I'm a scientist."

The woman became very interested. "You know, Mr. Chen, I am the chairman of our local school board. We are looking for a science teacher here. We have a brand-new school and wonderful children and a lot of new families moving here from the big cities to find fresh air. We can't pay that much, but you'll be back home. Why don't we get you a room at the new inn and you think about it, at our expense. At least you can rest in a new room with clean sheets. I bet you could use a nice rest after such a long trip."

Chen was tired, and this could be a great way to start his new future. He didn't know about teaching at the local school, but for one night, he would stay around. So Chen agreed, and the woman brought him to the inn, where he registered and left his small suitcase with a few clothes. She accompanied him to the school. He was amazed at how modern it was, how the science labs were filled with new equipment, and how attentive the students seemed to be. This was why China had made such great advances in science and technology. They invested heavily in it.

He spent the night at the inn, which, as advertised, had clean rooms, hot showers, and fresh sheets. By the next day he agreed to stay and teach through the summer term. In the meantime, he bought a new computer and down-loaded his USB drive with the data he had accumulated at Brookfield onto it. He thought that teaching was going to be a pleasure compared to what he had just been through. He placed his computer into his briefcase and locked the combination. To Chen, it was like sealing a tomb that would never have to be brought back to life. If Chen only knew.

CHAPTER TWENTY-TWO

New York, August 18, 2030

It took two months for D'Arcy to complete the necessary paperwork and filings for Lexington Bio to have an IPO. "You have a lot of traveling to do," he informed Steppler.

"Where to?"

"Shanghai. It appears that the Chinese government is most interested in the work that you are doing. I went over the Brookfield financials with an official of the government, General Han, discussing the one-hundred-million-dollar investment that was provided for you. Apparently, General Han had attended a conference in Atlanta where Chen had spoken and was quite aware of the company's research. When he asked about the use of the new proceeds, I explained that they included buying out your investors at a price of six billion dollars US, four billion if purchased within six months."

"He must have thought you were crazy."

"Actually, he said he would discuss it with me when we arrive in Shanghai."

"So there's a chance?"

"We'll find out soon enough. Any further funds will come from an investment conference in Shanghai that will be scheduled for the participation of global investors. This will give the raise international legitimacy."

"When do we leave?"

"September 7, less than three weeks from now. That means you have to put together a full investor deck to generate interest in Lexington Bio. If you are still as smooth in selling an idea as you were at business school, there should be no problem. You were the best of all of us. Remember, the major investor agreed to conclude the purchase within forty-eight hours. The investment conference is window dressing."

"I got it. Are you coming with me?"

D'Arcy smiled. "Damn right. I've got to earn another eight percent. By the time I finish with you, I can retire."

"Great," Steppler replied. "I hear a lot is going on in Shanghai."

"That's what they say. The business activity matches the temperature."

CHAPTER TWENTY-THREE

Chen was surprised at the seriousness of the students in learning science. He had twenty students to teach science, math, and technology. They all wanted to be entrepreneurs and start companies like Alibaba and Tesla. He was enjoying the routine and, with the money he had in the bank, could probably afford to spend the rest of his life at the inn, where breakfast was included and a choice of restaurants were available for lunch and dinner.

Over the past three months, he had grown to enjoy the simpler life. He was involved with his students, many of whom showed excellent promise, and he had no concerns about deadlines, Steppler, or raising money. Until he received an email from his friend, Tim Channing, back in New York: *Hate to disrupt your living the good life, but you need to take a meeting at the Shanghai Hilton on September 9. I think you will find it most interesting.*

CHAPTER TWENTY-FOUR

Monday, September 9, 2030, Shanghai

Chen Chu stood alone in the rear of the main ballroom of the Shanghai Hilton, unimpressed with the glittering chandeliers that flooded the huge space. To the attentive viewer, it would appear as if his posture had a hint of defiance. His arms folded firmly across the chest of his wiry body, his jaw set, his small dark eyes and chiseled ears focused intently on the speaker and his content. He seemed out of place wearing short sleeves, tight jeans, and canvas sneakers, an innocent among the wolves of international finance, sophisticated suited men and women seated on white cushioned chairs at round linen-covered tables sipping their lattes, enjoying croissants, taking notes on laptops, and checking stock prices on cell phones.

Chen recognized the chairman of the conference, who introduced the speaker. It was General Han Shi, the Batman.

"Welcome, everyone, to what China believes is a most exciting investment opportunity to participate in a company that we believe will be the future of healthcare in the world. That company is Lexington Bio, and we are most appreciative that the founder is with us today. As you know, the financial firm China Reform is close to making a substantial investment in Lexington Bio, but we want to share this opportunity with others in the global community. Therefore, my friends and fellow comrades, it is my pleasure to welcome our speaker, Mr. Philip Steppler, Chairman and CEO of Lexington Bio, to share the dream with you."

* * *

Phillip Steppler heard his name called onstage and took a deep breath. He fully realized what was at risk, not just the dreams that he had envisioned for so many years but, in reality, his life. He had no choice but to succeed. He stood upright, drew confidence from within, and walked out into the limelight to begin the presentation that he had rehearsed so many times.

From where he stood, Chen realized the interest that China had in his technology. If Jiang was correct, what was thought to be research in biotherapeutics was actually the development of bioterror, and without the antidote, they had nothing. Four billion was a small price to pay to ransom the world.

Chen's thoughts returned to the speaker, who was completing his corporate presentation to the overfilled room gathered to hear the results of Lexington Bio's new drug, LB182. Leaked information suggested it had the potential to be one of the great pharmaceutical discoveries of the twenty-first century and, if so, a unique investment opportunity. Those present were not disappointed.

"As the data shows," Steppler began, pointing out on his laptop connected remotely to the two huge screens on each side of the stage, "Lexington Bio has made significant progress in enhancing the body's immune system to seek and destroy virulent vectors, including its lethal efficacy against a host of viruses and their mutations. This ability to destroy not only the mother but its mutated offspring is due to the exceptional molecular activity of LB182, developed over the past twelve years in response to the terrifying effects of the COVID-19 virus with its high mutational burden. We believe that once LB182 is approved, a viral pandemic the likes of COVID-19 will never occur again. Our clinical results on treating severely ill viral patients with LB182 have already been sent to the FDA as well as the European and Chinese Health Ministries. We have a meeting date of October 15 with the FDA, and, to be honest, we believe we will be granted an expedited approval."

A burst of excitement filled the huge hall in affirmation of the pre-announcement enthusiasm that the medical and financial communities had anticipated. What investors heard was that LB182 was the key to unlocking the full potential of the body's ability to destroy the major pathogenic causes of death in the world.

Steppler paused for the initial excitement to fade, then went on. "In other words, we are presenting to you the long-sought treasure that Ponce de Leon spent his lifetime seeking, the precious fluid that would yield eternal life. And our projections indicate that following approval, LB182 will be the highest grossing drug ever marketed with revenues of one hundred billion dollars each year."

Chen finished the declaration himself, *assuming there was another pandemic.* The reaction was immediate and prolonged. The entire room rose to its feet in acclamation. No one had predicted the numbers would be that high. Steppler allowed the reaction to continue. As a student of crowd behavior, he had mastered LeBon's theories that large groups, when together, behave as a collective mind different from how they feel or think or act alone. And so he waited, allowing the hypothesis to prove itself, surveying the audience as it bonded together and began to unify in mass exhilaration, watching the transformation as individuals lost their decision-making abilities only to be swept into the driving force that found common cause in their insatiable addiction to their almighty god—greed.

Steppler monitored their behavior, judged their weakness, and waited for the moment. He knew it was imminent as he gauged their cries, quantified their eruption, and empirically sensed the inherent timing. Still, he waited, felt the conversion building, then the crescendo, then the peak as the room began to pulse. And then, finally, the explosion—the moment of transference—the masses had become a crowd. *Now!* he told himself, *Do it now!*

He raised his voice, and the room became electric: "Now, invest it all now, and you will never need to work another day."

The delivery was perfect, and the result was immediate. Cell phones sent transmissions from Shanghai to the world; emailed directives were dispatched globally to bankers, brokers, and A list clients: "Buy Lexington Bio at market."

Within minutes, Steppler checked his phone and was pleased. Lexington Bio's stock had sold twenty million shares and soared from $8.00 to $42.25 per share.

* * *

As Steppler walked into the wings following his presentation, he was met by D'Arcy.

"What did you think?"

"I think it worked."

"The stock went up?"

"Better than that."

"What?"

"General Han approached me as you were finishing the raise."

"And?"

"He's taking it."

"What?"

"The whole thing. He's wiring the funds within twenty-four hours."

"I don't believe it."

"Believe it. I went over everything with him, and I will send him the agreement as soon as I get back to the hotel. They had no problem with the four billion to pay back the investors. It will be a loan, so although they have no ownership, it will mean that they, in all practicality, will have a say in how the company is run, although they agreed that you will make all the decisions."

Steppler nodded. "That sounds fine."

"But they heard what you said about the FDA approving the drug. The loan will remain conditional based on the understanding that the FDA grants emergency acceptance within the year. Otherwise, they can demand immediate payment and the company assets. So you had better be certain of this before you sign. You have one year to make this work."

Steppler realized he had no choice. There was no other way he could repay Rapolo on time. "Let's do it."

"Fine, I will advise them we agree. Once General Han wires the funds to your bank, I will have Rapolo's money deposited into his account, which will be recorded as a return on investment. Rapolo will sign a note that the conditions of his investment have been satisfied, so everything is kosher. The new investment will be from a Chinese state-owned investment firm called China Reform."

Steppler couldn't believe it. "So this is now all legit?"

"That is correct."

"So you have saved me again."

"At least for the time being. For whatever reason, General Han believes your technology is worth a great deal. But remember,"—D'Arcy's face reflected the seriousness of the transaction—"you have one year."

Steppler left the podium flying high. His major problem was solved. As he made his way to the rear of the hall, the path opened as if Moses was walking through the Red Sea. On both sides, he was greeted by his new disciples, accompanied by a chorus of greetings. He was chatting confidently with his new investors, answering questions, and giving advice on investment strategies, not knowing what he needed more—the praise or the profits. But there was one exception: a young, well-dressed woman stood in his way, interrupting the adulation.

"Mr. Steppler, why didn't you mention Dr. Chen Chu's name in recognition of the role that he played? Isn't it true that it was his initial research that led to the drug's discovery?"

Steppler seemed taken aback by the question, and the surrounding investors noticed it. An unusual quiet penetrated the room, waiting for Steppler's response. Chen, having heard his name mentioned, straightened to attention, waiting for the reply and wondering who the young lady was. She had a striking face, a delicate jawline, and a pale complexion. Her long black hair reached halfway down her back, and she was wearing a black jumpsuit over a white shirt. Chen took a few steps toward her to hear Steppler's response.

Steppler took a long, deep breath before answering. This was a question he had never been asked, and he knew he had to be careful. "It is true that Dr. Chu was with us for a short time in the initial phase of our work, but he is not a signatory on the patents, nor was he involved in any further research. I believe he went on to other areas of interest." A weak smile crossed his lips as he added, "Hopefully, bigger and better things."

"One more item, Mr. Steppler. Is it true that you have a payment due of four billion dollars to one of your investors?"

Steppler gave a hardened glance at the young lady. "That was already paid."

He walked around her and continued through the ballroom, trying to pick up where he left off. As he made his way amid the mob of inquiring investors, he came to a sudden stop as if unnerved by recognition of the bespectacled individual in short sleeves and jeans standing near the back wall and staring at him as he passed by. And though their eyes met for the briefest of moments, the exchange was palpable. Steppler's composure was lost, his mind no longer enjoying the moment. The elation of his recent deal dwindled, and he turned away as he made his exit without another word.

Chen observed the response, a degree of retribution at the CEO's momentary loss of the cool, confident exterior that exposed the inner truth. Chen remained in place as if savoring the incident, observing the speaker as he made his way out of the room. Then, as if recalling something, Chen turned back, scanning the room in an attempt to find the young woman who asked the question. Who was she? What did she know? To Chen, who rarely paid attention to women, there seemed to be an unusual fascination. He continued searching, but when the crowd thinned, and she did not appear, he began to walk out of the conference when he heard a voice call his name from behind.

"Dr. Chu."

Chen turned to see who was speaking. "General Han."

"Nice to meet you again. As you see, we are very interested in the work that Lexington Bio is doing. We have been following your results, especially the Phase Two, which is undergoing review as we speak by the FDA. My contacts tell me the results were most favorable."

Chen responded. "I didn't realize that the FDA had already reviewed the data."

"They should be meeting shortly. There's very little that we don't know. But I wasn't aware that you are no longer involved with Lexington Bio. Is that true?"

"Yes, that's true."

"So you are not working on the project?"

"That is correct. Mr. Steppler is responsible for the company at this time."

The general gave a crooked smile. "Perhaps so, but we have taken a large position in Lexington Bio and are most concerned about our investment. We believe it is important for you to continue working on the project. We need to ensure FDA approval and Dr. Chu, I can make it very lucrative for you. Very lucrative. I would like you to consider that an offer."

Chen realized the danger he was in. "Actually, right now, I am working elsewhere."

"I heard something about your teaching high school science here in China, but I understood that was only a temporary position before you returned to the States."

"Actually, I am enjoying teaching."

"Yes, instructing students is very important, but please remember, so is China's national security, and that is my responsibility."

"So, you can't let anything go wrong."

"Glad to see you understand how things work here, and you certainly don't want to be on the wrong side."

Chen looked at the imposing figure opposite him. "And what side is that, General?"

General Han gave a devious smile. "To make certain that China is the most powerful nation on earth, and to achieve that, I will do whatever it takes. I look forward to your joining us."

The general removed a business card from his pocket and handed it to Chen. "Why don't you take a few weeks to think about it? Following that, I'll expect your call."

"Of course." And with that, Chen continued out the door and into the heat of a crowded Shanghai with one fear. Could General Han really force him to return to the project?

CHAPTER TWENTY-FIVE

October 15, 2030, 10 A.M.

The drive to FDA headquarters in Rockville was without discussion. Steppler and D'Arcy had too much on their minds to speak. Ever since the China trip, the press coverage of Lexington Bio had made Steppler the newest darling of Wall Street. The *Wall Street Journal*, *New York Times*, and *Barron's*, all had interviewed Steppler, along with appearances on CNBC and Bloomberg. In all instances, Steppler spoke confidently of the dramatic results of LB182, the flawless safety results and the assurance of expedited approval by the FDA. Only the *Wall Street Journal's* China correspondent questioned Lexington Bio's ability to deliver on their forecasts following the exit of their Chief Scientific Officer. As they passed through Delaware in Steppler's new Tesla, he took a call over the car's speaker:

"Steppler, here."

"Mr. Steppler, what a pleasant surprise. I checked the balance in our accounts, and sure enough, you returned our investment, just like you promised. Vito and I want to thank you for that. I have no idea how you did it, but you are quite a businessman. We are very appreciative and want to wish you the best with the FDA today. We enjoyed doing business. Thank you again, and anytime you want to eat on Arthur Avenue, just let us know. The meal's on me."

"Will do."

"Ciao." The call went dead.

D'Arcy looked over at Steppler. They both had a big smile. It was Steppler who spoke first. "You did it."

"But remember, you have one year to receive emergency approval. Otherwise, you will have another master."

CHAPTER TWENTY-SIX

October 13, 1:00 P.M., Rockville, Md.

They reached the parking lot outside of FDA headquarters at 5600 Fishers Lane. The FDA occupies the entire 93,000-square-foot modern four-story building called Element 12420, adjacent to the Twinbrook Metro Station in Rockville. From the exterior, the large structure looked more like a contemporary industrial loft than a government office building, with large warehouse windows and a facing of brick-colored cement. Inside was a sleek, modern decor, with glass-walled conference rooms, smooth slate floors, and high ceilings with exposed ductwork. Steppler thought it looked more like a nightclub than a government building that held sway over life and death.

As they entered the twenty-first century lobby with its shiny curving steel staircase that looked like it came from a Star Wars mother ship, Steppler and D'Arcy were greeted by Andy Cumberland, their regulatory adviser and Mitch Sedgewick, their operations manager responsible for the manufacturing of the product. Cumberland prepped the others on what was to occur and emphasized that they were only to respond if asked, "and keep those responses short and to the point. Remember, this meeting is only to listen. I have been here many times with numerous clients; we will be following a clearly stated process to obtain regulatory approval to market your product. So much depends upon a successful interaction with these people."

He looked directly at Steppler. "Phillip, understand something; they are here to help you through the process. They are not your enemies, so hear what they have to say, and we will do what they tell us to do. Unless I look to you to answer, let me do the talking. They know me, and I know them. If there are specific questions about the making of the drug, Mitch will answer. Phillip, you just listen, and we'll take it from here."

Steppler agreed and felt his mouth getting dry and the nape of his neck beginning to perspire, well aware of the importance of the impending outcome.

At eleven thirty, they were ushered into the elevator by a young woman, who introduced herself as Karen, a summer intern, along with a delivery man in a clean white shirt with the name *Hector, Ben's Caterers*, neatly scripted in red on it.

"Coffee smells good," Steppler remarked, trying to relieve his tension.

"Best on earth," Karen interjected with a smile.

Hector nodded. "I deliver here three times a day, so they must like it."

When they reached the third floor, Karen led Steppler and his group into a large office space with a conference table and chairs for twenty. Hector walked in with them, placing the coffee and Danish on the table as if he had done it many times before, and then left.

The FDA representatives, Pete Ward, PhD, Jerry Kagos, PhD and the Director of Biologic Medicines, Frederick Kosent, MD, introduced themselves and asked the visitors if they would like coffee or bottled water before they began. After a few minutes of informal chatting and bringing their coffees to the table, Kosent addressed the visitors.

"Gentlemen, thank you for allowing us to help guide you through what must seem like an unending series of steps. But please remember, our responsibility is the protection and promotion of the public's health, and that includes the control and supervision of all drugs, including vaccines and biopharmaceuticals, as in your case. And please understand we appreciate all of the hard work you have put into your product, and I must say; I am very impressed with the results you have obtained thus far. Today's meeting is to review your completed Phase 2 dosing data for your new drug LB182 and to discuss the initiation of your Phase 3 clinical studies. Is that correct?"

Cumberland responded. "That is correct."

Kosent continued. "Good, your data looks quite promising, but there are several . . ."

"Excuse me, I would like to clarify that."

The entire room looked at Steppler, especially Kosent, who apparently was not used to interruptions. "Mr. Steppler, you would like to modify the purpose of this meeting?"

Steppler's team looked at him with alarm, knowing he was flouting the instructions given to them by Cumberland.

"Well, actually, Dr. Kosent, it is my opinion that the results are so significant, and the threat of another virus so severe, that there is no need for any further studies."

Pete Ward looked at Kosent before responding. "And what do you suggest in place of further studies?"

Steppler continued. "I suggest that the drug receive immediate FDA Emergency Use Authorization to allow manufacturing in preparation for the next pandemic and be granted fast-track approval for marketing."

"Without further testing?"

"Absolutely, it's *rez ipso loquitor*. The results speak for themselves. Of course we would monitor the patients following their taking the drug."

The FDA members looked at one another. Kosent cleared his throat before responding.

"Well, actually, Mr. Steppler, your data is based on the completion of one clinical trial for a six-month period consisting of only ninety patients without any controls. We agree that your results, as described here, suggest an encouraging response, but without more robust participation, there is not enough data to draw clear conclusions. Your protocol originally advised us that after your Phase Two dosing study, you would be following with two further studies, each with four hundred patients."

Cumberland tried to intercede, but Steppler spoke over him. "No, Andy, I want to stress that I don't believe that there's a need to continue with further trials as the data is so overwhelmingly positive."

Jerry Kagos, the other FDA examiner, interjected. "And what about the need for controls as a comparator? How are we to know that any other drug would not have resulted in the same response? Isn't that the reason for controls in science? In other words, how many patients not receiving the drug or any other drug would have shown the same improvement? There is no data to give us that information."

Steppler appeared unnerved by the query, his voice growing edgy. "But, again, I repeat, with such outstanding results, would it be proper, even ethical, to deny those patients the one drug that would give them back their lives?"

Again, Andy tried to intervene, but Steppler put his hand up to stop him and became more aggressive.

"And what will you do with the emergence of another pandemic killing millions more?" Steppler's voice became more defiant. "Didn't you just tell us that your responsibility is the protection and promotion of public health?

Surely, the COVID-19 episode should have warned you to prepare for the next big attack, and I am offering you that public health protection now."

All you could hear in the room were the two examiners rustling their papers, waiting for the director to respond.

"Mr. Steppler," the director's voice was restrained, "we are well aware of our obligations to the citizens of our nation, and we try and meet them each and every day. The fact is, you are asking for an exceptional approval, which is rarely granted and only at the time of a national emergency. However, at this time, there is no emergency nor any threat of one. Furthermore, we believe that the vaccines and treatments that were developed for the previous COVID-19 should be most adequate to prevent any further attack. That is why your next studies need to be compared against those drugs, and we will see if there is a significant advantage."

All eyes darted from Kosent back to Steppler as if viewing a tennis match. D'Arcy realized that Steppler had placed all his bets on this meeting, and he was going for broke. If the drug weren't accepted now, there would be no tomorrow. Without Chen, without an approval, the one year agreement with General Han would already be lost. Steppler was getting out of control.

"No, Dr. Kosent, you are wrong!" Steppler rose from his chair. The fear of the consequences of rejection was taking hold, then anger, followed by accusations more suited for a courtroom drama than an FDA review meeting. While standing, he pointed his finger down at the director. "Mark my words, there will be another viral attack, one so virulent that you and your staff will be as unprepared as you were the last time, and then you will have to scramble to find a cure. And I will be the first to let the world know that you had the data and the drug to prevent it." Steppler was almost shouting, "I ask you once again, no, I demand that you grant LB182 Emergency use to prepare for the next pandemic."

"Let us worry about that when the next pandemic occurs."

At that moment, there was little left to say. Kosent gathered his papers. "I believe this meeting is over. You will be receiving our response within thirty days. Thank you, gentlemen, that will be all."

As Steppler's team rose to leave, Steppler had the last word. He realized he was about to lose his company. There was nothing left for him to do. Looking directly at the examiners, he called out with disgust. "Then you are all fools." He threw his business card on the table. "When the mutation strikes, and corpses are lining the streets, you can call me. Maybe I will answer."

* * *

November 6, 2030

The response from the FDA was received quickly and electronically. The FDA stated that the request for expedited approval of LB182 was declined. It also stated that the FDA would be pleased to discuss the Phase 3 clinical trials of LB182 should the company wish to pursue the agency's recommended regulatory pathway. Steppler stared at the email, anger, frustration, and fear consuming him at one time.

* * *

That evening, with the stress from the FDA's refusal and a half a bottle of vodka, Steppler fell asleep. By the time he had awakened, Lexington Bio's stock had already fallen 50 percent in market trading. His cell rang, and without recognizing the number answered it. He forgot the adage: Bad news flies fast, especially to all the wrong people.

"Mr. Steppler."

Steppler recognized the voice.

"General Han."

"I'm most concerned about the course of our investment in your company, especially with the reports in this morning's news programs. I understand that you lost your temper with the FDA. That was very foolish."

Steppler swallowed so hard he was certain that it could be heard over the phone.

"Actually, I was . . ."

Han interrupted the response. "Please, Mr. Steppler. There is no need to explain. But if you make another foolish move like that, I will make sure you are no longer involved with the company."

Han paused for a moment. "Tell me, Mr. Steppler, did the FDA give any guidance on how to achieve approval?"

Steppler realized his relationship with Han was going to be more difficult. "Yes, sir, they said they would reconsider the drug's approval should there be another pandemic."

"That's what they said? Another pandemic?"

"Yes, sir."

"I see. Well, we must remember that."

"Of course, General."

Han ended the call. He had a lot to think about. His future also depended upon it.

—{ B O O K   T H R E E }—

CHAPTER TWENTY-SEVEN

March 18, 2031, Wulajie, China

Chen completed teaching his afternoon physics class when his cell rang. He hesitated when no name was recognized before responding.

"Hello?"

"It's out."

"Jiang?"

"Yeah, it's me. I'm using a pre-paid cell without a GPS. I don't want this traced."

"Why? What's out?"

"Thanatos! I'm in my apartment about to start a needed week off when I received a call that two of my colleagues were working in the lab and reported having cold-like symptoms and taken to the containment hospital at the Institute. When I called a friend to find out what happened, I was told that the information was to be kept secret, but they both died within two days. The lab analysis found the cause of death. It was Thanatos."

"But how? You have protocols."

"Of course," Jiang responded. "The strictest, including level A disposable hazmat suits with fully independent internal environments, including breathing apparatuses. Following work, all safety garments are disposed of, and everyone goes through double disinfecting showers before redressing in street clothes."

"Then how?"

"I'm not sure, but there's been a lot of pressure on General Han to complete his research. As a result, he's taken a number of risks, including using Biosafety

Level 3 labs to shortcut his research. Those labs are much more vulnerable to accidents."

"Can the virus be contained?"

"He's certainly trying. He's demanding to know how this could have happened, going over every move we've made to determine how the accident occurred. But the pressure is beginning to get to him because if there's a spread outside of the Institute and they decide that Han is responsible, he will suffer the consequences. He's ordered all labs closed, saying it's for scheduled maintenance, but it's really to give him time to figure out what went wrong."

"Will it be reported?"

"Not for now. He's stopped all communication with outside sources."

"How long can he hide the deaths?"

"If he's lucky until he finds the source of the leak. Could be weeks, but there's another problem. The FDA examiners are due to inspect the facility in the beginning of May, and if there's a hint of a problem, the Institute will not be recertified. That means Hunan would lose all the recognition it has gained throughout the world, and Han would be held responsible."

"What's he going to do?"

"He's doubling down on finding the leak, but also the antidote."

"Can he?"

"He hasn't so far, and we sure don't have an antidote."

"Then I hope he has the answers before the inspectors arrive. Where's Han now?"

"He's up at the bat caves for one last try to figure why the bats are not vulnerable to the virus they're carrying. He still believes that he can find the source of their immunity in their blood. Each time he's tried, he's failed, but he insists he can find a means of preventing and treating the virus."

Chen thought the idea seemed sound, after all, something made the bats impervious to the virus.

"So you got out in time?"

"For now, but I will be responsible. If anything goes wrong, I will take the hit. He's going to want me to report back to the lab immediately."

"What are you going to do?"

"I need the break. It's been a tough year, and I've been working on finding the antidote nonstop. I have to get out for a few days."

"To where?"

"Haven't even had time to think about it."

There was a pause before Chen responded. "Then why don't we get together? You can meet me in Changchun."

"I would like that."

* * *

Chen's concern about Thanatos escaping from the Wuhan Institute had
him recall his visit to the site when General Han had first tried recruiting him.
The huge facility was located in a rustic setting in the hilly outskirts of Wuhan.
To Chen, it was high irony; nature in all its beauty contrasted with the potential extinction of man. Like Chen's lab at Brookfield, the main research lab at
Wuhan had a Biosafety Level 4 rating. However, surrounding Wuhan's central
lab was a series of Biosafety Level 3 research labs that were more vulnerable
to accidents, though still having to follow strict aseptic protocols. But Chen's
concern was that most of the growing number of maximum containment labs
in operation around the world were near urban centers, and Wuhan was the
largest and best known, with almost three-quarters of an acre of lab space. If an
accident happened there, it could happen anywhere.

Yet the question remained: how could the virus have escaped? If Jiang was
correct and shortcuts were taken for expediency, then the safety of the labs at
Wuhan could be questioned, and if Thanatos escaped, the result could be a
global pandemic the likes of which had never before existed. Chen would have
many questions for Jiang when they met in Changchung.

CHAPTER TWENTY-EIGHT

Changchun City, March 21, 2031

Changchun is one of the largest cities in northeast China, with a population of over seven million. Jiang had taken one of the high-speed bullet trains that traveled over one hundred and fifty miles an hour and met Chen as planned at the Holiday Inn Express on Jingyue Road.

They welcomed each other with a bear hug. "Chen, thanks for the invite. I really needed this break. Things are getting pretty uncertain in the lab. Bits of information are getting out, and if Han finds out who's responsible, that person will be eliminated."

"Has the leak been contained?"

"Don't know, but Han is leaving messages for me to report to the Institute. I haven't answered the phone, at least not yet."

Chen put his arm over his friend's shoulder. "You know, Jiang, I think it's time to change the topic. You're on vacation, so let me tell you about the itinerary I planned for us. And the first stop is the Puppet Emperor's Palace ."

Jiang laughed. "Never heard of it."

Chen gave a hearty laugh. "Jiang, you've spent too much time in chemistry and not enough in history. It's time for a review."

They walked the fifteen minutes to their first stop; Chen relating the history of the Imperial Palace of the Manchu State as if a tour guide. "Now it's a museum dedicated to Puyi, China's last Emperor. The palace was his home during the Japanese occupation of northern China in the 1930s and during World War Two. He was basically a puppet leader, a prisoner in his own home, hence the name the Puppet Emperor's Palace. The Japanese created it for Puyi to live in as the ruler of the Manchuko state, but of course, it was the Japanese who were in full control. In fact, Puyi had already abdicated his emperorship in 1911 when China became a republic, but it was deemed convenient for the Japanese to "promote" him to be the emperor of Manchuko since northeastern China was at that time under Japanese control. But not a bad place to be a prisoner since the property included a swimming pool, tennis court, golf course and horse track where Puyi practiced riding. Anyway, this is our first stop."

"Glad you brought me here. I'll consider it after retirement from virus hunting."

As they were entering the palace, Jiang's cell went off.

Jiang looked at the caller. "It's a friend who works with me."

Jiang answered the call. "What's happening?"

"I'm afraid a great deal. Han wants you to report here immediately."

"I'm way up in northeast China backpacking. It could take me days to get back."

"Okay, I'll let him know."

"I need to put you on speaker to hear better. Bring me up to date."

"Zhen died."

Chen saw Jiang grimace. "Zhen? How terrible. Was it Thanatos?"

"Yes." The voice on the phone continued. "But it's worse. She had gone home after work for a birthday party, and by the time she realized that her symptoms could be more than a cold, it was too late. She returned to the Lab and was taken to the hospital."

Jiang looked at Chen. "That means external transmission."

"It's already happened. Those at the party are already exhibiting symptoms. They've put her building and the area around it in full lockdown, complete quarantine. Han even tried giving her the bat serum, but it was of no help."

"So what's he going to do?"

"Everything he can to keep the news from getting out, including doubling down on security and sealing off the Institute. Several of our colleagues have already been escorted out of the lab by the secret police. We don't know if they've been arrested or worse."

"For what?"

"He'll think of some charge, but mainly to warn others. Word is out that Han has been called to an emergency meeting of the Central Committee in two weeks."

"He must be worried."

"He's trying to not show it outside of the lab. I think he believes the Party will go along with whatever he says, and all he needs to do is give an update on his work. He's got an ego the size of the Great Wall."

"Well, thanks for letting me know. I'll see you in a few days."

Jiang closed the call and looked at Chen with concern. They were both silent, trying to appreciate what a Thanatos leak could mean.

Chen looked at his friend. "He's arresting the workers. Are you safe there?"

"For now."

Chen thought for a moment. "And what about Han's bioterror program?"

"I've heard nothing. After all, how can he begin a state-sponsored bioterror attack if he doesn't have the antivirus yet? I mean, everyone would die." Jiang paused before continuing. "Not for lack of trying. You heard what was said about a last attempt at examining bat blood."

"You would think that has some merit.'

"Yes, but it failed. That means he has nothing."

They continued walking when Jiang interrupted the silence. "What about your work? That seems promising. Why did you stop?"

"There were some problems with the operation of the lab, business-wise."

"But I saw your Phase Two top line results you sent to the FDA. They looked great."

"General Han thought so. He offered me a job."

"I'm not surprised. They need something. What are you going to do?"

"Nothing, to be honest. I don't have my lab anymore, and I'm enjoying teaching these kids. Without a lab, I'm not in a position to try and save the world."

"But Han needs to, and nothing will get in his way to succeed. Right now, you may be the only one to have the answer. Last week he was asking about you. He knows where you are. He knows everything. If he has no answers, he will find you, and he has no conscience. And one more thing. He's running out of time."

"What do you mean?"

"Han may think he's too important to be criticized, but if Han is being called before an emergency meeting of the Central Committee of the Chinese Communist Party, he better be careful. Failure may mean the end of his career. I mean, here's a guy who has one of the top positions in China, a man with all the confidence in the world, who's never had to take orders from anyone, and now summoned before the ultimate power. Something's up. This whole New Order Plan was his idea. So, you better be careful."

CHAPTER TWENTY-NINE

Wednesday, April 3, 2031

The meeting of the Central Committee of the Chinese Communist Party, composed of two hundred Party leaders, was held in the party Chamber within the Great Hall of the People of China in Beijing. Han remembered the last time he had been called in, how his research had been overwhelmingly accepted, how he had been given a hero's welcome. And today, he would once again, as he had done throughout his life when adversity threatened, show that he could turn the tide from whatever direction it would run. As he confidently strode to the red-carpeted dais, he glanced at his protector, but the chairman appeared to avoid eye contact. Han was surprised, assuming that he and the most powerful man in China were in this together.

* * *

The members listened attentively as Han reported on pursuing his policy to achieve a new world order without the use of thermonuclear devices, saving China trillions of dollars and millions of lives. It was in the middle of this presentation, lauding his progress, when he was interrupted by Mr. Kim, the former premier.

"Tell me, General Han, it has been four years since you spoke to us explaining, no declaring, how China was to achieve world dominance without the use of military might. You told us that you succeeded in producing the weapon and demonstrated its potency by murdering an entire village, an act approved only by the chairman. But then you informed us that it would take four years to learn how to control it. Have you now learned how to control your mass destroyer?"

"Thus far we are . . ."

Kim interrupted him. "Yes or no?"

"No, sir, not yet."

"So, again, General, we ask you to tell us what kind of weapon can be effective when you can't control it. You'll kill more people in our country than outside it."

"Actually, sir, that is not entirely correct; we are working on a new . . ."

Mr. Kim was not used to being interrupted. "I have not finished speaking, General. As I was saying, you are not only unable to focus your attacks on where it should be deployed, . . ."

"But that is not.. " interjected Han.

Kim slammed his fist on the table and raised his voice. "I have not yet finished, General. Do not interrupt me again. I was saying you have not only lost control of your weapon, but you have also not been able to find a drug to prevent your own army from dying. I don't care what you are working on. Thus far, you have nothing, isn't that true, General?"

Han tried to control his reflexive anger at being questioned. "Yes, sir."

"And now, General, we are receiving reports that there has been a leak in your research lab. Isn't that true?"

Han responded slowly. "Yes, sir."

"And already three have died in spite of your bat serum. Isn't that so?"

"Sir, only two. The third is receiving the new antidote . . ."

Mr. Kim raised his voice. "Three, General Han, three. We were advised that the third one had died. Not only that, but she had also left the building. And you surely understand that if your virus gets out, you will be starting a global pandemic that begins here at home."

"Yes, sir."

"So where is all the progress you promised us? That is what the members here want to know. Our chairman has given you the extraordinary opportunity to lead, but what we want to understand is what you are leading us to. Have you and the chairman determined what you are going to do in a few weeks when May Day arrives, celebrating our great Communist past and encouraging our citizens to travel throughout China, visiting our historical sites, packing our movie theaters, restaurants, trains, and going to concerts? Shall the same policy be followed as ten years ago when the chairman wished to prove that COVID-19 had vanished by letting the masses loose only to see millions die and many more suffer?"

The chairman and Kim locked eyes for a brief moment as Kim continued.

"And one last thing," as Kim turned his attention to the members, "Isn't it true, General, that you made a substantial investment with government funds in an American company called Lexington Bio, and the success of that investment depends upon an FDA approval on an emergency basis? Isn't that so, General?"

"Yes, sir."

"And that approval has not yet been granted, has it, General?"

"Not yet."

"Because it was denied. Certainly, the members of the Council were not told of this."

Han heard grumblings of anger from the committee members around him as they received this latest information. He gave a glancing look at the chairman, whose taut facial muscles revealed his being taken by surprise.

"And I doubt that even the chairman was aware of that, isn't that so, General?"

"Yes, sir. That was done without his knowledge."

A shiver ran through Han as he realized he had gone too far with the most powerful men in China.

Mr. Kim looked directly at the chairman. "I, and many of us seated at this forum must insist that you be more careful when you assign China's Defense Policy to lab scientists. This is on you, Mr. Chairman, and frankly, many of us here today, including our military men, want to know how you decided to defend our homeland with microparticles rather than guns and missiles."

The members of the committee, several of them the heads of China's military, looked to the chairman for his response. It was the first direct challenge to his leadership the chairman had in many years, and he realized how his response must demonstrate his firm control of the Communist Party while addressing the discontent in the air.

"Thank you, Comrade Kim, I appreciate your bringing this information to our attention. He tried to restrain his anger. "General Han, I think it best for you to leave this room while we discuss the situation. We will call you in when we have reached a decision."

The chairman nodded at the security personnel in the hall. "Please escort General Han to the outer room."

It had been a long time since Han had been spoken to in this fashion. He slowly rose from his chair and as two guards ushered him out, felt the shame of defeat as the eyes of the powerful men focused on him. He entered an empty, bland room with two small chairs. He tried to sit, but the tension was so great he began pacing back and forth, unable to control his breathing, his pulse, or his perspiration. Was he to meet the same end as so many other past high-ranking men who failed?

Finally, the door opened, and Han was accompanied into the room and told to stand before the committee.

It was the chairman who spoke. "General Han, you have had a long and brilliant career as one of the leaders of China. You told us that merely the threat of your bioterror molecule would make the nations of the world tremble and fall before our feet without firing a single bullet. But now we learn that China is threatened as much as the rest of the world. That is not an advantage, General. In fact, it is an embarrassment, one that has already caused needless death to our people. The committee has decided to give you a last chance. You have exactly thirty days to find the antidote to control the virus and achieve the victory that you promised us without sacrificing our great army. Thirty days! You are to report back here on May sixteenth. Is that understood?"

"Yes, sir."

"Good, then you are dismissed."

Han saluted, turned on his heels as an obedient soldier, and with his back straight and his step in order, marched out of the room.

* * *

Han felt the disgrace, the humiliation, the embarrassment of being chastised in front of the nation's ruling members, a group that he had so often pictured himself leading once this chairman stepped down. But as he descended the curving marble staircase of the massive stone building, those emotions rapidly became hardened, and the fear of failure soon transitioned to the anger that always dwelled within him. Just as he had responded as a young man growing up in his small village to the insults and mockery, so he responded to these small minds that ruled China. How limited their vision, how constrained their understanding of what role China could play within the universe of nations and perhaps beyond. And yet, even the chairman failed to come to his aid.

As he slowly exited the huge bronze doors that opened onto a sun-drenched Tiananmen Square, he felt as if his world had been extinguished. What was he to do? As he looked out from the steps of the Great Hall of the People onto the massive parklike square of forty acres in the center of Beijing, he felt small for perhaps the first time in his life. What had happened to his dreams? As the cool breeze enveloped him, he tried to put in perspective what had just occurred. He was in the cradle of Chinese history. To the north was the Tiananmen Gate, named for the "Gate of Heavenly Peace," which separates the square from the Forbidden City, built in 1415 during the Ming dynasty; to the south was the Monument to the People's Heroes, the National Museum of China, and the Mausoleum of Mao Zedong who founded the People's Republic of China in the square on October 1, 1949. As Han walked back to his hotel, his shoulders slumped, his head no longer held erect, realizing that he was no longer to be part of Chinese history. He had failed. For want of a molecule, a kingdom was lost.

* * *

There was a hard knock on his hotel door. Han opened it to find two well-built, armed Chinese Security officers with an order to follow them. They accompanied him into the rear seats of a large black SUV waiting outside the hotel with a driver at the wheel. In spite of his questions, their only response was, 'You will find out soon enough.'

As Han rode through the streets of Beijing, flanked on either side by the officers, his mind was in constant motion, aware of the consequences befalling those preceding him who failed. When they had outlived their usefulness, they were purged from the party, often by being brought up on charges of corruption with mounds of purported evidence, removing them from their positions, and placing them into custody. Often, especially if holding state secrets, they were sentenced to prison or exiled to work camps as part of China's "re-education through labor" program for criminals and dissidents. Indeed, how many high-ranking Chinese officials were found dead weeks after being relieved of their duties? Han tried to prepare himself for the worst.

The SUV took the ramp off the highway, drove along Jingan Road, and then through a maze of small streets until it came to a stop in front of a small, dimly lit two-story building whose exterior had no address. A passerby would not think twice about its understated presence. Han and his security approached a single oak door on which was a small bronze sign that read *Bonica*.

The door opened, and he entered a room with subdued lighting that took a moment of adjustment. He was met by a man who gave the appearance of a well-groomed maître d' in a tailored black suit who, without introduction, ushered him through a dark space. As Han followed he observed the room contained only four tables, spaced far apart from each other, with a center round table containing a gold Buddhist statue. The dining tables were dressed in rich linen cloths and polished silver stemware that reflected the single overhead light. Fine art was displayed on the black walls, and Han realized he had been taken to a very private dining room for those who held wealth and power and whose lives demanded concealment. He made one other observation: No other diners were present. He was led silently to a small open courtyard that contained one table set for two. A chair was held out for Han, and he was advised that the other party would be arriving shortly. He checked his watch; it was 7:30 P.M. The man disappeared, and Han remained by himself. At 8:05, there was a slight commotion at the entrance. Two well-built men he identified as secret police appeared, accompanied by a third individual who slowly walked behind them. Han gripped the table until his hands turned white, preparing for what was next, but nothing could have prepared him for what then occurred.

"Please stand."

Han did as the police ordered and was checked for any weapons.

"He's clean."

"Thank you, gentlemen. That will be all."

As the men left Han's table, he realized who the third man was. It was the chairman. Han saluted, "Sir."

"Please, be seated."

Han did as he was told. The maître d' appeared with a bottle of wine, un-corked the bottle, and poured the wine slowly into the center of the chairman's glass. The chairman swirled the wine to aerate it, examined the bouquet and sipped the wine before acknowledging his acceptance. The man expertly poured five ounces of the red into the two glasses, wiped the bottle lip with a cloth, and walked away, leaving the two by themselves.

"That was quite a grilling you took today." The chairman smiled, looked at Han, and spoke quietly. "Welcome to dealing with China's most powerful. The fact is, they were correct. You told them you would find the antidote, and you did not. It was an embarrassment. Many of the members of the committee would like nothing better than to have me fail. The generals and admirals and other members of the Defense Department feel as if they have been treated as second-class citizens, that they are no longer needed, that their power is being usurped by your viral program that I have adopted as policy. They would like nothing better than to have me replaced, especially my old friend Kim."

Han responded. "I'm afraid I'm responsible. I am sorry that I have failed you in not being able to find the antidote, but perhaps I know where such a molecule exists."

"Then do what you have to do to obtain it. We don't have much time. Every day that you fail to find it is a day that the opposition grows stronger. I know your abilities and believe that you can succeed. That is why I convinced them to give you another thirty days. But remember, I can only give you thirty days. If you have not succeeded by then, understand you will be relieved of your duties. And Mr. Kim and his allies would like nothing better to relieve me of my duties, so you need to succeed."

"Thank you, Mr. Chairman. I will do what is necessary."

The older statesman thought for a moment. "I appreciate that, General. The jackals are at the gate, and they smell blood, mine. They have already fomented protests in Beijing, Shanghai and other cities challenging my policies. If your viral defense plan works, we may need to have it available sooner than you think."

At that point, one of the two men who accompanied the chairman came to the table and whispered something in his ear. The chairman thanked him. He turned to Han, "I'm afraid I must attend to another matter now, but you have my support." Handing him a card, he said, " Should you need to reach me in an emergency. It is for your eyes only."

"I understand."

"Good, then enjoy your dinner."

He waved to the maître d'. "Shu, I must leave, but please take good care of the General."

"Of course, sir,"

With that, the chairman exited the building.

Soon, waiters appeared and brought Han's dinner. Afterward, he would remember it as the finest meal he had ever been served. The wine, the charred and chunky octopus leg with green chili cream sauce and the huge slab of beef tongue that melted in his mouth. When the meal was over, Han knew what he had to do. He had been given one last opportunity to complete his mission. He understood how rare it was to be given a second chance. He had thirty days.

"Dessert, General?"

"I think just coffee."

"Of course, General."

As the coffee was served, a variety of sugar and sugar-free packets were brought to the table in a small silver bowl.

As Han began to plan out his assignment, he thoughtlessly played with the packets in front of him. Soon, he stopped and focused on the packets. Two were packaged in English, one colored pink and one colored yellow.

"Excuse me, Shu."

The maître d' walked to Han's table. "Yes, General."

"These packets are American?"

"Yes, sir. We have several types if you would like something different."

"No, this is excellent. Perhaps you can bring me half a dozen of each. I would like to take some back with me."

"Of course, General."

For want of a molecule, there would be no reason for a kingdom to be lost.

CHAPTER THIRTY

April 5, 2031

Han returned to the Institute and planned a series of moves to achieve his objective. He would have to complete the task by himself. He could trust no one else. There could be no further failures. He worked alone in the Biosafety Lab into the early morning hours, wearing his protective clothing and completing his efforts before the day shift entered. When he had finished his work, he went to his office and reviewed the list of Chinese undercover operatives working in the US, agents whose task was to acquire military technology and other classified information. These were individuals who were carefully trained to obtain trade secrets of US companies, especially in the area of biotechnology and gene therapy, and to ingratiate themselves with major scientific, academic and business contacts. It was a vast undertaking, and the General smiled at the thought that the United States had no idea of the extent to which Chinese companies partnered with American businesses to acquire their technology. The fact was that China's extensive cyber espionage operations made it possible to penetrate the computer networks of US government agencies, including advanced knowledge of FDA decisions prior to it being publicly announced. With that awareness, Han utilized a secure line to send a message to Sun Wei, one of his most trusted undercover operatives in the United States.

"There will be an FDA inspection end of April in Wuhan. The inspectors are Jerry Kagos and Peter Ward. I need to know their routine prior to making their trips, including who and where they meet with, what they have for breakfast, how they get to the airport, every movement from the moment they leave their homes to their arrival in Wuhan. I will contact you when I arrive. Will need protection."

His next call was to Jiang.

"Yes, General."

"Your friend, Chen."

"What about him, sir."

"I'm tired of asking him to work for us. Have him come to our labs immediately and begin the formulation of his antidote. If he will not come when invited then I will have him brought there. I want the formulation by the time I get back."

"Where are you going?"

"To have the FDA approve Lexington's drug."

"I thought that was refused."

"There was an exception."

"What was that."

"Another pandemic."

* * *

Late that night, Chen received a call from an unlisted number.

"Chen, it's Jiang."

"What's going on?"

"It's General Han. He's returned from the meeting with the leaders of the Party, including the chairman himself, and it must have been a disaster. The man has become obsessed with finding an antidote. He wants you to report to our lab immediately, and he means it."

"Immediately?"

"He wants the antidote by the time he gets back."

"Where's he going?"

"To get your drug approved."

"But it was refused."

"With one exception."

"And that is?"

"If there's another pandemic."

"But there have only been local outbreaks. Even the Hunan accident has been kept confined."

"What if he starts one?"

"What do you mean?"

"This evening, my assistant reported that the biosafety vault had been opened. Han had made a total of seven vials of Thanatos. Three are missing."

Chen became alarmed. "What are you saying?"

"The only other individuals with access to that vault besides myself are General Han and his head of Biomedical Security, Dr. Sang."

"Could Sang have taken them?"

"Sang would never go near that vault without permission. The General must have taken them."

"And you think he's traveling with Thanatos?"

"And I think he could use it."

"But why in the US?"

"Because if Han starts a pandemic, he has to blame it on someone."

"Even if he can't control it."

"Because he knows you can."

—| BOOK FOUR |—

CHAPTER THIRTY-ONE

Tuesday, April 15, 2031

Sitting in a first-class seat for the twenty-six-hour flight from Pudong International Airport in Shanghai to Washington DC's Dulles International on Lufthansa was a man wearing a well-tailored single-buttoned navy blue suit made from the finest lightweight Merino wool that draped his large athletic body, polished oxford shoes, and shaved head. His passport read Ling Shu. What he could not change was the deep scar running down his left cheek. He traveled under the protection of a diplomatic passport and was enjoying a cocktail while reading the daily edition of the Financial Times. Adjacent to him was a window seat on which was a small green satchel with a printed label: DIPLOMATIC BAG, THE PEOPLES REPUBLIC OF CHINA, and the number C15382. Although a combination lock secured the bag, the man knew its contents were protected under Article 27.3 of the Vienna Convention on Diplomatic Relations, which stated, "properly designated diplomatic pouches shall not be opened or detained, including inspection by X-ray." He would not be traveling with his QSZ-92 semiautomatic. Rather, he would be given a Glock G19 Semi carrying fifteen rounds once he reached his destination.

Upon arrival, the man retrieved his carry-on, placed the pouch into his suitcase, and walked to the Hertz counter. There, as arranged, he met his undercover agent, Sun Wei.

"General, good to see you. Here's the Glock G you asked for. I also have the schedule for the two FDA inspectors."

Han looked it over. "You're sure about the coffee?"

"Yes, sir. They have followed this routine for the past six years prior to international inspections. You should have no problem."

"Good, this will just be an attention-getter."

"I understand. Will you need further help?"

"Perhaps. "You're stationed in New York, correct?"

"Yes, sir, we have a safe house in Manhattan, close to the Embassy, and one out on Long Island."

"Okay, I'll be in the city in a few days. Stay there; I may need you."

"I understand, sir. Good luck."

When they parted, Han rented a dark-colored Ford Escape under the name of Peter Ling using a forged Kansas driver's license and Visa credit card as identification. He drove to a small inn off the interstate in Maryland, ate dinner in the dining room, watched the late news, and when there were no reports of a viral infection in China, went to sleep.

* * *

Friday, April 18, 2031

It was a clear morning, with the rising sun illuminating the blue sky in Rockville, Maryland, when a large figure in gray sweatpants, green sweatshirt, sneakers and black latex gloves exited his Ford rental and approached the open rear doors of a blue delivery van from Ben's Caterer's. Making certain the security cameras didn't observe him, he pulled the hood over his head and looked through the packages of deliveries until he found what he was looking for a package marked "FDA, third floor, conference room 304, Dr. Kosent." In it, he found two yellow packets of sweetener, croissants, coffee cups and napkins. It took less than a minute for him to replace the sweeteners with two similar-looking yellow packets before returning to his car. By the time the delivery man walked out of the deli, closed the van's rear doors, and drove away, the man was gone. The delivery driver drove out of the parking lot and made the five-minute trip to the FDA's office on Fishers Lane. Unknown to the driver, it was followed by a dark Ford rental.

* * *

That morning, FDA examiners Peter Ward and Jerry Kagos bade goodbye to their families and took Ubers to FDA headquarters to have their briefings with Director Kosent to discuss their scheduled international FDA inspections.

When foreign firms wish to have their medical products approved for use in the United States, they request the FDA to conduct examinations of their facilities to ensure that the drugs manufactured and intended for US distribution comply with US regulations and that any unsafe products are removed from the marketplace.

Over coffee, they discussed the trip objectives, reviewing the history of the drug manufacturers they were assigned to inspect. Following the meeting, the driver of a dark-colored Ford Escape observed as both men entered the idling Uber waiting outside the entrance. The driver of the Ford observed as both men began their drive to Dulles International Airport for a flight on Cathay Pacific 5722 to Changsha-Huanghua International Airport, with one stop in Hong Kong. It was a routine the agents followed numerous times over the past years, inspecting pharmaceutical manufacturing facilities throughout the globe, and both found the time in business class to review the respective files and get some sleep over the twenty-plus hour trip. This trip would be especially onerous as they would begin their inspection on Monday and spend three full days at the giant Hunan Institute of Virology. As always, they planned to meet with their wives at the end of the weekend for a homecoming dinner. There would be no such dinner.

CHAPTER THIRTY-TWO

Friday, April 25, Wulajie, China

It was at the end of the school day, and Chen was in the teachers' lounge sipping a coffee when the word virus caught Chen's attention. It was mentioned by a CCTV reporter interviewing a spokesperson from the Wuhan Viral Institute.

CCTV Reporter: "We are getting unconfirmed reports of a viral infection that occurred in Wuhan. Can you tell us anything about that?"

MSS: Yes, the Ministry of State Security is investigating a local outbreak that occurred several days ago in the Wuhan Institute Laboratories. China security immediately responded by sealing off the Institute, no one entering or leaving, and that containment will last seven days."

CCTV: Can you tell our viewers how this viral outbreak began?"

MSS: As far as we can tell, it may have been a bioterror attack. From the unusual virulence of the organism and massive tissue destruction of the deceased, there is concern that someone, somewhere, is doing GOF research.."

Interviewer: "Excuse me, GOF research? What does that mean?"

MSS: "GOF means gain of function, which involves taking a virus, for example, and modifying it to become more virulent, more powerful, more deadly."

CCTV: "And that can be done?"

MSS: Absolutely, modern biotechnology has enabled scientists to do this.

CCTV: "Are there any leads at this point?"

MSS: Let's just say that the first cases diagnosed were two FDA inspectors from Washington. Prior to that, there was no hint of disease in China."

CCTV: "And you think they carried the virus with them?"

MSS: "At this point, it appears to be the case, though a final determination has yet to be made."

CCTV: "Is there any possibility that the Institute could have had a leak during their laboratory procedures?"

MSS: "Absolutely not. The Wuhan Institute has security procedures that adhere to the strictest standards."

CCTY: "And what happened to the two Americans?"

MSS: "As far as we know, they left Washington on Friday and were in the midst of their first day of inspection at the Institute on Monday when one of the investigators collapsed. Medical support arrived within minutes, but he was near death, and the other was exhibiting symptoms. They were immediately brought into the Institute's hospital, but it was too late. Our concern is how, why, and where did they transmit the disease. The Institute labs are now totally sealed."

CCTV: One last question: Do you have the antidote?"

MSS: "The people of China can be assured that our scientists are finalizing such a drug as we speak."

CCTV: "Is there anything else that the people should know."

MSS: "Yes, we have issued a strong rebuke to the American ambassador. We believe this was a US-sponsored plot, and China is taking this most seriously."

Chen turned off the TV. So it happened just as Jiang had said it would. Han found someone to blame the outbreak on and let China State Television, CCTV, one of the chief propaganda arms of the Communist government, break the news that there was an infection at the Institute and deaths that had nothing to do with a leak. What a script, but so intriguing. How was it transmitted to the FDA inspectors? Regardless, the official explanation had its chilling effect, blaming everyone but China. Chen had to admit, it was brilliant. The fact that America was related to the infection was not a surprise. Who else was the Chinese government to blame? But was China ready to make a major international incident over this?

* * *

Friday, April 25, Wulajie

As Chen was about to leave for the day, the administrator entered the classroom, followed by a young woman.

"Dr. Chu, you have a visitor."

Chen looked up and realized he had seen her before. It was the young woman who confronted Steppler at his fundraising conference. He hadn't forgotten. She was as beautiful as the day he saw her. They shook hands.

"Dr. Chu, my name is Li Zhou. Perhaps you remember my family? We used to live next door to you. I think my brother was in your class."

Chen thought for a moment. "Zhou? Next door? Your brother was Zhong? Of course, I remember. What happened to your family?"

"Unfortunately, I was the only one that survived when the virus hit the village."

"I'm so sorry. My parents also died. I'm afraid that we were the only ones left alive."

Chen broke the silence that ensued with a smile. "You know, I remember that Zhou had a little sister who was always running into my father's herb garden. I see that you've grown up."

She blushed. "It happens. I was only eleven at the time. Your father was our doctor. I grew up on that tea your father made from the herbs in that garden. I remember my parents telling me that his son was the smartest student to have ever gone to school in Changchun. I always wondered what you were doing, and I learned that you were at Brookfield doing viral research."

"How do you happen to be here?"

"I came to see you."

Chen's eyebrows indicated his surprise. "Me?"

"I've been following your career. It's a story, and I'm a reporter." Li paused before continuing. "You see, after I was released from the hospital, they contacted my uncle in Cleveland, who was the only close relative left, and he invited me to come to live with his family. I went to high school there and then to Harvard for bioengineering and continued on to Harvard's Business School for a degree in finance. He was a wonderful person, and he taught me so much right up until his death last year. He was very proud of me. After that, I got a job at the *Wall Street Journal* covering biotech, and when they realized I could speak Cantonese, they assigned me to report from China. So, I've been on assignment here and wrote a series of articles on Lexington Bio, which is why I covered the conference when your CEO made his investor pitch. When I didn't hear your name mentioned, I asked him about that. He wasn't very happy."

Chen gave a slight smile. "Actually, I had left Lexington and returned to see what happened to my home. They asked me to teach here in the village, and having nowhere else to go, I agreed. And I'm enjoying it." Chen paused. "But why did you want to see me?"

"I saw Han Shi speaking to you at the conference. I have a source who read my articles on Lexington Bio and told me that the Chinese government is interested in your work as they are powerless to combat a possible new virus. Then, we heard of a potential viral breach from Wuhan. My source tells me that they offered you the opportunity to work with them and that you turned them down."

"True. I refuse to work for a country that would use my work for unethical purposes."

Li smiled. "I appreciate that. I was told that the next time you are asked, you will not be able to turn them down."

"Yes, Jiang Fang told me the same thing. I was asked again but have not yet responded. "

"Jiang Fang?"

"He's an old friend. He works at the Hunan Institute. But what is your interest in all this?"

Li copied down Jiang's name. "I would like your side of the story for a follow-up article I'm doing on Lexington. I will be at the Golden Arch for another day. I would like to ask you some questions. Will that be okay?"

"Sure."

She took a card out of her wallet. "Here. Let me know when it's a good time."

Chen realized that he was as interested in knowing more about this woman as much as she wanted to know about him for her story.

"How about now?"

She was as surprised as he was in asking. "Now? You mean you want to do our interview now?"

Chen felt his heart pounding. "Well, since you're here by yourself and as I am free, why not now?"

Li gazed at him for a long moment. "Then perhaps we can do it over some food. I haven't had lunch yet."

"Great."

"Can you give me half an hour to wash up?"

Chen smiled. "Sure, I can meet you in your lobby, say 3:30?"

"The Gold Arch?"

"That's where I'm staying since it's the only hotel in town. See you then."

* * *

As Chen returned to his third-floor apartment, the concierge called out.

"Dr. Chu, two big guys in blue jackets came in and wanted to speak to you; said they were friends of yours. I explained that you were out, but they insisted on waiting. When they showed me their badges, I had no choice but to let them in."

Chen seemed puzzled. "Friends? With badges? I have no idea who they could be. Are they still upstairs?"

"No, they left after about thirty minutes and told me they would be back. I just thought you should know."

Chen went upstairs to his one-bedroom apartment. The door was wide open, and when he entered, he was shocked by what he saw. Everything was in disarray, desk drawers emptied, newspapers and articles strewn throughout, the bookcase overturned, anything in the closets scattered on the floor, and even the bed had been stripped. Chen returned the chair to its original position and sat down to contemplate the situation, realizing that the warnings from Jiang and Li were to be taken seriously. The General was no longer asking.

CHAPTER THIRTY-THREE

Friday, 3:30 P.M.

"You were right!"

"About what?"

They met in the hotel lobby when Chen told her what happened.

"About them coming after me."

"What do you mean?"

"Two men broke into my apartment and tore the place apart. Fortunately, there was nothing to find, just some news articles. Anything of value is in my computer."

"Were you there?"

"I would have been if you hadn't been speaking to me. I suppose I owe you my life."

"Not your life. You're too valuable, but maybe a good beating."

"I suppose, but thank you."

Li thought for a moment. "You know, I think I've lost my appetite. How about we get some takeout and a few beers and take a look at your place? I'd like to see what they did, maybe even take some pictures. Remember, I'm a journalist."

* * *

When Li saw the apartment, she used her cell to photograph the mess. Together, they cleaned up and silently ate their Chinese takeout and drank their beers.

"Do you think it could work?"

Chen's eyebrows furrowed in confusion. "Work?"

"I mean your drug."

"I'm not sure. We've only done it on a small number of patients.."

"I know; I read the Phase Two application. But that was a different virus. Do you think it has a chance against this killer?"

Chen spoke thoughtfully. "I can't be certain, but it worked in the lab against it."

Li almost choked on her beer. "Are you saying that you tested this against the Thanatos virus that they found at Wuhan?"

"Yes, it was sent from there."

Li was trying to put this information together. "And your drug stopped it?"

"That is correct."

"So it could work?"

"The lab and animal results were most promising."

"Wow, that's amazing. No wonder they want you to work for them."

"But what about you? I heard you confront Steppler at the conference, asking him why my name wasn't mentioned. How did you know that I was involved with Lexington Bio to begin with? I mean, how did you find out that the work at Brookfield was based on my research?"

"For years, ever since I learned that someone else from my village survived, I followed you online. You were the only tie to my past, and I needed to know about you; otherwise, I had nothing. At Harvard, I came across your article in the journal and realized that you were carrying on your father's work—just applying the most recent bioengineering technology. I assumed you were still in China, but when I read that you were at Brookfield, I thought of coming to see you but wasn't sure you would be interested. So, instead, when I went for my MBA, I chose Lexington Bioscience for my finance thesis. It's how I got the job at the Journal. I showed it to them, and they liked what I uncovered. I followed Steppler and your sudden exit."

"But you seemed to know a great deal about Steppler."

"Not everything. I knew that something was shady when I didn't see your name mentioned, but I was never able to find out why. That's the reason I was sent to cover the conference. It's a big story. Investors lost a fortune, and the SEC began investigations, but no one was aware of what part you played in it. That became my assignment."

"Then I will tell you some of the story, but you will have to hold off on publishing until I say okay. Do I have your word on that?"

Li smiled and nodded. "Agreed, as long as I can take notes."

"Fine. Where do you want to start?"

"Well, first, I want to know why you left Brookfield. Your results looked flawless."

"But they weren't."

Li seemed surprised. "What do you mean?"

"Steppler changed some of the results, and when I confronted him about it, he told me to leave. Furthermore, the papers I signed with him when we formed the company gave me no ownership. He had complete control, owned the patents, and told me to get out."

"Wow, that's a bummer."

"I know. Totally my fault, but when I saw how he had raised the needed funding, I was so excited that I let him take care of everything. Never bothered to read the fine print. Just signed so I could get back into the lab."

"And there was nothing you could do."

"Nothing. I spoke to a lawyer friend of mine, a fellow named Tim Channing, in New York. He reviewed the documents and said I signed the agreement. It was airtight."

"I see." Li scribbled down the name as she ate the last of her meal. "And the technology, the formulation, dosage, and manufacturing ability? Who has that?"

"I do."

"And Steppler?"

He knows very little. I don't believe the patents nor the information provided to the FDA would be enough to reformulate the drug. Only I have that."

"And the original results that were changed. Are they enough to stop the project?"

"I don't believe so. They showed significance in terms of efficacy. The drug worked. I had no questions about that. I just didn't want to be involved with that kind of scientific inquiry."

"I understand."

"Does anyone else have access to Thanatos?"

"Besides me? Only if they had entry to the BioSafety Lab at Brookfield. I suppose Steppler would have the access codes, but as far I know, he never used them."

Li continued writing. "Did you know that Steppler was able to pay back his original investors with a loan that came from the Chinese?"

"That's what I heard. The Chinese want the drug desperately."

"Is it because they believe there could be another pandemic?"

Chen gave a coy smile. "Or for another reason."

"And that is?"

"They will start one."

Li hadn't thought on those terms. "You mean a state-sponsored bioterror program?"

"My friend Jiang told me that General Han is going to the US to have LB182 approved."

"How? They already rejected it."

"Apparently, the FDA gave it one exception, another pandemic. Jiang told me Han just left with three vials of Thanatos to demonstrate how easily a pandemic can start."

"You mean he's going to threaten the FDA?"

"That's what he said."

"Listen, Chen. The US has to be warned. If this is true, then you're talking about a deliberate attack on American soil . . . That can cause a war. It needs to be stopped."

"That's why you can't say anything. My friend is the only one who knows about this. They will know he leaked it."

"Innocent people are going to die. I need to tell my editor. It will be an unnamed source. He'll know what to do."

Chen thought for a moment. "Let me think about it."

"And you've got to get out of here. This isn't just a group of thugs. This would be a key element to China's foreign policy. They didn't just come to wreck your room. They came to force you to work for them. You were lucky this time, but maybe not the next. You have to get out."

The phone rang, and Chen answered. "Okay, thanks."

He looked through the blinds to the street outside. "This is the next time. There are two big guys waiting across the street wearing blue jackets. I was told those are the two fellows who went up to my room."

Li thought for a moment. "Pack up what you need. My room's at the end of the hall. I'll get my stuff. We have to leave."

"All I need is my briefcase, and I'll throw a shirt in there. Everything important is in my laptop."

"Good, then we've got to get to the railroad station. From there, we can get back to Beijing. I have some friends that can help us."

"My car's out back. There's a back stairway at the end of the hall."

As they met in the hallway, they heard the clatter of boots climbing the stairs.

"Li, this way."

They raced down the hall and reached the rear stairwell, making their way down to the lobby exit. Behind them, they heard yelling for them to stop. They ran to Chen's rental car. Chen started the ignition. In the rearview mirror, Chen saw the men sprinting toward them, shouting.

Chen floored the pedal, and the car leaped forward and out onto the main street.

"Chen, police."

Chen slowed as they drove toward the station. In front of them was a police checkpoint blocking the station entrance. "They must be looking for you. Where's the next station?"

"Changchun, two hours. We've got to try and get the train from here."

Chen made a quick turn to the left and sped the car through an alley that led to the parking lot behind the stores. Chen left the keys in the car, and they both got out.

"Li, they're only looking for me. You had better walk on the main street. I'll walk the back way and meet you."

"And what if you don't make it."

Chen realized that could happen. "Then you take my briefcase. My computer has everything in it. And, one more thing."

"What?"

"Call your editor. Tell him everything."

Li took the briefcase and walked to the main street, walking slowly, browsing at the shops on the way to the station. Chen walked behind the stores through the parking lot.

"Stop where you are."

Chen froze.

"Turn around slowly. I've been ordered by state security to stop anyone near the train station."

Chen followed the instructions. The policeman looked at a picture and then looked at Chen. He drew his gun.

"Looks like you're the guy they're looking for."

Fifteen minutes later Chen was delivered to the Wulajie police station.

* * *

—{ BOOK FIVE }—

CHAPTER THIRTY-FOUR

Sunday, April 28, 2031, New York

Dr. Sebastian Gogoli, the Chief Coroner of the City of New York, awoke with a start long before the sun had yet appeared on the horizon and looked out at the dimly lit cityscape. He was a short, bespectacled man in his early sixties with thin gray hair and a belt size two notches larger than it should have been. He was known throughout the medical world as a conscientious physician dedicated to his profession, a brilliant anatomist, and a stickler for details, everything you would want in a scientist whose chief role was dissecting bodies for evidence of the minutest pathologies or hints of toxins that could influence death. He had been at the Medical Examiner's Office for over twenty years, had seen almost every disease or injury known to man, was there for SARS, EBOLA, and MERS, and was the scientist to whom unsolved questions of mortality were asked. Yet, to Gogoli, each case was unique, each a challenge, for as coroner, he was responsible for investigating any death, be it from criminal violence, accidents, suicides, or signing death certificates.

However, for the past week, Gogoli had an unusually restless sleep, a recurring dream that continued to torment him. It was always the same—a grotesque bird with a body as black as carbon and as furtive as a stealth bomber. Its huge, expansive wings formed a sinister triangle that converged on a hawkish head, its conical dark pointed beak extending long beyond its massive body, its five-pointed outstretched wings undulating like an evil Batman machine that had no master, and when it soared, it caused the winds to blow and the heavens to echo the drumbeat of an unceasing heart that intensified the terror. A menacing smile seemed to part its mouth as it locked onto Gogoli's presence far below, a target to take hideous pleasure in the torture it was about to inflict. And then, like an enemy missile programmed to attack, it suddenly changed course and, at great velocity, dove directly at him, closer and closer until he felt its heat and its huge talons digging deep into his flesh. He struggled in his bed to escape, but it was as if he was entombed in stone. He tried to cry out, but any sound was silenced deep within his being. It was then that he awakened, dripping in perspiration, his body trembling. He would look around his room, examining the darkness, seeking the intruder, but nothing was to be found.

Why that dream? Why did it persist? Was it a reflection of the past? Or was it a sign, a portent of the future, something that was about to occur, something dark and terrible?

He sat silently on the side of his bed. His head bent into his hands as he shook off the images in his mind. He eased on his slippers and walked into the bathroom of his modest three-bedroom apartment in Chelsea, took a quick shower, brushed his teeth, shaved, and, while looking in the mirror, tried to assess how much he had aged. Where did the time go? He put on a pair of worn corduroy slacks, threw on a navy wool sweater with torn dark elbow patches that he had since his days as a medical resident, and walked into the kitchen. The window revealed it would be a rainy day. He turned on the flame under the teapot and went to the apartment door, and, with the aging ruin of time, strained to gather the Sunday Times from his doormat. It was during this morning ritual that he promised to begin visiting the new gym that had recently been built in the basement, a hopeless vision that it could somehow return him to the shape he was in before his marriage to Fredericka twenty-three years ago. He realized how fortunate he was to have her as his lifelong companion. She was an attorney, and they first met when Freddie was defending her client on a murder charge, and Seb was her expert witness. As soon as the case was over, he called her for dinner. Since then, the number of times they had not eaten together was few and far between.

He returned to the kitchen, poured a cup of boiling water, measured out one and a half teaspoons of instant coffee and two tablespoons of milk, directed his spoon to swirl to a mocha color, and sat down at the kitchen table to peruse yesterday's news. No wonder the world was increasingly receiving their information from the internet. If it was news, it had to be new. The world was spinning too rapidly for newsprint. Regardless, the morning's postings always seemed tragic enough to erase the persistence of his dream-filled sleep.

As he began to scan the headlines, a message crossed his cell. It was from Stan Galvin, the City's Medical Examiner. He checked the time. It was 7:15.

Why was his boss calling so early on a Sunday? *Hey Seb, sorry to bother you on your day off, but best to turn on CNN. We may have a problem.*

Gogoli walked into the living room and turned on the TV in time to hear the report.

Health authorities in China are trying to identify a mysterious strain of virus that has begun in the city of Wuhan in central China with a population of eight and a half million. The virus has caused severe fever and acute respiratory illness in several people. Imaging studies show invasive lesions of the lungs, heart, brain, kidney and liver. Authorities indicate that the patients observed had a complete shutdown of their bodily organs—all within twenty-four to forty-eight hours following initial symptoms. Treatment, including the COVID-19 vaccine and monoclonal antibodies that had been effective in previous strains, were of no value. It has been suggested that those infected attended a birthday party with a worker at the Wuhan Institute of Virology. The investigation is ongoing.

When Gogoli heard the words *mysterious strain,* he realized he had heard the same announcement years before. He would never forget the date, January 7, 2020. Was this a replay of that event or something new? He was certain of one thing; he had autopsied too many people with the COVID-19 virus back then to want a rerun.

His phone sang out its tone; It was Stan Galvin again.

"What do you think?"

Gogoli's concern was apparent. "I'm not sure. Could this have been a leak from the Institute? Let's wait a day or two to get further information."

* * *

Monday, May 1

It was Monday morning when Gogoli turned to CNN to see if there was anything further on the possible viral leak. The correspondent stationed in China was speaking: *The possibility of an outbreak of an unknown virus has now been reported in Hunan two days in succession. My sources advise that although the initial symptoms mimic COVID-19, they had excluded its reemergence as well as those of the deadly SARS and EBOLA virus. China has declared an immediate targeted city lockdown within a three-mile radius of the Institute, carrying out its zero-COVID-19 policy among the four million citizens within the densely populated cordoned-off area. Officials have ordered a work-from-home order, barring citizens from leaving their residences other than medical emergencies; local roads, subway stations, offices, apartments, and parks are sealed off, and mass testing is underway. When the quarantine zone tests virus-free for two days in a row, the lockdown will be lifted. No cases have been reported outside the quarantined zone to date.*

We also have an unconfirmed report from China State Security that the outbreak may be related to the visit of two American employees of the US Government who were visiting the Wuhan Institute this week and who reportedly died from the virus. Though not confirmed, evidence suggests that because the death of the two employees occurred within a day of arriving in Hunan, they were infected before they reached the city. China has already spoken sharply to the US Ambassador as to the possibility of an attack by Americans on Chinese soil."

Gogoli was transfixed by the report. An outbreak not caused by any of the past viruses? Then what was it? What organism could have such virulence to cause such massive destruction? If these reports were true, this was many times more pathogenic than, and Gogoli remembered all too well COVID-19 when over six hundred million people around the world were diagnosed with the disease, and six and one-half million had died. It was only eleven years ago when New York hospitals were overflowing with the sick and dying, city morgues full, and his staff couldn't keep up with the demand for identification or autopsies. It was a time when funeral homes could no longer accept additional bodies, cemeteries could not bury the dead fast enough, and the unidentified in mass graves on Hart Island saturated Potters Field.

'It seemed strange,' he thought, *'that the outbreak would involve the US. Was this simply a political accusation game, recusing the sickened nation of responsibility and blaming the convenient ugly Americans.'* But the thought of another powerful virus made him realize how futile the last battle was. All that heroism from physicians and nurses and ordinary citizens exposing themselves to a silent killer, and all without adequate protective equipment. And to what end? How poorly prepared we were, the greatest nation in the world with the most sophisticated medical technology, the finest hospitals, and medical academic institutions and yet unable to deal with the crisis. Within three months of the first case being diagnosed in the United States, COVID-19 had caused over 100,000 deaths and economic chaos, and two years later, over one million Americans had lost their lives. And now a rerun?' And yet, only an autocratic country like China could pull off such a tight quarantine. If it works, it's the only way to stop a plague without a vaccine.

As Gogoli went to his office that morning, he met the Medical Examiner in the hallway.

"Well, Seb, now what do you think?"

"Stan, I don't know what to think. Americans involved and our state department knows nothing about this? Why aren't we being alerted to this? We have to wait for the media to send this out? I sure hope the CDC is better prepared this time."

Stan paused, "You know what I'm worried about."

"I'm afraid to hear."

"You should be. Based on those reports of almost instant death, this could be the big one we've been waiting for: the end of life on this planet as we know it. COVID 19 was the prodromal, the dress rehearsal because opening night is about to occur. This country better start preparing now for what will surely reach our shores."

CHAPTER THIRTY-FIVE

Friday, May 2, 2031

General Han returned the rented car to the Hertz drop-off in Silver Spring, Maryland, and purchased a train ticket to Penn Station in New York. He took a hotel room in midtown, walked to Bloomingdales, and purchased a pair of khaki pants, a blue dress shirt, brown loafers, and a blue sport jacket, paying cash. He changed in his room, removed a black rectangular thick stainless-steel container with a hinged lid measuring two inches deep by five inches wide and four inches long from the pouch in his suitcase and left the hotel. It was about eleven o'clock when he felt the vibration of his cell. Han read the message sent from State Security over his mobile SAT phone that connects by radio through an orbiting satellite, assuring secure transmission. "We've got Chen Chu. He is in custody in Wulajie."

A smile crossed Han's face. He returned the message. *I want him taken to the Institute and have him working on the antidote immediately.*

Han continued walking along Lexington Avenue, slowing his pace to look through the windows of the lunch establishments along the way. It was noon, and the lunch crowd was already filling the avenue when he walked into several food establishments, looked around as if making a decision, but then walked out. Finally, he entered a busy Lexington deli and waited in a long line to order. While the counterman was busy with another order, Han appeared to be placing something on the counter and walked out. Without looking back, he walked over to Third Avenue and bought a ticket at a movie theater without any interest in what was to be seen.

⊣ BOOK SIX ⊢

CHAPTER THIRTY-SIX

6:00 P.M. Friday, May 2

Tony DeCarlo arrived a few minutes late for Friday evening's meeting of the Writer's Group, a collection of five hopeful unpublished writers. The meeting took place in a small room on the second floor of the local public library each week. They had varied backgrounds: a young attorney, a retired teacher, a newspaper reporter, a photographer and Tony, the most senior of the group. He was slight of build, of medium height, with balding black hair swept backward and olive skin in keeping with his Sicilian background. His dark eyes were alert as he followed the discourse of the writers around the table, each reading from the weekly new pages added on to the stories that they handed out.

He had a gentle voice with a measured rhythm that made his New York Lower East Side Italian origin more apparent. His writing was simple, with short words and small sentences, clear, distinct, with no attempt at sophistication or sophistry, and his stories were in the same vein. He had a lifetime of anecdotes, and he described them as being like a rat's tail, short and to the point. They were rarely more than four or five pages and all about his life growing up in an Italian neighborhood in the fifties and sixties. But in those four or five pages, you learned more about his grandmother Maria, his mother and father, his aunts and uncles, his wives and girlfriends and the businesses that he owned, sold, or gave up on then if it was as long as the twelve hundred pages of Les Misérables. You met the most colorful friends and acquaintances, all as if you were watching characters in a film, and the film would be "The Godfather." The stories he wrote of how his grandmother, upon hearing that a man in the neighborhood was ridiculing her granddaughter, went up to him and told him that if he ever did it again, she would cut off his balls, or the story of when the mafia chief came to his house for his grandmother's pasta. Each week, he would bring in another story, more surreal than the previous one but always interesting, and regardless of how sinister the plot was—it would always end with a smile. The other members told him that he had a unique voice and that his stories must be published because they could entertain and bring enjoyment to others. It was ironic because he confided that he never thought his stories were very good and that he never thought of having anyone read them. Sometimes, just a little motivation can change a person's life. He left that evening determined to have his first volume of short stories published.

CHAPTER THIRTY-SEVEN

1:00 P.M. Saturday, May 3, 2031

Tresh Jennine walked her parents to their car parked down the street from her apartment, where they had just finished lunch.

"That was quite a meal you prepared."

"You both deserve it. You're wonderful."

It was difficult for her father to hide the tears filling his eyes. "I've tried. Easy to be a father to you." His sleeve passed against his eyes. "How's work?"

She knew he would ask. He always did, always concerned that he had not provided for her as much as other wealthier fathers.

"My waitress job? It pays my half of the rent."

"And Karen?"

She smiled. "That's why I only have to pay half the rent."

Her mother asked, "Is she still going out with that fellow? He seemed like a nice guy."

"Richie? She is, and he is. Although she spends more time at his apartment than ours."

Her father paused before treading into territory that only he was comfortable in asking.

"And have you met anyone?"

"Meeting, yes, but no one special. Between work and preparing for auditions, I'm pretty busy. But the moment I meet that someone, I will give him your three-page questionnaire to fill out."

"And let him know I grade them personally, and only then will they be granted the final interview." He smiled before continuing. "And the auditions?"

"There's hope. I just got a third call back."

The glance at his wife revealed his pride. "I had a feeling this could be your time. You've worked hard at your craft."

"I'm not sure for what role they had me read for several, but I feel really good about it. Wish you didn't have to leave so early."

Her father opened the door for his wife. "I know, but we promised Aunt Susan and Cousin Fred that we would stop by. It's been a while since we've seen them."

"I understand. "

She closed the passenger door and walked her father to the driver's side.

"When will we see you again?"

"I'll try and get off for a weekend, but I can't promise."

"Your mother and I get it. You're a busy young woman, and we're both so proud of you."

He slowly eased into the driver's seat. "Well, then, young lady, until again. You know I love you."

She hugged him, always aware that his next heart attack could be the last.

"I know. I love you too."

She looked through the open window. "By mom."

"By Tresh."

As Tresh walked across to her building, she turned and, with a smile, called out.

"Hey, keep your fingers crossed and your calendar open. I may finally be making my debut."

She heard the response from across the street. "Can't wait."

With that, she gave a deep bow. Her smile couldn't be more infectious, and her father smiled back. "Better keep practicing those curtain calls."

She laughed. "Bye, Dad."

He raised his hand in a salute. "Bye, my little girl."

CHAPTER THIRTY-EIGHT

Han enjoyed the pleasant spring temperatures that New York had to offer. He planned his visit to the United States to last up to three weeks, depending upon the results of his work, and was constantly aware of the deadline given to him. He spent the days reading newspapers, listening to television, and overhearing conversations about any reports of unusual deaths, but only crime and mass shootings dominated the headlines.

There were many questions to be answered: *how powerful was Thanatos? Did the material stored in dry ice during the trip and the refrigerators in the hotels produce the same response as in China? What would Washington's reaction be? Had Chen made progress on formulating the antidote back in Wuhan?*

As he walked down Fifth Avenue, he admired the aging buildings that had brought New York to its great fame since the turn of the twentieth century. But he also realized that the twentieth century was long past, and the greatness of America had aged with it. In so many ways, he reflected on how the United States had been surpassed by others, from infant mortality to the inability to have a functioning government. Democracy had its day, especially liberal democracy. The idea of complete equality could never be achieved; satisfying everyone was a fantasy. He certainly agreed that the ideal should be equal opportunity, but surely not equal results. No, he thought to himself, China was the future. Autocracy had its advantages; limiting diversity allowed a nation to focus on where it wanted to go without concerns about the inequalities of the past, present or future. Just as Rome slowly withered into collapse, so he envisioned that the United States was on its downward spiral.

He spent the hours waiting for the verdict. Thus far, only general news reports about the limited spread of the virus in China had been covered, including the effectiveness of its isolation program, but nothing about its presence in the US. That was another major advantage of Chinese strategy. The immediate implementation of a Zero-COVID-19 policy with full lockdowns, even following minor outbreaks resulting in closed businesses and unemployment, is something that Western populations could never tolerate, although even China had learned there were limits to how many days the policy could be implemented. From the COVID-19 days, it was determined to be seven. He reviewed the schedule. If something were to happen, if the twenty-four-to-forty-eight-hour period for symptoms to appear held true, then a response should be reported by the end of the day. And certainly, with such a thing as a free press, it would bring headlines for the nation to realize what was happening. Han was aware that failure would not be tolerated, though he recalled the old Chinese proverb: It is better to attempt something great and fail than attempt to do nothing and succeed. But Han could not fail this time. How foolish the US government and their FDA were to dismiss the work of Lexington Bio. He was not so foolish.

CHAPTER THIRTY-NINE

4:00 A.M., Monday, May 5, 2031

It was four in the morning when Gogoli heard a continuous buzzing from his cell phone.

"Dr. Gogoli, it's Julio. We have a problem."

It was rare for Gogoli to be called into work so early. For coroners and murderers, cadavers could always wait an extra hour before finding out what killed them. Gogoli dragged himself out of bed, threw on whatever clothes were hanging over the chair, splashed his face with cold water, kissed Frederica gently on her forehead, and then quickly walked to the elevator, wondering what the emergency could be.

He hailed a cab that drove him straight east across the island of Manhattan from Tenth Avenue to the Medical Examiner's office located in the Milton Halpern Institute of Forensic Medicine building at 520 First Avenue. Security let him through, and he nodded to the sleepy receptionist sitting behind a counter under a sign with the ME's motto: *Science Serving Justice.* He walked to the end of the long, narrow, fluorescent-lit hallway and down the stairs to the morgue.

"What's happened?"

Julio reviewed the situation. "Two cases, both admitted at about the same time, two different locations, without any apparent cause and marked urgent, high potential risk."

Dr. Julio Perez was a thirty-one-year-old physician who had joined the ME's office two years previously following completion of the NY Forensic Pathology Fellowship program, which required both a medical degree and a residency in anatomic pathology. The program was not only the largest in the nation but also the most competitive, for it gave the individual the opportunity to learn forensic science with access to the New York Medical Examiner's laboratories, departments of forensic anthropology, epidemiology, emergency management, and the experience of court testimony. Over the past twenty years, over one hundred board-certified forensic pathologists from around the world have completed Gogoli's program.

"What can you tell me about the first one?"

Julio picked up the medical record and began reading: "James Davenport is a twenty-eight-year-old male who worked as an attorney at a large New York law firm. His girlfriend, who was out of town for the weekend, said that he complained on Saturday night of burning up and having difficulty breathing. She told him to go to the ER at Whitestone Hospital, which he did and was placed on a ventilator. Imaging indicated severe inflammation with invasive lesions of the lungs, heart, kidney, and liver. He was fading in and out of consciousness all Sunday until his heart gave out, and he died Sunday night. The treating physicians had never seen anything that killed so fast and were concerned that this could be something we should see immediately. There was no significant medical history, just the usual childhood diseases and vaccines. He died within forty-eight hours of first complaining of symptoms to his girlfriend."

"So quickly?" That caught Gogoli's attention. "What could have caused that? You want to go over the symptoms again?"

"Fever, respiratory distress, inflammation throughout the body, breakdown of bodily organs, and death, all occurring between Saturday morning and Sunday night."

Gogoli's mind began running in overtime. "You have labs?"

Julio reviewed the chart. "Everything is way off. Increased white blood cells. neutrophils, LDH, ALT, AST, total bilirubin, creatinine; cardiac troponin, d-dimer; prothrombin time, procalcitonin; c reactive protein, along with decreased lymphocytes, and albumin. I mean, there's nothing within normal limits."

"And the second case?"

Julio picked up the medical record. "It's almost a copy of the first. Fred Smith, a sixty-five year old male who started to feel ill Saturday evening and whose fever spiked Sunday morning. His daughter said he had a temperature of one hundred and three and had difficulty in breathing. She called 911, and he was brought by ambulance to the ER and put on a ventilator. Imaging indicated severe inflammation with tissue loss in the lungs, heart, kidney, and liver. Same response, fading in and out of consciousness all night until his heart gave out Sunday night. The treating physicians who worked through COVID-19 thought this may be of a viral nature but much more powerful. They sent the body over for an immediate evaluation. The patient had a history of prostate cancer, childhood usuals, but otherwise healthy."

"And the symptoms again?

Julio reread the report.

Gogoli saw the relationship. "And I bet the labs are similar."

Julio reviewed the chart. "Almost exactly, everything way up. Two different people from different parts of the city. What do you think?"

Gogoli pondered the history. "I think it's here."

"What?"

"China, same symptoms, unknown viral infection, and deadly."

Jesus put the chart back on the desk. "Then we should move them to do the autopsies."

Gogoli nodded. "Agreed. Bring them into the Airborne Infection Isolation Rooms and check that the room has negative pressure to the surrounding environment. What's the ACH in there?"

Julio answered: "A minimum of twelve air changes per hour. We have it connected through a HEPA filter to prevent the virus from spreading out."

Gogoli approved. "Good. Then, get the team together and review the procedures. We're in emergency mode. We have to know what we are dealing with."

CHAPTER FORTY

Julio put the automatic call into the Airborne Infection Team, and within fifteen minutes, the two residents and six nurses gathered in the outer room. He reviewed the precautions.

"We're going into maximum PPE on these cases. We're not certain what we have, but it could be a viral outbreak and all procedures we've trained to do must be strictly adhered to. We will be moving both cases into the isolation rooms where the negative pressure keeps airflow and anything in the air inside the room. Once there, we only exit on an absolute need basis until the case is closed. Everyone is to wear double surgical gloves interposed with a layer of cut-proof synthetic mesh, fluid-resistant gowns, waterproof aprons, goggles or face shields, and NIOSH-certified disposable N-95 respirators. Surgical scrubs, shoe covers, and surgical caps should be used as usual."

Julio looked at the team members, several of whom were not present when COVID-19 hit.

"And one more thing. Be careful; do not contaminate yourself. This is real. We don't know for sure what we are dealing with, but it's possible it's more lethal than anything we've met before."

The group looked at each other and understood what was at stake. They changed into their PPE equipment, checked the isolation rooms and the interior pressure differential, and moved the cadavers in for autopsy.

Gogoli began in Room One, examining the gross features of the lifeless body of James Davenport lying on the narrow stainless-steel table within the well-lit, white-tiled aseptic sanctuary and dictated his notes while the two residents observed.

"Now, remember what I am about to do because if my instincts are correct, you will be responsible for repeating these many times over the next weeks. Most important, we must determine what pathogen did this, so we're going to do a lot of swabbing to collect samples for the lab to evaluate. Why so many swabs? "

The first resident answered, "Because there must be enough material to be analyzed by both the CDC and ours."

Gogoli nodded. "So please observe. First, I will collect the postmortem nasopharyngeal specimens using synthetic fiber swabs with plastic shafts. Why? Why not the calcium alginate swabs or swabs with wooden shafts?" The second resident responded. "Because they may contain substances that inactivate some viruses or inhibit PCR testing."

Gogoli was pleased. "Good. And once I have the specimens, what do I do with them?"

The second resident answered, "Place the swabs immediately into sterile tubes containing 2-3 ml of viral transport media, making sure that the nasopharyngeal specimens are placed in separate vials from the lung specimens."

"Good, then what?"

"Refrigerate the specimens at two to eight degrees centigrade, send one set of vials to our lab and ship one overnight to CDC on ice pack."

"Excellent."

Gogoli then began by collecting the upper respiratory tract specimen by inserting a swab into the nostril parallel to the palate.

"Notice how I leave the swab in place for a few seconds to absorb secretions. Make certain you swab both nasopharyngeal areas with the same swab."

Gogoli then removed the scalpel from the sterile stainless-steel tray and began the Y-shaped incision from both shoulders to the sternum that continued down to the pubic bone. He flapped back the skin and underlying tissues, noted his observations, and then removed the rib cage and abdominal cavity along with the underlying neck and chest anatomy, allowing examination of the deeper organs. He then collected the lower respiratory tract specimens and asked for the lung swabs, collecting swabs from both the right and left sides. He removed the heart-lung block and, after wiping the surface of each lung with an iodine disinfectant and drying the surface, inserted a swab as far down into the tracheobronchial tree as possible on both the left and right sides. Then, using a sterile scalpel to cut a slit in the lung, he inserted the swab to collect a sample from either side. After ninety minutes of careful dissection and examination,

Gogoli returned his scalpel to the autopsy tray. Perspiration saturated his forehead above the green surgical mask, and one of the surgical nurses blotted the
area with gauze.

" And I want you to be certain to remove tissues from the lung, upper
airway, and other major organs and fix them in formalin for evaluation. And
please note there was no previous history on this patient. Forty-eight hours ago,
he was a healthy young man."

When he completed the procedure, Gogoli placed the white sheet back
over the cadaver, removed his PPE, and disposed of them into the red hazard
waste container. Dr. Perez then repeated the procedure on the second case with
Gogoli assisting.

CHAPTER FORTY-ONE

10:00 A.M. Monday

It was ten in the morning by the time a tired Sebastian Gogoli removed his PPE, scrubbed, and sat down in the outer room. He contacted both Stan Galvin, the Medical Examiner, and Jeffrey Moss, the Assistant Medical Examiner, indicating a matter of urgency. Twenty minutes later, they met in Stan's office.

"What happened?" Gogoli took a deep breath and handed a report to each of the physicians. "Two tough cases. "

Jeff perused the report. "Unknown virus?" He read it twice with a worried look on his face. Stan reported the same finding. "Ditto. Unknown virus. You did the autopsies?" Gogoli continued. "Just completed them. The two men live here in New York, and from the symptoms and the autopsy results, they appear to be similar to what is being reported in China. And whatever it is, it seems much more virulent than COVID-19."Stan was concerned. "We better notify CDC."

Gogoli added. "We've already expedited a set of specimens to them. They should have it in a few hours, and I kept a set for us. We gave it as top priority. The labs will be using the polymerase chain reaction test, which detects the genetic material of the virus." Stan added. "Fine, and call Priya Majmadur in on this. If we're about to go through round two of a viral invasion, we're going to need her help. She's down the block at the School for Public Health. I think if Jeff calls her, she will make time to come over."

Gogoli was inquisitive. "How's that?'

"She was his resident."

He turned to Jeff. "In epidemiology?"

"No, In cardiovascular surgery."

CHAPTER FORTY-TWO

Monday, May 5, 12:10 P.M.

Priya Majmadur smiled at Jeff when she entered the ME's office. "Been a while, but your message said it was urgent. What's up?"

Jeff extended his hand in greeting. "Hi Priya, thanks for coming over. And you know Sebastian Gogoli, our chief coroner."

"Only by reputation."

"Yes, nice to meet you." Gogoli continued. "We were at your conference last year when you warned us to start preparing for the next invasion. Well, I just completed two autopsies. Both clinicals and labs strongly suggest that the virus that is overseas is now here."

Dr. Majmudar pursed her lips and nodded slowly. "Tell me about them."

Gogoli reviewed the cases. "The postmortem readings are still coming in, but whatever this is, it's much more virulent than SARS or COVID-19. In all my experience, I've never seen anything so powerful."

Priya thought for a moment. "And you say medical history was non-significant?"

Gogoli responded. "As far as we know. The EMs were just received." He handed several electron micrograph images of odd, brightly colored spheres with wheel-like structures extending from them and handed them to her. "Can you identify what it is?"

Priya viewed the three images before responding. "The virus looks the same as COVID-19, but the virulence is certainly different. But why? Is there a subtle mutation that EM cannot pick up that makes it so powerful, or is the body not able to defend against it for some other reason? The fact that healthy men can be overwhelmed so quickly is difficult to appreciate. Didn't these patients receive the COVID-19 vaccines and the annual boosters?"

Gogoli responded. "According to their histories, they did.."

"So that tells us that the vaccine was of little value, and that means we have a mutant for which we have no defense."

Gogoli's cell went off, and he answered. "Yes? When? I'll be right down." Gogoli looked at the others.

"Another case just came in. Same history. Death within forty-eight hours of symptoms. I've got to go."

Priya made a few notes. "Jeff, we need to know what we're dealing with. That means, who are these individuals? Where have they been? With whom? Did they know each other, live together, work together, anything that would suggest they received the virus from a common carrier."

Priya looked through the charts. "We have to do these two ourselves. If word gets out of a killer virus, the country could go amok. You take James Davenport, and I'll take Fred Smith. Let's see what they may have in common."

* * *

1:13 P.M.

Jeff spoke to James Davenport's girlfriend, Angela. She was still in shock over his death, and he told her how sorry he was.

"How was this possible? He was perfectly healthy."

Jeff began his questions as gently as he could. "So he was fine on Friday?"

"Absolutely. I was at my sister's babysitting for the weekend, but I spoke to him. He didn't get home from work until seven, heated up some frozen pizza and went over to his writer's group at the library. He called me about ten and told me he was going to bed."

"And the weekend?"

"He worked all day at home because he and his boss had a big trial on Monday, and he had to prepare. He called me Saturday night and told me he was burning up and had difficulty breathing. I told him to take his temperature. It was one hundred and two. I told him to get to the ER immediately and let me know what they say."

"And that was the last time you heard from him."

"Yes.

"And you didn't see him all weekend."

"I wish I was there."

"Tell me about the writers' group."

"I'm not part of it, but James has always wanted to write a book, and he goes every Friday night with several others. You would have to call the public library to get the other names. "What could have happened?"

"We're working on it. As soon as I know more, I will let you know. Thanks, Angela. I'm so sorry, but there is nothing you could have done if you were with him."

* * *

Priya called Fred Smith's daughter, Wendy, and related her condolences.

"My father was a great man. He was one of the founders of a big law firm, very charitable, well-known throughout the city and the country."

"When did you first know he was not feeling well?"

"I spoke to him on Saturday evening. His cousins had visited him that afternoon, but after they left, he mentioned he was feeling tired and was going to bed early, probably working too hard for the trial on Monday. When I called later, he said he was getting out of breath and felt hot. I told him to take his temperature. It was one hundred and two, and he could barely speak. I called 911, and they took him to the ER. I never saw him alive again."

Priya made her notes. "What about Friday? Any idea where he was?"

"At his law firm. He practically lived there. Law was his entire life."

"What was the name of his firm?"

"Bowman, O'Leary, Smith and Shapiro in Midtown Manhattan."

Priya wrote everything down. "One last thing. You mentioned a visit from his cousins on Saturday. Can you tell me their names?"

"Yes, Robert and Fran Jennine, and Judy Taggert. The funeral for my father will be tomorrow."

"I understand. Thank you for your help, and again, I'm so sorry for your loss."

* * *

When Jeff and Priya finished their interviews, they compared notes. "So both attorneys at the same firm and worked together. Were they together on Friday?"

"Let me check," Jeff called back to Angela. "Fred was his boss. In fact, they had lunch together on Friday in the office. I remember because he bragged about how he had a salad for lunch. Wanted to impress his boss. I've been trying to get him to eat a healthier diet."

"So he ordered in?"

"Actually, he went to a deli where he always buys his lunch, a place called Maxwell's Coffee Shop on Lexington Avenue."

As Jeff ended the call, Stan walked in. "Find out anything?"

"Two potential niduses of infection, a coffee shop and a law firm. The two deceased worked at the same law firm and lunched there on Friday. The food came from a place called Maxwell's Coffee Shop."

"And the law firm?"

Jeff checked his notes. "Bowman, O'Leary, Smith and Shapiro."

Priya followed up. "That's the connection. They worked for the same firm! Was the CDC notified?"

Stan responded. "Gogoli contacted the CDC, as protocol requires."

"What about notifying the politicos? The feds need to be alerted."

"I'll call my contacts and get as much info as I can. Jeff, best you work with Priya. Let's meet back here, say five."

Priya nodded. "And Jeff, see if someone can go online to the law firm's website and print out some photos of Fred Smith and James Davenport. Perhaps someone at the coffee shop remembers them coming in on Friday. Find out about the deaths, I'll call the law firm. Same kind of interview. Anyone else sick? How did it spread? etcetera."

"Priya, one last item," Jeff raised, "What do we tell the press? If it's a story, they'll find out."

"Let me think about that. For now, let's not say too much. But anyone who has had contact with these two men is to be quarantined. Let's see if we can contain this situation. Meet you back here at five."

CHAPTER FORTY-THREE

Monday, May 5, 2:30 P.M.

The lunchtime crowd at Maxwell's Coffee Shop had emptied out when Jeff arrived and introduced himself to one of the workers whose name tag read Miguel. He asked who had been working take-out Friday lunch.

"Yeah, either me or Carlos works lunch take out. One pours drinks, and the other packs food. This past Friday? Carlos did the drinks, and I wrapped the food order."

"Is he around?" Jeff asked.

"Yeah, he's in the back. I'll get him."

Carlos walked out. "You lookin' for me?"

"Yes. How have you been feeling?"

"Fine, what's up."

"Just checking on a few things." Jeff removed the photos from his jacket pocket.

"Would you happen to recognize these men"?

Miguel and Carlos looked at the photo. "Yeah, the young guy. That's the lawyer. He comes in every day and orders the same thing: meatball hero and a coffee. Nice guy."

Jeff pursued the questioning. "Did you see him on Friday?"

"Friday? Busy day. I mean, he's always here, although, come to think of it, I didn't see him today. He okay?"

"That's what we're checking."

"Let's see, Friday. Yeah, hey Carlos, that's when you told me to make up two garden salads for the lawyer, no meatballs. Remember, I says you sure, and you said yeah, his boss ordered one, and he ordered the same thing to show he's healthy."

Carlos nodded. "Right, and I poured the coffees to go."

Jeff handed them his card. "If you hear of anyone getting sick, give me a call."

* * *

Priya made the call to Bowman, O'Leary, Smith and Shapiro, identified herself, and asked for the managing partner.

"That's Mr. Baskins. I'm sorry, but he's not expected until later this afternoon."

"I see. Well, it's quite important, so please have him contact me ASAP."

"Perhaps I can help. I'm the office manager."

"Can you tell me if any personnel called in sick today?"

"Today?" No one called in sick, but we're missing Fred Smith and his associate, James Davenport. I haven't been able to reach them, and they were supposed to be on trial. We don't know what happened, but we had to ask for a delay. This has never happened before."

"And no one else?"

" According to the records, everyone else is here."

"Okay, thank you. Just have Mr. Baskins call me."

"As soon as I can reach him. He's at a meeting out of town. He should be checking in at the end of the day. I'll send a message to call you."

* * *

It was 5:00 when Stan, Jeff and Priya reconvened in Jeff's office.

Stan opened. "I received a message from James Ryan at CDC. The reports of the two Americans in China having the virus are true. They worked for the FDA and had made a routine inspection visit to the Wuhan Institute of Virology. They both died after the first day of the inspection."

Priya went over her notes. "But how? Where did they come in contact with the contagion? Here? On the plane? At Wuhan?"

"The timing suggests that they had it before they reached Wuhan," Jeff interjected. "If this is the same virus, then death occurs 24-48 hours following symptoms. The reports suggest that they experienced symptoms upon arrival, which implies there must have been a contact before they left for China."

Priya thought about the sequence. "Then let's review the New York cases. Let's assume exposure occurred sometime on Friday when they were together for lunch."

Jeff added. "I checked out the deli. The guys there made them salads and coffees. Neither of them had any symptoms."

Priya tried to understand the events. "Then, if the lawyers had lunch together, how was it transmitted to them? What was the connection? Was it the food?" Assuming they left their homes for the office and only met each other at work, then what happened at work?"

Priya's cell rang. "Yes, Mr. Baskins, thank you for calling."

"Sure, I've been in conference all day. So what's the emergency?"

"What I am speaking to you about must remain confidential. Two of your employees passed away over the weekend from a possible viral infection. We are trying to trace how that could have happened."

"What two?"

"Fred Smith and James Davenport."

"What?" Baskins' response was truly anguish. "Fred? How's that possible? He started this firm. And James was his associate. So that's why they didn't go to trial on Monday. I assumed they wanted a delay for further preparation."

"Yes, and now you understand why it's so important for us to check your staff for symptoms."

Baskins was worried. "So you think it could have spread?"

"That's what we're trying to determine."

"Oh, I'm so sorry. What a tragedy."

Priya continued. "I spoke to your administrator, and she said no one else reported ill. Even so, we will need to trace if either Fred or James were in contact with anyone else at the office. This is purely preventive. In most cases, we believe that the symptoms appear within forty-eight hours. We're already past that, but we need to be sure."

Baskins paused before replying. "I know they were preparing for the trial late Friday. They were still in the office when I left . . . Is this another COVID-19?"

"We certainly hope not. But let's keep that possibility between us for now. By the way, we understand that Fred and James had lunch together on Friday. Do you know where that would be?"

"Sure, Fred's office. He never leaves his office when in trial preparation."

"That's good to know. So it's okay for us to send over a team to check for symptoms?"

"Yes."

Priya ended the call. "We may have some luck. The lawyers stay in their office when preparing for a trial."

"So James goes out to the deli for lunch, comes back to the office, and they never leave again until evening."

"Yes, except for lunch."

Jeff nodded. "it seems this revolves around the deli."

Priya reviewed her notes. "Yes, it seems so."

There was a pause for thought when Priya suddenly spoke up. "Jeff, do you have a car?"

"Yes, why? Are we going somewhere?"

Priya smiled. "First thing in the morning, Rockville, Maryland. We need to check out the two FDA agents that died in China. If what you are suggesting is true, then perhaps they did have the disease before they got on the plane."

Jeff nodded. "Then I'll give the FDA a heads up that we'll be there around noon."

"Make it ten."

Jeff seemed surprised. "Ten? What time do you want to leave?"

"Six."

"You're a tough taskmaster."

"If I recall my surgical residency, you were much tougher."

CHAPTER FORTY-FOUR

Monday, May 5, 5:30 P.M.

Tresh was at work setting up tables for the evening diners when her cell went off. She checked to see who was calling but didn't recognize the number. With all the rogue calls everyone was getting she was about to disconnect, but, for some reason, hesitatingly answered. "Yes."

"Is this Tresh?"

Still cautious, she responded. "Yes."

"Tresh, this is Joe Marks, the casting director for "The Princess Bride."

Tresh's heart began racing, and that nervous jolt entered when something special was about to occur.

"We want to thank you for spending so much time with us during the auditions." She heard the phone ringing in the background, and Marks excused himself to take the call. To Tresh, it sounded like another rejection, and she was so hoping for this one. But she girded herself up, recalling what her father had advised her when deciding to be an actress. "Remember, there are fifty-two cards in a deck, and there are four aces. Those aces can either come up in the beginning or at the end, but your job is to keep drawing cards until the ace appears. Just keep auditioning.' Guess this was not going to be the ace. "Anyway," she said to herself, "it's the first time that a casting director called her for the rejection rather than one of their lackeys."

The voice returned. "Sorry about that. As I was saying, thanks for your time. We were very impressed, and we would like to cast you as the princess. That means you are our lead. Congratulations. We hope you will be able to join us."

Tresh could not believe what she had just heard. She sat down on the nearest chair, her hand shaking, her heart beating overtime, trying to get the words out, "Thank, Thank you very much. Yes, I would love to join you."

"Wonderful. You didn't list your agent's name, which is why I called you directly. Do you have an agent?"

"Actually, I haven't; I mean, I don't have one."

"Then have your attorney call me, or we can refer you to an agent if you can't find one, but we need to get the paperwork done, and there's a lot to do. Opening night is in eight weeks at the Broadhurst Theatre, and we'd like you to come in tomorrow to meet with us. I will message you my contact info."

Tresh ended the call and rested her elbows on the table. What had just happened? She didn't know whether to laugh or cry. She just sat there, numb to all sensations around her. Finally, she picked up her cell, made the call, and when no answer was asked to leave a message.

"Mom, Dad, I was just given the lead for a new musical. We open in eight weeks at the Broadhurst Theatre on Broadway, and I'm to meet with them tomorrow. I'm going to need an attorney."

She knew what they would say. "Congratulations, darling. You did it and earned every bit of it. As for an attorney, call cousin Fred. He's the finest attorney there is."

Tresh ended the call and began to cry softly.

"Something wrong?" Karen Ash was Tresh's roommate.

"No, something wonderful. I just got the lead in the musical I auditioned for."

They hugged, and tears came to both sets of eyes.

"The casting director called. He wants to speak to my attorney or agent. I'll call my dad's cousin. He's an attorney. I'm sure he can help."

She patted her face with a napkin, went through her contact list, and pressed the number. "Hi, this is Tresh Jennine. May I speak with Fred Smith? Fred's my cousin."

"Fred Smith?" The receptionist hesitated before adding, "Just a moment, please."

It took several minutes before a man answered the phone. "Yes, this is Marty Shapiro, I'm Fred's partner. How can I help you?"

Tresh sensed something was wrong. "My name is Tresh Jennine, and Fred is my cousin. I need his advice."

"I see. Is there anything I can help you with?"

"I just got a part on Broadway, and I need an attorney to represent me."

"Well, congratulations! I'm sure we can arrange that for you. I have your number and will have someone get back to you."

Tresh was growing suspicious. "Well, I would really like to speak to Fred?"

Shapiro paused. "Tresh, I am so sorry to tell you that Fred passed away yesterday."

Tresh tried to appreciate what she was being told. "What? How? I mean, my dad was with him on Saturday."

"We're not sure what happened, but he missed work on Monday, and his daughter called with the terrible news. I'm so sorry."

Tresh slowly clicked off the phone, trying to understand what could have happened. Finally, she pressed a contact number, but it went to voice mail. "Mom, Dad, I heard some terrible news. Cousin Fred passed away."

CHAPTER FORTY-FIVE

Tuesday, May 6, 10:00 A.M.

Jeff pulled into FDA headquarters on Fishers Lane, and he and Priya went to the third floor to meet with the Director of Biologic Medicines, Dr. Frederick Kosent.

Following the introductions, Priya went right to the point. "We are interested in discussing the two FDA representatives, Pete Ward and Jerry Kagos, who were doing international investigations in China. We need to trace their activities from the moment they left here until they reached their destination. Can you help us with that?"

"You don't believe that Chinese propaganda that our agents were somehow involved?"

"That's what we're checking."

Kosent viewed his log. "We met here on Friday, April 18, for the usual review of their itinerary at 10:30 in the morning. Following the meeting, they had a car waiting to bring them to Reagan International and flew out from there."

"And how were they feeling at that time? Did any of them seem ill, or were they ill previous to the trip?"

Dr. Kosent answered immediately. "No, they were healthy when they came in and had all their vaccinations. We go over that with them just prior to international visits."

"So they had their annual COVID-19 immunizations?"

"Absolutely. They contacted us as they were checking in to their hotel in Hunan and would begin their inspection at the Institute according to plan."

Priya asked. "So that would have been Monday or Sunday our time."

"Correct. They completed the day's inspection and apparently fell ill at that time and called for medical help. We were told that they went into respiratory distress, taken to the hospital and died within twenty-four hours."

The phone rang, and Kosent picked up. "Bring them right in." A knock on the door, and a delivery man brought in coffee.

"Any coffee drinkers?"

Priya and Jeff looked at each other. It was Priya who asked, "No, thank you, but is coffee brought here every day?"

Kosent tried to follow the logic. "Why yes, several times a day."

"And is it possible that Ward and Kagos had coffee that morning?"

"Yes, they were both coffee drinkers. What does this have to do with their illness?"

"I'm not certain, but that's why we're here. Do you remember if you also had a cup?"

"I'm certain I did. I enjoy a cup at that time every day."

Priya looked at Jeff. "And how many people working here have coffee every day?" Jeff asked.

"Must be at least fifty people."

"And did any of them get sick or stay out of work?"

"No, and we checked thoroughly when we heard about Jerry and Pete."

Jeff continued. "And you were the only ones in this room at that meeting?"

"That is correct."

"And do you know if anyone at their home, wives or kids reported any illness?"

"We checked. They did not."

Priya then interjected. "Then what was different about what you had that morning and what they had? I mean, do you have milk, and they don't?"

Kosent thought for a moment. "Actually, they have it with sweetener, and I don't. Why is that important?"

Priya responded. "It may be. Dr. Kosent, was the coffee delivered specifically to you for the meeting, or could it have been distributed to any of the rooms?"

Kosent thought for a moment. "Specifically to us."

"Well, thank you for the info.. "

Jeff added. "Dr. Kosent, one more thing. Where's the coffee from?"

Kosent went over to his desk and brought back a cup. On it was the name: Ben's Caterer's, with the address.

Priya and Jeff got up.

"Thanks, Dr. Kosent. You've been very helpful."

When they reached the car, they both began to speak at the same time. "Ben's Caterer's."

Jeff plugged it into the GPS. "It's five minutes away."

It was 10:45 when they entered as preparations were being made for the lunch hour. Jeff showed his badge and mentioned that he needed some information.

"Who usually delivers morning snacks to the FDA?"

"That's Hector. Wait, I'll get him."

Priya seemed surprised. "You have a police badge?"

Jeff smiled. "You mean you didn't know. Stan wants all his assistant MEs to go through police training, not only because they will be doing forensic police work but also to cooperate more closely with local and federal investigators. That means we have to attend the police academy as part of our training and have joint membership in both the police and Medical Examiner departments. Actually, I was in the first class. I may not be a sniper yet, but I do have to schedule visits to the firing range."

Priya gave him a skeptical look. "I'll be sure to keep my distance."

At that moment, a thin young man came out. "Hi, I'm Hector. You want to speak to me?"

"Hector, I'm Officer Moss, and this is my partner, Dr. Majmadur. Do you do the deliveries to the FDA in the mornings?"

"Yes, sir."

"And has anyone here reported being sick over the last few days?"

"No, everyone's working."

Priya then asked. "Tell me, Hector, I see you're wearing gloves. Do you always wear gloves?"

"Yes, ma'am. Everyone here wears gloves for food preparation and delivery. Ben insists on it."

"And do you pour the milk and sweetener before you deliver?"

"No, ma'am. I just pour the coffee and throw in the packs of sweetener and deliver it."

"So everything is delivered unsweetened and black?"

"That's right."

"And no one has ever reported being sick over the past week?"

"Not that I know of."

"Thank you, Hector. Have a healthy day."

* * *

As Jeff reached the entrance to I95, Priya's phone rang, and she recognized the caller. "It's Sarah, my resident. I'll turn on the speaker."

"Priya, we've completed the exams at the Law offices. No one had symptoms, but I'm about to enter Fred Smith's office. It's been locked since he was last here on Friday, preparing for a trial. We brought our viral protection gear just in case. What do you want us to do?"

Priya glanced at Jeff. "First, I want that office sealed immediately, and when you go in, you need to put on your safety equipment. Call me when you get in."

It took fifteen minutes for Priya's cell to ring. "Okay, we're in. The remains from lunch are still in the trash. Want anything specific?"

"Place everything from lunch, including the lunch wrapping and coffee cups, into sealed specimen containers. If you notice any sweetener packs, be very careful; they could be the contaminant. We're thinking that the virus had something to do with lunch. Not certain how long the virus can survive, but have the labs done stat."

"Okay."

* * *

Priya broke the silence on the drive back to New York. "Jeff, I've been meaning to ask, how did you get to the ME's office? The last time I saw you was when you were chief at Metropolitan Hospital. I mean, you were by far the top cardiothoracic surgeon on the East Coast, chairman of the department. How did you get to here?"

Jeff hesitated before responding, thinking about those past events. "I suppose the stress was taking its toll. And one day, out of nowhere, I get a call from Stan Galvin, a med school classmate, and he offered me the job."

"So that was it, one phone call?"

"Well, actually, that wasn't the way he put it."

Priya looked at him. "Then how did he put it?"

"He said, and I still remember his words, 'I need you with me. It's time we brought modern technology to find the bad guys. I suppose when he mentioned finding the bad guys, that's what made its mark."

Priya studied his silence and understood.

"I heard what happened to Barbara. I sent you a condolence. That was awful."

He took a quick look at her before returning his eyes to the road. "Yes, it was personal, very personal, and a rough part of my life. I lost someone I loved to bad guys trying to steal a pocketbook and killing her because she resisted. Probably for the first time in my life, I found myself helpless to fight back."

He paused. "I kept hearing the words of Edmund Burke: All that is necessary for the triumph of evil is that good men do nothing, and I realized that I'm not capable of doing nothing. I suppose after the murder, I knew that I needed a new direction, a fresh start, and maybe a new life and Stan's call helped with that decision. So I gave the hospital notice that I would not be returning, and with no ties to bind, I packed what little I had. As they say, the rest is history."

Jeff smiled as he glanced at Priya. "That seems like a long time ago."

She returned the smile. "I met Barbara once when I was a first-year resident, and she was giving a lecture on pediatric surgery. I asked her a question afterward; she was smart and lovely."

"That she was."

The silence continued until he broke it. "But what about you? The last time I saw you was when you were a young resident, single, and incising the pericardium. I was certain you were going to make a great heart surgeon. What changed?"

"Well, still single, but I left your program because I thought I could make a larger impact on society than the repetitive mechanics of picking up a blade and making anatomical repairs. I guess I was more interested in the social aspects of medicine."

"And now you're one of the top viral epidemiologists in the world."

"I enjoy what I do, especially the challenge to free this world of disease."

Jeff's cell rang. "Moss here. When? What? Okay, Seb, thanks for the update."

He turned to Priya. "I have the feeling you are about to be challenged. That was Gogoli. Six new deceased just arrived for autopsies, all part of a writing group that meets at the local library. The morgue is full. But something else: the ORs are full. The virus must be affecting the heart because every cardiothoracic surgeon on staff has been called in. Whatever is happening, it's spreading quickly."

Priya interrupted the silence. "Quarantine everyone. That means a complete lockdown for those who had any contact with this writing group. We have to stop it now."

CHAPTER FORTY-SIX

Tuesday, May 6, 2031

General Han sat on a Central Park bench in the warm glow of the early sun, his carryon beside him, as he perused the morning papers for some mention of his virus. It was an obituary on the front page of the *New York Times* regarding a Fred Smith that caught his attention. Smith was a major figure in New York as an adviser to mayors, senators, and large corporations. Audrey Martinez, the Times reporter who had links to anyone and everyone in the city, wrote of Fred's childhood in Brooklyn with parents who survived the Holocaust, went on to Harvard Law School, and established one of the most prestigious law firms not only in the city but in the nation. She also included the cause of death based on the results of the autopsy and a source suggesting that he was a victim of a powerful new virus recently found in China. How it was transmitted to the United States was unknown. As of this time, there was no known cure. She gave it a name: The Red Mutation.

Han read it again before it brought a restrained smile to the corner of his lips. The Red Mutation, he liked what she called it. It was also what he was waiting for, the first mention of the virus and its pathogenicity. The General knew that he needed more than one case for America to appreciate the virulence, rate of transmission and potential for a pandemic, but the first case was enough for him to continue to the next step. That will be all that is needed for Lexington Bio to be called.

Han rose from the bench, rolled his carry-on behind him, walked out of the park, and became part of the masses going to work. As he walked down

Fifth Avenue looking for an early morning taxi, he passed the seductive window displays of Bergdorf Goodman.

"*How interesting. Most of the fabrics and their final designs were made in China.*' It soon became clear to him that America doesn't want to work anymore, they only want to sell what others have made and reap the profits. *That's fine. We will soon be making everything, and then one day, you will be told there's nothing for you to sell. China will no longer supply you with chips for the technology that runs your computers, cars, planes and missiles. Even if my nanoparticle doesn't work, we will use economic terror.* Hadn't he just read in this morning's *Times* the results of a ten-year study analyzing American students and the educational changes made to improve diversity? The results indicated that without access to challenging educational programs, students who had the ability and interest to go beyond the average could no longer do so. This most severely affected the minority students who, with no programs to go beyond the medium, remained frustrated in being prevented from achieving the education they deserved. As a result, they did not have the needed educational skills to reach the heights of opportunity afforded those who were in educational systems that offered students of all backgrounds the advantages of advanced course content, such as AP studies. Han had read the article carefully. The effects on medical care in the United States for those students graduating from medical schools that no longer required testing for admission were not yet reported. No wonder America was falling behind in every category of intellectual and technological pursuits. To Han, it was another example of how the *country would collapse like Rome.*"

The cab brought him to JFK Airport. One hour later, a passenger with a driver's ID of James Seng from Toledo, Ohio, was on a Jet Blue flight to San Francisco.

* * *

Li Zhou read the Audrey Martinez piece on the front page of the *New York Times* online in the *Wall Street Journal*'s Offices in Shanghai. The cause of death of the prominent New York attorney was a powerful new virus recently found in China. As was reported in China, death occurred within twenty-four to forty-eight hours following exposure. Was this enough for her to set off the alarm that she had discussed with Chen? After careful thought she would wait for confirmation. She contacted the Journal's New York Office and asked to speak to Nick Robinson, the Managing Editor.

"Yes, Li, how are things in Shanghai? We're hearing reports of an outbreak in Wuhan."

"Seems to be controlled here, but Nick, that's what I need to discuss. Let me know if any cases besides the obituary in today's Times are occurring from a viral attack. If so, better call me back ASAP."

"You're onto something?"

"Depends on what you tell me."

"Will do."

CHAPTER FORTY-SEVEN

Tuesday, May 6, 3:00 P.M.

Four hours later, Jeff and Priya were meeting with Stan at the ME's office when Priya's cell rang. It was from one of her residents. She turned on her speaker.

"Hi Sarah, did you get the labs?"

"As Dr. Moss suspected, the packets of sweetener tested off the charts, and the cups were also positive for the virus. The lab is doing the characterization on the virus now, so at least we'll know what it looks like. How did it get into the sweetener?"

"That's what we have to find out. Speak later."

"If the sweetener was the cause in both Maryland and here, then there's only one way that could have happened."

Stan realized what Jeff was saying. "You mean a deliberate attempt to cause another pandemic."

"That's how I see it."

"So you're talking mass murder. I'm afraid this is way over our pay grade. I'll get DePalma on the phone. If we have a maniac walking around the streets of New York, we need the NYPD on this."

CHAPTER FORTY-EIGHT

Tuesday, May 6

Li Zhou received the news from Nick Robinson, the Managing Editor at the Journal's New York office. "Sure sounds like you're on to something. Cases are starting to crowd the Coroner's Office and filling up the ERs. How did you know?"

"I have it from a reliable source that this is a bioterrorist plot being spread from a Chinese Agent, a General Han and head of the Wuhan Institute of Virology."

"Wait, are you saying there may be a bioterrorist on the streets of this city?"

"That's exactly what I'm saying. Something about not approving the drug from Lexington Bio, and this is a warning to have it approved, or there will be a full pandemic."

"Listen, Li, that's quite an accusation you are making against a Chinese General and head of the Institute. I'm going to need a second source to confirm this; otherwise, we can't run it. Do you have a second source?"

"The source is someone within the Institute."

"And when you spoke to him, he was certain of this?"

"I never spoke to him. Someone I spoke to had spoken to him. That's how I know about this."

"And do you have the name of the original source?"

"Nick, I can't give you that information."

"Then all we have is hearsay. It's too big a story for the Journal to make such serious charges without named sources. If you come up with something more, let me know immediately, and we'll front page it."

"Well, can you at least mention it to someone who can look into it?"

"Li, let me think about it." Nick scribbled '*Call NYPD?*' on his pad. "But get that confirmation."

Li was disappointed. There was nothing else that she could do. She knew Nick was right about a second source, especially when getting involved with such an accusation against a major Chinese official, but there would be no second source, and she could not give up Jiang's name. It was a dead end. An old quote she learned at school came through her mind. Something about:

> *For want of a nail, a shoe was lost*
> *For want of a shoe, a horse was lost*
> *For want of a horse, a kingdom was lost.*

Li hung up the phone. She needed another nail. All she could do now was hope for Chen's safety.

CHAPTER FORTY-NINE

Tuesday, May 6

It had been four days since Chen was arrested in Wulajie and transported to the Hunan Institute. Security police had taken him through a long, narrow, poorly lit hallway that smelled of mold and brought him handcuffed into a small windowless cell. The room was cold and bare. Whatever paint remained on the degrading walls was a depressing gray. Two old wooden chairs were set in the middle of the space above, which was a dull overhead light that swung on a rusty chain whenever the door was opened or closed. Chen understood his fate. He would be brought to General Han to complete the antidote, confirming the destruction of Thanatos. From there, the future would unfold exactly as Han had planned. Once he had the antidote, his bioterror program would allow China to threaten the world. The nations would have a simple choice: either accept death or bow to China's demands. The General was right. The road to conquest was no longer missiles and bombs but an invisible force that could overwhelm the human condition.

Chen also had to make a choice. Either agree to cooperate, be forced to cooperate, or prepare to die. Was this his fate? Was this what was being asked of him? He saw no easy answer. Any choice would bring the world to its knees. And did his death matter? Would enough experiments be capable of reproducing what he had begun? What did the gods want? Was this his mingyun, his destiny?

CHAPTER FIFTY

Tuesday, May 6

The eyes in the ME's office were on Li Zhou of the *Wall Street Journal* reporting from China.

"I am here outside the Wuhan Institute. The scene is chaotic. Our sources suggest that severe measures are being undertaken to determine the cause of the leak. As previously, strict measures have been issued to prevent further spread of the disease both inside and outside the Institute. The Security Police had sealed off the Institute with reported deaths now up to eleven workers. The days of lockdown are back in an attempt to limit its spread. Reports now indicate that outside the Institute, twenty-two cases have been diagnosed, all resulting in death. There have been two new cases reported in the last twenty-four hours. Officials, aware of the past protests by Chinese citizens, have emphasized that the orders of containment and disruption of daily life would last for only forty-eight hours. Chinese leaders learned with COVID-19 that there are limits to what the people will accept, even in a country that disregards individual rights."

CHAPTER FIFTY-ONE

Tuesday, May 6, New York, 4:30 P.M.

It didn't take long for Chief of Detectives Anthony DePalma to arrive at the ME's offices when he heard the word bioterror. DePalma had been chief for the past eight years. He was not interested in looking for the top spot of chief of police—he didn't need the politics. He was the oldest of three brothers, all of whom, like their father and uncle before, had joined New York's finest and worked their way up the ranks. An ex-marine, DePalma was a veteran officer, popular with the men he commanded, with a reputation as a demanding but effective leader, a no-nonsense law enforcement professional. He worked the twenty-four-seven stressed hours with the calmest exterior and had overseen many of the city's high-profile murder cases. He had a slightly prognathic jaw that suggested respect and a full head of black hair still worn in a military crew cut. He kept his six foot, two hundred and ten pounds in trim condition. He spoke softly, a man of few words, but when heard, conveyed an air of authority.

Jeff introduced DePalma to Priya, who updated him on the results of their investigation of the two New York attorneys. "What we think happened is that the symptoms appeared circa one to two days following the ingestion of a sweetener they added to their coffee. They both had lunch from the same deli in midtown. Within forty-eight hours, they complained of symptoms and were taken to the hospital. Each died within twenty-four hours. We believe the same scenario occurred with the two FDA agents. In those cases, it appears that the contact occurred while they were at an FDA meeting with the head of the department where they had coffee and sweetener."

Jeff added the missing thought, "Except the department chief, Dr. Fred Kosent, did not have the sweetener, and the others did. Which suggests.."

Priya finished the thought, "That the sweetener contained something besides sweetener, as at the deli in Manhattan. We tested the sweetener packets; they tested highly positive for the virus. This was intentional."

DePalma thought for a moment. "And motive? Blackmail? Ransom money? Holding the world hostage?"

Jeff responded, "Unknown."

DePalma cut in. "But if intentional, who would have access to the virus?"

Priya answered. "The largest cache of viruses is found in China, at the Hunan Institute of Virology."

DePalma continued. "So you're suggesting that China may be involved? Perhaps the name Red Mutation is spot on. But does that mean that they have agents responsible for planting the virus here?"

Jeff offered, "Possibly, and placing the blame on the United States."

DePalma was skeptical. "Or a rogue group working independently?"

Jeff answered. "Domestic terrorism? Also possible, but there have been no warnings, no demands, and no recognition by any group. And how would they get their hands on something like that?"

DePalma made a note. "Then that's what we need to find out. How many dead thus far?"

Jeff replied. "Two confirmed by autopsy and lab results, in addition to the two FDA examiners in China. Five from a book group at a local library are having autopsies done at this time. We suspect they are of the same viral origin. We have checked on their contacts. Many of them are already in ERs, and for anyone exposed, we have tried to enforce strict lockdowns. China has done its part. Lockdown has kept new cases to a minimum. I hope we can minimize this also."

"So who's behind it?"

DePalma's cell interrupted the discussion. "Yes, Darlene, when? Really? Okay, that could be helpful." DePalma closed the call.

"We just received an interesting piece of information from Nick Robinson, Managing Editor at the *Wall Street Journal*. One of his reporters has a secondary source that suggests this is a bioterror incident, but there's no confirmation, and the source remains unnamed. The reporter claims that the person behind this bioterror plot is a major figure in China and that the outbreaks here are a warning as to what could happen if the FDA does not approve a certain drug.

Nick won't print it because of a lack of confirmation, but we should know that someone in our city may be threatening us to approve a drug or else there will be a pandemic."

It was Galvin who stated what the others were thinking. "Is this possible?"

"Well, we're about to find out." DePalma looked at Jeff. "Jeff, I'm going to need you to lead the investigation from our end, and I'll contact the FBI and Homeland Security. We'll need all the help we can get."

Stan looked at her. "Priya, you have more experience with viral pandemics than any of us, so you should really be running point on this from the transmission end. What will you need?"

Priya thought for a moment. "If this individual has the ability to spread the virus, then we need to stop him immediately. This is more lethal than anything we've seen, and it doesn't look like our immune systems can put up a defense. All we can hope for is our old methods of quarantine and trying to find out who has been intentionally spreading it. Without a vaccine, a lot of people are going to die."

"I'll tell you this," replied Stan, "the idea of having our FDA agents involved in this gives cover to whoever is responsible for spreading it."

Jeff nodded. "And very effective, I must admit. The US accounts for over half the drug sales in the world, and our FDA agents travel throughout the world certifying laboratories."

It was Priya who responded. "Does that suggest that a single individual could be the perpetrator?"

Jeff nodded. "Based on what Chief DePalma said, it certainly is possible."

DePalma made another note. "So, explain this payback idea for not approving a drug. Can we check what drug wasn't approved? "

Priya nodded. "I'll speak to Kosent at FDA."

"And Priya, how do we defend ourselves if this individual can't be stopped?"

Priya nodded. "Without an antidote, we have nothing. All we can do is inform every hospital, physician, and healthcare worker in every city and state as to what to look for and to report anything unusual to a command center at the CDC. That means cooperation on the state and federal levels, same scenario as COVID-19, but this time we're going to need an immediate response."

It was Stan Galvin who gave the signal. "I'll put a call into my contacts at the administration. Let's see how they can help. Something needs to be done before the deaths start filling the coroner's corridors."

Stan paused before turning to Priya. "Anything we've left out?"

"Yes, a meeting to coordinate. How about tonight at 7:00? Send out invites to whomever we think should be on that call. I don't know how long a containment strategy can be effective if this starts spreading." She paused before continuing: "I was just thinking of something Churchill said some seventy-five years ago. "Plagues prepared and deliberately launched upon man are being pursued in laboratories to poison not only armies but whole populations—such is how military science is advancing." Priya pursed her lips in fear. "I guess we've advanced."

CHAPTER FIFTY-TWO

Tuesday, May 6 Hunan

Hours had gone by when Chen was startled by the sharp metal sound of a door being unlocked. An officer of Chinese Security, followed by two security agents, entered. His name was Colonel Hu Ming, and Chen realized he was not one to be taken lightly. He was short and stocky, with a face so scarred that it looked like it went through fifteen rounds with the top middle weight boxer. Ming looked at Chen, hunched over in one of the chairs.

"So, you're the scientist who will be helping us fight this virus?"

Chen looked up. "Actually, I will not be helping you."

Ming smiled as if pleased that Chen would not cooperate.

"I am so sorry to hear that. I know that General Han was looking forward to working with you. I'm sure the General had planned for such a contingency, but if I were you, I would strongly rethink your position. I've been known to be quite successful in having people change their positions.

* * *

Colonel Ming was in his office when there was a knock on the door.

"Ah, and you must be Doctor Jiang. I understand you're an old friend of Chen's. Well, he and I are just getting acquainted with each other. He was telling me that he preferred not to cooperate on General Han's project. I suggested that if he chooses to begin, it will save me a great deal of effort and him a great deal of discomfort."

Jiang looked at Ming. "What are you going to do with him?"

"If he chooses not to cooperate, we will use a little persuasion. Probably place him into residential surveillance for a few days; that should change his mind."

Jiang was surprised. "You're talking about enforced disappearance."

"So you know how we help our friends cooperate. We'll be easy on him, at least for the first few days. When he's ready to help, I will call you, and you can get him set up in the lab. In the meantime, I don't think you're needed here any longer. Why don't you go home for a few days? We'll let him look around for a while, and if he insists on not helping, we will begin our introduction."

Ming went over to the desk and wrote a note. "Here, this will notify security that you are allowed access to the facility. The place is sealed off. No one gets in or out without my authorization. The pass will get you through."

"Listen, colonel, before you send him to surveillance, let me speak to him. General Han needs his help, and I know him. Perhaps he will listen to me if he still refuses to help."

Ming looked intently at Jiang. "Fine, if after a few days, I still need you, I will call you in. But if you can't get his cooperation, I will."

* * *

When Jiang had left, Ming made a call that was routed through a Chinese State Security Service. Han Shi felt the vibration as he crossed Van Ness in downtown San Francisco.

"Han."

"General, it's Ming. I just met with Dr. Chu."

"Is he in the lab?"

"Yes, sir. He's being shown where everything is."

"Good. And Jiang Fang?"

"I believe he's going home for the night. He looks pretty tired. But we do have a small problem. Dr. Chu has chosen not to cooperate."

Han bit his lip as his eyes looked up toward the heavens, not in prayer but more like making a decision. He had hoped this would not be the case.

"Then do what you have to do. But remember, I need him working."

"Yes, sir. In a few days, he'll be begging to help us."

CHAPTER FIFTY-THREE

Tuesday, May 6, 5:45 P.M.

Stan Galvin called the two physicians that he had trained with and who had positions that could be of help. James Ryan at CDC and Tom Crantz in the administration. Ryan was an Associate Director at CDC, and Stan spoke right to the point.

"Hey Jim, do you have confirmation on the virus?"

"Just got it. I'm afraid we concur. There's a lot of concern here."

"Here, too. It seems that Hunan has it under control, and we believe that we have those in New York stabilized, but it's a killer. And what's worse, it may have been done purposely."

"By whom?"

"Not sure. We've already made NYPD and the FBI aware, and Priya wants a meeting of everyone involved to start coordinating a national response. We're going to need your help and the administration's."

Ryan tapped his pen on his desk. "Fine, I'll speak to Tom Crantz. He has to get the President on board. And Stan, the press has already been calling. They smell something's up. Everyone wants something on what they're all calling The Red Mutation."

"Yeah, here too."

* * *

Ryan's call to Tom Crantz followed. Crantz was a classmate of Ryan's at Harvard's Med School and, like the others, went into public health. After being stationed in DC for a number of years, he rose through the ranks with hard work and smart decisions and was chosen to head the Department of Health and Human Services.

"Tom, we need your help."

"The virus?"

"Yeah, it's here."

"I know, and we've been told to keep a low profile on it. We need a coordinated effort from the top, which means the CDC and the President. I hear this is much more virulent than the COVID-19."

"You got that right. Stan already has evidence in the morgue, and the press is getting a hold of it as we speak. Priya Majmadur wants to have a meeting of essential personnel to coordinate. And you're right about the President. We're going to need his help if we want to avoid another COVID-19."

"Okay, I'll call Will Porter, his Chief of Staff, and let him know. Let's see if the President will take a meeting."

"Good. And we're having a conference call at seven this evening."

"I should be able to make it. Send me an invite, and I'll see if I can get Porter to join us."

* * *

Tuesday, May 6, 7:00 P.M.

The Zoom meeting began as scheduled. Priya opened the conversation. "Thank you all for participating. Our concern at this time is that the cases we've seen here in New York and those at the FDA may be part of a Bioterror plot. We can't be certain, and the information at this time is incomplete, but if there is someone out there capable of planting this virus, then we must be prepared for a potential catastrophe. The Chinese have informed us that although they kept the infection to a minimum, those who were infected died. Maybe we've finally learned that once it's here, it just doesn't go away."

"Is that how the rest of the world feels?" Stan asked.

Ryan responded, "They are already working on the problem. The Netherlands has already announced a plan to incorporate a full lockdown should the virus be transmitted. France is tightening rules, and London is prepared to declare a "major incident" should another pandemic occur. Tomorrow, the European Health Commission will meet to begin to review the mandatory preventive steps learned from COVID-19."

"And Asia?"

"They're already stepping up preventive measures such as airport temperature screening and notification requirements by doctors to report patients with symptoms to the authorities. Singapore, Taiwan, and South Korea have already set up quarantine task forces, as has India and Pakistan. But so far, no new cases have been reported."

"Thanks, Tom, good to know." Priya checked her laptop. "We have Fred Kosent from the FDA on the call.

"Didn't think we'd speak again so soon."

Priya explained to the others that she and Jeff visited the FDA that morning. She continued. "Fred, we're going to need vaccines or some therapeutic to stop this. That means we'll need help from government and private industry working on this, and you have connections to both."

"My staff has already arranged for an eight-thirty conference call this evening with the NIH and CEOs from the biotech firms that worked on the last round of vaccines."

"Fred, what about a report that the cases we are seeing may have purposely been transmitted because a drug wasn't approved."

"I heard something about it. I already have someone checking into it."

"Thanks."

"May I interrupt? This is Will Porter, the President's Chief of Staff. The President has just called for an emergency national TV and radio broadcast this evening at 9:00 P.M."

Priya was surprised. "Really, what's he going to say?"

"We're working on the script now. We know he's going into a preventive mode to inform the public but to be honest, we never know what he's going to say."

"What's he going to prevent?"

"The Media from blasting fake news. So, he wants his message carried by all the networks. He is mad as hell with all this talk about a plague that will destroy the world. He's getting calls from his wealthy backers wanting to know what's going on. He's telling them there's nothing to be concerned about, that the reports they are receiving are overstating the situation."

Priya was amazed. "What about his medical advisers? Surely, they're telling him about the potential severity."

Porter gave a critical laugh. "You wish. His doctors are afraid to tell him that his high school science education does not qualify him to give medical guidance to the 350 million people in this country. He insists that the media that complained of needing more back in 2020 were wrong, and he doesn't want anyone in the administration to discuss anything about the virus but himself. It could disrupt the economy, which he believes is essential for reelection. And it's not just the virus. He doesn't want anyone to say anything about climate change, wildfires, flooding, heat waves and storms. He gave an order that the only discussion with the media is to be limited to immigration and the economy. To be honest, I believe there would have to be a lot of bodies piling up before he would believe this virus will be a problem."

At that moment, Jeff felt his cell vibrate, and he checked the incoming message: "All one hundred and fifty residents in a nursing home have died in San Francisco. The cause is unknown, though there's concern it's of viral origin."

Soon, others had the same message across their cells. When Priya read hers, she realized this viral invasion may have just begun.

"My friends. I think all of you have read the message that just came across the screen. I have the feeling that unless we find an effective therapy, the only way that this virus can be stopped is if it runs out of humans to infect."

It was Stan who gave the final announcement. "Just got word from our coroner. Another two bodies were brought in for autopsy. Same symptoms as the others."

CHAPTER FIFTY-FOUR

Tuesday, May 6, 9:00 P.M.

Stan's office was crowded, with all eyes glued to the television awaiting the president's speech. The airwaves that had been covering the tragedy in San Francisco and the new report of cases in New York now quickly switched to the White House. The cameras focused on the President seated behind his desk in the Oval Office, wearing his tailored blue serge suit with a power red tie. He had his prepared script on the teleprompter before him.

"I hope all of you had a beautiful day. Here in Washington, the cherry blossoms were in full view, and I am looking forward to spending the weekend out on the golf course.

"I am here to discuss with you the media filling our airways with information that is false and purposely being vented in an attempt to destroy the incredible record of economic growth and prosperity in our country. Never before have so many Americans held jobs; it really is amazing, and such high wages, especially for our wonderful citizens of color. But now, in an attempt to turn your attention from our incredible record of achievement, the media is blasting headlines and airwaves with unsubstantiated stories of a new pandemic, a new virus, what they call The Big One, that will make COVID-19 seem like a sneeze. They even gave this new virus a name, Thanatos, the Greek god of death.

"Well, as your elected leader, I am here to tell you it's never going to happen. Why the World Health Organization just released a statement that read, *"There is limited information to determine the overall risk of this reported cluster of illness of unknown etiology, and that it does not recommend any specific measures*

for travelers and advises against the application of any passenger or trade restrictions
based on the current information available on this event."

He looked away from the monitor and, directing his attention to the cameras, went off script. "And that is from the World Health Organization, such an important group of dedicated people who the *New York Times* and other news outlets with an anti-American agenda accused me of refusing to fund. Again, false news. The fact is, I specifically decreased our WHO funding to ensure that other nations would step up and pay their fair share. And indeed, just as I predicted, that is what happened. No one is a bigger advocate for the WHO than me, and I am pleased to have the situation under control. So go out, enjoy the weekend, enjoy your prosperity, spend your money at the malls and your local stores, for I can assure you, nothing will ever harm you, not while I'm around."

The television then switched to a reporter interviewing Dr. Gregorius Faricci, Director of the Institute of Allergies and Diseases. "Do you agree that there is no need for concern about this new, unidentified virus?"

Dr. Faricci responded. "Based on the new reports from the nursing home in San Francisco and the cases in New York, I would say there is plenty of concern. While the cause has not yet been confirmed, I will tell you that the symptoms and immediate death surely must raise the flag of fear for all of us. So let me say, while it is impossible to predict how this new virus will play out, based on preliminary studies of its virulence, this virus could be on track to be the deadliest this world has ever encountered."

The interviewer persisted: "But after the COVID-19 pandemic, aren't we more prepared than ever to meet this outbreak?"

"Unfortunately, if anything, we are less prepared now than we were for COVID-19, and you saw what that outcome was."

At that point, the President, who was standing nearby, rushed over to the interviewer and pushed Faricci away from the microphone, which caused him to stumble backward to the floor.

"What did he say, the bum? He doesn't know what he's talking about. There's nothing to prepare for. These guys are always thinking doomsday. That report of some kind of bug in that nursing home hasn't been confirmed. If anything, it has more to do with the food they served. And the cases in New York, it's false news. Ever been into those hospitals? The place is filthy. It's a wonder anyone who goes in comes out alive." He turned to Faricci who was on the floor, "Get a life."

Stan muted the television. "Well, you heard what the plan is, there is none, and you heard what the director of the Institute of Allergies and Diseases had to say, poor guy, that there has been no further preparation for an outbreak since the last crisis."

"Damn it." It was Priya. "Someone has to take this seriously. I don't care what the President thinks. We can't sit here while people are dying." She paused and lowered her tone. " Ten years ago, we had a President's Task Force to deal with COVID-19. We only met once, but it included our top scientists. The time has come to organize a new one. The past administrations already cut most of the funding for infectious diseases, believing that COVID-19 was a fluke and never could happen again. Well, personally, I couldn't give a damn what the president thinks." She turned toward Stan, "And we have to find out who the psycho is that's behind all this."

"We'll get right on it." It was DePalma. "Jeff, I'm assigning someone from the detective squad to help you."

"Who were you thinking of?"

"McDougal, young, capable and one of the smartest to have earned his detective badge in a long time."

"Fine, send him over, and we'll start him right away."

Priya made a note. "Great, and I'll start getting some truth out there by giving Audrey Martinez at the Times the real story, and that will include an announcement of a new Task Force meeting."

Jeff was surprised at the strength of her declaration. "When?"

"Today's Tuesday. We'll call it for Friday morning. That should give time for those who wish to attend to make arrangements, and the others can do it virtually. My staff will get the invites out immediately."

"Is the President invited?"

"For what reason? You heard his response."

"Priya, you better be careful. You're about to go up against the president of the United States."

"Damn right, I am."

CHAPTER FIFTY-FIVE

Wednesday, May 7, 6:00 A.M.

When America awakened, they were greeted with headlines on every major newspaper:

> *New York Daily News*: "Prez says Live It Up while Death Hits the City Streets."
>
> *Washington Post*: "New Killer Virus Arrives in US"
>
> *LA Times*: "Virus at our doorsteps. Hundreds Dead in San Fran Nursing Home."
>
> *New York Times*: Virulent Virus Spreading on both Coasts. Emergency meeting of a new Pandemic Task Force. Scientists, Politicians and First Responders scheduled to meet in New York."

* * *

The President, as usual, began his morning with a cup of black coffee while watching the news on his favorite channel. As he waited to hear the poll numbers from his speech, he saw an interview with reporter Audrey Martinez on CNN:

"In spite of the President's suggestion Tuesday night to the nation to spend the day at the mall, one of the top epidemiologists in the country, Dr. Priya Majmadur, warned the nation that they should begin to plan, if it becomes necessary, to stay at home or wear a double mask and gloves. We have no idea what we are up against, but it's a killer." On Friday, Dr. Majmadur will lead a panel of experts and politicians in an attempt to organize a response to the new viral threat. The conference will be held at the New York School of Medicine. At last count, including the San Francisco Nursing Home, almost two hundred deaths have been reported in the US. When asked why she was calling for the meeting, she responded: "This time, we will be prepared."

* * *

The response from the President to the interview was short and predictable: "Who let this information out? I didn't authorize this meeting. Find out who did and when you do, they're fired! And who is this Priya Majmadur?"

It only took a few hours for Priya to receive a message short and to the point:

The President wants to know who this Priya Majmadur is, who organized the President's Task Force without his clearance. He wants to see you before you have that meeting. You are to report to the White House Thursday at 4:00 P.M., and he's in a fury. I'll meet you there. Tom Krantz

CHAPTER FIFTY-SIX

Wednesday, May 7, 11:00 A.M.

Tresh Jennine slept late following a long first cast read-through of the script that lasted late into the night. It was the first time that she could sleep without the worry of preparing for an audition. She heard the phone, turned over to find the time and took the call. It was eleven in the morning. What a treat. She didn't even bother to read who was calling and figured it could only be one person. She gave a sleepy hello. "Mom, is that you? I've been trying to reach you guys."

"Hello, is this Tresh."

Tresh did not recognize the voice.

"Yes, this is Tresh."

"This is Dr. Julio Perez. I was wondering if I can speak to you about Robert and Fran Jennine. Your name was listed as a contact should there be a medical problem."

Tresh sat up, wiped away the webs from her eyes, and answered with concern in her voice. "Is there a problem?"

"That's what I wanted to discuss with you."

Tresh's voice began to quiver, "What do you mean, is something wrong? I spoke to them two days ago, and my mom said they were tired and going to bed early. They assured me they were fine."

"I see."

"I tried calling them, but there's been no answer."

"I'm afraid I have bad news."

"What do you mean? What's wrong?"

This was the part of his work that Julio had the most difficulty dealing with. Training to be a physician is based on learning the science of medicine, but the emotional requisites, the empathy needed to appreciate the art of medicine is a human factor that cannot be taught. You enter your training with a certain set of emotional tools based on the kind of individual you are, how you were raised, and what impacted your young life. But, the physician lacks the training to break the news of sudden death. In the end, you respond with the humanity within you.

"Your parents became ill on Monday."

"Ill? With what? I just saw them on Saturday; they were fine."

"A viral infection."

"A virus? I heard there was an outbreak in China, but the President just said there was nothing to worry about. Well, how are my parents? When can I see them?"

Julio waited, trying to be as gentle as he could with the finality of his message.

"I'm afraid your parents have passed away."

The cry of anguish at the other end of the phone would remain in Julio's mind for a lifetime.

"No, no, it's not true. I didn't know anything about it. No one told me."

Julio waited for the cries to diminish. Soon, another voice came to the phone.

"Hello? This is Karen Ash, Tresh's friend. What just happened?"

"I'm afraid that Tresh's parents passed away, and the ICU at the hospital left several messages but wasn't able to reach her. Would it be possible for you to bring Tresh to my office so we can speak?"

"Yes, of course."

Julio gave her the address, put down the phone, his hand shaking, and walked the corridor to the ME's office, where Stan, Jeff, Gogoli and Priya were speaking.

A tear was visible as he sat down.

Gogoli was the first to speak. "Julio, what happened?"

His voice could barely be heard. "I just told a young woman that both her parents had passed away from the virus, and she didn't even know they were ill. She's coming now for me to meet with her."

Priya put her hand on his shoulder. "We have all experienced this, and I fear that this is only the beginning. I would be glad to be with you when you meet her, but I think it best for you to do this yourself. I will tell you one thing: you need to protect yourself from the death around you. For me, I picture myself with a white light that covers my body as if a shield that allows me to maintain my role as healer and not be affected by the state of health of those I'm treating. You may wish to try that. You have a long and special career ahead of you, and you must learn to defend yourself. But if you need me, I can be with you."

Julio looked up at her, wiped his tears away, and stood. "No, I can do this myself, and thanks."

The others understood. They had all experienced it in their own lives as physicians. The stress doesn't only affect the family of the dead but also the provider, who treats their patient with all of their skills and hopes to help them heal. To those healthcare workers who invest so much of themselves into their patients, only to see them die takes a heavy toll on their psyche. If anything, what was learned during the COVID-19 crisis, where death haunted the halls of hospitals day after day, the stress on those providers must be appreciated and somehow dealt with. That is what Julio and all the others will have to deal with, and when you add that mental agony to the physical stress of working with death twelve hours straight, you wonder how much energy is left to prevent the mind and body from breaking down. Where does the healthcare team find the source of compassion and kindness when they have lost so much? That is the part that others don't appreciate.

CHAPTER FIFTY-SEVEN

Wednesday, May 7, Noon

"Dr. Perez?"

"Yes."

Julio stood as two young women entered his office.

"I'm Tresh, and this is my friend Karen." Tresh's face was moistened with tears, washed of makeup, eyes red, flush with emotion, and her long blonde hair hastily brushed. "Tresh, thank you for coming, and Karen, thank you for being a good friend. I know how difficult a time this must be."

"What happened?"

"Your parents were brought to the hospital Sunday night after your father called 911. They were both having symptoms of fatigue, which led to fever and difficulty in breathing. They were taken directly to ICU, but in spite of all their efforts, your mother fell into a coma and passed away yesterday. Before your father was put on a respirator, he kept asking how she was. Finally, they put him on a respirator, but his heart stopped in spite of all efforts to revive him. He was brought into surgery, but the virus had caused so much destruction to the heart's tissue that nothing could be done. He died last night. The doctors at ICU tried to reach you and left several messages but were unsuccessful."

Tresh tried to control her sobs. "He had a heart problem and was on medication. But it's my fault. I was in rehearsal and had my cell turned off. It's all my fault."

Karen put her arm around Tresh. Julio did not want her to blame herself. "It's not your fault. This was a terrible virus. There was nothing that could have been done."

"But I didn't even say goodbye. They were my biggest fans. You have to understand. I just received my first role on Broadway and . . ." She couldn't finish the sentence and took tissues from Julio's desk. "Can I see them?"

"Of course. I had to do an autopsy on them to determine the cause of death, and I will need you to identify them."

Julio picked up his phone and pressed a number. "Hi, this is Dr. Perez. I'm going to bring Tresh downstairs." He turned to Karen, "It's best if you wait in the lounge area."

Julio led Tresh down the stairs and handed her a gown, gloves and mask. The bodies had been covered with clean white sheets. Julio uncovered her mother's face first. She looked at her face.

"Yes, this is my mother, Fran Jennine."

It was difficult for Tresh to control her tears, and Julio stepped away, respecting her privacy. She spoke in a hushed voice. "Oh, Mom, I'm so sorry. I don't know what happened, and I ask you to forgive me for not being with you. At least you will be with Daddy. I will never forget you. Thank you for being my mom. I love you."

Julio waited until she finished and then recovered the sheet over her mother. He then guided her to another gurney and removed the sheet covering her father's face.

"Is this your father?"

"Yes." With that, the tears and cries exploded, echoing through the enclosed chamber.

"Oh, daddy." She bit her lip, trying to control the love, the sorrow, wiping her arm over her face, trying to stop the torrent from cascading to the floor. "Why? I am where I am because of you. You won't be there for me to thank you for everything you have done, all those years, sitting with me at the piano, singing while you played, you're teaching me about music and voice and theater. I will never forget you. Please take care of mommy. I love you."

Julio tried to shield himself with the light that Priya had suggested, but he couldn't help dropping a tear when he heard her final testament.

They walked upstairs and found Karen. Julio did his best to comfort her. He had her fill out several details for the death certificate.

"Can you tell me if your parents were with other people over the past week?"

She thought for a moment. "They were at my apartment on Saturday and then left to visit his sister Judy and Fred Smith, his cousin."

Julio recognized the name. "Fred Smith?"

She thought for a moment. "Yes, Fred is an attorney, and he passed away this week. Wait, are you saying there is a connection?"

"I'm afraid so. And your aunt, what was her name?"

"Judy Taggert."

"Taggert." Again, the name sounded familiar. "Do you have her contact number?"

Tresh went to her cell phone and gave it to Julio.

"Tresh, I will need to follow up on this. Thank you for your help. I am so sorry for your loss, and if there is anything I can ever do, please call me."

He watched as the two women walked out arm in arm, a scene he would soon be repeating many times on a daily basis.

Julio walked into the ME's office. "Seb, do you recognize the name Judy Taggert?"

Gogoli looked up. "Taggert? I did her autopsy this morning."

CHAPTER FIFTY-EIGHT

Wednesday, May 7, 9:00 A.M.

Detective Joe McDougal was wearing jeans, a tee shirt, sneakers, and a Yankees cap when he entered Jeff's ME office. "

"Jeff Moss, I'm Joe McDougal. I've been assigned to help you out on this viral situation."

Jeff eyed his new partner. *So much for first impressions.* "Great, we've got a lot of work to do."

McDougal was a tall, lanky kid with a genuine smile that showed his white teeth, a perfect accompaniment to his good nature. Orthodontics had worked. He was in his early thirties, single, graduated from St. John's University, where he was ROTC, played some basketball but was never a starter, and an honor student in software engineering. Following graduation, he spent two years in Afghanistan in Intelligence, completed his service obligation and then returned to the States to work in a tech startup for a year before realizing he didn't want to spend the rest of his life behind a desk. So he decided to do what his older brother was doing, keeping his city safe. After graduating from the police academy, he quickly rose through the ranks.

He accompanied Jeff to Maxwell's Coffee Shop. Miguel recognized Jeff. "Hey, you're the detective that was here before. What's up?"

Jeff told him that he was investigating a case and would like to see the video surveillance equipment.

"We'd like to check the security camera footage from the previous Friday."

"Sure, let's go in the back and take a look, but I'm not an expert at this."

They went into the office, and Miguel showed them the video equipment. "As I said, I'm not expert at this, and I gotta go up front and start preparing for lunch."

Jeff seemed surprised. "I'm not really up on all this new equipment."

"I should be able to help."

Jeff looked at McDougal as if his partnering had already paid off. McDougal sat down and replayed the output of the previous Friday.

"Always good to have a computer wiz around."

McDougal gave him that innocent smile. "Copy that. Before I entered the Academy, I was at a tech startup."

"Didn't suit you?"

"Guess not."

"What about the big dollars? Didn't you want to be another Gates?"

"I suppose it wasn't my thing. I always thought about having my own company, but my brother's a cop and the stories he told always excited me. So here I am."

McDougal began the playback from lunch hour Friday: "There, stop there." Jeff looked at the photocopies he made and pointed at one of the figures in the takeout line. "That's James Davenport, the lawyer. Wait, what just happened? Take a look at the guy in front of Davenport." McDougal replayed the scene in slow motion. "There, he comes to the counter, and that must be Carlos. He's about to take his order, but the guy walks away."

McDougal replays it again. "Not hungry? I mean, he waited online all that time, and when he finally gets to the counter, he doesn't want lunch?"

Again, Jeff pointed to the figure. "Take a look at what he does with his right hand."

McDougal studied the action frame by frame. "Is he wearing a glove? What's he doing with a glove on a beautiful spring day? Sure enough, looks like he's wearing a latex glove. Now what?" McDougal continues to forward the replay, studying each frame. "See that? The guy is removing something from his pocket and places it into the container of sweeteners on the counter."

"Sure seems like it. Wait, Joe, can you increase the close-up?"

McDougal made the adjustment. "There, what do you see?"

McDougal sharpened the focus as best he could. "No question looks like he's dropping two packets of sweetener into the basket. That means whoever took those packets was by chance."

Jeff smiled knowingly. "And I'll bet a year's pay that's not sweetener, that's virus, and you're right, the victims weren't targeted, it's all random. But where would he get it from? And how did he make it into a powder and place it into the same packets as the other sweeteners? Can you get a good picture of him?"

McDougal played the video from a second camera that viewed whoever was entering the shop. "Looks like the guy's pretty savvy. He has his hat covering his face, has his jacket collar up, looks to see where the cameras are, and keeps his back to it at all times."

McDougal switched back to the camera, viewing the counter area. "And when he approaches the counter, he pulls his hat over his face and keeps his head down. Sorry, Jeff, all we can do is approximate his size but no face. How big was Davenport?"

"The medical history said six two."

"Then this guy is bigger. What do you figure, six four?"

"Maybe more, and he's built like a bull. Can you get us a picture?"

"I can do better. These days, the standard equipment is pretty sophisticated. I can isolate the images and send them over the internet. Let me have your email, and I'll send you a copy."

"Wait! Check out what happens to the young lawyer, Davenport. Keep advancing the tape."

McDougal went frame by frame. "See that! When he's handed the bag containing his lunch order, he picks up the packets of sweetener, places it into the bag, and leaves. There's the proof you need."

"Yes, but who is the big guy?"

* * *

As they walked out, McDougal had a thoughtful look. "But you asked a great question. How did the perp get that packet, especially if it was filled with virus? Is he some kind of chemist? Does he have his own lab? Did he have someone make it for him? And where would he even find the virus?"

"Joe, you're asking all the right questions. See if you can get a list of every lab in the New York area that works with viruses."

Joe nodded. "Copy that."

As they walked down the avenue, Jeff felt his cell vibrate; it was Priya.

"Yeah, Priya, what do you have . . . Really, that refines our search. I'll check it out."

He turned to McDougal. "We may still have one more chance to ID this guy."

McDougal seemed surprised. "How's that?"

"That was Priya Majmadur. She's an epidemiologist overseeing this case. She just reported that the three coffees were specifically delivered to Dr. Kosent's office for the FDA meeting with his investigators. That means we're talking targeted murders."

"But what we just saw was a case of random targets."

"Yeah, but why the difference? Feel like taking a nice drive through the countryside?"

"Sure, I've got nothing on my plate. When?"

"Now."

"Now? Where we going?"

"A deli in Rockville, Maryland."

"That's a long way. Must have great sandwiches."

CHAPTER FIFTY-NINE

Thursday, May 8, 9:45 A.M., New York

As Jeff's 2028 Mazda pulled onto the New Jersey Turnpike, they heard the radio report about the investigation taking place regarding the West Coast nursing home.

McDougal looked up from working his computer. "What do you think? Same guy?"

"Possibly. I already put a call in to the San Francisco Police Department for the officer in charge of the investigation to get back to me with any information. Let's see what he comes up with."

It was 1:15 when Jeff pulled into the strip mall in Rockville, where Ben's Caterer's was located. The place was still busy with lunch orders as Jeff and McDougal entered. As they looked around, marking where the surveillance cameras were located, he heard someone speaking to him.

"I remember you. You're the cop that asked questions."

Jeff smiled. "Good memory. I have a few more questions. I need to look at your surveillance footage."

"That's something I can't help you with. Let me ask Ben, he's in the back."

They were ushered into the back and introduced to Ben, a short, dark-haired fellow with a touch of gray, of medium height, in his fifties and a pleasant smile.

"Anything in particular?"

"Yeah." Jeff checked his notes. "April 18, a Friday. What time do you deliver coffee to the FDA in the morning."

"FDA? Deliveries are at ten, noon with lunch and through the afternoon. Depends on who's ordering."

"What about Dr. Kosent?"

"Kosent, sure, that's at ten."

Ben's cell began to ring. "Hello, yes, hello, Mrs. Bellows . . . today at two? That's cutting it close, but I'll get it done. Same as last time. Lunch for fifteen. Of course."

When he ended the call, he turned to his guests. "Listen, I'm a little busy. Do you need me here, or can you do this yourself?"

McDougal answered. "Sure, I'll take care of it." They sat down, and McDougal searched the system. "Okay, Friday, April eighteenth, for an early delivery. Let's start at eight."

They went through it frame by frame, repeating it several times.

McDougal shook his head. "Sorry, I don't see anyone coming into the shop for coffee. What about the perimeter cameras facing the parking lot in the back?"

McDougal began at the 9:00 recordings. A handful of cars were already in the rear parking lot, including a white delivery van with Ben's Caterer's printed in red on its sides. At the nine-forty time period, a man is seen leaving the back of the building and carrying bags to the van. He leaves the rear panel doors open and walks back into the building.

"That's Hector, the fellow we just spoke to," Jeff observed. "Now, let's wait. If something is going to happen, it should be when he begins the delivery. Meanwhile, the food smells good back here. Want something?"

McDougal smiled. "Sure, a buttered roll and coffee, light, and a teaspoon of fresh sugar, no packets."

Jeff smiled and left as McDougal continued examining the screen.

It took five minutes before the young investigator shouted out: "Hey, Jeff. Better get in here. I found something."

Jeff returned with the order, "What's up?"

"Take a look at one of the cars in the rear parked several rows behind Ben's van. At the 9:45 mark, as soon as Hector returns to the building, someone gets out of a dark-colored Ford Escape and walks to the back of Ben's van. He looks around as if making sure he's not being seen and inspects the bags Hector just put in there."

Jeff pulls up a chair. "What about his face?"

"Nothing. He knew how to avoid recognition."

"Then what?"

"Watch!"

"Wow, that's him! The big guy."

McDougal nodded. "Exactly, and he's wearing gloves but no face ID. Anyway, after the guy checks the packages, he opens one of them, takes out something, puts something back into the same bag, and then leaves."

Jeff is reviewing the scene. "Yes, but then what."

McDougal speeds forward and stops at the 9:50 mark. "Hector returns to the van, closes the doors, gets into the driver's seat and drives away."

"Okay, let's slow this down. First, can you read the label on the package the guy is carrying?"

McDougal freezes the frame as the package is being placed into the van. "All the packages are the same, white with Ben's logo on it."

Jeff sits forward and stares at the screen. "Looks like some writing on the package. Can you check?"

McDougal begins to adjust the controls, magnifying the image and fine-tuning the focus.

"There, that's clear enough to read. FDA, Third Floor Conf."

"And what did he remove?"

"This should give us a good magnification." McDougal made some adjustments, and the removed contents can be clearly seen.

"Packets of sweetener. Same MO as in New York."

Jeff pulls up his chair. "That's him. Can you give us a picture of the guy?"

McDougal focuses on the individual. "Still can't get a facial visual. This guy sure doesn't want to be seen. All we see is some big guy wearing dark pants, a sweatshirt, and sneakers. He pulls the sweatshirt up to hide his face as he looks around. That's all we have before he returns to the car."

"Okay, see anything on the other rear camera?"

McDougal goes through the same exercise.

"It confirms the other camera, just a different view, Nothing new."

"But wait," Jeff places his finger near the screen. The driver appears to be following the van out. Can you get a plate number?"

"McDougal keeps turning dials, focusing the view. "Bingo, Virginia Plates, SJ3479. It's a rental."

"That's our man. I'll message DePalma. Find out who rented it."

"Let's ask one last question." McDougal followed Jeff into the store.

"Hector, at about 9:45 on that Friday morning, the video shows you delivering packages from your van. The package is marked FDA third floor, Conference. How many conference rooms are there on the third floor?"

"Only one, Dr. Kosent's."

"And what is usually in the package besides the cups of coffee?"

"Oh, spoons, napkins and some packets of sweetener."

"Hector, thanks. That's all we needed to know."

* * *

Two hours into the return trip, Jeff regarded his new companion. "You haven't said a word; what are you working on?"

"Following up on the New York State's Department of Health database of labs working with viruses. There are ninety-seven listed, but seventy-eight are clinical diagnostic labs that test blood or urine specimens for patients, such as Quest or Lab Corp. That leaves nineteen involved with viral research, but fourteen of those are companies that, since the COVID-19 threat passed, are no longer actively pursuing viral research. That leaves five institutions still involved: NYU, Columbia, Mount Sinai, Brookfield and New York Medical College, but only Brookfield's website indicates it's still working on viral research in one of its labs, a company called Lexington Bio. It's the only one with the highest clearance."

"What kind of viral research?"

"Not certain. The website said it was down for updates, and to be honest, I'm not sure what we're looking for. A mad scientist? A disgruntled worker? A rogue foreign agent? A terrorist-linked group?"

As Jeff drove along the New Jersey Turnpike, he thought about the same question. *What was he looking for?*

"Let's visit Lexington first thing in the morning and see what comes up." When there was no reply, he looked over at McDougal. He was fast asleep, his cap hiding his face.

Minutes later, Jeff's message buzzed, and he took a quick read. It was from Captain Joe Franco of the San Francisco Police: *Hey Jeff, got your note. Nothing yet on the nursing home case—will get back to you as soon as some info in.*

CHAPTER SIXTY

Thursday, Noon, May 8, Wuhan

Jiang was at home when he received the message from Colonel Ming: "He's all yours. You have forty-eight hours to change his mind, or I will do it for you. Forty-eight hours starting now." Jiang checked the time. It was noon. He rushed into the street, looking for a taxi. From out of the shadows, he heard his name called.

"Jiang Fang? Dr. Fang?"

Jiang turned to see a young woman approaching him.

"My name is Li Zhou, I'm a friend of Chen Chu. I was with him when he was arrested in Wulajie."

"What were you doing in Wulajie?"

"I was born there, and Chen's family lived next door to us. Now I'm a reporter for the *Wall Street Journal* and was following up on a story investigating Lexington Bio when the state security agents came after him."

Jiang was cautious. "I see. Well, how can I help you."

"He mentioned you were a friend, and I'm worried. I know what they do to make people change their minds, and I know he won't."

"What do you want me to do?"

"You go inside; that means you have access. If you can get Chen out, I have contacts that can help him get to the West. We've got to do something."

"I'm going to see him now."

Li handed Jiang her card. "My contact information is on here. Please let me know. If you can get him out of the Institute, my friends can get him out of the country."

Jiang studied Li's face, looking for something to help determine her authenticity.

"I'll think about it."

* * *

Jiang showed his pass to the head of security that surrounded the Institute and was led into a distant section of the building that he had never been to before. From its decayed appearance, he realized it must have been part of the original structure that had been out of use since the early days of the Communist Revolution and was now employed for a different purpose. The guards brought him to a thick steel door, partly rusty, that creaked when opened by security. As Jiang entered, a small dull light was switched on, and the door relocked. It took a minute for Jiang to adjust his eyes to realize he was in a room no more than the size of a closet with stone walls. As his pupils dilated, Jiang was able to make out he was in a small cell without a bed. There, on the cold stone floor, he saw the folded form of a body wrapped in a gray sheet. Jiang walked over and looked down. It was Chen. There was no movement. What had they done to him? He bent over and placed his hand on Chen's shoulder.

"Chen, can you hear me? It's Jiang." When there was no response, Jaing kneeled on the cold floor and felt for a pulse. At least there was life. Jiang softly repeated his call. Chen's body moved slightly. Jiang gently lifted Chen's head off the stones and called his name. This time, Chen opened his eyes and studied the face before him.

"Jiang, is that you?"

"Yes, Chen. You were sleeping. Do you have any water?"

Chen's eyes blinked as if trying to wake up. "Water? No, only at night."

"Let me see what I can do." Jiang walked over and knocked on the door. A guard opened it. "I need some water, now!"

The guard was not certain what to do, and Jiang repeated the command. "Water, now!"

Within minutes, he was brought a bottle of water. Jiang brought it into the cell and held Chen's head up as he sipped the liquid.

"What have they done to you?"

"Want me to cooperate. I'm forced to sleep on the floor, fed one small meal a day with water, and interrogated for hours with questions that have nothing to do with anything. They threatened that if I did not help them, they would charge me with furnishing Chinese state secrets to the FBI. They want the antidote, but I will not cooperate, and I couldn't if I wanted to. The only drug remaining is back at the Brookfield Institute with all my equipment. Nothing can be done here."

Jiang realized there was no use in arguing. "Listen, Chen, I met a young reporter from the *Wall Street Journal*. She says she knows you."

"Yes, her name is Li, she's a friend."

"She says she has contacts who can get you out of China and back to the States. Can we trust her?"

"Yes. But how can I get out of here? These guards are watching me constantly."

"Let me think about that. I'm going to need some time."

Jiang knocked on the locked door, and two young security guards entered.

"I want Dr. Chu to be given full meals, new clothes, and brought to my lab to begin his work. I am not pleased with how you have been treating him. He is an important scientist who is going to be helping us."

"But the colonel gave us orders."

"You did not understand the orders. Now do as I told you, or I will report your conduct to the colonel. If I do, he will not be happy. "

The two guards looked at each other.

"Now!"

"Yes, sir."

CHAPTER SIXTY-ONE

Thursday, 8:00 P.M., May 8, Wuhan

Jiang spent the remainder of the day walking aimlessly through an empty Zhongshan Park, trying to determine what to do. What was he to do? What could be done? Finally, he exited the park and walked the streets of Wuhan. As he placed his hand in his pocket, he felt Li's business card. He had to make a decision. Almost by force of habit, he looked around to see if he was being followed. He quickened his pace, making turns into side streets until he felt there was no one to hide from. He took out Li's card and sent a text message. Moments later, he received a reply. *Meet you in an hour.*

Again, being certain of not being followed, he walked quickly down JieFang Avenue to the DongBu Shopping Center. There, he entered a small, darkly lit café called Coffee Ba and took a seat at a rear table, ordered a Latte, and waited for Li. At nine o'clock, she arrived.

"Thanks for getting back to me. I've been busy."

Jiang seemed surprised. "Doing what?'"

"Making plans, just in case you can get him out."

"What kind of plans?"

"There's an economic conference in Frankfurt starting Saturday morning, that's the day after tomorrow. I told the Journal that I want to cover it and will need a photographer with me. They approved it. If you can get him out, I can get him on a Cathay Pacific flight to Frankfurt in the morning."

"What about documents?"

"I made arrangements. It will take a few more hours."

"And you understand what will happen if you and Chen are caught. The Secret Police will show no mercy."

"I know."

"You would be taking a huge risk. Once they find out that Chen is out, they will seal the borders."

Li looked at Jiang closely. "I understand, but you would be taking an even greater risk. Everything you have accomplished would be in jeopardy."

"I suppose."

Li's upper lip moved over her lower lip. "There's one other problem."

"What's that?"

"It's a twenty-six-hour trip, which includes a ten-and-a-half-hour stopover in Hong Kong. I'm worried that we won't have enough time to get there before the Security Police start looking for him. Every security agent will have his picture, and every flight out of China will be checked. But it's not just in China. If Interpol is contacted, they'll issue a Red Notice that puts Chen on the fugitive list and is wanted for prosecution. That means law enforcement throughout the world has the right to arrest him if he arrives in their jurisdiction."

Jiang's face tightened as he thought for a long minute. "Perhaps there is a way. I've been given forty-eight hours to try and convince Chen to change his mind, or he will be handed over to the Secret Police."

Jiang looked at his watch. "That means we have about thirty-nine hours before they come for him, which is Saturday at noon. What time are you to arrive in Frankfurt?"

"Six, Saturday morning."

"That doesn't leave us much time for error, but if you can get him to your conference before noon, no alert would have gone out."

Li took a moment, trying to put it all together. "That could work, but how will you get him out?"

"'I'm not sure. What time does the flight leave?"

"Eleven thirty in the morning. I would need to get him to the airport by ten at the latest, and we would have to leave for the airport by nine."

"It's now nine. That gives us twelve hours. Give me an hour to try and figure this out. If I don't get back to you by then, assume nothing can be done."

"Okay."

"One more thing. If you get him to Frankfurt, what then?"

"I'm still working on that."

Jiang got up and shook Li's hand. "That's a big gamble to take for a news story. You're sure it's not more than that?"

She smiled.

"Then good luck." With that, Jiang walked out.

CHAPTER SIXTY-TWO

Thursday, 10:30 P.M., Wuhan

It took longer for Li to receive the message from Jiang than planned: *"Meet me midnight outside Banli De Express Hotel, 5344 Hanhuang Rd. I will be wearing a black hat and hopefully have Chen with me. When you see us cross the street, blink your lights three times if it's safe. If I'm by myself, then you'll know nothing could be done.*

Li's heart began to pound, and tears formed in her eyes as the promise of hope turned into the fear of reality: What if nothing could be done?

CHAPTER SIXTY-THREE

Thursday, 11:30 P.M., Wuhan

Jiang figured the best chance for him and Chen to make it out was just prior to the midnight change of security that surrounded the Institute. Inside, Jiang went to his lab and found Chen reading a book.

"I see they're taking better care of you."

"For the moment."

"That's why we've got to get you out of here."

"Listen, Jiang. You're my best friend, but there's no way they're going to let you take me out. Do you see the guards outside the door? If you're caught, you'll be severely punished. It's best you leave now and thank Li. Perhaps if I help General Han, he will someday release me."

"Chen, it's more important for you to get out than me. Now, let's not have an argument."

As the whistle blew, announcing the shift of guards, the door to the lab opened, and a man wearing a lab coat with Jiang's name written on it announced, "I have to leave."

As the man exited the building, he was stopped at the perimeter by a young corporal starting his shift.

The corporal looked at the lab coat: *"Dr. Jiang Fang."*

"That is correct."

"Papers!"

The security pass signed by Colonel Ming was handed over.

The young corporal examined the pass.

"Where's your photo?"

"That is my photo."

The guard focused his flashlight on the man's face. "This doesn't look like you."

"It's an old photo."

The guard looked at the pass. "Why would Colonel Ming give you a pass to leave? No one is to leave."

"Because I'm an important scientist here at the Institute. Are you questioning the colonel's authority?"

The young guard thought for a moment. "Stay right here; I need to find my commander."

"It's getting late, and I need to leave now."

"You stay right here. I just came on duty and was told no one is to leave."

"I must leave."

"You stay here, or I'll have you arrested."

It took fifteen minutes for the guard to return with his commander. The young guard looked around. "Sir, I don't know where he is. His name was Jiang Fang, and he was just here."

* * *

Twenty minutes later, Li saw a figure walking slowly out of the shadows toward her car. As it approached, the hotel lights revealed a dark-colored baseball cap. She flicked the headlights three times, and the figure waved, slowly making his way toward the car. Li realized that he was alone. Chen could not be freed.

Suddenly, Li saw the bright beams of a vehicle pull up behind her. In her rearview mirror, she saw several men in a van, the headlights almost blinding her. Her hands tightened on the steering wheel. As she looked in the rearview mirror, she saw a man in a suit getting out of the van. Moments later, there was a knock on Li's window and the man in the suit was motioning for her to lower it. They must have found out. She thought about driving away but realized it would be hopeless. There was no escape. She opened the window. "Yes, yes, sir," she managed to say.

The man looked at Li. "Mind moving your car forward? We need to move some heavy equipment into the hotel."

She almost choked. "Yes, sir. I'll be leaving now."

As the man returned to the van, Li's passenger door opened, and a figure slid onto the seat. It took a few moments before she calmed enough to look at the passenger sitting next to her. It wasn't Jiang.

"Who are you?"

The man removed his hat. Li stared at the man, trying to understand what was happening.

"Chen, it's you!"

"It's me."

"How?"

"Jiang made me switch places with him. He said it was more important for me to get out. I tried to stop him, but he refused to listen. He gave me one of his lab coats and gave me his security pass and papers.

"But?" She kept staring at him.

"Li, I think you better start driving."

She got on the highway and gave him a quick look. "Are you okay?"

"Yes, they just put me on a diet for a few days, but I'm fine. They've been giving me full meals since Jiang spoke to them."

"And Jiang?"

"He told me he could get out."

"How?"

"He said he'd figure it out."

"But Jiang is taking an awful chance. Won't they see that you are missing, and Jiang took your place?"

"I doubt it. They never really looked at me; just brought my meals into the room, and others removed it. They don't care whom they are guarding."

"Then when will they find out?"

"In about thirty hours when Colonel Ming returns and realizes there's been a switch. By the way, where are we going?"

"To friends outside the city where you'll be staying for the next few hours until I pick you up. They have your laptop. We have a flight to make first thing this morning, and I have to pick up documents for your new identity."

They rode on along the mostly empty highway in silence, the lights of the city melting away.

CHAPTER SIXTY-FOUR

Friday, 9:00 A.M., New York

It was morning when Jeff and McDougal met outside the Brookfield Institute on the Upper East Side of Manhattan. McDougal confirmed that he spoke to the four institutions that reported having been once involved with viral research. All said they no longer had labs running viral studies, and their scientists were now assigned to other projects. That left only the Brookfield Institute, who responded that they had one company working with viral research but with no recent activity. If they needed to know more they should speak to Doctor Geoffrey Ballan.

Jeff and McDougal entered the building and were directed to Dr. Ballan's office.

"The only group doing research here on viruses was a company called Lexington Bio. It was run by a brilliant researcher, Dr. Chen Chu."

Jeff was taking notes as Ballan spoke.

"And where do I find Dr. Chu?"

"I'm not sure. The project was financed by a Philip Steppler, and Chen has not been seen in several months."

"What were they working on?"

"On a molecule to enhance the body's ability to destroy the most pathogenic viruses."

"And was he successful?"

"Chen believed the molecule had the potential to destroy any virus, including any mutations of the original COVID-19."

"Even effective against the one transmitting now?"

"That is correct."

Jeff was surprised. "You mean a universal vaccine? What happened?"

"They completed their Phase 2 studies with dramatic results and went to the FDA to ask for immediate emergency authorization based on their limited Phase Two data without the need for further definitive clinical trials."

"And?"

"They were denied."

Jeff nodded. "Wow, sounds like it could have been the magic bullet."

"Perhaps, but Chen did not attend the FDA meeting. He had left before that. Some say that he went back to China. I haven't spoken to him since then, but the stock, which was riding high, has lost over ninety percent of its value."

"And no one knows where Chen is? Did he have any friends or family here?"

Ballan thought for a moment. "Actually, one of my former graduate students helped Chen with his business plan and they became friendly. The fellow's name was Channing, Tim Channing. Tim was very bright but decided research wasn't for him, left the program and went to law school. He's practicing here in New York at a large corporate firm. You might speak to him."

"And Steppler?"

Ballan sat back in his chair. "An interesting fellow. I met him at a social function, and he mentioned that he wanted to finance promising research. I hooked him up with Chen, and Steppler raised the needed funds. But after Chen left and Steppler's run-in with the FDA, I haven't seen or heard from him."

McDougal glanced at Jeff. "Run-in? What do you mean?"

Ballan continued. "It was reported that when the FDA refused to approve Lexington Bio's new drug, he stormed out of the meeting."

"Do the Chinese have anything to do with this?"

"Absolutely, they're the ones who gave the money to Lexington to continue their work on the antivirus."

That's all the information that Jeff and McDougal needed. They thanked Ballan and exited the building.

"What do you think?" McDougal asked.

"I think the Chinese need a Thanatos antidote and will do anything to get it."

McDougal nodded. "Agreed."

CHAPTER SIXTY-FIVE

Friday, 10:00 A.M.

Jeff and McDougal entered the law office of Stippling, Groton, Marcy and Minion and were ushered in to meet Tim Channing.

"Sure, I worked with Chen when he was at Brookfield. Good man. I saw him before the Lexington Bio FDA meeting. We met for coffee, and he told me he was leaving for home—back in China. His relationship with Steppler turned out poorly. The guy screwed him royally, giving him no ownership of any part of Lexington Bio for his own inventions. Basically, Steppler needed the money to finance the research and finally turned to some unsavory characters probably trying to launder their money. Chen did return to China, where he's teaching high school in his hometown."

Channing scrolled his cell and made a note on paper. "Here's his email. You should be able to contact him. I can't tell you where Steppler is, but he held an investment meeting in China organized by a James D'Arcy, an attorney here in New York. If you can get hold of him, you should be able to get a fuller understanding of what is happening. His office is only two blocks away."

* * *

Thursday, 11:00 A.M.

D'Arcy was reluctant to speak about his relationship with Steppler, citing attorney-client privileges protected him. That changed when Jeff threatened to mention his name to the media and his involvement. With that, D'Arcy agreed to speak under anonymity and explained how Phillip Steppler, an old classmate, came to him for help with financing and that he made an introduction.

"And what do the Chinese have to do with this?"

"They provided the financing. Four billion to take the original investor, a fellow named Rapolo, out of the picture."

Jeff whistled. "Four billion? They must have wanted that drug badly."

"Very badly. I arranged the transfer with the Chinese."

"Any idea with whom you were speaking."

"Yeah, a man named Han, a big wig in China. The guy's a general and head of the Wuhan Institute of Virology."

Jeff and McDougal looked at each other. "Did you ever meet him?"

"Sure did. In Shanghai. He introduced Steppler to the Chinese investors."

"Have you seen him recently?"

"Not since the China trip."

Jeff gave D'Arcy his card. "If you see him, give me a call. I'd love to have a talk with him."

"No problem."

"One more thing." It was McDougal. "Could you identify this General Han if you saw him?"

"That's an easy one. Big guy with a scar running down the left side of his face as big as a canal."

When they left D'Arcy's office, McDougal looked at Jeff.

"What do you think?"

"I think we've received a lot of info, and we better sort this out."

CHAPTER SIXTY-SIX

Friday, Noon, ME's Office

"Where do we find a giant with a big scar?" McDougal was going through the day's interviews at the office when Jeff received a message from the San Francisco Police Department: "Sending videos should be of interest."

Jeff clicked on the link and studied the images from the San Francisco nursing home.

"Hey, McDougal, "Tell me what you see."

McDougal looked at the attachment. "Okay, a big guy is walking into a room. A woman appears to be sleeping in her bed. He comes over, dressed like a doctor, takes out a needle and injects it into the patient's arm, then walks out."

"But you can't see his face. It's the same problem. Physically, the guy looks the same as in the security tapes we've reviewed, but in each case, we can't get a make on his face."

"No, but let's keep looking." McDougal advances through the images, another room, another patient. "Still can't see his face."

He continues his replay. "Okay, now he's in another room, but wait." McDougal examines the scene. "Jeff, take a look. As he's about to inject the patient, she looks up at him and screams, reaches up and pulls the guy's mask off. He quickly puts it back on, but I see him clearly. Look at the guy's face. The left side has a deep scar running through it. Never saw anything like this. Looks like he was hit with a bayonet. What was the name D'Arcy gave us?"

Jeff checked his notes. "Han Shi."

"And what was the name that the reporter from the *Wall Street Journal* gave to her editor?"

Jeff went through his notes again. "A General Han, a bigwig in the Chinese government."

"Jeff, we've got our man."

"I think you're right. Send this over to Chief DePalma. Tell him this is our guy. If he's got a scar that big, someone in this country will recognize him."

"What next?"

"I've got to walk over to the Medical Center. I'm already late for Priya's meeting with the President's Council, and we've got to bring her up-to-date."

CHAPTER SIXTY-SEVEN

New York, Friday, Noon, May 9

The President's Task Force was already in session when Jeff found his seat next to Gogoli. "Can't believe they all came."

Gogoli smiled. "The media is keeping them up-to-date. They don't want a repeat performance. The agony of COVID-19 is still fresh."

Jeff looked at the filled chairs around the large conference table, reading the place cards in front of the seated members: Priya Majmadur, M.D., Ph.D.; Fred Kosent, M.D., FDA; Stan Galvin, M.D., Ph.D., Chief Medical Examiner City of New York; Tom Crantz, M.D., Secretary of Health; James Ryan, M.D., Ph.D., CDC; Omar Sheila, Ph.D., Homeland Security; Jason Furman, M.D., Ph.D., and other notables.

Priya was in the midst of speaking. "The fact is, after reviewing the data from colleagues in Hunan, in San Francisco and here in New York, we realize we are encountering a virus that is acting and structured differently than those we have met before. Our models show that once this virus starts it spread, it will double every second day. That means within a week, it would be the dominant variant, and with the rare exception, once you have the virus, you die. Unless we can disarm this mutant, its logarithmic transmission could result in the loss of 80 percent of the world's population within three months.

An undertone rippled through the room as Priya continued. "And even if we find the antidote, please remember that some thirty percent of our population may choose not to receive it. So, what do we know about Thanatos? Our bioassays confirm that the virus has a unique feature. What had been a well-established COVID-19 sequence of the furin cleavage has now undergone a significant change. Using RNA sequencing and computer models of the surface spike protein, we have determined the molecular interactions occur when the spike grabs onto a cell-surface protein called ACE2, the virus's gateway into the cell. Once the virus attaches to the cell-surface protein, it doesn't let go, regardless of all the antibodies and vaccines it has been tested against."

What Priya did not report was that the virus may have been genetically engineered, nor did she mention that an unidentified individual or individuals were spreading it. In other words, there was no mention that terrorism had come home.

"Are you talking in terms of global extinction?"

"To some degree, Dr. Furman, I fear so."

Dr. Jason Furman was a Professor of Genetic Biologics and Bioengineering at UCLA. "Do we know how such a mutation occurred? Was this simply by natural selection, that is, by random, or genetic recombination or even laboratory insertion?"

Priya responded, "At this point, we do not have that information."

"One last question for Dr. Kosent." Again, it came from Dr. Furman. "Before we go home and tell our families that the world is about to end, are you saying that there is no drug that the FDA is aware of that can fight this thing? I mean, you must be aware of hundreds of drugs that never received approval for one reason or another. If the problem is with the mutation of the spike protein was there not one of them that attacks the remainder of the virus? Perhaps that way, the treatments could work even as the virus mutates."

The entire group looked to Kosent. "You make an interesting point, Dr. Furman, very interesting. If we could take a short break, I would like to review some information." As Kosent began searching through his laptop, a slight murmur from the other attendees was heard. Kosent kept his eyes focused on the screen, scanning through previous proposals and results from Phase Two and Three clinical trials that had been refused acceptance by the FDA for various reasons.

Priya was speaking with several members when Jeff approached her. "Priya, sorry to interrupt, but we need to talk."

Jeff walked her to the corner of the room and spoke quietly. "Do you remember a company called Lexington Bio headed by a fellow named Steppler?"

"Sure, years ago. I thought the FDA rejected their drug based on insufficient data. We figured Steppler was another brash entrepreneur with no scientific background."

Jeff responded. "Not according to Dr. Ballan at Brookfield. I just met with him, and he said the studies showed positive results,"

Priya looked up as if the sun had just appeared through the clouds. "You're saying Geoffrey Ballan believes the drug had potential. Ballan is one of the best scientists around. We better speak to Kosent. If the FDA reviewed this drug, then we need to know about it."

They walked over to Kosent and sat down in the chairs next to him.

Priya began, "Fred, do you remember a Lexington Bio company with a fellow named Steppler?"

Kosent looked up from his screen. "Lexington, sure. Difficult to forget. Steppler demanded that his drug be approved for antiviral activity without going through Phase 3 studies."

"Fred, Dr. Moss just spoke to Geoffrey Ballan. Ballan says he felt the drug had potential. What did you find?"

"If I recall correctly, the results looked excellent. Give me a moment."

Kosent opened a file and read a summary. "Yes, the study was based on ninety patients, no controls, but almost one hundred percent positive results, and the few that did not respond died from underlying diseases."

"And the safety profile?"

"No untoward responses of significance. The profile was clean. But remember, they only worked on ninety patients."

"Fred, is there any chance that you could approve this drug on an emergency basis? "

Kosent thought for a moment. "Priya, you're asking if FDA would grant an emergency approval based on the data already presented."

"Yes, people are dying, and we have nothing. If you don't have any problems with safety, then would you at least approve it for those who are dying?"

Kosent thought for a moment. "Based on the ninety patients, it could be done."

"Thanks, Fred, that's good to know, that's very good to know."

"And where do I find this fellow Steppler?"

"Never saw him again and prefer not to. He was one difficult individual."

"I think you should let the group know."

Fred looked out at his colleagues. "My friends, we may have something."

The room became silent. Kosent looked up from the screen. "I'm not certain if it would work, but yes, perhaps . . . perhaps there is one possibility."

Priya concluded the meeting. "Listen up, I think we have a drug that the FDA already reviewed. Dr. Kosent will review his data with you. In the meantime, Tom and I have to catch a plane. We have a meeting this afternoon with the President."

As they walked out, Priya spoke to Jeff. "We're going to need this fellow Steppler. He's the only one who has the lab that made the drug."

"Ballan said he hasn't seen him since the FDA meeting."

"Then how do we find him?"

Jeff put his hand to his chin as if in thought. "If you are going to see the President, tell him to inform the media that the FDA will be giving emergency approval to Lexington Bio's drug LB182. The stock will go on fire, and Steppler will realize that he has a chance to get an approval. He'll come out of the woodwork. "

Priya looked at Tom Krantz and smiled. "I think we have a plan."

CHAPTER SIXTY-EIGHT

May 9, 4:00 P.M.
Friday, The White House

The meeting took place in the Oval Office as scheduled. Tom Crantz and Priya were ushered in while the President was watching an old match on the Golf Channel. He looked up for the moment to greet his guests.

"Good afternoon Tom, and you must be Dr. Mamadur? Please sit down."

"Good afternoon, Mr. President. Actually, it's Majmadur."

"Whatever. Anyway," he glanced up from his reading, "You see what time it is? I should be on the golf course right now, but when I heard you hatched a little conference in New York without my authorization, I'm only going to be able to fit in nine today."

He looked at Priya. "Perhaps you're not aware that nothing gets done in this country without my approval, whether it's foreign affairs or domestic. Yet, you took it upon yourself to call a Presidential Task Force and tell them that this could be the most severe attack this nation has ever experienced. Are you aware how scared you are making my people? Do you have any idea the effect this will have on the markets? On the economy? On the confidence that the nation and the world will have in me. There is an election coming up. Do you think this nation could survive if I wasn't here to bring them the greatest prosperity they have ever had? And your CDC is back to giving advice from ten years ago! Does anyone have any idea what they are doing? Each day, you give a new guidance, and the people think it's a joke. One day, you make them wear masks, then you tell them there's no need for masks, then only a certain type of mask, then you say distance yourself from others by six feet, then, forget that, make it three;

then you advise them to wash their hands while singing Happy Birthday. Really, it's a joke and you can't blame my constituents for laughing at whatever is being touted that day. Isn't there anything new to tell us in the past ten years? What do you do with all the money that's been given to you for your so-called research?"

Priya was surprised at the directness. No diplomacy, no thought as to what was best for the nation, just what was best for him politically. And she countered in kind, as she did in defending herself when her older brothers tried to bully her growing up.

"Actually, I am aware of those factors, Mr. President, but understand that our guidelines are based on what we learn from the most recent studies. Science is not static; our guidance is never final as we continue to gain new information. Perhaps it would have been better to not have revised our guidelines following each new study. Perhaps it is too confusing to the population to give them so many updates. I'll grant you that. But does that mean we should do nothing in the meantime? That, Mr. President, is what science is—learning, adapting, and modifying our conclusions based on the most recent and peer-reviewed data. And it takes leadership to explain that to your constituents. But you didn't explain that; instead, you made it seem like our top scientists were fools. And there is media that repeat that they are fools, even though they knew better."

The President seemed stunned for the moment. It was rare for someone to stand their ground.

"The fact is, Mr. President, that I was informing them of the facts, and that is something you, as our leader, must do also. The nation cannot have these mixed messages sent to them, scientists telling them one thing and you the opposite. When people hear mixed messages, they will follow the one that makes them the most comfortable. I don't want them comfortable; I want them to be scared, so scared that they will do the right thing."

The President had not heard anyone confront him so directly. He stood up and raised his voice. "Don't ever tell me what to do. I am the President of this nation, and I will tell them when to be afraid."

Priya took a moment to respond, and when she did, it was in a soft and calming voice.

"First, Mr. President, please speak to me as a gentleman. Second, it is because you are the president that I am here. Right now, we are going to need you to act in a responsible manner. You need to listen to your scientific advisers. And third, if you want a sycophant, get a dog, but if you want someone to tell you the truth, then you will sit down and listen. Ten years ago, a virus infected over one billion people on this globe and ten million of them died. Yes, that was a different administration, a different leader, but we don't want to repeat the same mistakes."

The President was not certain how to respond. He had never, at least not since he was a teenager, been told what to do so pointedly. Even at his military academy, he rarely obeyed without an argument or at least a silent curse. He stared at Priya and seeing eyes more afire than his, surprised himself and sat down.

She paused as if to emphasize the reality. "That virus, Mr. President, was but an appetizer. What is now being served is the main course, and unless you mobilize this nation and the world's resources to counter this onslaught, you will bear the responsibility of the death of eighty percent of the world's population. Eighty percent!"

The President rose from his chair and turned to look through the window overlooking the nation's capital.

"Is China involved?"

"We believe so."

"Our reports are telling us that there is a great deal of internal turmoil in the upper levels of the Communist Party. This is war, but how do you fight it?

"Not with missiles."

"Then get me a drug that works."

"I think we might have one."

It took a long moment for the President to appreciate what he was just told. "You have a drug?"

"It's going to take some work, but for the first time, I believe we may have something."

The President sat down in his chair and doodled with a pen on a piece of paper. Finally, he looked up. "Fine, Dr. Majmadur, you have full authorization to do whatever you have to do."

Priya smiled. "Thank you, Mr. President, but please understand that it will take time to manufacture and distribute it. Until then, all we can do is limit the damage. That means people may have to work from home where possible, and face masks must be a legal requirement in public indoor areas such as theaters, houses of worship, eating establishments, and sporting events if they're allowed to leave their homes at all. Right now, it has been kept to a few localized areas, and we're trying to cordon those areas off to prevent transmission. But without a drug, you must be ready for turmoil in the economy and the markets as investors and consumers adjust to the new reality. If this variant races across the country, teachers, parents, and workplaces will need to brace for the impact. The people will be afraid, and that means lawlessness may occur as the population seeks to do anything to survive. They may march on food stores, on pharmacies, and our medical systems will be ill-prepared to handle the increased burden and expect chaos to businesses, especially leisure establishments like gyms, bars, restaurants, nightclubs, and hotels. And there will need to be lockdowns, and that will result in staff shortages. But all this, Mr. President, will depend upon the speedy success of our pharmaceutical intervention because the restrictions that will be imposed on people's lives will not be tolerated over time. If thirty percent of the population refused to follow guidelines of masks and vaccines the last time around, imagine what will rise up this time. And that is where your leadership must come into play, for we will need to have a national conversation about the way forward and what other mechanisms need be employed to protect your voters."

"My voters? My voters won't follow those guidelines."

"Then you must change that, and that could be a challenge. If certain media still can't declare that a past president won the election, then you will need to convince them to state that vaccines work. They know it, but the ratings love alternate theories."

"No problem, but I must tell the media that we have found a drug."

Priya handed him a typed message. "Then tell them this, that we may have a drug, and that the drug was made by Lexington Bio, headed by Phillip Steppler, whose research labs are located at the Brookfield Institute. The FDA hopes to meet with Mr. Steppler shortly."

The President's smile filled the Oval Office. "I will do as you say, and six months until the election. Perfect.."

* * *

That evening, the President held an emergency press conference. "My fellow Americans. I want to advise you that my administration, working with America's top scientists, is pleased to announce that a drug may have been discovered that will destroy this terrible virus. The drug was made by Lexington Bio, headed by Phillip Steppler, whose research labs are located at the Brookfield Institute. The FDA hopes to meet with Mr. Steppler shortly. Further work is being carried out as we speak, and once the formulation has been finalized, production by the nation's top pharmaceutical manufacturers will begin. Until then, I urge our citizens to stay at home and, if not possible, to wear masks. And finally, when the drug is available, everyone, including my dearest followers, must take it. Thank you, and God bless America."

CHAPTER SIXTY-NINE

Saturday, May 11

By the time Steppler got out of bed, his name and the emergency approval of Lexington Bio's drug filled the world's airways and newspapers. He was trying to understand the consequences when a call to his private cell came through.

"Good morning, Mr. Steppler."

Steppler recognized the voice. "General Han."

"Congratulations, I hear the FDA wants to meet with you about an approval for LB182. You were correct about the original denial having one exception—a new pandemic. I assume you still have access to your lab at Brookfield."

Steppler hesitated. "Yes, sir, I do."

"Good, I will be visiting the lab on Monday, the day after tomorrow. We will need the access codes to enter, so please meet me there. I will let you know when. Good luck at the FDA. We certainly need that approval."

"Yes, sir."

Steppler felt the perspiration run down the back of his neck. What was he to do? If he went to the FDA, what was he to say that he could discuss the molecular structure of the drug, or the method of producing a lab batch, or explain stability, dosage, route of administration? No way. Yes, he had some science background, but he certainly wasn't involved with the assays that Chen had supervised. In spite of having Chen's laptop, many of the notes appeared deleted or missing, and his former assistants were not able to fill in the missing blanks. Even the patents only gave a general description of what Chen had created, but the actual dosing, combinations of herbal extracts and amounts were never stated. Steppler needed Chen, but why would Chen even want to work with him again? He realized that his actions had come back to haunt him. And yet, if he was to satisfy the General, he had to bring Chen back. But where to find him? The last he saw him was at the investment conference in China, but how to get a hold of him? He knew nothing about Chen's personal life, only his relationship at Brookfield with Dr. Ballan. Perhaps that was his only chance. It was a Saturday. He called the Institute, explained who he was, and that he needed Ballan's cell number; it was an emergency. He made the call and left a message.

"Dr. Ballan, this is Phillip Steppler. I need to get a hold of Chen. We have an emergency at the FDA. Can you help me with that?"

* * *

Jiang was in his lab when he asked the guards to bring in Chen.

"He's not there."

Jiang acted surprised. "What? How's that possible? Of course, he's there."

Jiang went with the guards to check the room where Chen was held. "I want the entire building checked. Find him!"

Jiang checked the time. Colonel Ming arrived exactly at the forty-eighth hour.

"Ah, Jiang. Did your friend Chen decide to cooperate?"

Jiang straightened himself and calmly said: "He's gone."

"What?"

"I asked the guards to bring him to the lab, and they said he's gone. I have them searching the building. My understanding is that he was under security watch twenty-four-seven. I have no idea how they could have let that happen."

Minutes later, the guards returned. "We put the entire place on alert. No one has seen him."

Ming was beside himself, both for the professional error of having lost a prisoner under his supervision and the retribution he feared after telling General Han.

He walked into his office and called the General.

"Yes, colonel. How's our prisoner? Cooperating?"

"General, I don't know how it happened, but he's missing,"

"What?" Ming could feel Han's rage.

"The entire place is on lockdown. No one has seen him."

"I want the entire area secured. That means side streets, highways, airports, and notify Interpol. I want him back in Hunan."

"Yes, sir."

"And colonel, could Jiang have anything to do with this?"

"I'm not sure. When I got here, Jiang was in the lab and had told security to bring Chen in. The guards reported he wasn't in the cell."

"Well, if we don't have Chen, we will need Jiang."

"I understand, sir."

"But you are to keep him under close surveillance and no slip-ups this time. A lot is going on here and a tight schedule to meet. I need you and Jiang to get here immediately. And just to be safe, I don't want Jiang to have any computers or phones. Understand?"

"Yes, sir."

"Good, now let me speak to Jiang."

He gave the phone to Jiang. "Jiang, without Chen, you're going to have to help put the antidote together. Go to my office. On my computer, the password is HanShi323. You will find a file marked Chen Chu. I need you to download the files that include his FDA application and the patents. Bring those with you."

"Yes, sir."

"Good. Now let me speak to the colonel."

"Yes, general."

"Colonel, Jiang needs to download two files for me. I gave him the password. Shouldn't take more than twenty minutes. Remember, I need you here as soon as possible."

* * *

When Ming had completed travel arrangements, he checked on Jiang. "Almost finished?"

"Just about."

As Jiang was about to power off, he noticed a file named *Wulajie Study–Thanatos 2021*. It was marked High Security. Jiang checked the cover page and realized that it contained the entire study on the village deaths he had asked Han about when he first visited Hunan. Jiang thought for a moment and then took an empty USB drive and began the download.

Ten minutes had gone by when Ming entered the office. "Hey, you ready yet. We have a plane to catch."

"I need ten more minutes. One of the downloads wasn't complete."

"Not complete? General Shi said it should only take twenty minutes. "Let me see what you're doing. He told me only two files."

Jiang's heart began to pound. If Shi found out, he could be charged with treason. He needed more time. Ming looked at the computer screen. "What's Thanatos?"

Jiang got up and blocked the screen. "Listen, colonel. These are highly secret files. I'm the only one who has permission to see them. I'll be finished in another ten minutes. General Shi didn't realize how much material was on these files." Ming thought for a moment. "Fine. Ten minutes, or I'm calling the general."

Jiang was almost finished when Ming walked in

"Finished?"

Jinag's heart was racing. And then the flash drive stopped its download. "Finished."

"Then let's go."

Jiang put the flash drive into his pocket and walked out of the lab, to which he hoped he would never return.

CHAPTER SEVENTY

Saturday, May 10, 7:30 A.M.
Frankfurt, Germany

It took the taxi fifteen minutes early on Saturday morning to drive from the airport to the Frankfurt Marriott, located in the city center and directly across the street from the entrance to one of the world's largest convention centers. The huge conference room where Chen and Li sat was filled with economists, financiers, and others controlling the world's money supply where the Economic Forum was being held. Li took notes, recorded certain speakers, and took pictures for the article she would have to submit to the Journal for publication. It was noon by the time the morning program had ended. They walked across to the hotel lobby and sat at the far end. As Li scanned the room, she saw several policemen speaking at the front desk. She checked the time; the forty-eight-hour grace period was long over. She approached the desk and listened to the conversation. After several minutes, she returned to Chen.

"Interpol. There's a general alert out for you, but they're looking for a Chen Chu, not the Hu Seng on your new papers. We better stay out of sight for a while. It's going to be a problem getting a plane out of here."

"Any suggestions?"

"Not yet. But we better stay incognito until we think of something."

They moved to the far corner of the large lobby, fatigued from their trip. Chen picked up a magazine from a nearby table, Li finding a copy of the London Times. As Li lazily scanned the front page, her eyes came to a sudden stop. She could not believe what she saw. Her eyes dilated as she read the front page story under the fold. It was an article on Lexington Bio. Li couldn't read it fast enough. She gave Chen a gentle nudge and whispered. "Chen, it's all over the news."

"What?" he said sleepily.

"Read this. The FDA is giving emergency approval to Lexington Bio to develop their drug for distribution against the virus. They are looking for your CEO, Phillip Steppler."

Chen was amazed. "The FDA is approving my drug to deal with the virus?"

"They think it has the best chance to prevent a global pandemic."

"And what does Steppler say?"

"They have no idea where he is. He hasn't been heard from in a long time."

Chen smiled. "Yes, I assume that would be the case. If General Shi is after me, he's certainly after him."

"But Steppler knows nothing without you. Who knows how to contact you?"

"Only my attorney, Tim Channing."

"Then we must speak to him."

"What good would that do?"

"Because if Steppler wants to save the company, he has to get you back. You're the only one who can produce the drug."

"If I want to produce the drug."

"What do you mean?"

Chen was silent for a few moments. "I'm not sure. In some ways, I feel that this drug has caused all the trouble. I mean, it's because of the drug that I've been kidnapped, imprisoned, and now fleeing to save my own life. In some respects, I wish I wasn't involved at all."

Li smiled sympathetically. "I understand. I suppose you are being asked to sacrifice your comfort here for a less personal mission but one that may be of great significance. I guess you have to decide." She paused. "What would your father do?"

Chen looked into her eyes. "You are very wise, Li. Yes, what would my father do?"

Chen opened his briefcase and removed the photo of his mother, father, and himself as a young boy in the herb garden planting seeds and showed it to Li.

She smiled. "I remember this garden. It was in your backyard. I still remember the names of those herbs that your father gave to my family."

He smiled. "Yes, I remember. But look at the back."

She looked at the back of the photo.

"It's all I have left of my father. He gave it to me when I came home from university. It was in my pocket when they took me to the hospital. It has served me as a guide at decisive turns in my life, as if my father is here, advising me with this one phrase."

Li read it out loud. "*He who sacrifices his conscience to ambition burns a picture to obtain the ashes.*" She handed the photo back to Chen.

"What do you think he's telling you?"

Chen spoke deliberately. "That helping people, like he did in our village, healing them, counseling them, allaying their physical and emotional problems, should not be motivated by personal comfort, for the greatest gain is to profit others."

He looked at her, lifted her hands to his lips, and kissed her gently. "You're right. We should call Tim. If there is even the slightest chance that I can help others as my father did, then I need to try.

CHAPTER SEVENTY-ONE

Chen's call to Channing's cell was made when Tim was about to leave his office. Chen introduced Li who discussed with the attorney her thoughts.

"Sorry to bother you on a Saturday."

"No problem, I finished whatever I was working on. I'm on the way to the office now to get some work done. Chen said you are a good friend. What's happening?"

"I read the FDA may be approving Chen's drug. That means if Steppler wants the drug accepted, he's going to have to meet with the FDA, but he knows nothing about the drug. That means he needs Chen, and my understanding is that you're the only one who knows how to reach him. So Steppler will have to speak to you, and when he does, I want the contract that gives Chen no ownership ripped up and a new one drawn. In fact, he deserves to get what he gave Chen."

Tim smiled at the aggressive stance that Li was suggesting. "Sounds like a plan. By the way, where are you?"

"It's a long story, but we're in Frankfurt, having escaped a Chinese jail. The Chinese have the virus, but they don't have the antidote. That's why they need Chen, and that's why they have Interpol on our scent. Somehow, I've got to get Chen back to New York without being arrested and returned to China."

"Interpol is checking all passenger flights?"

"That's what I heard, and although he's flying with a different passport, we can't be sure he won't be stopped when we land. Any ideas?"

"Without trying to get through the incredible red tape of getting the State Department on board, it's a problem, even with a changed passport. Is he still flying as a Chinese citizen?"

Li realized the problem. "He is."

"Then that's a toughie. Let me get back to you. Send me your contact info."

"Will do."

* * *

Tim Channing sat at his desk digesting the problem. He was fully aware of the International Criminal Police Organization known as Interpol, the inter-governmental organization that helps coordinate police in one hundred and ninety-five countries. A few years back, he had a case of money laundering across borders, and Interpol enabled him to access needed information on organized crime, including names, fingerprints, and even stolen passports. And Li was correct. If China wanted him back, their first move would be to utilize Interpol to send out an arrest warrant for Chen with his picture. There would be little chance of Chen boarding a passenger flight out of Germany or any European country without being caught.

CHAPTER SEVENTY-TWO

It took an hour for Ballen to return Steppler's call. "I have no knowledge of where Dr. Chu is. It might be best to speak to Tim Channing, an attorney who practices here in Manhattan. He may be able to help you. By the way, Mr. Steppler, the FDA has been trying to reach you."

* * *

Half an hour later, Channing's thoughts were interrupted by the office phone. Tim had a good idea who would be calling on a late Saturday afternoon. He answered the call.

"Mr. Channing, my name is Phillip Steppler, and I was referred by Dr. Ballen at Brookfield."

Steppler explained that he needed to locate Dr. Chu.

Channing smiled at Li's perception. "Mr. Steppler, I may be able to help you, but I doubt that Dr. Chu would be interested. I can tell you that there would need to be a reallocation of ownership of Lexington Bio and a revision of the provisions. In other words, based on the work that Dr. Chu did and the funding that you provided, a ninety-ten split would be required."

Steppler thought for a moment. He knew that he had little choice and that giving Chu ten percent of the company, about to make billions, was better than he had thought."

"I believe that giving Dr. Chu ten percent is fair."

Channing laughed. "No, Mr. Steppler. I believe you misunderstood the conditions. Dr. Chu is to receive ninety percent of ownership. You will have ten percent, which is ten more than you gave to Dr. Chu. Furthermore, you will also reassign, or I should say, return ownership of the patents to Dr. Chen, and a board of directors will be appointed to help advise the company with respect to business, legal, research and marketing strategies. You will not be on that board. In other words, Mr. Steppler, for Dr. Chen to return, you will simply be a silent partner."

Steppler couldn't believe the terms.

Channing continued. "And, Mr. Steppler, knowing how anxious your investors are for that drug to be approved, I would suggest you agree immediately. If not, Dr. Chu is not interested. What do you say, Mr. Steppler?"

Steppler realized he had nothing to bargain with. Without Chen, he had no remaining chips. He recalled the old axiom: ten percent of something is better than a hundred percent of nothing. "Fine, I agree."

"Excellent, Mr. Steppler; I will have the papers drawn up immediately. By the way, how much money is left in the Lexington Bio accounts?"

Steppler thought for a moment. "Seventy-five million. Twenty-five million was used for the preclinical research, the GMP manufacturing of the drug to be used for the three clinical trials, and payment for the Phase Two human trial."

"Good. Then, stop by my office in an hour with all the original ownership and corporate documents. I will have the transfers for you to sign. That means Dr. Chu will have full control of the finances, and you will no longer be an assignee on the accounts. And one more thing, Mr. Steppler, do you remember a gentlemen named Sam Rapolo? I will need his telephone number."

Steppler complied.

Channing was pleased. "Thank you, Mr. Steppler. I will see you in an hour."

* * *

Within minutes, Sam Rapolo received a call.

"Mr. Rapolo."

"With whom am I speaking?"

"This is Tim Channing."

There was a pause on Rapolo's side. "You mean the Tim Channing that helped put my associate Mr. Torcantino into permanent residence."

"I wasn't aware he was an associate of yours."

"No, I stand corrected." Rapolo gave a slight laugh. "I only read about him in the papers. What can I do for you, Mr. Channing? Do I need my lawyer present?"

"Nothing like that. Actually, I have a favor to ask. There is a scientist who worked on one of your projects recently, a special drug to kill viruses. This individual had some trouble with a foreign country, and he escaped. He's now in Germany, but the police are checking all airports. I can assure you he did nothing wrong, but he and a friend need to get back to New York to finish the project. Can you help them?"

Rapolo hesitated before responding. "I believe I know of the individual of which you are speaking. The man's a genius, and his company's name was mentioned all over today's paper along with our friend Steppler. And where is he in Germany?"

"Frankfurt."

"Let me get back to you."

* * *

It took Sam Rapolo thirty minutes to return Tim's call.

"Okay, here's what I can do for my scientific friend. He's to go to Frankfurt Airport. On the far north end, there's a small field about three miles outside of the main terminal. I have an associate, I mean an acquaintance, who manages the air cargo warehouses there. What they do is take in cargo, build up and break down the pallets, handle the containers, and load and unload the aircraft. They got a midnight flight goin' to Logan Airport in Boston. If he don't mind not having first-class passenger service, my friend can get him on that cargo delivery. No one's gonna bother him comin' or goin'. Once he gets to Logan, he will be part of the crew and can get out of the airport as needed. How's that sound?"

Tim smiled. "I had a feeling you could help him. And he's traveling with a female friend."

"No problem. So then tell them to get there by eleven thirty and ask for Hans. He's the night manager, but he knows what's up. Give my regards to that genius and have him bring some sandwiches and drinks. They don't serve no dinner. And Mr. Channing, you should know that I have now retired. That genius has made me a rich man. And, Mr. Channing, for future reference, please remember that I have no knowledge of any activities of any previous businesses and associates, capiche?"

Tim smiled. "Capiche."

CHAPTER SEVENTY-THREE

Frankfurt, Germany

They arrived at the airfield at about the same time that Li received Tim's email. She sat in the small World Cargo waiting room, read his note, and viewed the new contract with Chen, making several suggestions to clarify the financial aspects. She soon realized that Chen had little interest in the details of the business. It was almost as if his brain could only focus on the areas needed for scientific analysis. Financial arrangements were certainly not part of that equation.

"Chen, are you following me?"

Chen shrugged his shoulders. "To be honest, I'm really not interested. For whatever reason, I have never been interested in finance, figuring everything would work out in the end. I seem to only be interested in the new work I'm doing, not capitalizing on what I had already done."

Li nodded slowly and quietly frowned. "I'm afraid this is how you got into the trouble to begin with. You have to know what is happening to your company."

Chen smiled. "I prefer not to. You're the businessperson here. You do it. From now on, you're the chief financial officer of the company. I just can't get involved. I'm a lab guy. Give me a lab, and I'll be happy. You take care of everything else."

Li shook her head. "You are incorrigible. That's a full-time job. I already have a job."

Chu smiled. "Then leave your job. As the new CFO, you should double your salary."

Chen thought for a moment. "Does the company have any money?"

"According to the papers I just received, there's a balance of seventy-five million."

Chen smiled. "Then triple your salary."

Li quietly shook her head out of frustration.

Chen continued. "I'm serious. I want you with me on this project. Who else can I trust? At least I will have you and Tim Channing to guide me through the legal and financial work that needs to be done, and maybe Dr. Ballan can join us. The fact is, Li, I need you."

Li stood and walked around the room, looking out at the plane that was being loaded. Finally, she returned to her seat and looked intently at Chen. "Fine, I accept, but there is a lot of work to do. According to the new contract, you will be President of the company and will own the controlling interest. I'll ask Tim if he will take care of the legal aspects, and I will run the financial area, but you must approve everything, and you must take an interest in the workings of your company."

"I will try my best." With that understanding, he took the pen and signed the document. Li emailed it back to Channing, adding that Tim should contact Dr. Ballen to set up a meeting with the FDA. Li added that it would be best to keep Chen's involvement confidential; Chinese agents were hunting him.

By the time they arrived in Boston, they received the final agreement with Steppler's signature. The deal had been completed, and the meeting with the FDA had been set.

CHAPTER SEVENTY-FOUR

Rockville, Maryland

Chen, Li, Tim Channing and Geoffrey Ballen entered Phillip Kosent's conference room at the FDA.

"Dr. Chen, a pleasure to meet you. When I received the notice that Lexington Bio was taking the meeting, I assumed that Mr. Steppler would be here."

"Mr. Steppler is no longer actively involved with the company," Li responded. "My name is Li Zang, and Mr. Channing and I will be assuming the legal and business responsibilities of the company. Dr. Chen will be the Chief Scientific Officer."

"I see." Kosent nodded to Ballen, "And Geoffrey, good to see you again. Last time was at the Cancer Society meeting in Dallas. Are you now part of this project?"

"I am. Dr. Chen talked me into being responsible for the operations of the company."

Li added. "Dr. Ballan will be Lexington Bio's new Chief Operating Officer."

"Well, then," Kosent began, "Let's get to work."

Kosent's cell rang. "Yes, please bring them in."

The door opened, and into the room entered Jeff, Priya, Gogoli, and Stan. Introductions were made. "I thought we would have the entire team here from New York, as well as James Ryan from the CDC, Phil Crantz, head of Health and Human Services, and Drs. William Power and Roseanne Filber representing our largest pharmaceutical companies. I believe this is everyone that is needed to get this project going."

Kosent opened the meeting. "Thank you, everyone, and especially Dr. Chu and your group. Priya, perhaps you can start."

"Sure. In spite of our efforts to keep the virus contained, we need to be prepared for the contingency that somehow, somewhere, there will be a leak. I suggest that our work focus on the two aspects of the problem. The first is to determine whether Dr. Chen's drug can help us. The second is to prevent the person or persons responsible for the release of this deadly pathogen from doing further harm. For that, I will ask Dr. Moss to give us an update."

Jeff went through the identification of the perpetrator and how he was connected to China's ruling hierarchy and was involved with the Hunan Institute of Virology. The FBI has been notified, and local police departments throughout the states have received an internet emergency dispatch along with his photo and description from previous background checks. This will all be made public starting on the six o'clock news and a reward for anyone giving information leading to his arrest. We hope that by blasting his photograph on every television station and media outlet here and in Canada, someone will turn him in."

"Question," it came from Li, " So this is a single individual?"

"That is what we believe. We have followed hot spots in Maryland, New York, and San Francisco."

Chen interrupted. "Let me ask you, Dr. Moss, would the name of that perpetrator be a General Han Shi."

Jeff and Priya looked at each other. "You know General Han?"

"Han arrested me and tried to force me to work for him. Thanks to Li, I escaped and just got into New York. I believe he is still here. He needs an antidote and will do anything to get it."

Jeff was surprised at how much Chen knew. "If that's the case, then he will not hesitate to find you. We will need to make arrangements for your safety until he has been apprehended."

"Well, Dr. Chen," it was Priya. It seems that our fate is up to you. We saw your Phase Two results. What do you think?"

Chen responded slowly. "I believe that the pandemic virus is identical to the one that we tested in our lab. It's Thanatos."

Kosent gave a warning glance at Priya. "You have Thanatos in your lab?"

Chen nodded. "Yes, we tested our molecule against Thanatos before the funding dried up."

"Where did you get it from?"

"From the Wuhan Institute in China by a friend who works with Dr. Han in his lab. They heard my presentation at the Atlanta meeting and wanted to know if it could work against Thanatos."

"And did it?"

"It did."

Jeff interjected. "Could anyone else have had access to it?"

"Only if Wuhan supplied it, and I don't believe that happened. Every time you start transporting these viruses, there's the possibility of transmission. There are strict procedures and a great deal of administrative paperwork. Brookfield is a certified Biosafety Level 4 laboratory equipped to handle the deadliest viruses. We sent in the government documentation, had it approved, and it was shipped to us under tight security protocols in biohazard-sealed vials. Once we received it, it was placed into the secure bio lab section, where the viruses are stored. It was in that area that our experiments were carried out."

Kosent followed up. "Dr. Chen, how effective was your molecule against Thanatos?"

"It not only prevented the death of the animals but destroyed the virus on contact."

Kosent and the other members present were amazed.

Jeff was now concerned about security. "And who has access to that lab."

"Only Phillip Steppler and I, and you need both a retinal scan and a combination lock for entrance. Access is tightly controlled and under video surveillance."

"So you don't think there could have been a leak from your lab."

"Not while I was there."

"And the lab in China? Could that have been the source of a leak?"

Chen responded. "I was told it was possible."

"By your friend?"

"Correct."

Jeff followed up. "Are we able to speak with him?"

"I wish we could. He saved my life. But, there have been reports of a number of the scientists at the lab having gone missing. I don't know how he is or where he is, but he got me out of prison at his own peril."

Kosent interjected. "From our review of your Phase Two clinicals, there should be no reason why we can't grant you an expedited approval."

Priya followed up. "But that still will take time to have the drug manufactured. How soon can you get your drug to Bill and Roseanne to begin manufacturing?"

Chen thought for a moment. "I'm not certain. It's been a while since I was in the lab, but if I can get the team back to the lab, it shouldn't be that long, assuming all the needed materials are still in the freezers."

Priya continued. "And how long to get the manufacturing process up to speed?"

Bill Power spoke first. "Fortunately, we still are producing the COVID-19 vaccines for the annual booster shots. We can transition those lines to the new molecule rather easily. We could start producing in quantities within six weeks for the material transfer to be completed, assuming we have the needed ingredients."

Roseanne Filber added, "I think Bill is correct. Figure six weeks, and that's working round the clock."

Priya followed up. "And global production?"

"For that, we will need manufacturing from the Chinese, the Indians, the Israelis, and our European partners."

"Can we trust the Chinese?"

The group turned to Jeff. "We'll know that after I find General Han."

Priya made some notes. "Dr. Krantz, how long for US distribution?"

"Once we get the drug, we can start to get it to the drug stores within two weeks."

"And the rest of the world?"

Krantz thought for a moment. "Using all the global agencies that are presently vaccinating and utilizing all the existing immunization sites that are still functioning, it could be months."

"And to get everyone vaccinated?"

Krantz shook his head. "Everyone vaccinated, six months."

"So we're talking at least a year." Priya echoed. "By then, we could lose a billion people."

There was a deep silence at the table, with the realization that mass production of the vaccine, even working round the clock, allows for no shortcuts. It takes time.

"I have another idea." It was Chen who received the participants' attention. "How much drug do you need immediately? That is, if you can isolate those that may have been in contact with the virus, all you would really need is enough drug to administer to those hospitalized or to administer to those in direct contact with the infected."

They turned to Priya. "As of today, if we had one million doses to treat the hospitalized and infected, we could end this attack immediately."

Chen stood up from the table. "If you will excuse me, I need to make a call."

Five minutes later, Chen returned to the room.

"I just spoke to Mitch Sedgewick, who overlooked the manufacturing of our drug for the clinical studies. We have three million doses stored in the lab freezers available immediately for human use."

A relief was let in the room. "That may be enough to stem the tide."

It was Jeff who responded. "Then we need to return to New York now. If you have the drug, then we need to make sure it and you are safe and secure."

With that, the meeting ended.

* * *

With Chen and Li dozed off in the back of Jeff's car, still exhausted from their escape, Priya asked the remaining question. "What if there really was a serious episode, and millions were infected? Who is going to receive the three million doses of vaccine?"

"You mean," Jeff asked, "who is to live and who to die? The last time I played God was my last heart surgery. Could I save this person's life, or was there no hope? Do I spend my time and resources on each and every patient that walks in, or are certain cases so terminal, such a poor prognosis, that I must tell them there is no hope? I'm sorry."

Priya thought about Jeff's remark. "Back to medical rationing. Only the young, only the healthy, only the productive members of society? That's always been the question."

"But this goes further, " Jeff continued. "The prognosis for everyone here will be the same. They will all die. So, whom do we choose to save? Yes, you could say those with terminal diseases or those with poor long-term prognoses should be weeded out, but we are talking about something else. Do you save the government? Do you save the medical personnel? The teachers? The entrepreneurs? Whom? We have no criteria for that. The question of medical rationing has always been discussed but never put into widespread use."

Again, there was silence until Jeff responded. "Who did Noah save before the flood?"

"You mean each species to preserve life on earth?"

"Yes."

"This is not a medical question." Priya asked, "Then whom do you speak to?"

Jeff glanced over at his passenger. "My rabbi."

CHAPTER SEVENTY-FIVE

The moment that Colonel Ming notified Han that they had arrived in New York, the general called Steppler.

"Mr. Steppler, it's time for us to get to the lab."

"What do you want me to do?"

"Give me access to Brookfield. I will meet you at noon."

At noon, Phillip Steppler was greeted at the Brookfield entrance by the security guard.

"Mr. Steppler, haven't seen you in a while. Going into the lab?"

"I am. And Chris, I have guests coming in from China. Please direct them to the lab when they arrive."

"Sure, when they get here, I'll send them over. And, by the way, I see your name all over the news. I hear the FDA is approving your drug. Congratulations."

"Thanks."

Han, Jiang and Colonel Ming arrived moments later and were told to go straight down the hall. Lexington Bio facilities were at the end. Han and the others entered the double doors.

"Well, Mr. Steppler. Good to see you again." Han looked around. "Didn't realize you had so much space."

Han and Jiang began a thorough review of the equipment and supplies in the outer lab before entering the Viral Secure area. They put on the required protective suits, and Steppler opened the lock to the inner door with the retina entry scan and the combination lock. The three of them entered while Ming remained outside doing guard duty.

The viral lab was in perfect order, seemingly maintaining its aseptic condition. All microscopes, assay equipment, scales and a dozen other instruments were covered as required.

"Place looks like it's ready to begin formulating. What do you think, Jiang?"

"Very impressive. They even have the new monitors."

"Mr. Steppler, I must say I am surprised. I didn't realize how sophisticated your lab is. From what I see, this lab is ready for the final formulation of Chen's antidote."

When Han had completed his initial inspection, he sat down on one of the lab benches.

"You know, Jiang, I'm thinking that there may be more here than we realize." He looked at Steppler. "If I'm correct, you were to follow up your Phase 2 study with the two large Phase 3 clinicals."

Steppler nodded. "Correct, but we never began those clinicals."

Han ran his fingers over his scar as if delving deep into thought. "But, when you made the drug for Phase Two, did you also manufacture enough for the two clinicals—that was four hundred patients in each of the two arms of the experiment?"

"Yes, we believed we would save time and money by making the clinical-grade drug for all the patient studies at once."

"For eight hundred patients and multiple testing? That's got to be a ton of vials made up. So where are all the unused vials of drug?"

"I really don't know. I've rarely been in this section."

"Jiang? Certainly, if they were saved, they would have to be stored in very cold temperatures."

"I would think so. There must be storage somewhere here."

They searched the room, and at the far end, there was a steel door secured with a combination lock.

"Any idea what's in here, Mr. Steppler."

"I don't, general."

"Let's try the same combination you used for the outer door."

Han entered the combination, and the door opened.

"Well, what do you know! A room full of freezers. Jiang, what do you think?"

Jiang walked into a room lined with a bank of six massive freezers with outer doors having touchscreen temperature monitoring systems.

"This should be it. They all have operating glycol temperatures of -20°C to -30°C."

Shi was all smiles. "Well, Mr. Steppler, please, do us the honors, open the doors and let's see what we find."

Steppler opened the side-by-side doors of the first freezer. Inside, countless vials were placed upright in containers that looked like egg cartons. Han walked deeper into the room and opened all the freezers. Each one was filled with vials the same as the first.

"There's got to be several million doses here. Congratulations, Mr. Steppler. Looks like you have saved us a great deal of effort. To be honest, we thought we would have to start the development ourselves, but it appears that the completed product is here. I don't believe there is a need to make anything. We just need to bring some samples back to our labs."

As they walked out of the sterile room and removed their safety equipment, Jiang asked: "What are you thinking of doing, general?"

"Probably best to bring two of the freezers back to Wuhan with us, and we can do a few quick studies on some of our villagers. If it is as effective as I think, we will reverse engineer to duplicate the exact formulation and begin manufacturing. Jiang, find a company that can remove the freezers from here and keep them frozen during transport to JFK Airport. I'll arrange for the plane, and I want this picked up tonight."

Ming seemed alarmed. "Tonight? That could be a problem."

"Not for the money you will offer them."

"Yes, sir."

"What about the other freezers?" Jiang asked.

The general gave a wicked laugh. "Those we will unplug. We don't want anyone to have what we have."

He turned to Steppler. "And Mr. Steppler, let's keep this to ourselves. If this works out, you will be making a lot of money."

For whatever reason, Steppler did not mention his recent transaction with Chen. With that, the Chinese contingent exited Brookfield Institute.

CHAPTER SEVENTY-SIX

McDougal and Jeff were in Jeff's office while Chen and Li were relating Chen's imprisonment and escape.

"But there's a bigger issue, and that is an entire bioterror program that General Han has initiated. If the threat of Thanatos being released is made, Han believes that whoever has the antidote will be able to hold the world hostage. No longer will there be a need for nuclear weapons? It's as simple as that."

"But," Jeff added, "the threat can only be of significance if he has the missing antidote."

It was McDougal who completed the thought, "Your molecule."

Chen continued. "Correct, and he sold the entire plan of replacing armed conquest with a nanoparticle to the Chinese Communist Party and its chairman. But for the world to believe he has the antidote, he has to prove it."

Again, McDougal answered. "And that's why Han needs the FDA to approve Lexington's drug."

Chen agreed. "Yes, the Chinese and even the European Regulatory authorities can give their approval, but the FDA is the most respected regulatory agency in the world. If they say it's safe and effective, the world will agree. And all he needed to prove was the virulence of Thanatos in a few places here in the US."

Jeff nodded with a satirical smile. "Well, he certainly accomplished that. But what does he need to do to secure the antidote?"

Chen responded. "Well, he tried to force me to do that; otherwise, I'm not sure. My friend Jiang and his colleagues at Wuhan worked on it for years but have consistently failed. I suppose the only other way is to get into the Lexington Laboratory."

"But how would he gain entry if you're not there."

. "By having Steppler with him."

"And," Li added, "the general probably believes that Steppler still owns Lexington."

"And Chen," McDougal asked, "where are the vials of vaccine stored?"

"In the freezers."

"And how many did you say were there."

"For eight hundred patients and plenty left over for stability and other studies, I was told three million."

* * *

By the time the evening news had been broadcast, half the nation had seen the image of Han Shi. By morning the remaining populace who relied on print or social media also were aware. Han Shi would be the most wanted individual in the nation. All leads would be funneled to the staff at the Terrorism Hotline: 888-NYC-SAFE. Any considered viable would be sent directly to Anthony DePalma's office at One Police Plaza on Park Row in the Civic Center in Manhattan. If any of those were further screened and remained viable, it would be sent to either Moss or McDougal. If it led to an arrest, DePalma would be notified.

CHAPTER SEVENTY-SEVEN

It was late afternoon in their hotel room when Jiang told Ming to make the arrangements. Ming was in the middle of watching the Russian versus French soccer match on television.

"Colonel, I need you to call PA Roadway to send over a refrigerated truck. And make sure that it can maintain the freezer compressors on the ride to the airport, so have them provide a generator powered by either propane or, if possible, the electric system of the truck."

"Hey, I don't work for you. You do it."

"Listen, colonel, you have to do it. I don't have a phone."

Ming shook his head in frustration. "Fine." He reached into his bag and threw one of the burner phones that he had bought at the airport to Jiang. "You take care of the trucker and explain what has to be done." Ming turned back to watch the game. It was the first time Jiang had a transmitter in his hand since he left Wuhan. He didn't know if there would be anyone to receive it, but he sent an email on Chen's old address:

Chen, I am in NY. Tonight, Han will take two of the freezers with your vials and destroy the rest. JF

Ming looked over as Jiang was typing. "What are you doing?"

"Ah, trying to figure out if I should message or speak to them. It's complicated. I'll try calling."

When they had completed their tasks, Ming messaged General Han while Jiang went into the bathroom."

"Damn!"

"Jiang, what's the matter?" Ming was laughing, "you lose something in there."

"Yeah, the cell phone fell into the sink full of water. It went dead."

Ming finally stopped laughing at his joke. "All right, give it to me, and I'll see if I can get it working."

Jiang couldn't let Ming examine the phone and see his message. "Forget it, it's not operating."

Ming raised his voice. "I said give it to me. Perhaps I can get it to work. I don't like using so many of these phantom phones. One might be traceable."

Jiang realized the predicament. "Okay, I'll be out in a minute."

Jiang filled the sink with hot water, submerged the phone, and waited.

"Hey, what's going on in there? Give me that damn phone. You're not supposed to have it. If the general finds out, I could be in a lot of trouble."

"Fine, be right out." Jiang flushed the toilet and removed the phone from the water.

"Here. Sorry, it's still wet." Jiang threw the phone onto the bed.

"Okay, let's see if it works." As Ming dried it off and pressed the 'on' switch, his phone rang.

"Yes, general."

"It's all over the evening news!"

"What is?"

"Turn on the TV!"

Ming threw the wet phone back on the bed and picked up the channel changer. He never even noticed the small banner news item moving across the bottom of the screen on almost every channel:

Wanted - Information on the whereabouts of Han Shi. Reward for information leading to arrest. Call the Terrorism Hotline.

Ming was alarmed. "General, you need to move, or you'll be found."

"I know. We've got to get to the lab immediately.

"Did you make the arrangements?"

"Yes, sir. The truck is outfitted with generators and will pick up the freezers at ten tonight and bring them to JFK."

"Good, then you and Jiang pack everything and get our immediately. Nothing should be left behind. The flight is scheduled for midnight. If all goes well, we will be on that flight back to Hunan. Understand?"

"Yes, sir."

Ming ended the call. "Jiang, we've got to go. The general wants us in the lab. Pack everything. Nothing is to be left behind."

As Jiang threw his few belongings into the carry on, he kept his eye on the cell phone which had been thrown on the bed.

As Ming went to clear out the closet, Jiang grabbed the cell, threw it in with his clothes, and zipped up the piece of luggage. They paid the bill in cash and caught a taxi to the lab.

* * *

Han checked the calendar as timing was now everything. He had been in the United States for a total of twenty-three days, traveling from coast to coast. He had seven days left until the thirty-day deadline. He was confident that he had what he needed: enough drug to engineer the molecule and the remainder to give to each member of the Central Committee and their families. The fact that his name, description and photo had been circulated throughout the nation's security forces was simply another challenge to meet. Staying away from being captured would become more difficult, but riding in the refrigerated trucks with the freezers would work out perfectly.

CHAPTER SEVENTY-EIGHT

It was eight in the evening when Steppler met Han, Jiang, and Ming at the entrance to Brookfield. As they walked past the security checkpoint, Chris greeted the visitors and went back to watch the Mets game. Between innings Chris finished his coffee and doughnut when he noticed the directive flashed across the TV screen with the general's face: *Wanted - Information on the whereabouts of Han Shi.* It included the telephone number to call and the reward notice. Chris almost spilled the drink. Didn't he see that fellow enter with Steppler?

He walked into the Lexington Bio lab to confirm his suspicion. As Han walked out of the biosafety lab, he saw Chris looking at him.

"Can I help you?"

"Uh, no, just, ah, checking how everyone is doing."

The general smiled. "Sure, I understand. Han put his hand inside his jacket. "Guess you know who I am."

"You, I mean, uh, I mean a friend of Mr. Steppler."

"I'm afraid there's no reward tonight."

In one smooth motion, Chris lay on the floor, a bullet through his forehead. Steppler couldn't believe what he saw. "What was that about?"

"He was in the way." He called to Ming. "Put his body in one of the offices."

* * *

By eight o'clock, Chen, Li, Jeff and McDougall had finished the two pies they ordered from a Second Avenue Pizzeria not far from the ME's offices. They had already spent hours going over all that had happened to Chen over the past year. Finally, he had a moment to open his computer.

"Jiang is alive!"

Li looked up. "What?"

Chen was reading his mail.

"Jiang sent a message. Listen to this: *Chen, I am in NY. Han taking two freezers with vials and destroying the rest. Help. JF*

"When will that be done?"

"He doesn't say, but if the general returns to Wuhan with drug, he could reverse engineer the whole molecule."

"Can he do that?"

"He certainly could. China is not concerned about patent protection. Jiang also said that Han will destroy the rest of the freezers. That's all the drug we have."

"When was it sent."

"An hour ago."

"Then we should get over there. McDougall, call DePalma. Tell him Han Shi may have just entered Brookfield. We'll meet him there and bring backup."

CHAPTER SEVENTY-NINE

8:20 P.M.

The refrigerated truck with a crew of three from PA Roadway arrived at the loading dock behind Brookfield thirty minutes early.

"You have the generators?"

"Yes, sir, as requested." The driver wore a tan uniform with his name in red written on the left side, 'Cliff.' "We checked the specs on your freezers. Should have no problem maintaining the temperatures."

"Good. You need to get into safety suits, take the freezers out, and wait for us."

The men moved the two freezers out to the truck and began loading them onto their high-capacity machine skates that lifted the cargo.

Han then turned to Jiang. "You need to work on the remaining freezers. Remove the plugs from the power outlets, open the doors, and raise the temperature to as high as it will go. Those vials should be defrosted within thirty minutes. Within an hour, any bioactivity should be lost. And Ming, go out back to check on the truck. I'll be there in a moment."

As soon as Ming opened the door to the main hallway, he heard the sound of police sirens. "General, the police. We've got to get out of here."

"You go. A few more things to tidy up."

When Ming left, he spoke to Steppler. "Is it true that you signed an agreement to give Dr. Chu most of your ownership?"

"Yes, I . . ."

"How much do you still own?"

"I believe ten percent."

"Good, sign this paper that you are leaving to my investment company all of your ownership as of this date."

"Why would I do that?"

"Why?" The general removed the gun from his shoulder holster. "Because I'm asking you to."

"But, I'm not.."

"Listen, Steppler. I'm going to count to three; either sign it, or I'll pull the trigger."

Steppler realized he had no choice. Han handed him a pen, and he signed the agreement."

"Thank you." Han put the document into his jacket pocket. At that moment, the alarms went off throughout Brookfield. Jiang ran out of the Biosafety lab. "What's happening?"

"The police are here. Did you destroy the vials?"

"Sorry, general, I didn't. If the virus spreads, people are going to need it."

"I told you to destroy them."

It was Steppler who interceded. "He can't destroy those vials. It's all we have."

"Shut up, Steppler. Jiang, if you don't destroy them, then you're of no use to me."

Han pointed his gun at Jiang. "Now, what's it going to be?"

Steppler realized Han was out of control. "You're out of your mind." He charged Han, throwing his full force against the big man's knees as he learned from his football days.

The general was taken by surprise. He fell backward, firing off three shots before his head hit the edge of the lab counter behind him, stunning him.

When Ming heard the shots, he ran back into the lab and saw the general on the floor, the back of his head bleeding. "General, you've got to get out of here. The police are here."

Ming helped the big man up and walked him down the hall toward the loading dock as the police gained entrance to the building. By the time Jeff and the others arrived, there was no one at the Security Desk to let them in. Chen entered the security code and opened the door. As they walked in, they heard gunshots from down the hall.

"That's coming from the lab. End of the hall."

The detectives withdrew their guns, and Chen followed them to the lab. As they opened the door, the body of Phillip Steppler was on the floor. Jeff checked for his pulse. There was none. Two shots had entered his chest.

"We've found another body! Still breathing."

Chen ran over to the detective. "It's Jiang!" Chen's cry resounded off the empty walls. Chen knelt next to his friend, a reflection of when Chen was in prison, and Jiang knelt to save him.

"Jiang, do you hear me?"

Chen saw Jiang's shirt was drenched in blood. "Dr. Moss, I need your help!"

Jeff rushed over and evaluated the situation. "McDougal, call 911. Tell them we have a single gunshot wound to the abdomen." He turned to Chen. "He's lost a great deal of blood. I need bandages or clean towels, quickly."

Chen rushed to a closet and reached for the emergency kit. He ripped open the envelopes and handed them to Jeff, who covered the stomach area of bleeding and kept pressure on the wound."

"What do you think?"

"Not sure. It depends if the bullet caused organ damage. He's going to need emergency surgery; he's phasing in and out of consciousness."

"Jiang, I'm Dr. Moss. Stay with me. Chen, a cup of water."

When Chen returned, he placed the towels under his friend's head.

Jiang's eyes opened slightly. "Chen." Jiang's voice could barely be heard, and Chen bent over to hear.

"Han wanted me to pull the plugs on the freezers and destroy the vaccines. I wouldn't do it. He and Ming left in the truck to JFK with two freezers full of your antidote. He's going to reengineer your drug."

"It's okay, Jiang. Don't speak, keep your breath. We'll get you to the hospital."

"How's Steppler?

"I don't think he made it."

"I'm sorry. He tried to stop Han from shooting me."

Chen saw his friend trying to breathe. "Don't speak, save your energy."

"Chen, in my pocket, it's for you." It was the last words he spoke before falling unconscious.

Chen cradled his friend's head in his left hand. It didn't take more than five minutes for the EMTs to arrive from across the street at University Hospital. They put him on the stretcher and wheeled him out.

Chen looked at Jeff, "Is he going to be okay?"

Jeff's facial muscles tightened. "It's going to be close. It looks like it got an artery. I'm sure they'll do as much as they can."

CHAPTER EIGHTY

The truck carrying the general, Ming and their cargo turned up First Avenue toward the RFK Bridge when Han spoke to the driver.

"We're making a change in destination. Take us to Teterboro Airport in New Jersey. This time of night, it shouldn't take more than half an hour."

"Hey, forget it. We were told to take this stuff to JFK, and that's where we're going."

Han took out his revolver. "Don't make this hard on yourself; you're already making triple your wages. Take us to Teterboro, or you're going to lose a leg. Now, what will it be?"

The three workers looked at each other. "Okay, mister, whatever you say."

"Good, very smart. Once you get there, you'll drive behind Atlantic Aviation. A Bombardier Global Eight Thousand private jet will be waiting for takeoff. Pull right up to it, and the cargo handlers will take the shipment onboard. Each of you gentlemen will get a healthy bonus if you keep this trip between us. You think that can be done."

They nodded. "Yes, sir."

"Excellent."

He returned to the rear. "Colonel Ming, did you see what happened to Jiang?"

"I think your shot hit him. There was a lot of blood."

"That was a mistake. If we can't find Chen, we'll need him to make the drug."

He made a call to his secret agent in New York. "Sun Wei, General Han. A fellow named Jiang Fang was shot and probably taken to University Hospital. Find out his condition and get back to me."

"Yes, sir, I'm fifteen minutes away."

* * *

In the lab, Chen told the others that Han had left in the truck to JFK with two freezers. "He's going to reengineer the drug."

"Okay, let's get a hold of JFK to start." DePalma made a call to Air Traffic Control. "Hold any airfreight flights leaving for China until I arrive. NYPD should be arriving shortly if there's any trouble." He then called headquarters. "Send two units to JFK air freight. I'll be there in thirty minutes. I want all airfreight planes bound for China to be thoroughly searched. We're looking for two laboratory freezers with General Han Shi on board. He's already shot two men."

Chen then told him what Jiang said about Steppler's death.

"So Jiang refused to destroy the vaccine. That took a lot of guts. And give a lot of credit to Steppler. He gave up his life to try and stop Han."

DePalma turned to Jeff. "We better get over to JFK, and Chen, better see how Jiang is doing. Then get back here and make sure the drug is safe."

* * *

As Chen walked across the street, he called Li and told her Jiang was in University Hospital and she should meet him there. Ten minutes later, Li walked into the waiting room, and they anxiously held each other.

"How's Jiang?"

"I haven't heard. Apparently, they took him into surgery, but I don't know more than that."

"What happened?"

"It was General Han. He shot both Steppler and Jiang. Jiang lost a lot of blood, and Jeff said they'd have to do surgery to try and stop the bleeding."

"And Steppler?"

"He tried to stop Han. He may have saved Jiang's life, but it cost him his own. He died."

"So he wasn't all bad."

"I suppose greed can get the better of anyone."

"How can I help?"

"I don't know how long Jiang will be in there, but I need to get back to the lab to check the remaining vials. If you could wait here and keep me up-to-date on his condition, that would be great. I'll get back as soon as I can."

"Okay."

As Chen exited the room, Li sat down, nervously checking her messages, constantly looking up to see if the door to the OR was opening and pacing back and forth as she looked out at the city lights. In a short time, a nurse walked out of the OR. Li went up to her.

"Hi, my name is Li Zhou, I'm a friend of Jiang Fang. They brought him in with a bullet wound. Can you tell me how he is doing?"

The nurse gave a caring smile. "All I can say at this time is that the wound was to the stomach. He's lost a great deal of blood, but the surgeons are trying to stop the bleeding and determine how much damage has been done. It could be a few more hours before they know the results. My shift is over, but I'm sure the doctors will advise you.."

"I see, thank you."

* * *

From a seat several rows behind Li, a man dressed as a successful businessman wearing a gray-striped suit, white shirt and conservative blue tie was hidden behind the day's *New York Times*. Rather than focusing on the editorial page, he was more interested in attending to the events that were transpiring before him. After the nurse had left, he walked to the rear of the waiting room and made a call. "General Han, it's Sun Wei. I'm at the hospital. Jiang is in surgery. They're trying to stop the bleeding, although they're not sure if they can save him. But, of interest is that a young woman named Li Zhou is here and told the nurse she's a friend of Jiang's."

There was a pause at the other end of the call. Finally, Han responded. "Li Zhou, yes, we have photos that Interpol has identified of her and Chen traveling together. They are supposedly good friends, very good friends. I believe she's the reporter from the *Wall Street Journal* who covered Lexington Bio. I think it would be most interesting for me to meet her. Is she by herself?"

"She is."

"I don't care how you do it, but I want her brought to me. Can you do that?"

"That should not be a problem, general."

"It's 10:30. I will message you the instructions. We leave at midnight."

"I will make arrangements."

CHAPTER EIGHTY-ONE

Chen entered Brookfield's high-security lab and checked the vials. They had been saved, but as he looked through the freezers, he realized that he might have been given the wrong count of active vials made for the clinical studies. Of the three million vials, only half were active that contained the antidote, and half were the control vials containing only water. That means, with five hundred thousand vials in each freezer, half were controls and half were the antidote. The vials were identical in size and shape, with the sole difference being a coded number placed on the label of the vial. And because this was a fully blinded study, neither the recipient of the vial's contents nor the investigator who administered the drug would know whether they were being given the antidote or the control. Only one person, the chief investigator, held the key to the code, and that individual was Chen. Whoever had given the original count of remaining vials had no way of knowing what was active or what was control.

He called Priya and gave her the updated number. "Priya, General Han took two freezers with him back to China, each containing two hundred and fifty thousand active and two hundred and fifty thousand controls. That means all we have left are four freezers with a total of one million antidotes and one million controls. What do you want me to do?"

Priya thought for a moment. "So, not as much as we thought. All we can do is hope that it will be enough. I'll get an update count from CDC in the morning and see what arrangements they can make to have the drug transported to the areas where the nidus of infection is present. If it can be done soon enough, there's a chance we can stop this."

Chen agreed. "Then make those arrangements. We're going to need to break the code to send you only the real antidotes."

"No, that will take too much time. Just send me the codes identifying which is antidote and which is control. We will let the doctors administering the drug have the code. They will be responsible for administering only the antidote and throwing out the rest."

"Okay, I'll leave a note for Dr. Ballan to have everything ready for you in the morning. Jiang was hurt, and I need to be with him."

"Will he be okay?"

"I'm hoping."

"Send him my best."

* * *

Sun Wei left the paper on the chair next to him and walked out into the empty hall of University Hospital. It took no more than ten minutes for a maintenance worker to direct him to a door whose sign read Lounge: "Medical Staff Only." He knocked and, when there was no response, entered the empty room which was part lounge and part lockers. Used white lab coats spilled over the laundry hampers, and half-filled coffee cups were left on the tables for the weekend crew to clean up. Sun Wei opened several of the lockers until he found a white jacket with the ID tag clipped on the pocket and put it on. He instantly became Dr. Frank Miller. Minutes later, he returned to the OR waiting room.

"Are you Li Zhou, Jiang's friend?"

"Yes, is he all right?"

"That's what I would like to discuss with you. If you come to my office, I can give you an update.

CHAPTER EIGHTY-TWO

Jeff and DePalma arrived at the airfreight terminal at JFK and met with the NYPD captain, who reached the site first.

"There's been no refrigerated truck delivery this past hour, and no air-freight's scheduled for China tonight. You sure you have the right intel Chief?"

DePalma seemed puzzled. "That's what we were told. Perhaps the truck hasn't arrived yet. Stay here until midnight and then post a unit here until morning. If there's no activity, let me know. We'll check the info on our end. Maybe there was a miscommunication."

* * *

It was midnight when the Global 8000 departed the tarmac at Teterboro Airport. General Han and Ming, after checking the freezers in the cargo hold, walked forward into the passenger cabin. The plane had plenty of juice to power the freezer compressors.

"How's your head feeling, general? That was a nasty fall."

Han gently touched the back of his head where a bandage had been placed. "It's fine. Takes more than that to slow me down. Talking about slowing down, how's our young reporter doing?"

Ming looked over at Li. "Still sleeping like a baby. Sun Wei must have given her enough propofol to keep a horse in dreamland for quite a while."

Han grinned. "Well, if she wakes up, she's going to find the dream has become a nightmare."

Colonel Ming settled into his chair, looking through a magazine, and Han went to the cockpit to speak to the pilot.

"How's the bird behaving, captain."

"It's a dream, general. This baby has more speed and range than any private jet I've flown. It's a beauty. To be honest, it flies itself. If you want to try it, I'll go back and sit in that cabin."

The general laughed. "I don't blame you. The cabin is fitted out like the royal suite in a top hotel. No, I think I'll let you guys fly this eagle, and I'll go settle in. How long until arrival?"

The co-pilot checked his gauges. "Flying time from New Jersey to Shanghai is fifteen hours, sixteen minutes. The plane has a top speed of Mach-point-94, which means it's the fastest business jet ever made. We'll be cruising at Mach point 92, which is seven hundred mph. That's two hundred miles faster than a commercial airliner. General, you picked a winner."

The general returned to the cabin and walked over to the well-stocked bar. He poured himself a scotch, took a deep breath, and sat down, removing his shoulder holster and placing it on the side table.

"Ming, want a drink."

"No thanks, general. I think I'll just read."

"Well, enjoy the trip. I may just sleep until we get there. It's been a busy day."

Han tilted the chair back, sank into the soft leather seat and closed his eyes. Ming resumed his reading when he felt the vibration of his cell. He answered the call.

"Ming." Ming sat up straight when he recognized the voice, quietly responding. "Yes, sir." He focused intently to the voice, responding with a "Yes, sir, I understand" at several intervals. Finally, he hung up and had a thoughtful air about him.

Ming turned his attention to the general, observing him as he dosed off, his eyes never leaving the deep facial scar as if contemplating what to do. After several minutes, it was as if Ming made his decision. He rose from his chair, walked over to the table where the general had placed his Glock Semiautomatic and removed it from its holster. As Ming returned to his seat, he slid the general's Glock under his belt and sat down.

*　*　*

The flight was smooth, and after half an hour of keeping his eyes on the General, Ming's eyes became heavy, and he soon fell asleep. Two hours had passed when the general awakened and saw Ming sleeping, observed that Li was still sedated, and went to the restroom. He washed his face, placed his hand over his bandage, saw no bleeding and returned to his seat. It was then that he noticed his weapon was no longer in its holster on the table.

Han looked at the floor, trying to determine where the Glock was. Finally, he walked over to Ming and gently opened his jacket. He saw the Glock under Ming's belt. Still having difficulty understanding the situation, he reached down and removed the pistol. Ming stirred but didn't awaken. Han returned to his seat and placed the Glock next to him on the side table.

CHAPTER EIGHTY-THREE

Chief DePalma received the call at three in the morning. "There has been no freight truck seen and no airfreight plane leaving JFK for China all night."

DePalma called McDougal. "Joe, check all flights from New York area airports that carried cargo and departed for China anytime over the past six hours."

Within half an hour, McDougal reported back. "There were no commercial flights out at that time. All I could find was a delivery made to a private jet, a Global 8000 at Teterboro that left at midnight. The flight plan has it going north-northwest over Ottawa, flying west of Southampton Island, then on to Prince of Wales Island, Prince Patrick Island, and then over the ocean onto China. It has a fifteen-hour arrival time in Shanghai. It just passed over Ottawa."

DePalma clasped his hands together on his desk. "Then we have a problem. We're not going to be able to stop a flight to China carrying a Chinese general over Canadian territory. I believe General Han has outsmarted us."

* * *

Ming began to stir. He awoke with a start and, becoming aware that he had drifted off, looked over at the general, who appeared to be sleeping. As with a sudden recall, he placed his hand over his belt and realized that the general's gun was no longer there. He looked at the seat and the floor but found nothing. Han opened his eyes and smiled. "Looking for this, colonel?" The general's gun was pointed at Ming. "Colonel, before you tell me what's going on, I need to ask you for your weapon. Please throw it over to me, very slowly."

Ming took the weapon out of his holster and tossed it onto the floor near Han.

"Now, why don't you tell me what this is all about?"

"General, I was informed by phone that the Central Committee issued an arrest warrant for the chairman and his supporters, and that includes you. The generals of the armed forces have decided that the chairman's Bioterror Program is no longer operable. You have been relieved of command and to be brought back to China for trial. The Party has lost confidence in you and your plan."

Han thought for a moment. "Well then, if that is what you were told, that's fine. I'm sure when I get back, we will have this all straightened out. Meanwhile, I respect your actions. Now, colonel, I will have another drink and go back to sleep, and hopefully, you will wake me when we arrive at our destination."

"Thank you, sir, I appreciate your cooperation. I would like to have my pistol returned, just to be sure we are in agreement."

"Of course."

The general picked up Ming's weapon and walked over to his seat. Han must have been concerned about any action that would spoil the cream-colored leather seats because the force of the big man's fist onto Ming's cranium came as a surprise. The resulting concussion had Ming almost unconscious by the time the general put his hands about the colonel's thick neck and silently compressed the airway until no life remained. Ming slowly sank into his chair. "Enjoy the rest of your trip, traitor."

Han returned to his seat, removed a card from his wallet, and called the number he was once given should there be an emergency. The phone rang several times before it was answered.

"Yes."

"It's General Han. I just heard."

"I'm glad you called. It's time to see how effective your defense policy is. Do you have the antidote?"

"I have enough for now."

"And for the future."

"Being taken care of."

"Good. I've been informed that some of my oldest friends, Mr. Yang, Mr. Kim, even some of the military staff have scheduled a trial for us."

"When will that be?"

"In two days. We are to report to Shanghai, to the Hall of the People."

"What will you do?"

"Meet and figure it out. There's an old military air base called Datuopu, just outside of Changsha, the capital of Hunan Province. It should be safe from our detractors. It's rarely used anymore, having only an old single runway. That should give us the privacy and security we'll need. I can be there in three hours.

"I'll be there."

The general ended the call, looked over at Li, who was becoming restless and quietly walked to the cockpit.

"Gentlemen, I am sorry to bother you, but we need to change our final destination."

* * *

Han returned to the passenger cabin and heard a cell phone ring from Li's pocket.

It was a message from her Journal colleagues in China. *Generals dismissing bioterror program as failure. The chairman is being accused by Mr. Yang and his followers as traitors. Sources say will be put on trial.*

The general smiled. He will not let that happen. He looked through her phone's directory, preparing to make a call.

CHAPTER EIGHTY-FOUR

University Hospital, New York

"How's he doing, Doctor?"

Chen was in the waiting room when the surgeon walked out of the OR. He wasn't sure where Li was and assumed that she was somewhere in the hospital or back in her apartment resting. She was not responding to his calls.

"Your friend has an amazing drive to live. We were able to stop the internal bleeding, and we gave him antibiotics to prevent infection, but he's not out of the woods yet. If you wish to see him, you can go in for a few minutes. He's still not fully conscious."

Chen entered the room. Jiang was by himself, unresponsive, the only sound being that of the respirator with its continuous inhalation-exhalation rhythm and the intermittent beep of the heart monitor. He sat silently at the foot of the bed, as in vigil, until he realized there was little more that he could do. Chen stood and quietly said goodbye to his friend and began to walk out when he passed the open closet containing Jiang's clothes. Remembering Jiang's last words to check the inside pocket of his jacket, Chen found a USB flash. Intrigued, he took it with him and walked across the street to the lab, where he inserted it into his computer's port. The name of the file was "Wulajie Study–Thanatos 2021." Chen was fascinated. It was a write-up of the virus that infected his village ten years ago. What kind of study was carried out in his village? He began to read.

The first section was filled with alphabetical listings of names, many of which Chen recognized from his village, each assigned a number. The second section had a list of those numbers, followed by the autopsy and lab results as to the cause of death. Chen soon understood the significance of the paper and focused on the reasons for the death of the villagers. In every case, the lab findings indicated death from an unknown powerful viral infection. Autopsy results revealed that every resident died from the same described condition: *Death from massive tissue destruction of all organs caused by unknown virus,* with one exception—he couldn't find why his father died. His father wasn't even listed. How was that possible? Surely, it must be included, but where?

Chen skipped down to the end of the paper and found the bibliography and citations needed for publication but no mention of his father. He scrolled back to the last page and found a small footnote that contained a single result. It was for the number 110. Why was this separated? He read the report. It was different; this individual did not die from a viral infection. Why? He kept reading:

The findings of subject #110 were found outside of the village boundary. It included pathologic features similar to those observed in cases of sudden death, including acute pulmonary congestion and edema, myocardial disarray and fracture. Forensic toxicology indicated large concentrations of suxamethonium chloride detected in the heart blood and skin tissue. Cause of Death: Homicide caused by suxamethonium poisoning, resulting in immediate death.

Chen scrolled back to determine who #110 could be. Poisoned? Why? His finger moved down the listed numbers to one hundred and ten . . . No, it couldn't be - he checked again - tears filled his eyes as he stared at the name. It was his father.

Chen turned to the last page of the manuscript. Who did this research? There were only a few lines written at the end of the manuscript. It read: "This paper was carried out by Han Shi, MD Director of the Wuhan Institute of Virology. It is an epidemiologic study regarding the lethal response to a new virus introduced in the remote village of Wulajie in northeast China. All comments or questions should be directed to Dr. Han.

* * *

Chen's body collapsed into his chair as tears swelled in his eyes. "He did it. He killed everyone. He killed my parents."

Chen returned to the hospital and sat in the chair next to Jiang's bed. He wiped his eyes with his sleeve and whispered words that could barely be heard: "Jiang, it's Chen. I read the report you left for me. Now I understand. I will find him, I promise. Get better, my friend. Get better." For a fleeting moment, Chen thought Jiang's eyes opened and closed.

* * *

As Chen walked out of the hospital, he felt a vibration from his cell that brought him back to the present. He recognized the caller.

"Li, where have you been? I've been calling you for hours, but you haven't picked up. I'm here at the hospital but can't find you."

"Ah, Dr. Chu."

The caller was not Li. "Who is this?"

"Dr. Chu, this is Dr. Han. Li is with me and is fine for the moment. But how long she remains fine depends on how long it will take you to return to China."

"If you hurt her . . ."

"Dr. Chu. That depends upon you. I am going to send you instructions as to where you are to go. If you need any notes on how to prepare the antidote for manufacturing, then go to your lab and bring them with you. A car will be waiting for you outside Brookfield in fifteen minutes. If you notify anyone, you will not see your friend again. Is that understood?"

Chu had no choice. "I hear you."

"Good. See you soon."

Han's next call was to Sun Wei. "I need a pickup of Dr. Chen Chu outside of Brookfield in fifteen minutes and bring him to the same airport where you brought the woman. I will make arrangements for a plane to transport him back home."

"Yes, sir. I will take care of it personally."

─┤ BOOK SEVEN ├─

CHAPTER EIGHTY-FIVE

At sixteen hours into the flight the Global 8000 made a minor course correction following Han's instructions and landed at the Datuopu Military Air Base in Hunan Province.

The chairman and Han greeted each other.

"You have the antidote."

"I do."

"Good."

"But, Mr. Chairman, why did this happen?"

"Because two days from now, I am to be elected to another five-year term to lead China to its full potential. Instead, I was informed that my old friend Mr. Kim and his associates met behind closed doors with three hundred and seventy Communist Party senior officials, informing them that they had established a new leadership team backed by several of the heads of the military. Supposedly, they have assembled a new Politburo Standing Committee made up entirely of his allies with the power to replace me."

"How has he done that?"

"By telling the Party heads that I no longer hold to the party's axiom of collective leadership, that I seek too much authority without the need to consider other opinions before making policy decisions."

General Han realized the situation. "How can I help?"

"You already have."

"How's that?"

"I will tell you. When I was a student at Oxford many years ago, a wonderful and wise friend of mine studied the Torah, the Jewish teachings on how to live a good and honest life. He taught me a line from a psalm that I will never forget, written by King David. It said the stone the builders despised had become the cornerstone. You, Han Shi, provided that stone, but our friends rejected it without thought. What you have created in our laboratory will become the cornerstone of our success."

* * *

It was afternoon by the time the general and Li arrived at the Institute. She was placed in an empty office and guarded by members of his security team; Han had his assistant connect both freezers to outlets to maintain the required temperature. The chairman reviewed the plan that General Han was to carry out.

CHAPTER EIGHTY-SIX

The truck backed in at the Brookfield rear loading area. Priya and Ballan spoke as the freezers were transferred into the truck.

"So you think there's a chance?"

Priya gave a long exhalation. "I'm praying. I went over the situation with Ryan at CDC. He verified the case numbers at four hundred thousand hospitalized and three hundred thousand with symptoms in three main areas of concentration. CDC has already made arrangements to send the antidote to the hospitalized patients immediately and the surplus drug sent to any outbreak zones. The President has given them whatever they need."

"Thanks to you, Priya."

"Without his help, we would have no chance. The Airforce is delivering the drug, and the National Guard will bring them to the local hospitals."

"Priya, one more thing. The antidote has stability for two weeks at room temperature. No need to keep it frozen within that time."

"That makes it easier. Thanks."

* * *

Hunan, China

When Chen arrived, the General greeted him with anticipation. "Well, my friend, thank you for joining us, although I must say I preferred that it not be this way. Your lady friend is most interesting. We spoke briefly on the plane about politics, about her criticisms of China's policies, domestic and foreign. She is quite up on everything."

"When can I see her."

"She is in an office down the hall, and you can see her shortly. But first, a few questions. "How long after administration of your drug does immunity take effect?"

"Almost immediately."

"And how many vials of drug do you prescribe?"

"Our studies showed only one was necessary to build up immunity. No need for boosters."

"I see. Very interesting. So, whoever takes your drug now will be protected from Thanatos?"

"That is what we found."

"Excellent." The general motioned for one of his assistants to remove from the freezer several vials and give them to Chen.

"Chen, I am giving you the honor of administering your drug to myself and a friend. Then you will describe to my scientists the required materials and methods needed to manufacture the drug. Once that has been done and tested, you and your friend are free to leave or stay as you wish. That is all I need from you."

* * *

Han went into another room to bring his 'friend' out. Chen recognized the chairman but tried to hide his response. He had both men roll up their sleeves. Chen washed his hands, put on sterile gloves, was handed a syringe, and, reading the numbers written on the labels, selected a vial from which he withdrew the contents and injected it into the chairman's arm. He repeated the same process for Han, filling a second syringe from a different vial that he had selected and injecting it into Han's arm.

"As you know," Chen said while looking at Han, "you now have all the protection you need. Congratulations."

Han thanked Chen and called in two members of his security team to accompany him to see Li.

"Give them a ten-minute reunion and then bring him to the lab." He then turned to Chen. "As you know, I removed two of the freezers from Brookfield and brought them here. You can work with them if you wish. I will be back in a few days."

"May I ask where you are going?"

"To the Communist Congress that meets tomorrow, The chairman invited me personally."

CHAPTER EIGHTY-SEVEN

For many of the three thousand members of the Communist Congress, the inauguration of a chairman was an event they had been looking forward to for the past four years. And though the People's Hall would be filled with long and tedious speeches testing even the most faithful of the party, the sumptuous dinners, flowing drinks, and time with old friends made it worthwhile. But this year was to be especially memorable, for reelecting the chairman to a third term would not only break a two-term tradition but grant a level of autocratic power not seen since the days of Mao, a return to a dictatorship that would allow him to remain in office indefinitely.

To the senior delegates, the election of a chairman had always been finalized and orchestrated long before the convention. There was never a question of who won at the ballot box, for to challenge the chairman was a death wish. That is why the outpouring of applause to accept the chairman's formal nomination suddenly came to a halt with the announcement that a second nominee was to be offered from the floor. To the vast majority of delegates, it was a complete surprise. Yes, they knew of the growing resistance to the powers being sought, but no one would dare raise a voice in protest. Whoever was to be nominated had better have the backing of powerful, organized insiders.

The name was Kim, the former Premier and a member of the powerful Politburo Standing Committee. A hush filled the hall as Mr. Kim rose to address the delegates.

"Mr. Chairman, many of the delegates here today are concerned that you wish to remain the party chief for a third term. Yet, over the past ten years of your administration, you have caused an economic slowdown with your draconic COVID-19 policy, raised geopolitical tensions by inflaming China's ties with the United States and the West, insisted on defending Putin and his reckless incursions into foreign lands, ruthlessly placed Hong Kong under your control resulting in what was once a global leader in economic activity only to become a second class center for entrepreneurship and business, spent billions of dollars to fund infrastructure projects around the world only to find that those projects were poorly planned, poorly constructed and now forcing the nations that house those project to undergo expensive repairs or throw them out entirely, and finally, failed to advance our goals of returning Taiwan to its mother. The fact is, China is less secure today than it was when you promised us wealth and power ten years ago."

Mr. Kim paused, and scattered sounds of applause were heard in the great hall. "And most concerning, much more concerning, is that you have jeopardized the security of our people by reducing our defense budget, dramatically decreased our military personnel, and downgraded power from our generals all because you believe that growing viruses will make China the most powerful nation on the globe."

Again, Mr. Kim paused, but this time, jeers against the chairman filled the hall. "That is a fairy tale that has no basis in reality. You yourself have reported that your program has not found an antidote to the virus you call Thanatos. The fact is, if you let that virus out, everyone dies. That's no weapon, Mr. Chairman. That's existential suicide for the entire globe."

As Mr. Kim sat down, long, thunderous applause followed until the chairman stood from behind the dais, confidently regarding the mass of faces focused on him. "Members of the Politburo Standing Committee, members of the National People's Congress Standing Committee, and delegates of the Communist Congress, Mr. Kim has brought up serious accusations against me and my administration. I appreciate the open debate of our next Five Year Plan and your participation representing all of China. This is true democracy of the people, and I applaud Mr. Kim's challenge. May I suggest that Mr. Kim and I have an opportunity to defend our positions formally in forty-eight hours in this hall of social justice? In the meantime, my administration has worked hard on making this congress a special event for all of you over the next week. As a result, if my old friend Mr. Kim agrees, I suggest that we go back to our rooms and prepare for this evening's special gala opening banquet that I am sure will be one you will always remember."

The chairman looked at Kim with a smile, who stood and declared, "I agree." With that, the delegates left the room, the banquet hall was set up by myriads of workers, and the kitchen staff completed their food preparation.

***

The chairman was correct. It was a meticulously orchestrated evening they would never forget. The immense banquet hall was set to seat just over three thousand, with dazzling crystal chandeliers illuminating the room floating above a sea of lavish Chinese handmade sculpted carpet with a design of pink and cream floral medallions over a brilliant red background. The long dais in the front of the room that spanned the width of the hall was reserved for over one hundred leaders of the Party, including the seven members of the Politburo Standing Committee, the senior members of the NPC Standing Committee, the newer members of the Committee, and the commanding officers of the Army, Navy, Air force and other military departments. The remainder of the room was filled with round tables seating twelve, each with table settings made of the finest silver, elegant linen tablecloths with colored floral centerpieces and gold-colored upholstered chairs.

There was one other detail that the chairman included. Above eighty-seven of the table settings on the dais was placed a special card bordered with gold foil that identified the name of a key leader of the Communist Party. The instructions given to the waiters were specific: these special high-ranking members of the Party were to be served a special mushroom noodle soup cooked by one of China's greatest chefs, Tai John. Tradition has it that Chairman Mao himself chose this recipe for special events, and Chef John took great care in selecting its ingredients of tender Chinese noodles, fresh umami flavors, rich mushrooms, a fine oyster sauce, light and dark soy sauce, fragrant green onions, ripe Bok choy, and a teaspoon of chili garlic for a spicy kick. A close observer would have also noticed one addition to the recipe not part of Mao's tradition: a special flavor supplied by General Han Shi. All agreed it was the most lavish opening gala they had ever attended.

CHAPTER EIGHTY-EIGHT

Two days later, the spectacle of a real convention election battle added immense intrigue to an otherwise staid and preorganized event not seen before in Chinese politics. The three thousand delegates of the NPC arrived at the closing ceremony of China's twentieth Party Congress that took place in the Great Hall of the People in Beijing only to discover that there would be no election. Rather, they read the headline being transmitted on the internet via CNN.

UNKNOWN VIRUS ATTACKS EIGHTY-SEVEN TOP CHINESE OFFICIALS; CHAIRMAN ALIVE! PAST CHINESE PREMIER KIM AND SUPPORTERS NEAR DEATH! SECRET SERVICE INVESTIGATING.

AFP footage, shared on Twitter, showed a large number of Party and Government officials missing from their seats of honor on the Dais of the Great Hall of the People during the Party Congress's closing ceremony. China offered no explanation. BBC's China correspondent suggested that the most likely reason was "China's power politics on full display." The voting resulted in a new ruling Central Committee headed by the chairman, paving the way for his third term. There was no opposition.

* * *

Chen read the Twitter lines and realized what had happened as General Han entered the lab.

"You're back early."

"More important for me to be sure everything was working out here than attending a dinner that only adds weight."

"I see the antidote protected the chairman."

"That it did, and you saved our nation."

There was a knock on the door, and a security agent entered with a package marked for General Han. A note was attached that read: "General, thank you for your service to the nation. As a measure of my respect for you and what you have accomplished, I am asking that you accept the position of Premier of the Party. There is no one more loyal or qualified to help lead us to a new age. And by the way, I have enclosed some of the most delicious soup served at the conference. Sorry, you weren't present. As long as we have been inoculated, enjoy. The chairman."

Perhaps for the first time, Han was truly happy. His dream of power, prestige, wealth--anything he could have ever wanted had been achieved. Even revenge, if there was anyone left to be revenged.

"Chen, want to share some of this soup. It's Mao's favorite recipe, and the chairman sent it specially to me. Have some, as long as you've taken your antidote." Han laughed. "You deserve it."

"No thank you, you're the one to be rewarded. You are a loyal ally."

"Why, thank you, Chen. Glad you see it that way."

Han opened the container and slowly tasted the soup, trying to enjoy every spoonful. He paused between mouthfuls and asked. "Tell me, Chen, any chance of your staying around. I've been named the new Premier of China, which means I am second in command of the most powerful nation on earth and heir apparent. I could give you whatever you or Li wanted. You could be the Director of the Wuhan Institute, gain wealth beyond your imagination, beautiful homes, jewelry, anything you could ever wish for. Whatever you want is yours."

Chen waited until Han had finished his soup. "Your offer is very generous. I would need to speak to Li before accepting it. Perhaps you could give me a day to discuss it with her."

"Absolutely."

He brought in his Chief of Biomedical Security. "Dr. Sang, this is Dr. Chu. Please bring Dr. Chu to his friend Li. They are free to go."

Chen realized he had heard Sang's name mentioned before but couldn't place when.

"Thank you, general. And one more thing. I would like to spend a little more time in the lab. There may be one more study that I think could be very helpful if I was to stay."

"Of course, anything." Again, he spoke to Sang. "Dr. Chu may want to do some work in the lab. Whatever he orders, you are to comply with immediately."

Sang saluted. "Yes, general,"

"Chen, I must leave immediately for Beijing to be sworn in as the new Premier. Call me when you have decided."

"Absolutely. Perhaps I will come to Beijing to see you personally."

Han was pleased that his offer was being so seriously considered. He couldn't remember a better day.

"Then see you in Beijing." He gave Chen his contact information. "Call me as soon as you arrive. You'll be the first to see my new quarters."

* * *

Chen was ushered in to meet Li. They embraced, spoke to each other of what had occurred to each of them, and were pleased that they both seemed healthy. Chen went into the lab with Sang and surveyed the two freezers.

"Dr. Sang, is the virus limited only to the city of Wuhan?"

"That is correct. And with the strict lockdown, only limited to a small perimeter around the Institute."

"How many have been hospitalized?"

"As of this morning, twelve thousand."

"And those that have developed symptoms?"

"I have reports of an additional thirty-two thousand who are isolated either in their homes or in shelters."

Chen thought for a moment. "Here is what I want you to do." They put on protective gear, and Chen pointed out the labels on the vials. "The labels that end in odd numbers are to be immediately destroyed. They have already expired and are of no threat to anyone. However, the vials that end in even numbers are to be immediately distributed to those hospitalized with the virus, and the remainder are to be distributed to those with symptoms. The lockdown you have imposed within the area around the Institute need only last two more days. If no one develops viral symptoms within that time, then there is no more need for a lockdown. That must be done immediately."

"Yes, Dr. Chu."

It was at that moment that Chen realized where he had heard Sang's name before. It was Jiang who mentioned it in regard to the missing Thanatos vials.

"One last thing, Dr. Sang. The general mentioned that if I needed access to the biosafety vault, I should speak to you. I need that opened at this time."

Sang seemed confused. "The general mentioned that?"

"Why yes, how else would I know to be asking you to give me access? He also stressed that I should be wearing my protective uniform if I wish to inspect it."

Sang was hesitant. "Yes, I suppose so. Of course, Dr. Chu, come with me."

When Sang opened the vault, Chen found several vials and a thick notebook. He counted the vials of Thanatos. There were four, just as Jiang had said.

"Dr. Sang, please bring me four of the even-labeled vials from the freezer."

Minutes later, Sang returned with the vials.

"Thank you, Dr. Sang. Now, better start your work with the even-labeled vials for distribution immediately. When I am finished here, I will let you know, and you can relock the vault."

When Sang left, Chen mixed the antidote into the vials of Thanatos and left them in the vault. He then looked through the notebook, realized it contained the method to construct Thanatos, and lit a match. Chen then removed his biohazard clothing, told a security agent to notify Dr. Sang that he had completed his work, and he and Li walked out of the Institute. When Sang returned to the vault, he found the four vials undisturbed. However, there appeared to be one change: Instead of a notebook, he found a glass vial filled with ashes. Perplexed, Sang locked the biosafety vault and went out to oversee the administration of the antidote to the sick citizens of Wuhan.

* * *

Chen told Li of the general's offer and how he would make his decision within twenty-four hours. They spent the day visiting the sites of Wuhan and took the evening flight to Beijing, stayed over in a fine hotel and in the morning prepared to visit Han. Chen called Han's number, and a woman answered, mentioning that the general was not feeling well, but would like for him to visit. She would notify security that his taxi would be arriving.

"Chen, are you actually thinking about accepting the general's offer?"

"Li, I'm not sure, but even if I don't, I need to say goodbye."

CHAPTER EIGHTY-NINE

At 9:45 A.M., Chen and Li took a taxi to Zhongnanhai, a large complex of buildings located west of Beijing's Forbidden City. The driver took them through the southern entrance at Xinhuamen, known as Xinhua Gate, or "Gate of New China," located on the north side of West Chang'an Avenue. Chen had to give his name to the security agents who checked the taxi before letting them through.

The driver was surprised. "You must be very important people to allow us to drive in. I've only been here twice in my twenty years of driving."

On either side of the entrance, walls were written in large letters: "Long live the great Chinese Communist Party" and "Long live the invincible Mao Zedong Thought." As the driver passed through the entrance, he came to a wall that blocked the view of the compound. "See that sign that says 'Serve the People.' It supposedly was written in the handwriting of Mao Zedong himself."

"This place is beautiful. What is it?" Chen asked.

"It used to be the imperial gardens, and those buildings on the right are the offices of the Politburo Standing Committee; opposite them are the central headquarters of the Chinese Communist Party, and next to them are the offices of the central government or State Council. I'm taking you to those buildings in front of us: the office of the CCP chairman himself, and next to it is the office of the Chinese Premier. *Zhongnanhai* is like saying the "White House" in the US or "Downing Street" for the British government, and it is where the state leaders carry out their day-to-day work, like meeting with foreign dignitaries. Not even China Central Television is allowed to show the outside of the buildings.

"Does anyone live here?"

"Oh, yes. The government provides the top leaders with beautiful apartments, though many also have homes elsewhere in the city."

As the driver pulled up to Han's building, a security agent opened the taxi door. "Li, best to stay here with the driver. I don't know how long I will be, but wait for me."

Chen was brought to a large double-door apartment and was greeted by an assistant.

"You must be Dr. Chu. Please come in, doctor. General Han is not feeling well and is in bed. He seems to be getting worse."

The assistant led Chen through a grand apartment and opened the door to the bedroom, leaving Chen and Han alone. The big man was lying in bed, blankets wrapped about him, perspiration lining his head and face.

Chen moved a chair next to the bed and sat down.

"Chen, you made it. Thanks for coming," he said weakly.

"General, what's wrong?"

"I don't know. Hopefully, it's just some bug that I will get over shortly. They put me on an antibiotic, but it's not helping."

"I see."

"So you've decided to stay and join me."

"Depends on what you will offer me."

"Anything you want, just tell me, and it's yours."

Chen answered softly. "Can you give me my village back, my family, my mother, my father?"

The general seemed taken aback. "What do you mean?"

"I read your report."

"What report?"

"The Wulajie paper you wrote. You sacrificed my village to test your virus."

"Oh, that. Yes, that was an important experiment. It showed us what was possible in place of bombs and bullets. It's the basis of my foreign policy. Don't you realize what I, no we, accomplished? Sacrificing a few poor citizens to conquer the world."

"My father and mother were two of those poor citizens."

The general was weak, but paused before responding, as if thinking back to when he did his experiment. When he did speak, Chen heard the anger in his voice. "They deserved it. Growing up, they treated me like an animal. They destroyed me and gave me this face for a lifetime. I could never let them get away with it. That's why they died. It was payback. But I remember your father.

He didn't suffer like the others; I gave him a special drug that put him out of his misery immediately."

Again, Chen spoke just above a whisper. "And I will do the same for you."

"What do you mean?"

"You don't have just any bug, general. You have Thanatos."

Fear spread over Han's face like a curtain being drawn. "What do you mean? You gave me the antidote just like the chairman."

"The vials your assistants gave me were stored for the clinical studies. You should have known that every active has its control. I must have given you the control by mistake. Apparently, the chairman had the real antidote. You are dying, general, just like the village you destroyed."

Han tried to raise himself but was too weak and fell back onto his pillow. "It's over for you, general, and for your plan of using Thanatos to conquer the world."

"What do you mean?"

"Dr. Sang was kind enough to open your vault where your store of Thanatos is kept.. You should know that I destroyed every vial that you had and burned your notebook containing your procedures to engineer the mutation. Quite brilliant, I may add, but it will never be made again. When the chairman finds out that you and your defense policy no longer exist, he will be replaced as a failure, and your name will go down as the evil fool you are."

Again, Han tried to get up. "You bastard. No, don't do it. I'm the new Premier of the Party. Finally, I am to rule China. I will have you exterminated."

"Now you know why I'm here. You had your payback. Now I will have mine. Your report said you killed my father by injecting suxamethonium chloride. Then I will give you the same courtesy. Picture my father as you draw your last breath."

As Chen stood up, towering over the failing man, Han tried to cry out. In one silent motion, Chen placed his arm around the general's neck and inserted the narrow gauge needle through the dying man's right carotid, injecting its contents. Within a moment, the silence of death came to its terminal state as the frail body crumbled onto the bed.

The door opened, and the attendant asked if everything was all right.

"Oh, yes. I believe the premier has fallen asleep. I would not wake him until six o'clock. He needs a good eight-hour rest before he is disturbed. After that, I think you will find him a new man."

"Thank you, doctor."

CHAPTER NINETY

As Chen entered the waiting taxi, he told the driver to take them to Beijing Capital International Airport, Cathay Pacific Airline.

"Where are we going?" asked Li.

"Home." He looked at his watch. It was 10:30.

"What did you tell the general?"

"That I prefer not to accompany him on his new journey."

* * *

Cathay Pacific flight 335 left Beijing Capital at 12:05 and arrived in Hong Kong at 4:25 P.M. Chen and Li then boarded Cathay Pacific flight 882, departing at 5:45 for the thirteen-hour flight to Los Angeles on an Airbus A350-1000 and then on to New York's JFK. At six o'clock, Chen looked down as they flew over the China Sea, thinking how the general would be sleeping much longer than his scheduled awakening.

CHAPTER NINETY-ONE

New York City

Chen and Li went directly to the hospital. It had been three weeks since they last saw Jiang. His room was empty. They spoke to a nurse who mentioned he was released the week before but was seen for a post-op two days ago. He had recovered from his wounds.

Chen and Li were surprised. Where would Jiang have gone? Perplexed, they walked across the street to speak to Professor Ballen.

They entered the new Lexington Bio lab, filled with scientists and assistants, busy carrying out their work. Chen and Li walked around the lab, speaking to the new researchers, pleased that the company was working at full capacity with formulation procedures being analyzed, assayed, re-assayed, and the most recent bioanalytical tests carried out to be certain of purity and activity of the molecule on a twenty-four-seven schedule. When they completed the tour, they knocked on the director's door.

"Dr. Ballan, how are you?"

"Ah, my dear friends, you came back. Heard you had quite an adventure. Seems every time you go home something explosive happens in China."

Chen laughed. "Blame it on Thanatos. But, Dr. Ballan, where is Jiang? We went to the hospital, but they said he was dismissed."

"Jiang is doing fine. The surgery went perfectly."

"Do you know how to reach him?"

"Jiang, yes, I saw him today. He healed well, and he's been pretty busy. He should be somewhere around here. As you can see, a lot is going on since you left. We're days away from sending your molecule out for mass manufacturing.

If there's ever another pandemic, we will have enough stored for humanity to survive. Did you see your stock price? The company already has a valuation of over fifty billion dollars. Li, you're quite a CEO."

"I had nothing to do with it. It's been Tim Channing and you who have been responsible for the restructuring, and once the story got out, the company has become the darling of Wall Street again. The media has let everyone know that Lexington Bio is the future of healthcare."

"Tell me, Dr. Ballan," Chen asked, "what happened to the million vials of antidote that was sent over to Priya?"

"They were immediately sent to areas in the country that had patients hospitalized with Thanatos. Unfortunately, we lost about twenty-five thousand, but the four hundred thousand that had symptoms and received the antidote survived. Another three hundred thousand vials were given to individuals who had tested positive for the virus. Amazingly, that completely stopped further loss and further spread. What you have accomplished is beyond any accolades that can be given. You have literally saved the planet. And by the way, the President called to congratulate you. He said if you want to run for the Senate, let him know, he'll back you. And Chen, I heard that you're on the shortlist for the Nobel Prize. You have become a hero."

"Wow, I'm sure not any hero and I certainly don't deserve the Nobel."

"Well, we'll know soon enough. I believe they begin announcing the list of winners in October. I myself was nominated but never made the final cut. But to be honest, you've made me realize that I've had enough."

"What do you mean?"

"I've decided to retire. I've spent my whole life in a laboratory. Never had a wife or a family, and never felt I had the time to settle down. It's time for the next generation with fresh energy and new ideas to work here. I've already handed in my resignation as of December 16 of this year."

Chen was surprised. "Then what will you do?"

"Something I always wanted to do, just go up to my country house, finish the books I've always wanted to read, pay attention to my overgrown gardens, and breathe the clean air." And then, with a twinkle in his eye, he looked at Chen and said: "Maybe even grow some herbs."

"But who will take your place?"

"The Board has already chosen someone very qualified, I must say. Come with me. I'd like you to meet the new director."

Ballan led them to the new director's office, where he asked the administrator if the new director was available.

"Of course, go right in."

Chen and Li walked in. "Jiang! What are you doing here?"

Ballan was beaming. "Meet the new Director of the Brookfield Institute. Who knows more about viral research?"

They greeted each other, though a little gentler than in the old days. "Jiang, you look great."

"Feel great. So, I heard you had a trip to Wuhan."

Chen and Li looked at each other. "I suppose."

"I heard some virus killed a lot of the Politburo. From the reports I read, it sounded like a virus I used to work with called Thanatos."

"Yes, I guess General Han needed to prove to the world the great achievement of his life."

"But Han also died right after he was appointed premier."

Chen nodded. "Yes, I was there when he passed away. It was the Wulajie report you gave me that was his undoing. He must have taken the wrong antidote. "

Jiang smiled. "I can imagine."

"And Dr. Sang was kind enough to open General Han's biosafety vault for me. I don't think we will have to worry about Thanatos or the method of preparing it any longer."

The three friends sat down and went over the past three weeks. "By the way, make a note, a few of us are giving Dr. Ballan a retirement party - and it's going to be formal. We'll surprise the old fellow. December 16. I'll let you know more as we get closer, but we're both going to need a tux and Li, a formal dress. The challenge will be how to get Ballan to wear one."

It was good to see them together again.

CHAPTER NINETY-TWO

Six Months Later
December 10, 2032, Stockholm, Sweden

The invitations were received, the travel arrangements were made, and the required formal attire was purchased and fitted. To Chen and Li, spending the week in Stockholm was one celebration after another until finally, the day came when the Nobel laureates took their seats in Stockholm's huge Concert Hall. The ceremony began with a flourish of trumpets heralding a proclamation of great importance. The President of the Nobel Committee walked to the podium and spoke a few words in Swedish, followed by the announcement in English:

"For the contribution awarded to the individual who has conferred the greatest benefit to humankind in the field of physiology or medicine, the Nobel Committee is honored to present the 2032 Nobel Prize to Dr. Chen Chu for his brilliant discoveries and applications concerning the effectiveness of ancient herbal medicines in destroying the most virulent of all pathogens, the Thanatos Mutation. Dr. Chen, I speak for the citizens of this earth when I truly say thank you for saving this planet."

As the audience stood and applauded, Li squeezed Chen's hand as he was escorted from his front-row seat by two royal guards in formal dress uniform up to the podium. With a smile that could be seen around the world, he shook hands with Sweden's King Carl Gustaf the Sixteenth, who presented him with the Nobel diploma, gold medal, and a check for ten million Swedish Krona. Chen put the prizes on the dais and adjusted the microphone to offer the required remarks.

Chen appeared hesitant as he looked out at the sixteen hundred guests in the huge chamber decorated with twenty thousand white, yellow, and orange flowers donated each year by the Italian city of San Remo, where Alfred Nobel died on December 10, 1896. After a moment, he looked down at Li, smiled, and reached into his suit pocket to withdraw his speech. He was just beginning to appreciate the significance of the tribute he was receiving.

"Your Majesty, Your Royal Highnesses, Your Excellencies, Mr. Chairman, members of the Nobel Committee, ladies and gentlemen. I thank you and am overwhelmed by this honor. But it is not to me alone that this prize is given, but to those who came before me, my father, his father, and the generations of those who realized the power of the natural world around us. And I want to thank my mentors, especially Dr. Geoffrey Ballan, who gave me the opportunity to think, to experiment, to create. It is said that when God created the world, he only completed ninety percent of it. The remaining ten percent is for man to finish, among them peace and health. Peace is a goal I leave to those who can guide man to control his evil inclinations. To control our emotions, I believe, is the greatest challenge we have met throughout history. I suppose we, as scientists, chose the easier path: finding a drug to cure man's ills. That is what I chose to do.

"In a way, the path I chose is similar to the one taken by the man whose name appears on this prize. Alfred Nobel was a Swedish chemist and engineer whose inventions made him a wealthy man, best known for his discovery of dynamite and gun powders. As he aged, he assumed that he was honored by all who received his largesse. And yet, one day, he was quite surprised to read that his own obituary entitled 'The Merchant of Death' is dead. The paper had mistakenly reported that the death of Alfred's brother was of his own demise. But to leave a legacy as 'The Merchant of Death' made him realize what the world thought of him, and to alter that remembrance, he rewrote his will specifying that his fortune be used to create a series of prizes for those who confer the "greatest benefit on mankind."

I was also influenced by a 'Merchant of Death,' a man who developed a mutation that wiped out my family and my village to prove how he could also destroy mankind. Yet, unlike Alfred Nobel, he reveled in his deadly accomplishment. In response, I devoted my life to finding a means to stop that Merchant of Death, and for that, you have so honored me. I will leave to others far greater than me the challenge of finding a drug to bring peace to this world, but for the opportunity to prevent the scourge of a viral plague, I humbly accept this honor and thank you for your kindness."

* * *

Later that night, Chen and the other laureates attended a gala banquet at Stockholm's City Hall attended by 1,300 people. Chen wore his first tuxedo, and Li wore a beautiful long gown. It was a night they would never forget.

* * *

They returned to New York late the next day, fatigued from the past week's events. Chen was greeted as a hero, making the rounds of talk shows, morning news interviews, and newspaper articles that proclaimed him the man who stopped The Red Mutation and saved the planet. At the end of the week, Chen received a call from Jiang reminding him of the small retirement dinner they were to have with Dr. Ballan. Chen got a haircut, Li had her hair done, and they were to meet Jiang, who would wait for them in a taxi at eight in the evening.

What Jiang hadn't told them was that a limousine would be picking them up without Jiang and taking them to an intimate restaurant to be seated at a table for four and that the evening was not to be only a farewell to Dr. Ballan. It was when the limousine driver let them out on Broadway between thirty-sixth and thirty-seventh in front of a large, elegant building that they began to become suspicious.

Two doormen were standing next to each door to welcome them. Chen and Li were surprised. "What is this?"

"Welcome to Gotham Hall"

"It looks like an ancient Roman amphitheater."

"It originally was built along those lines for the Greenwich Savings Bank back in the twenties."

Chen looked at Li, "This is where we're having an intimate dinner?"

As the filigree brass doors opened, they stepped onto the inlaid marble floor into the Grand Ballroom. The couple thought they were back in Sweden as they looked up, amazed at the gilded ceiling, in the center of which was a three thousand square foot stained-glass inset.

The couple held hands as they were slowly escorted into a dimly lit room largely hidden in shadows. Moments later, the lights came up, and Chen and Li realized the ballroom was filled with tables and chairs and standing next to them were people applauding, and the same trumpets that they heard in Sweden welcoming the Nobel laureates were once again echoing from the granite walls and solid limestone Corinthian columns at each end of the hall's oval-shaped space.

There was constant applause as they were ushered through the tables to the far end of the ballroom, where a small, intimate table for four was present, with Dr. Ballan and Jiang waiting for them.

"What is this?"

"We said we would have a table for four."

"But what is all of this?"

"Just a few people who want to repay their respects to New York's Nobel Laureate. The mayor thought this would be more appropriate than a motorcade down Sixth Avenue.

"The mayor?"

"And the governor, and every politician that's in office, or wants to be in office, and every A-lister who wants their names printed in tomorrow's Page Six. And one other group."

"You left someone out?"

"Yeah, your friends."

With that, Dr. Ballan walked up to the microphone and asked everyone to be seated.

"Good evening. What a pleasure to see so many people here in this beautiful room to honor my retirement."

Laughter filled the room.

"Actually, tonight's gala began six months ago when preparations were made to reserve this room and complete all the needed functions to have this party of two hundred and fifty to honor someone more special than one who is retiring.

Tonight was to have been a quiet dinner for four, celebrating my retirement from fifty years of scientific research and the last fifteen as Director of the Brookfield Institute. A great deal has happened since those early days when we were determined to begin a program for advanced scientific studies. Tonight, I am proud to say that we are now recognized as one of the leading scientific research organizations in the world.

But obviously, those four of us invited to the intimate dinner realized that the dinner had grown. The reason is quite dramatic. We are here to honor one of the great scientific achievements in world history: the formulation of a molecule that can destroy the most powerful viral pathogens man has ever been exposed to. And the fact that the pathogen was man-made shows the extreme methods that a madman will devise to gain power.

"So tonight, before I officially retire on this last day of my work, it is my pleasure to introduce the individual who we truly wish to honor, the real reason why we are all here, Dr. Chen Chu, winner of the 2032 Nobel Prize for Physiology and Medicine.

Chen, I know this is a surprise, and I know you would prefer to be spending tonight in the laboratory, but please come up to the dais. And with him, I invite up our Governor and Mayor who helped to make this evening possible.

As the guests stood, the three figures walked up to the dais. They shook hands, and the governor walked to the microphone.

"Dear Dr. Chu, this is one evening when the two parties are in unanimous agreement -so the mayor of New York City, and I got together to make up a Key to the City and the State - this key has great benefits for it is good for one lunch either in Albany or here in the city. We are not responsible for the food. Mr. Mayor, if you will do the honors."

At that point, the mayor picked up a giant key and presented it to Chen. Everyone laughed, and Dr. Ballan asked Chen to say a few words.

Chen smiled and looked out at the guests. "Governor, mayor, senators, congressmen, and ladies and gentlemen. What a complete surprise. I had no idea my friends cooked up this incredible evening. I was invited this evening to honor one of the great scientists of our century, the leader who made Brookfield Institute what it is today, my role model for anything I have accomplished, including wearing this tuxedo, and that is my dear friend and teacher, Dr. Geoffrey Ballan."

Chen began to applaud and hugged Ballan while the audience stood and cheered.

He turned to his professor. "You know, Dr. Ballan, if this keeps up, I may become a professional master of ceremonies." Everyone laughed.

"In addition to being here for Professor Ballan, I want to thank you for wishing to honor me for receiving the Nobel. That also comes with generations of names whose curiosity led them to question, explore, and create. As I have said many times, creativity is an attitude. It doesn't matter if you choose to involve your life in the arts or the sciences, writing a Boadway play, creating a new dance, painting a fresh canvas, or finding a better way to arrange a program such as this. Regardless, it all takes the creative portion of our minds. I simply chose science. The honor I received and the honor you offered me this evening is something I will never forget. For it not only required the scientific background of pioneers before me, like my father and grandfather, who gave me the tools to inquire, search, and remain true to myself.

"Being able to stand here before you is also a testament to the strength of this nation and how fortunate for me that you allowed me to be a part of you. I am so proud that this will be my new home." Again applause.

"I also must give tribute to those who, without their help, a deranged terrorist might still be spreading death around the globe. Drs. Priya Majmadur, who coordinated the fight against the spread of the virus, Dr. Jeffrey Moss, Detective Joe McDougal and their Chief of Detectives Anthony DePalma, whose investigative genius tracked down the perpetrator. I must thank Drs. Sebastian Gogoli and Julio Perez, who first realized what we were dealing with here in the US; Nick Robinson of the *Wall Street Journal*, who realized the significance of the bioterror reports from China; Dr. Fred Kosent of the FDA, and two very special people, Tim Channing, a true friend and a very special person, and Sam Rapolo, who I offer my gratitude and my friendship."

"And finally, there are three special people that are here tonight that have allowed me to be here with you. I already gave tribute to Doctor Geoffrey Ballan, my teacher, my guide, and my mentor. Without him, there would be no antidote for this viral killer. To Doctor Jiang Fang, my closest friend, who risked his life for my freedom and who, with Dr. Ballan's retirement, has been named the new director of Brookfield Institute. And finally, a young woman who grew up next door to me in my small village, who, like me, survived the murders of our village, and who became a brilliant scientist and writer, who brought me from prison to freedom. Li Zhou, please join me here at the dais. As Li walked up to the stand next to Chen, he kissed her and spoke quietly to her for a moment as the applause continued.

"By now, you have all heard through the media how Jiang and Li engineered my escape. But there is another reason that will make this evening so memorable. He paused and looked at Li. Her face lit up, realizing what Chen was about to do.

"There are so many things I can tell you about Li, but I can boil it down to one statement: Li has accepted my proposal for marriage."

The response was not just applause but whooping and hollering from all parts of the room. It was a joyous moment, and the orchestra immediately responded with music for the occasion.

The Governor and Mayor walked over, gave their congratulations, and spoke to the couple, who looked at each other and nodded their heads.

"My friends," the governor said with a broad smile as he extended his arms for quiet in the room. "Please be seated. I have a special announcement to make."

Slowly, the guests quieted down and took their seats.

"After speaking to the happy couple, I would like you to know that according to Section eleven of the New York State Domestic Relations Law, a valid marriage ceremony may be performed by the current governor of New York or the mayor of New York City. After consultation with the two aspiring single individuals who desire to get married, the mayor and I suggested the couple could save a great deal of money and time if we perform the ceremony tonight. I will need a vote on that from you: All in favor?"

The crowd cheered their approval, and with no nays, the governor and mayor stood before the lovers.

"Do we have someone to walk Li down the aisle?"

Li looked at Ballan. "Dr. Ballan, would you walk me down the aisle?"

Ballan was overwhelmed. "Me? Why me?"

"Because without you, none of this would have happened."

"You mean I'll have a daughter after all?"

"We're also looking for a grandfather."

The mayor looked to Chen. "And a best man?"

"Jiang, would you do me the honor?"

Tears formed in his eyes. "It would be my greatest pleasure."

The Governor and Mayor took turns in offering a marriage oath, and after the "I do's" the crowd gave out a roar that could be heard in every theater on Broadway. All agreed they had never been to such an affair that ended in a surprise wedding. It was quite a night; forget Broadway. This was the hit of the season."

As the guests poured out onto the Avenue in high spirits, the whole Thanatos team gave their congratulations. Jeff, Gogoli, Galvin, DePalma, McDougal, Priya, Crantz, Ryan, Kosent, Channing, and even Sam Rapolo immediately gave the new couple a large monetary gift. Tim Channing was pleased to see it was a personal check from a well-known bank with Sam's signature.

* * *

When everyone had left, Jiang and Ballan, Chen and Li remained at their table for four, and two bottles of empty champagne remained. Around them, the workers began their cleanup.

Ballan gave a heartfelt smile. "Wow, what an evening. Talk about creativity!"

Jiang, who played a major role in emptying the champagne bottles, stood, slightly unstable, and said, "Chen, you always were great at setting off chemical reactions. But this one nearly blew it off the roof."

Ballan spoke softly. "You've made me so happy. You know, it was the biggest mistake I ever made. To spend my life by myself. I had one chance, I suppose, but it flew away before I could catch it."

THE DENOUEMENT

Six weeks of marriage and bliss had flown by. They stayed in the city, looking for an apartment to rent, visiting museums, concerts, Broadway shows, friends—the best that New York had to offer.

By now, Lexington Bio was in full production, working to supply the world's needs.

The stock had soared to new heights, and in spite of charging a minimal price, profits were pouring in. Chen and Li had become very wealthy.

They finally planned a trip to an unknown destination for a honeymoon and, before they left asked some old friends to their new apartment. It was still sparse, but Li ordered in, and the guests at the table were not of the demanding sort: Ballan came, and Jiang, and Priya, and Jeff. The conversation revolved around the control of Thanatos in China and the prevention of its virus from spreading throughout the world.

"Oh yes," Priya remarked. "There will always be outbreaks of other mutations, but never anything like Thanatos."

Ballan put down his cell phone. "I just read a report that China's chairman was found guilty of treason, to be replaced by a new and younger generation of Communist Party leaders. Perhaps they will see the world more collaboratively."

It was Jiang who added. "Perhaps."

"Listen, Li and I have made some decisions."

"And what is that?"

"Well, since we've already made enough money to last us and any little ones for a lifetime, we are donating all of our holdings in Lexington Bio to the Institute. Tim Channing is already making the arrangements. Jiang, perhaps we can have the Institute add a teaching area to fund young scientists with great ideas."

Jiang was taken by surprise. "You mean the Chen Chu Teaching Foundation. With that kind of funding, we can attract the finest minds in the world."

"So Chen, what are you thinking of doing with your time?"

"Well, Priya, the first thing is, with Li's help, I would like to be as good a father as my father was."

Priya looked at Li. "Is that happening?"

Li smiled. "I think it is."

Priya gave her a big hug, and all offered congratulations.

Chen gave a big smile and continued. "And, with your permission, Jiang, I would like to teach some of those young scientists myself now and then."

Jiang nodded, but it was Ballan who interjected. "Tell me, Chen, what will you teach them?"

"I will try to teach them what my father taught me."

"And that was?"

"*He who sacrifices his conscience to ambition burns a picture to obtain the ashes.*"

ABOUT THE AUTHOR

The Red Mutation is Barry Libin's third work of fiction filled with the suspense and drama of his previous works. Libin combines his knowledge of science, history, and current political conditions to tell a tale that makes it hard to differentiate between what is real and what is fiction.

His first book, *The Mystery of the Milton Manuscript* is based on John Milton's great epic poem, Paradise Lost and the secrets that surround it. His second novel, *The Vatican's Vault* is a thriller that introduces the reader to the search for the great Temple Treasure of King Solomon. He and his wife live in Florida.

www.ingramcontent.com/pod-product-compliance
Lightning Source LLC
Chambersburg PA
CBHW011404010726
47495CB00009B/2772

*9 7 8 1 6 2 0 0 6 1 0 7 7 *